Axe-Identally Married

The Maine Lumberjacks

Book 3

Daphne Elliot

Published by Melody Publishing, LLC

Editing by Beth Lawton at VB Edits

Cover by 50's Vintage Dame

 Created with Vellum

Dedication

To every woman who has ever felt ashamed of her body. You are not too big, too small, too short or too tall. You are just fucking right. Remember that you are worthy of passion and deserve a person who will worship every glorious inch of you.

Never settle for anything less than goddess status.

Prologue

Willa

"Blow on the dice, gorgeous," he growled, his lips ghosting over the shell of my ear.

I obeyed. Then, with my lip caught between my teeth, I smiled up at him.

"For good luck." He raised another shot of tequila, and I did the same. So did Bob and Phyllis, a couple in their '70s. They had remarkably excellent party stamina for septuagenarians.

"Roll the dice, hockey boy," Phyllis hollered.

We were up. That was all I knew. I had little knowledge when it came to gambling. It wasn't really my thing. In fact, I'd never done it before tonight. The closest I'd come in the past was sleeping in before a big test and skipping my usual last-minute cram session.

If I had to guess, I would have picked blackjack as my game of choice. It seemed to be the most academic way to lose one's money at a casino.

But here I was, at the craps table, throwing down come

bets and field bets and yelling about something called the pass line.

Cole was in his element, being goofy and dramatic and rolling successfully time and again. We'd attracted a small crowd, in addition to our new friends Bob and Phyllis.

My brain was hazy from the tequila, the pure oxygen, and the wild stimulation of a Vegas casino floor. Not to mention the sensation of Cole Hebert's very large, very strong hand wrapped tightly around my hip. As the night had progressed, he'd touched me more and more.

And I was just drunk enough to let him.

"We got married here, in Vegas," Phyllis said, swaying to the music. "We were young, silly and in love. Just like you two."

I froze, my heart lodging in my throat. Cole and I were not in love. We were two lonely people hanging out in Vegas while our friends and family were all coupled up and drinking fancy wine with the hotel's sommelier. Two lost souls forced together to endure a weekend centered around an engagement and babies and family. Things that felt miles away for me, and likely for Cole too.

Bob leaned in and kissed her wrinkled cheek. "The best decision I ever made. I knew I couldn't let this girl get away."

My brain was flooded with affection for these two. They were adorable. The sweet elderly couple from Virginia had come to Vegas, where it had all begun, to celebrate their fiftieth wedding anniversary. They'd defied the odds and had made it work for decades. Theirs was the kind of story I was inclined not to believe. Though I deeply enjoyed it anyway. Like fiction. A Hallmark movie. The plot sweet and entertaining, yet implausible.

Cole rolled another seven, and the crowd gathered around the table cheered.

He looked down at me, his eyes molten chocolate. "What do you think, Doc? Last bet? How about a hardaway?"

Caught in the magnetism of this man, I would have agreed to anything at this point.

"That means…"

He smiled. "A pair. Let's go big."

"And then you two should go find a chapel," Phyllis said, holding her martini glass high. She wore jeweled glasses on a chain around her neck and had meticulously styled gray hair.

Bob agreed, beaming at his wife. Though his pink-and-green striped polo strained over his belly and he had a round, kind face, he had the posture of a former military man.

Cole hovered close, his enormous frame all but engulfing me, and kissed the side of my head.

My heart fluttered. Had anyone ever done that before? I couldn't remember a single time. The gesture was so intimate and gentle.

He grinned at me. "You're on. If I roll a pair, let's get married."

It was preposterous. Totally absurd. But while I was caught in his gaze like this, and with the way he looked like he wanted to devour me, while the people around us chanted, it seemed like a very sensible thing to do.

It was the dress. I was high on a sexy dress. A girl like me didn't experience many glamorous nights in her life. Getting all dolled up in Vegas and spending the evening with a hot man hanging off me had clearly gone to my head. And the drinks. All those free drinks.

God, his touch felt incredible. It was rare that I felt small in the presence of a man. But Cole Hebert completely dwarfed me. And his tactile nature, the way he was always touching me in some way, made my insides melt.

When he licked the salt for the tequila shot off the inside of my wrist, I was a goner. This was too much fun. And I'd been so desperate for fun, craving it, for so long.

So after I blew on the dice, I looked up at his dark eyes and said, "You're on, Hebert. Snake eyes, and we tie the knot."

He took a slow sip of his drink, attention locked on me the whole time, and then offered me the glass.

I knocked it back, relishing the way it burned down my throat.

The noise level increased as he theatrically shook them with one hand and splayed the other wide across my ass.

My heart pounded against my chest. I wasn't good-girl Dr. Savard here. Nope, I was Willa the wild child, cleavage on display, making myself comfortable with the hot guy getting handsy, and actually winning at craps.

I wasn't just drunk on tequila. It was the dress, his hands, and the crowd that had assembled and cheered us on.

Tonight, I wasn't just Willa.

I was the woman I'd been striving for, the one who'd always been a little out of reach. Who did what she wanted and took what she deserved.

So when I clutched his shirt and kissed him hard as the crowd roared, I felt like I was flying.

"Let's do it."

I should have known that all casino games are rigged.

I was a good girl.

Polite and hard-working. I always put away my grocery

cart and gave my loose change to the Salvation Army bell ringer during the holidays. I promptly returned my library books and never made a fuss.

I even flossed daily.

I did not go to Vegas and randomly marry my best friend's ex.

Before tonight, I would have bet my life that I was the last woman on earth who would stand up in front of an Elvis impersonator and say "I do."

But maybe I wasn't such a good girl after all…

Chapter 1
Willa

36 Hours Earlier....

With a long breath out, I surveyed the decadent pool. Lila and Magnolia were stretched out under one of the exclusive cabanas, drinks already in hand. Everywhere I looked, there were fountains, marble columns, gauzy curtains and uniformed staff scurrying around to meet the needs of the guests, all of whom were clearly having a better time than I was.

"Get your sexy ass over here," Magnolia yelled as she hopped up and waved at me.

When I begrudgingly approached, she planted a smacking kiss on my cheek and threw her arm around my shoulders. "Smile, Doc. You're on vacation. Now sit and drink this shit. It's expensive."

Leave it to Magnolia to make sure no luxury was spared this weekend.

Vegas had never been at the top of my list of dream destinations, but right now, I'd have taken a weekend in Cleveland. I needed a break. I was in way over my head and flailing. So Sin City would have to do.

Magnolia had flown in from New York yesterday, and naturally, she had booked the nicest suite this place offered.

I'd arrived today. All I wanted to do was collapse for a few hours. Then I'd try to pretend to be human.

All my life, I'd had a toxic relationship with sleep, and lately, it had been wearing on me. I was only thirty, but some days I woke up feeling one hundred. It was the same story every year. After college, I'd take better care of myself. Then after med school. After my internship. After residency. Yet even now, after a year of fellowship and becoming a full-fledged board-certified physician, I was still pushing and grinding all day, every day.

Since I was a little girl, this had been my dream. To follow in my father's footsteps, to make my parents proud, and to carry on the family legacy.

Dr. Walters had agreed to cover for me this weekend, though only after a lot of grumbling and several rambling anecdotes about how back in his day, there was no such thing as work/life balance and we younger generations couldn't keep up.

With my fill-in secured, I'd pulled an all-nighter so I could get my charting and coding done, the bane of my doctor existence, but necessary. In order to keep the lights on and the patients healthy, we needed to be paid. It wasn't pretty, but I'd done it. I'd finished my list so I could party in Vegas.

The plan had been to sleep on the plane, but once I discovered the free WI-FI, I worked on posting an ad for a nurse practitioner. As the only practice in the county, we desperately needed the help. Dad disagreed, but I'd happily take a pay cut, and I was confident that if I found the perfect person, he'd come around.

Once I'd gotten the posting completed, I'd caught up on emails to my former mentors. The popular opinion there was that I'd dropped off the face of the earth, which got me paranoid about new studies I may have missed, so then I speed read a dozen journal articles to make sure I was caught up on any and all major breakthroughs in family medicine. It was cold and flu season, after all. I needed to keep current.

By the time I reached the Bellagio, I was dead on my feet.

My friends had texted, notifying me that they were already at the pool, so I let the bellhop lead me to the suite Magnolia had booked. Gorgeous didn't even begin to describe the luxury. The king-size bed in my room was covered in a downy comforter that looked like it was made from clouds and piled so high with pillows I wondered if I'd need a stepstool to get into it.

In order to keep my eyes open, I'd turned on my energizing playlist and set to work gently hanging all my cute Vegas clothes in the closet.

Retail therapy had gotten me through the last year.

For most of my adult life, I'd believed that if I enjoyed frivolous, feminine things, it would make me unserious. And I was very, very serious, and I had been since birth. But in the last few years, I'd begun to appreciate the simple pleasures that came in the form of good shoes, a skincare routine, and a fresh manicure.

Maybe it was finally earning that board certification.

Maybe it was turning thirty. Or maybe I just didn't give a shit anymore. But slowly, I was figuring out what I liked.

And I liked clothes, I liked color, and I liked makeup. I was tired of wearing black in an effort to look slimmer.

Growing up, I'd been ashamed of my body. Always wondering why I couldn't have long legs and skinny arms and a flat stomach. I'd spent decades trying and failing to achieve the feminine perfection that magazines and TV had taught me to covet.

So, naturally, I was the kid who refused to get in the water at pool parties, and I spent my summer wearing long pants instead of shorts because I was embarrassed of how thick my thighs were in comparison to the skinny legs it seemed all my friends had. I'd layer multiple sports bras to flatten out my chest.

Eventually, I gave up. There was no time to obsess about my body or stress about the diameter of my hips or my round face while slogging through med school.

During that time, the strangest thing happened. The less energy I gave to concerns about my body, the more I began to enjoy and accept it.

After grueling shifts at the hospital, I'd mindlessly scroll Instagram, discovering that it was filled with gorgeous women of all shapes and sizes giving fashion and beauty advice. I saw girls who looked like me—really well-groomed and stylish versions of me—looking hot as hell rocking their curves.

It started as a few pairs of heels.

Then I uncovered an unrealized love of dresses and skirts. Each garment I slipped on made me feel feminine and put together. After decades of hiding beneath jeans and baggy shirts, a cute dress with a swishy skirt felt revolutionary.

Next I found facials and cycling classes and coconut-oil deep conditioner.

And pretty soon, I had left the chubby ugly duckling behind and had become an actual grown woman who had her shit together.

While residency in Baltimore hadn't afforded me many opportunities for glamour, I'd been ready for my New York debut.

For my fresh start.

Willa 2.0. The Willa who practiced self-care and bought nice clothes that flattered her curves rather than black stretch leggings from Target and oversized T-shirts.

The staggeringly confident doctor who made the city her bitch, all while looking great.

After all, the three of us—Magnolia, Lila, and I—had been dreaming of this day since high school. While our twenties had taken us on diverging paths, I had been counting down the days until I could move in with my best friends, have more control and autonomy over my career, and truly figure out who I was and who I wanted to be.

But after years of dreaming and planning, that vision had been wiped away and redrawn. When my beloved, brilliant father suffered a stroke, I'd moved back to my tiny hometown and had spent the last few months caring for him while taking over his medical practice.

"Get over here and get a drink," Magnolia ordered, snapping me out of my reverie. "And take off the caftan. Get some vitamin D."

My pool outfit was the result of a late night and a bottle of wine.

I'd never worn a bikini before. In fact, throughout my entire childhood, I swam with a T-shirt on. So this was a big step for me. But the plus-size models on the website had looked incredible, and I had been feeling sorry for myself.

Maybe it was too sexy? But was anything really too sexy for Vegas? I was thousands of miles from my parents and the townsfolk who'd known me my whole life. All these attractive strangers were too busy drinking and enjoying the sunshine to care about my cellulite and soft tummy.

The top was bra style, with underwire cups, necessary for my 36H girls. But the cups were low-cut and had straps that crisscrossed over my breasts. The bottoms were high-waisted, with additional crisscrossing straps up the sides of my hips.

I'd donned a gorgeous hat, a sheer black-and-white caftan, and jeweled flip-flops. The outfit was magazine-worthy. But as the moment where I'd have to take off the cover-up loomed, I was gripped by fear. Sure, other curvy girls rocked bikinis all the time and were gorgeous doing it. Even here, at this very pool, women of all shapes and sizes wore a variety of swimwear, each one as badass and sexy as the last.

But me?

Lila held out a champagne flute, wearing an expectant look. She didn't carry even an ounce of self-consciousness about her appearance. Why would she? She'd been a freaking beauty queen and had been parading around in skimpy outfits since grade school.

Magnolia slid her sunglasses down her nose and raised an eyebrow.

Seriously, it was like my friends could read every negative thought that had swamped me since I stepped out into the heat. And the last thing I wanted to do was ramble about my pool-based body terrors on minute one of my well-earned vacation.

I was thirty years old. I had an MD, for God's sake. If I couldn't be brave now, what was the point? So I closed my eyes, said a silent prayer that a tit wouldn't pop out of this top, and took off my cover-up.

And was immediately met by whistles.

Yup, my drunk friends were catcalling me.

"Fuck, you're hot," Magnolia said, raising her glass in my direction. "You're giving sexy bondage, and I'm here for it."

"God, you have the best tits. I'm so jealous," Lila said, cupping one perfectly respectable C-cup with her free hand.

A heated blush crept into my cheeks. My friends were so kind to me. But as I took the flute out of Lila's hand and scanned the pool area, determining that no one was staring, my pulse steadied. The villagers weren't gathering with their pitchforks and torches to chase me away for looking like a troll in a swimsuit. *Every body was a bikini body.* I repeated the mantra in my head a few times.

It was what I'd so adamantly reminded myself of over the last couple of years. But that knowledge didn't miraculously quell the seizing fear gripping me, telling me that I wasn't good enough. That my wide hips and fleshy upper arms disqualified me from having a happy and productive life.

But I'd spent too much time and money in therapy to go

there now. So I pulled my shoulders back, smiled at my friends, and downed the glass of champagne in two sips.

Empowerment flowed through me. I was with my girls, I looked hot, and I didn't have to worry about work for a couple of days.

It was time to have some fun.

"You are so getting laid this weekend," Mags declared. "Now drink up. Our girl Lila is engaged, and we managed to evacuate you out of Maine for three days. We're celebrating."

I stretched out on the fancy teak chair, working to calm the voice in my head that was yelling at me to cover up.

But I was rocking my bikini, and I'd just have to drown out the negative thoughts with another glass of bubbly. Because Magnolia was right. While I may have a mountain of work, a Maine winter, and my ailing father waiting for me at home, for now, I was on vacation.

And there was no telling when I'd have another chance to cut loose.

So I'd rock my bikini, and I'd drink and dance and gamble.

Watch out Vegas, Wild Willa was coming out to play.

Chapter 2
Cole

I climbed out of the pool and scanned the area, in search of a towel. Water was good for loosening up my hip, which was stiff and sore from the long flight. I'd been pushing hard in rehab and was making great progress. But folding my six-foot-seven frame into a commercial plane seat was uncomfortable on a good day, never mind after hip surgery.

I'd even sprung for extra legroom, but my knees had still been in my throat.

Halfway to where my brothers were camped out with beers and burgers, a woman across the pool standing near Lila caught my eye. When her form registered in my mind, I froze.

As I took her in, she pulled a flimsy dress thing over her head, revealing a black bikini.

She was stunning, her honey-blond hair falling past her shoulders and big sunglasses and a floppy hat obscuring her face. Medium height and endless curves. The bikini was insane, with skinny straps everywhere, drawing attention to her wide hips, the nip in her waist, and her breasts. Round, full, incredible breasts.

"Cole," Owen barked.

"Stop staring at Willa," Finn said, raking his fingers through his long hair and pulling it into his signature man bun.

"Ahem," Gus grumbled. "It's Doctor Savard. Show her some respect. She's not a kid anymore."

My pulse pounded. *Willa?*

I'd known her my entire life. Smart, cute, very serious, and far from my biggest fan. In fact, I'd venture to guess she hated my guts after the fallout with Lila. Willa and I had never had a single thing in common. She'd been one of those perfect kids. A straight-A student and president and captain of every academic team. Not to mention that after high school, she'd gone on to graduate from college and then medical school, carrying on her family's legacy. She didn't just think she was always right; she knew it.

But *damn*.

I turned, regarding her again as she took a sip of champagne. Heat gathered in my groin in a way that could very easily get me in trouble since I was wearing nothing but a pair of swim trunks. Because I had no idea what she'd been hiding under that doctor's coat.

"She's an excellent doctor," Gus said. "I learned that the hard way."

"You're gonna have to explain," Jude said, his tone subdued, as always.

Gus adjusted the brim of his baseball cap while Owen was back to making moony eyes at Lila. "I had to have an STI test." He shuddered. "But she's a great doc. I was mortified the entire time, but she was nothing but professional."

I could see it. The Willa I knew was stern, coldly professional, and brilliant. It figured that a body like hers would be attached to such an intimidating personality.

The topic of conversation turned to football pretty quickly, and I pretended to be absorbed in the book I was reading. *Daring Greatly*. Debbie had given it to me, and everyone in the knitting group was always going on about the author, Brene Brown, so I figured I should check it out so I knew what the hell they were talking about next time.

But damn, was this book fucking me up. I'd spent the plane ride reading and thinking and experiencing far too many emotions. Brene said courage was contagious, but I wasn't even sure what courage meant anymore.

All I knew was that I was the opposite of courageous. I was a coward.

I'd hidden behind my talent and my dad's money for most of my life. And when things had gotten tough, when I'd been faced with the consequences of my actions, I'd spiraled and lashed out, hurting the people I cared about.

I loved Debbie more than I loved just about anyone in this world, and I appreciated that she wanted to help me, But I was pretty certain that I was a lost cause.

So rather than engage with the group, I read and snuck looks at Willa.

Eventually, Gus, Finn, and Jude headed back up to their rooms to shower. Owen had arranged for a chef to create a gluten-free tasting menu for the whole crew, so a quick rinse-off was probably a good idea. But the weather was incredible, and the view, with the ornate fountains and topiaries, was hard to ignore. All this decadence was a far cry from the landscape of rural Maine.

But all the Italian marble in the world did not hold a candle to the woman on the other side of the pool. It was bad. It was so wrong to stare at her. But I was fascinated.

Of all the women to catch my attention, Willa Savard would be the last one I expected. But I'd clearly been blind my entire life. Because bodies like hers were the kind that had been painted on the sides of bombers during World War II.

Owen stood and towered over me, glowering. "Stop staring and put your tongue back in your mouth." At his annoyed tone, I immediately flashed back to childhood, back when I was the baby brother tagging along and always getting it wrong.

With a nod, I lowered my head and sightlessly stared at my book. The last thing I wanted was to argue with my second-oldest brother. This was his weekend, and our relationship, which had previously wavered between hostile and nonexistent, was just beginning to improve.

For months, I had been on my best behavior. I could keep myself on Owen's good side for the next couple of days, then he'd be back in Boston, and I could go home and hash all this out with my therapist.

She'd challenged me to identify my values and priorities. What I'd known from the beginning was that my family was at the top of my list. I'd do anything to repair the damage I'd done and build strong relationships with my brothers and with Debbie. So I had to suck it up and behave.

Owen offered me a hand, and I accepted, hauling myself to my feet.

I grabbed my hat, book, and hotel keycard from the wrought-iron side table next to my chair. Then I followed him toward the lobby.

As we approached the elevators, he stretched his arm out, stopping me with a hand against my chest. Expression serious, he pushed his glasses up his nose and regarded me. "Please don't."

I said nothing. At this point, I was used to his lectures.

"She's not some puck bunny. She's a doctor." Brow arched, he angled in closer, the subtext clear. She was too good for me. She was Lila's best friend and the town doctor. And I was, well, me.

Washed up.

A loser.

The family fuck-up.

Living with Debbie.

He didn't need to say it out loud. I knew the song by heart. I'd been singing it my entire life. I wasn't good enough. Never had been and surely never would be.

Not good enough for him or the rest of my brothers. Not good enough for my hometown, the NHL, or Lila.

Willa had now been added to that list.

Gaze lowered, I gave him a nod. "Message received."

He pushed the elevator button, and when the doors slid open and we stepped inside the car together, he hit the buttons for our respective floors without a word.

I was lucky he'd even invited me out here. I couldn't screw up his weekend. We were here to celebrate his love for Lila. Though he'd recently proposed, it would probably be a while before they actually got married. She'd moved to Boston to attend graduate school and was totally focused on her studies. So Owen had planned this lavish Vegas weekend for their families and closest friends.

It was a welcome break all around. For the last few years, my brothers and I—hell, our entire town—had been through hell. We'd watched our father get arrested and learned the shocking extent of his crimes, and we'd lost our family business and the respect of our community.

On top of it all, I'd torn my labrum and lost my pro hockey contract. I was sleeping in a twin bed in Debbie's house and completing my court-mandated community service. Good times.

When the door opened on his floor, he clapped me on the shoulder, his casual good-guy smile firmly in place. "See you at dinner."

My chest tightened as the doors closed, and my mind raced with excuses I could make to spend the rest of the weekend in my hotel room alone. Food poisoning, a migraine. A work emergency had come up for Noah, and he had bailed at the last minute. I should have done the same.

Owen and Lila probably would have preferred it that way. She and I had been broken up for well over a year by now, but it was still awkward. How could it not be? We'd been together for eight years.

But I was here, and I'd be a good brother. I'd plaster on a smile, laugh when it was called for, and toast the happy couple. I'd table my issues and push through.

It was my only option.

I couldn't go looking for trouble.

Sadly, trouble always seemed to find me.

Chapter 3
Willa

Dinner was delicious but exhausting. Lila had found an incredible person who treated her like a queen. And this lovely group of people celebrating their love together like this was wonderful. She deserved it. I couldn't have been more pleased for her.

So why was I so out of sorts?

I'd begged off karaoke, opting for quiet time to think.

I walked for a while, enjoying the cool night air and taking in the sights and sounds of the Vegas strip before heading back to the Bellagio.

Out front, I sat on an ornate bench, watching the world-famous fountains, soaking in the peacefulness of the moment.

"Can I join you?"

Startled by the deep voice, I turned. Cole Hebert, of all people, stood behind the bench, hands stuffed in his pockets. He was so damn tall I had to push my shoulders back in order to crane my neck far enough to look him in the eye. His dress shirt was unbuttoned, and he'd rolled up the sleeves. It was unfair how effortlessly handsome he was. *Jackass.*

"Sure." I shrugged.

Cole and I had grown up in the same town and graduated together, but we'd barely said more than a few words to one another. For many years, he'd dated my best friend. Even so, I kept my distance. I'd had a front-row seat to their dysfunctional relationship, and while they were wrong for each other, I was ride or die for my bestie. Plus, he was the epitome of an entitled jock, and I, well, I was me.

His large, strong hand caught my eye as he ran it through his hair, and a flash of color on his wrist caught my eye.

"What's that?"

He held out his wrist so I could take in the two beaded friendship bracelets. They were made of crimson, white, and black beads, the color of the Lovewell Lynx, our town mascot.

"My team made them for me." He shrugged. "I coach now."

One read *Coach*, with hearts on each side.

I ran my fingers over the beads of the other, politely ignoring how close our bodies were. "What does this one say?"

"Lady Lynx." He twisted it around so I could see the lettered beads. "I tried explaining to them that, as a species, lynx are not gendered and can be male or female." He shrugged. "But if I've learned one thing in the last couple of months, it's that there's no reasoning with eight-year-old girls."

I nodded, smiling. It was strangely endearing that he was wearing a suit and still rocking his friendship bracelets.

"You like kids." It was a statement, not a question.

Lila had confided in me after their breakup that one point of contention for them was Cole wanted children someday and Lila did not. According to her, they both thought they would eventually change the other's mind, but after several years, it became clear that would never happen.

He nodded. "Always have. I love coaching and sharing my love of the game."

"And you're an uncle."

He smiled. "Best job ever. Merry is the coolest, and I can't wait until Baby Thor and I can get into trouble together." He laughed to himself. "And now Gus. That kid's gonna be so serious. I'll have to work extra hard to get laughs there, I'm sure."

I smiled. This was a side of Cole Hebert I'd never seen before.

We stared at the fountain in silence for a few minutes, my mind spinning with thoughts about whether coming on this trip had been a mistake. I was too tired and stressed to enjoy myself, and I didn't want to drag down my friends with me.

I was content to sit in silence like that, but then Cole put his elbows on his knees, hung his head, and in a soft voice, said, "That dinner was awkward."

A dark chuckle rumbled out of me. "You don't say." As much as I disliked him on principle—because he was Lila's ex-boyfriend, of course—I couldn't help but feel bad for the guy. His ex was engaged to his half-brother. His clean-cut, corporate, responsible, successful older brother. I was an only child, but even I could see how that could sting.

Shaking his head, he sighed. "Not for the reasons you think."

"Then start talking," I said, shifting his way.

"I'm happy for Lila. She's incredible, and she deserves all the good things."

"Correct," I said with a firm nod. Lila and Mags were my ride or die. Always had been. Honestly, my ability to refrain from throwing this giant asshole into the fountain was a testament to how evolved I was.

"I know, I know. And I agree. I'm not good enough for Lila. Owen is."

My heart twisted a little at his resigned tone. They had been wrong for each other from the start, sure. They were fundamentally different people. But I hadn't expected to see him like this.

"It's just—while I'm grateful to be included in this with my brothers, it only underscores how far removed I am from them. I've always been the odd man out."

Head tilted, I surveyed him. The entire town knew that Cole's father had knocked up Cole's mom—his secretary—and then left his wife and five sons. Cole, despite his innocence in the entire saga, had never quite fit in with the rest of the Hebert brothers.

"It's my own fault," he continued, tugging at his hair in a way that was strangely endearing. "I keep fucking up and making things worse."

"I wasn't going to mention your arrest." But I might as well now that he was alluding to it.

Cole's antics were town lore at this point. He'd been acting out for attention since childhood. And he'd gotten plenty of attention for being a great hockey player. My psych training didn't go beyond one rotation during my internship, but even I could see what was going on.

Head still bowed, he turned and quirked a brow. It was unfair how handsome he was. Darker and taller than his brothers, he carried his big frame with the grace of a ballerina. "Why? The whole town knows. No sense in ignoring the obvious."

Giving in to my curiosity, I asked, "Why'd you do it?"

"Wish I knew. I was drunk, high, and lashing out. I was mad at myself and my father. And I threw a tantrum like a fucking child."

Despite the topic, a trickle of appreciation ran through me. This man was far more emotionally honest and self-aware than I had expected. As a person who carried around a lot of anger at herself, I felt for him. I put a hand on his shoulder, hoping to imbue a little comfort. "We all fuck up. You don't have to keep punishing yourself."

Focused on the ground in front of him, he shook his head. "Not true. You don't fuck up."

I scoffed. "Of course I do."

He sat up, dark brows tugged down dubiously. He didn't want my pity. That was clear. But for a man I had pegged as an emotionally constipated jock, Cole Hebert was full of surprises.

"Sure, Willa."

My hackles rose at his tone. "You don't know me. I've had my share of fuck-ups."

"Really? *Oh no.* Did you once get an A-minus on a test?"

He gasped and fanned himself like he was going to faint.

"No." Shaking his head, he shifted to face me. "No, I've got it. You wore white after Labor Day? You once threw away a plastic bottle instead of recycling it?" He was chuckling now.

While I was annoyed that he saw me as an uptight goody-goody, it was nice to see his morose demeanor lighten up a bit.

I rolled my eyes. "You done?"

He laughed. "You know you're cute when you're annoyed."

Cheeks heating, I turned and faced the fountain. The last thing I wanted was to be on the receiving end of any of this man's flirtation, so why was I overwhelmed with the sudden urge to flirt back?

I didn't like Cole. Not a bit. He was not a good person. And even if he was, he was my best friend's ex.

Unsure of how to respond to his comment and seriously considering running back to my hotel room, I kept my mouth shut and my focus set on the lights and water shooting from the ground.

"You gonna tell me why you're here, staring vacantly at the fountain and not partying with your friends?" he asked, low and deep. "Or are you just gonna sit there while I die of shame beside you?"

Relief washed through me. He was letting me off the hook. I couldn't begin to articulate all the reasons I was anchored to this bench right now.

Finally looking at him, I lifted my chin. "No one has ever died of shame."

"You sure about that?" His dark eyes twinkled.

The Hebert blue eyes were famous in our town. Cole was the only brother with brown eyes. And in this light, they weren't just brown, but gold and a little gray. Beautiful and strangely complex.

"I am a physician," I said, leaning into an annoyed tone. "I've read a lot of medical journals, and I've never once come across a peer-reviewed, double-blind, placebo-controlled study of shame-related deaths."

He threw his hands up and let out a huff, then he nudged me with his giant shoulder. "Fine. You got me there, Doc. So why so glum? I shared my story."

The spark that ignited inside me when his shoulder bumped mine should have sent me on my way. I should have been hightailing it back to my room so I could read and get a good night's sleep. Instead, I opened my mouth and let my honest thoughts spill out. Must have been the exhaustion. Or maybe the alcohol my friends had been forcing on me since I arrived.

"Just trying to reset. It's been a rough few months."

Cole's lips turned down. "I'm sorry about your dad. He's been my doctor since birth, and he's always been kind to me. He saw me a lot as a kid. I was always dealing with broken bones and various childhood injuries from trying to keep up with my brothers."

My heart clenched. My dad was one in a million. The town was filled with stories like Cole's. "Thank you."

"How's he doing?"

"Better." I swallowed past the lump in my throat. "A lot better. He and my mom are headed to a rehab facility in Portland after Christmas. He'll get intensive physical and occupational therapy while he's there." Licking my lips, I ducked my head. "We're lucky he's alive, but you know my dad. He wants to come back from this stronger than ever, and regaining what he lost will be hard."

"I can't imagine how difficult it must be for him. Is he still struggling?"

I nodded. "Cognitively, he's great. Just more tired than usual. The big issue is his hands."

I looked down at my own. No rings, short nails, sturdy fingers. Doctor's hands, my father had always said.

"Hands are a big deal to doctors," I explained. "Not just surgeons. They give us access to our patients, allow us to learn about them and assess symptoms. So to not have his hands..." It was unthinkable. I studied my hands again, my throat tightening as I thought about my dad. The larger-than-life man who'd kept an entire county healthy and never missed a piano recital or an opportunity to help me with my math homework.

Cole gave me a gentle nudge. "So you're filling in for him?"

I nodded.

"For how long?"

"Forever. Even if he makes a full recovery, he's in his sixties and was planning to hand the practice over to me eventually. I thought I'd have a few more years for training and for enjoying life somewhere other than Lovewell, Maine, but here I am."

"And you're a real doctor already?"

A hint of irritation sparked through me like it did every time someone discounted me. I'd faced this question regularly since taking over the medical practice in town.

"I'm board certified in internal medicine," I said slowly. "And completed X and Y."

"Sorry." He winced. "I wasn't trying to offend you. You're so young."

"I'm fully qualified. And Dr. Walters came out of retirement to help out."

A shudder racked Cole's body. "He's still alive?"

"Yes," I said. "And still as charming as ever. But he's a damn good doctor. He's only in three days a week, but it's a big help to me."

"Sounds like you have a lot on your plate. Vegas is a great place to cut loose."

I nodded. "That was my plan. But." I pressed my lips together, working through a way to explain my thoughts to someone like him. "My friends..." Sighing, I shook my head. "Things are different now. Lila is off living in Boston, going to grad school, engaged and living her dreams." I was happy for her. She deserved it all. But all this change was unsettling. "And Magnolia is globe-trotting. Dating someone new. Wheeling and dealing and lending me a house."

"You feel left behind," he said softly.

A dull pang echoed through my chest. That was exactly it.

He held my gaze for a long moment, and understanding passed between us. "Welcome to the club," he said, lowering his head. "Want me to teach you the secret handshake?"

I smiled, grateful for the levity he'd brought to the conversation. "Is it complicated?"

"Nah. Mostly shaking your fist at the universe and moping."

Strangely, a little bubble of joy erupted inside me. "Ooh. I'll be great at that."

"So," he said, sitting back on the bench, "in celebration of your induction into the left-behind saddie club, let's have some fun."

"What are you suggesting?"

"Nothing in particular. But if you want to get a little wild and forget about your troubles for a day or two, Vegas is the place, and I'm an excellent wingman."

Huh. The sensations that continued to spark inside me were damn confusing. The last person I expected to hang out with in Vegas was Cole Hebert. But he wasn't wrong. We were the two odd men out here. We'd both been left behind by our people.

I pushed my hair behind my ears, hit by the strangest urge to open up to him. "I thought I'd have a few years in New York with my friends. We had plans. Well, I had plans."

"What kind of plans?"

"To get more training and become an awesome doctor, obviously," I said. "But also to start living for me. Develop my friendships, find hobbies, have the kind of experiences everyone lives through in their twenties."

"But you're thirty."

"Thanks for the reminder." I glared at him, though there was no heat behind it. He was just stating the obvious. "But I spent my twenties in med school, then completing an internship and residency. I put everything I had into my career." My shoulders slumped at the thought. "I'm grateful. Don't get me wrong. I've been counting down to the moment it would finally be my turn to get a little wild. Make some mistakes, be silly, figure out who I am beyond medicine."

He nodded, his eyes softening.

Why the hell I was telling all my innermost thoughts to

the hockey bro who'd screwed over my best friend was beyond me, but I felt at ease with him.

It was bizarre, really. I was not what would be considered smooth around guys, especially super-hot, massively tall, built guys like Cole. But he was strangely easy to talk to. Maybe because he was my best friend's ex-boyfriend and firmly off limits? That had to be the reason.

"Then you have come to the right place." He straightened, his lips tipping up on one side. "Vegas has a way of bringing out the wild. And I can help."

Dubious, I inspected him from head to toe. Why on earth would someone like him want to hang out with someone like me? "Really? You are a Vegas expert?"

"A washed-up pro athlete with no prospects? Please, this place was made for people like me."

I'd never seen him like this, self-deprecating and a bit silly. This man didn't fit into the mold of the guy I'd known my whole life. The guy who'd always taken himself way too seriously and thought he was better than everyone else.

"Are you playing golf with the rest of the group tomorrow?"

"No." I shook my head. "You?"

"Fuck no. I hate golf."

Seriously? Could've fooled me. Cole's demeanor screamed popped-collar golf bro. "You seem like a golfer."

With one brow cocked, he put a hand to his heart. "I take offense to that. My dad was obsessed with golf." He wiped at the front of his shirt absently. "And since I've spent my life hating him, I decided at a young age that I hated golf. I'm sure it's a delightful way to spend a day, but I've come this far. There's no going back now."

I laughed, again taken aback by his honesty.

"Since everyone else is playing golf tomorrow, why don't we meet up and have some Vegas fun? We can forget about our troubles and ignore the way all our people have left us behind."

The thought alone settled me in a way I didn't think possible.

I should sleep, maybe get a massage and catch up on my journals.

But when he looked at me like that, his brown eyes sparkling, there was no way I could say no.

My impression of Cole Hebert—and growing up in a small town with someone made it impossible not to make and hold on to those impressions long past their usefulness—was that he was an entitled, arrogant jerk who lived a life of minimal consequences and maximum partying.

But if our conversation tonight was anything to go by, there was more to the story. And despite my better judgment, I was curious.

"Okay," I said softly, dipping my chin. "Tomorrow."

He rubbed his hands together, grinning. "I won't let you down. You wanna get wild, Dr. Willa Savard?"

I laughed and nodded. "Why not?"

"Then I am the man for the job."

Chapter 4
Cole

A faint buzzing roused me, but my eyelids were glued shut. And fuck, my back hurt like a mother.

The buzzing sound stopped, then started again. On repeat. Buzz. Buzz. Buzz.

Fuck.

I picked up my head and forced my eyes open. Blinking, I took in my surroundings. Why the hell was I on the couch in my room? The white sofa was large, but not anywhere big enough to serve as a suitable bed for me. My knees hung over one side and my injured hip was screaming.

Groaning, I rolled off the couch. I hit the floor hard, pulling a pillow down with me. Pain shot through my hip as I flipped onto my good side. Breath held, I adjusted my position, desperate to ease the discomfort. Had I lost a fight last night? Why did everything hurt?

And what in the fucking hell was that noise?

Before I could figure it out, a terrified scream pierced the air.

I sat up straight, all my breath escaping from my lungs, and came face to face with Willa, who was standing before me in a strapless bra and panties, once again screaming at her phone.

"Oh my God," she said, digging one hand into her messy hair and giving it a tug. "Jesus."

She hopped from one foot to the other, making those incredible breasts bounce, and for an instant, all the concern that had swamped me disappeared.

But a sniffle caught my attention, and when I snapped out of my stupor and zeroed in on her face, my gut sank. She was crying.

"How could this happen?" Turning, she kicked at the ottoman. Then she collapsed onto the couch I'd just rolled off, and the waterworks began in earnest.

I jumped to my feet, wincing as pain tore through my hip.

I was wearing a pair of boxer briefs and my dress shirt from the night before, which was completely unbuttoned. Confused and thirsty, I hobbled over to her, desperate to make her feel better.

"Willa," I said softly. "What's going on? Can I help?"

She picked her head up and focused her puffy eyes on me. Her makeup was smeared beneath them, and tears rolled down her cheeks. "Everyone knows," she sobbed.

Frowning, I searched her face for a hint as to what she was talking about.

"That we got married."

Married. That word had me dropping onto the cushion beside her. Shit. We'd done it. And she was devastated about it. While the details were hazy, I remember having a lot of fun yesterday.

"How could I be so irresponsible?" she sobbed. "I never lose control." She was mostly talking to herself, but each word was like a knife to my chest.

This was all my fault. I was the one who had started it. Something in her had called to me, and I'd wanted to help her, to put a smile on her face. But as usual, instead of doing any good, I'd fucked everything up.

"What was in those tequila shots?" she hissed. "Peyote?"

I couldn't respond. The shame of hurting yet another person was too much to manage in my current state.

My self-loathing was interrupted, thank fuck, by a knock at the door a moment later.

At the sound, she startled, her spine snapping straight. And with a squeak, she jumped up and ran to the bathroom.

With a harsh breath out, I went to the door.

Heart in my throat, I pulled it open, and instantly, I was flooded with relief. "Good morning, sir," the bellhop said, beaming. "And congratulations."

He wheeled in a silver cart covered with an enormous floral arrangement and every type of fancy breakfast food known to man.

As he passed, I snagged the card stuck in the bouquet and tore open the envelope.

To the newlyweds, it was an honor to witness your love. Congrats on a beautiful future together. Your friends, Bob and Phyllis.

As I reread the words scrawled on the crisp white paper, memories came flooding back at high speed.

It took a moment to realize the bellhop was standing by the open door. Shit. I scooped my pants up off the floor, yanked out my wallet, and tipped the man.

When he was gone, Willa poked her head out of the bathroom.

She had on a fluffy robe. It was really cute.

I handed her the card, and as she silently read it, her eyes widened, as if the events were snapping back into place for her too. "They are so lovely," she said, wiping away a tear. "But what the eff did we do?"

With a sigh, I cataloged my memories.

First, we crashed the pool party with the DJ, and then I convinced her to take a helicopter tour over the Hoover Dam. It was expensive, but so worth it.

What came next was hazy, but I closed my eyes and willed images to the surface.

Ah. The gondola ride through the canals at the Venetian.

She dared me to zipline over the strip.

I dared her to play drag queen bingo.

We had dinner after that. She went up to change first, and then she came down into the lobby wearing that dress.

It was green, and it dipped and clung and draped in the most tantalizing ways. The instant I saw her, I was lost.

We met Bob and Phyllis and chatted the night away, all while hitting the tequila. That was when all my honorable intentions went out the window.

Swallowing thickly, I studied her drawn face. "We got married, Doc."

"I know we did," she said, still studying the note, frowning. "I wasn't blacked out, just out of my effing gourd."

With a sigh, she stood, picked up the silver coffee carafe, and attempted to pour herself a cup. As she tipped the carafe, she spilled it on the white linen tablecloth, leaving a good-sized stain.

"Shoot."

"Let's sober up," I suggested. "Then we can go get it annulled. People get stupidly married in Vegas all the time. I'm sure it's easy."

"You're missing the point," she said, pinching the bridge of her nose. "We'll get it annulled, of course. The problem is that everyone already knows."

"Who?" I popped a piece of croissant into my mouth and had to bite back a moan. Damn, that was good.

Her lower lip wobbled as she settled beside me again. "The town."

"Impossible."

She shook her head and pulled her phone from the pocket of her robe. When she unlocked the screen and slid a thumb down it, there were dozens of text messages.

She opened one from Bernice, who owned the diner, and then from her friend Becca, who owned the salon. Both included a blurry photo. The image was of us. I was carrying her through the hotel lobby. She was still in that gorgeous green dress, but she was wearing a white veil.

A buzz like the ones I'd been dreaming about vibrated through me then. I hopped up and dug under the couch cushion, finding my phone lodged there, along with my key card, just as the device buzzed again.

When I caught sight of the screen, my chest tightened. Dozens of texts and missed calls. And as I scrolled through them, bile rose in my throat.

"Apparently, Gail Thomas saw us in the lobby and took that photo."

My stomach plummeted. Fucking Aunt Gail.

She was Debbie Hebert's overprotective sister and the town gossip. She'd come to Vegas with Debbie, and she never resisted the urge to glare at me.

She was loyal to a fault when it came to her sister and her nephews. Thus, she despised me. As if it had been my fault my asshole of a father cheated on his wife with my mother and broke her sister's heart. She taught Sunday school, delivered meals for the food bank, and had worked at the bank for years. But behind her pious façade, she was pure evil.

Shit. If Aunt Gail knew, then she'd surely already made a scandal out of it.

Willa curled up against the armrest, attention locked on her phone and tears streaming down her face again.

Sniffling, she looked up at me. "My parents," she said softly. "What am I going to tell them? They will be ashamed of me."

My heart sank. They were the kind of loving, supportive parents any kid would be fortunate to have, and it was a well-known fact in town that they were proud of their daughter and all her accomplishments. Of course they'd be horrified by all of this.

Eyes closed, I cursed myself. Fuck. I had to fix this. I'd been on a downward spiral for months. I couldn't drag Willa down with me. Not bothering to question where this protective instinct came from, I put an arm around her and pulled her close.

"Blame me," I said. "I got you drunk and took advantage of you."

Thankfully, I hadn't taken advantage of her in *that* way. I'd woken up on the couch, and one of the not so hazy memories lodged in my brain was of heading straight for the couch to pass out when we finally got back here. There had been plenty of kissing—that part I remembered clearly—but by some miracle, we hadn't gone further.

"No. I was an active and willing participant. And we had so much fun. Drinking, drag queen bingo, and after we won all that money at craps. I got carried away." The smallest smile tipped her lips as she looked up at me.

My breath hitched. Even depressed and hungover, she was knock-you-on-your-ass beautiful. All green eyes and full lips and long lashes. How had I been blind to this for so long?

"I blame Bob and Phyllis," I said, feigning indignation. "They're a terrible influence. They 100 percent pressured us into substance abuse and an ill-conceived marriage."

The giggle that escaped her filled me with warmth. Damn, it felt good to cheer her up.

"Yes," she said, biting back a smile. "Those wild septuagenarians led us astray. That defense will clearly hold up in the Lovewell court of public opinion."

I squeezed her a little tighter. "You're a doctor, not a lawyer."

The lightness in her expression evaporated, and she put her head back in her hands. "Don't remind me. I'm the town doctor. I'm supposed to be reasonable and trustworthy. It's hard enough already, having grown up there. People don't take me seriously or actually listen to my medical advice.

They'd rather treat me like the child they knew decades ago."

My phone buzzed in my hand for what had to be the fiftieth time since I'd found it. Curiosity took over, and I checked the notifications. The texts were mainly from acquaintances and varied between *congratulations* and *are you okay?*

"I know this seems bad," I said slowly, tapping the button on the side to make the screen go dark, "but we'll fix it. We'll get an annulment, and in time, they'll all forget. It won't take long for you to go back to being the dependable doctor."

"If it were only that easy," she said, fixing her glassy eyes on me. "You're a man. The world forgives your mistakes and boneheaded decisions. Women in my position are held to a higher standard."

Though I had no right to argue with her on that point, she needed to see that everyone made mistakes.

Before I could come up with a reasonable response, she was actively crying again. "My d-dad," she stuttered. "His health is so fragile, and God, he will be so disappointed. How could I make such a terrible decision? I'm a selfish bitch."

I hated seeing Willa cry, but the way she spoke so harshly about herself made the protective instincts inside me flare.

"We had fun and got carried away," I said, keeping my tone soft. "It's not a good look. I get that. But it's not a tragedy—"

She raised her head, her eyes sharp and her face fixed in a glower. "Maybe for you. Everyone expects the worst out of you."

Shit.

Her words hit me like an arrow to the heart.

I'd thought we'd bonded. I thought she could see past the reputation that had been haunting me. I'd opened up and shared things I'd only ever told my therapist. I'd hoped that maybe she thought I was more than an irresponsible fuck-up.

But she was just another person for whom I'd never be good enough.

Chapter 5

Cole

My research on Nevada annulment procedure—which was way more complicated than I had anticipated—was interrupted by a loud banging on the door.

With a gasp, Willa looked up from her phone. She was doing her own research. Likely reaching the same conclusion about our predicament: getting out of this marriage would be a hell of a lot harder than getting into it.

"Open up, Cole."

My gut bottomed out. Fuck. Owen was my biggest critic, and clearly, he'd heard the news.

Focusing on keeping my breath even, I headed toward the door. I grasped the handle and eyed Willa over my shoulder. "You can head back to your suite if you want to."

Rather than scurrying off, she straightened and shook her head.

Okay, then.

The instant I'd pushed down on the handle, Owen barged inside, his face red.

"Explain yourself," he demanded, shaking his phone at me. "Why are you pulling stunts?"

Lila appeared behind him, stepping into the room quietly, her face grave.

At the sight, I was hit with another wave of embarrassment. I'd married my ex's best friend. During said ex's engagement celebration weekend. I studied my hands, unable to even open my mouth, let alone come up with an explanation.

"You couldn't let Lila and me be happy, could you? You're jealous, so instead of standing back and doing the mature thing, you went and ruined it. And the worst part is that you dragged Willa along with you."

I gritted my teeth. Why the fuck did he have to bring Willa into this? She had enough to deal with.

My gut churned. Of all my fuck-ups, this came close to topping them all. And for all the shitty days I'd suffered through, this one might have been the worst. Not only had I screwed things up for Willa—a genuinely kind person who'd made me feel as if I wasn't such an embarrassment—but now my brother and ex-girlfriend hated my guts too. Excellent.

"I told you to stay away from her," he gritted out, his nostrils flaring as he got in my face. "How on earth did you convince her to marry you?"

Just like that, the progress that we'd made these last few months evaporated. It was clear in this moment that Owen would always hate me. Not because he was marrying my ex-girlfriend, but because we were too different, and the past had imprinted too deeply on us.

I shouldn't have even come. I should have stayed home

and said no thank you. I was destined to fuck everything up and cause problems from the get-go.

"I can't believe you." Sneering, he shook his head.

"Owen, stop," Lila pleaded, grasping his arm. "There has to be an explanation."

She looked at me. Those big brown eyes pleading for me to make this make sense. Lila was too kind and trusting for her own good. Her whole life, she'd looked for the best in everyone. Especially me.

As much as Owen's anger hurt me, her disappointment hurt so much worse.

My tongue was heavy, as if it had swollen in my mouth, making it impossible to speak. And shame, red hot and powerful, flooded my nervous system. I'd love to say I was a stranger to this sensation, but it had become all too familiar lately.

Owen paced from one side of the room to the other, his hands on his hips. "I can't believe you. Though I suppose I shouldn't be surprised. Of course you'd pull a stunt like this."

As my throat swelled and my gut burned, I lowered my head and let him fume. There was no reasonable explanation for last night. Even if it had nothing to do with Owen or Lila, I'd still gotten swept away, stupidity winning out.

I wasn't trying to cause embarrassment or hurt. I'd only wanted to cheer up a pretty girl.

Owen stopped in front of me, his chest puffing out, and crossed his arms. "You're a fucking disgrace," he spat, shaking his head.

"Excuse me," a distant voice said. The sound was so soft I could barely hear it over the string of self-loathing comments running through my mind.

I was still enshrouded in the thoughts when Willa stepped between Owen and me and poked a finger into his chest.

"You need to apologize." Her voice was calm, but her body was tense.

Owen grunted. "This has nothing to do with you."

I stepped to Willa's side, ready to push Owen back if he said another shitty thing to her.

Beside me, she narrowed her eyes and pulled her shoulders back. Willa was usually kind and pleasant, but furious Willa was terrifying. Those plump pink lips pressed into a hard line, and those dark eyes were practically black with anger. "Okay," she said, her tone eerily tranquil, "I guess I'll have to repeat myself. Please calm down and apologize to your brother. Then we can have an adult conversation."

Owen's jaw went rigid, his focus locking on me. "This is between me and my brother. I told him to stay away from you. I told him to behave."

"Behave?" Finally, irritation bled into her voice. "Do you hear yourself right now?"

Lila stepped up next to my brother. "Guys, let's sit down."

It was as if Owen hadn't heard her. He was gaining momentum, already tugging at his hair, his face turning redder by the minute. "Of all the dumb shit for you to do, you had to drag poor Willa into it with you."

I'd heard far worse, especially after my drunken vandalism spree, from my family, as well as the county judge. This kind of disappointment wasn't new. Owen would run out of steam eventually and leave. Then I could wallow alone. It was a fairly predictable pattern, and one that I only had myself to blame for.

But before he could go on a full dad rant, Willa planted her hands on her hips and said, "It was my idea."

Lila, who'd had her head bowed and was picking at her nails, went ramrod straight, and her gray-blue eyes went wide. "What?"

Willa grasped my hand and gave it a firm squeeze. "Cole and I have been seeing each other in secret."

Owen's mouth fell open, and he blinked at Willa, as if trying to make sense of this new information.

"We kept it a secret," she continued, her lip curled in disdain as she scrutinized my brother, "for obvious reasons."

A smarter man would speak up, tell her she didn't have to cover for me, apologize, and set to work fixing this mess. But clearly, I was not that man. Instead, I stood, rooted to the thin carpet, while my wife of eleven hours stared down my older brother.

"We did not pull a stunt. We were not thinking about you and your precious engagement, but way to show us how self-centered you are," she said to my brother, her tone syrupy sweet. "We got swept up in our passionate love for one another." She squeezed my hand again, the small gesture like a life raft during a hurricane.

My mind was still spinning, my heart pounding. But with Willa at my side like this, I already felt less shitty. Not because she was lying—in fact, I hated that she felt the need to lie for me—but because she was defending me. No one ever defended me. No one ever took my side. Even if this was only for a moment and a total lie, it filled me with more gratitude than I'd felt for anyone but Debbie in years.

Lila sputtered, "So—so you two...?"

"Yes." Holding her gaze, I picked up our joined hands and kissed the top of Willa's. "For a few months."

Lila nodded, her face a mask of confusion but also curiosity.

Willa shrugged, affecting a challenging expression. "Sorry if this is an inconvenience for you." She was staring straight at Owen, who was now the one frozen to the spot. "I realize that the timing was not ideal, and that is my fault." She peered up at me and gave me a warm smile. All for show, of course. "I've been in love with Cole for years, and the opportunity arose, so we took it."

"You never told me," Lila said softly, hurt swimming in her eyes.

Fuck, I hated myself for my role in all this. The two of them had been friends since childhood, and I was the asshole coming between them.

Willa stepped forward and hugged her friend hard. "I'm sorry you had to find out this way. But what you and Owen have is incredible. Yes, we got married last night, but we're still here to celebrate the two of you."

Lila hugged her back. The sight sent a pang of jealousy through me. While they were settling things, my own brother was still staring at me suspiciously.

"So," Willa said, fixing her focus on my brother again. Her tone was friendly, but her facial expression was glacial. "Feel free to apologize for verbally assaulting my husband."

With a jerky nod, Owen growled out a "sorry" and clutched Lila's hand.

"We'll see you at dinner," Willa said, threading her arm through my elbow and leaning against my bicep.

As the door shut behind them, we stood, frozen, waiting for their footsteps to fade down the hallway.

When the room was deadly silent, I turned to her. "What was that?"

Her cool façade instantly crumbled, and she covered her face with her hands. "I don't know why I did that. I was so mad. The way he was talking to you pissed me off." She stomped her foot for emphasis.

I had to bite back the smirk threatening to overtake me. She really was gorgeous when she was angry.

"He spoke to you like you were a—"

"Loser?" I interrupted. "The family shame? Not his real brother?" I had no idea why I was baring all my deep insecurities, but the woman had just gone to bat for me in a huge way, so what the hell?

It was strange, to have an ally like this. When it came down to it, my brothers would always side with Owen. He was the responsible, reasonable one. He commanded respect.

I was the runt, the leftover, the half brother. And after this morning, I had no doubt that all the progress we'd made over the last few months was slipping away. I had nothing and no one, and I only had myself to blame for it.

She crossed her arms over her ample chest—even in this moment of upset, I couldn't help but notice how ample—and glared at me.

"Cut that shit, Cole. We got into this mess together, and we'll get out of it together. Owen can suck an egg."

A laugh rumbled through me unexpectedly. I hadn't heard that expression in years. "But we still have to get the marriage annulled. Or get divorced or whatever. Deal with the legal stuff."

Pressing her lips together, she studied my face for a moment. Then she waved a hand. "We will, of course."

The pause made my heart skip a beat. The reaction confused me, but it was hard to deny that I wanted to spend more time with Willa. Get to know her. Maybe even become friends. Because she was fucking awesome.

How the hell had I never noticed before?

"But in the meantime," she said, "no one treats you like that and gets away with it. Got it?"

"I'm used to it. Everyone hates me," I admitted. "For what happened with Lila and then how badly I behaved after..." I trailed off, not in the mood to recite my rap sheet again.

She narrowed her eyes. "What happened with Lila? That's not fair. You were wrong for each other, and you both made mistakes."

Huh. That was unexpected. I was used to being the asshole who broke the heart of the sunshine beauty queen. She broke up with me, but that didn't stop the town gossips from spreading the word of my misdeeds.

"Thank you for saying that."

She nodded. "I get it. You wanted different things. Lila told me everything. About how you really want kids and she doesn't. So while you hurt my best friend, and I'm allowed to be mad at you for that, I can't hate you. Relationships end, people move on, and hopefully, we all learn something in the process."

Chastised but also a little amused, I nodded.

"And—" Now she was poking me in the chest. I was easily a foot taller than her, but clearly, my size didn't intimidate her. "I can't believe you stood there and let Owen speak to you like that. You tower over him. You could take him out with one punch."

"I'm not a fighter," I said, spreading my arms. Even as a kid, I was huge. Everyone had always been afraid of me, on and off the ice. But I'd never been a violent or aggressive guy. Maybe if I had been, I'd have had a longer pro career.

Head tilted, she smiled. "Good. Toxic masculinity is such a turn-off."

Heat crept into my cheeks at the comment and the way she assessed me. This conversation had taken an interesting turn.

"Really?" I said, taking a step toward her. "And what are your turn-ons?"

She spun and strutted toward the bedroom, her ass swaying in the fluffy robe. "Stop flirting, Hebert," she called over her shoulder. "We've got damage control to do. Now order more coffee from room service. I've got to work up the courage to call my parents."

Chapter 6
Willa

How did one explain this kind of predicament to their parents?

Hi Mom and Dad. Sorry, but I'm struggling to handle the pressure of my chosen career and family obligations, so I went to Vegas, wore a bikini, got drunk, and married a virtual stranger.

God, I was the worst.

More than anything, I wanted to go back to my suite and shower, but Magnolia would no doubt be waiting for me, and I could not face her right now, especially after lying to Lila.

She'd been texting my phone nonstop, and with every message, my guilt grew.

MAGNOLIA

What the shit is going on? Why didn't you come home last night?

Did you really get married?

Are you okay? How did this happen? Do you need me?

I mean it. If you're in trouble, you know you can ask me for anything. I can make some calls.

Seriously. I can help. 50K in small bills in a duffel bag? A gun? A jet to take you out of the country? Please text me back so I know you're okay.

What the hell? You never worry me, and now I'm worried. I know a hostage negotiator. Met him at a scuba retreat in Belize. Don't ask. But I can call in a favor.

I'D BEEN SO FOCUSED ON WHAT A SHITTY DAUGHTER I was that I had completely forgotten that I was also, in fact, a shitty friend to Lila by not only marrying Cole, but by lying to her and claiming to have been in love with him behind her back.

But the way he lowered his head, with his broad shoulders slumped while his brother belittled him, had hurt my heart. Cole wasn't perfect, and he may not have even been a good person, but he was a person, and he deserved to be treated like one.

The consensus was that, in general, doctors had God complexes. For me, though, it was more of a justice complex. And when I saw unfairness of any kind, I felt called to respond.

So before I could think better of it, I was on my feet, defending him and spinning wild lies. Lies I'd eventually have to untangle.

Before I could dive into that, though, I had to confront my parents. I couldn't risk the town rumor mill getting to them first. Luckily, the odds were good that they hadn't yet heard. They weren't gossipy by nature, and on top of that, on Saturdays, they drove down to Bangor to shop and have lunch with friends.

Cole had given me a T-shirt and running shorts—that were a little tight on my ass, but otherwise fine—to wear, and I was camping out in his room, drinking coffee and panicking. It wasn't my finest moment, but I was in uncharted waters right now.

First things first, I had to give Mags proof of life. If I didn't, God only knew what kind of reinforcements she'd called in. After that, I could deal with my parents.

WILLA

I'm okay. No need for cash, weapons, or hostage negotiators. I'll be back in a bit to tell you everything.

MAGNOLIA

Thank God. Are you sure you're okay? I'm here for you.

WILLA

Thanks.

THANKFULLY, COLE WAS GIVING ME SPACE. SO FAR today, he'd hugged me when I was wearing nothing but a bra and panties, then we'd held hands, and he'd even pressed a kiss to the back of mine. Things had been a bit too intimate, and I needed a moment to wrap my head around it all.

Over the last twenty-four hours, I'd discovered that he was a lot different from what I'd imagined. But that didn't mean this was anything other than a drunken mistake.

As I sat on the luxurious king-size bed, staring at my phone, he came in, sat next to me, and gently bumped his shoulder against mine. Despite needing a breather, I was strangely comforted by his presence.

"I know you're embarrassed," he said quietly, "and I know we've gotten ourselves into a big mess. But I have an idea."

As he spoke, I kept my head lowered and my focus fixed on my phone.

"What if we pretended for a bit?"

I straightened and blinked at him. "Pretended what?"

He shifted and turned so I could only see a sliver of his profile. "That it wasn't a drunken mistake. That we're together. In love. And that we impulsively decided to get married."

Turning, I tilted to one side so I could see his sweet, concerned expression. "Be serious," I said softly.

"I am serious." His shoulders slumped. "You don't want to upset your parents and risk your father's health."

"Or my reputation as the town doctor," I added.

"Exactly. And you stood up to Owen. Knocked him right off his high horse. You spun this situation from an irresponsible mistake into a sweet love story."

My heart thudded at the way he described it. He wasn't wrong.

"And I know how embarrassed you are." He trailed off, studying his hands.

I nudged him with my shoulder. "Let me be clear," I said. "I'm embarrassed about the drunken Vegas wedding, not about my choice of groom."

A slow smile spread across his face, causing a deep dimple to form under the thick, dark stubble of his right cheek. "Thanks for saying that."

I shrugged.

"I'm pretty sure I've now ruined my relationship with my brothers. Again. After months of rebuilding and trying to show them I'm worth it, they'll no doubt go right back to thinking the worst of me."

I felt for him. As much as I worried about letting my parents down, they would never turn their backs on me. I couldn't imagine a world where I didn't wake up every single day certain of their love.

Cole didn't have that. Not with his parents. And he was so desperate for his brothers' approval. So desperate to connect with them.

"How would it work?" It was silly, really, piling another irresponsible decision onto the mountain we'd already made. Surely it would be better to face the consequences now, then deal with the fallout and move on.

"We handle it the way you did with Owen and Lila. Tell people that we've been secretly dating for a couple of months and got swept up in the moment in Vegas. Go home and stay married for a bit. That way you don't risk your career or your dad's health."

"And what do you get out of this?"

"With any luck, it'll keep my brothers from hating me for fucking things up again. Or at least hate me less. Also," he trailed off, "I'd really love to move out of Debbie's house. Get some space. Figure out my plans for the future."

Yesterday, between drunken dares and helicopter rides, we'd talked a lot about his future. His voice had been filled with pride when he talked about the work he'd done on RiverFest and how he was thinking about going back to school to complete his bachelor's degree.

My cottage did have a spare bedroom, and I was barely home anyway.

But...

"I'm not sure." My stomach twisted. A fake marriage? That was a bridge too far. I needed to stay focused on my patients and the practice. Learn and train and become the kind of doctor my dad and grandfather had been before me.

I didn't even have the time or energy to date, never mind fake a whole-ass marriage.

"I'm a great roommate," he added, his brows lifted hopefully. "Debbie trained me well. I do laundry and cook, and I'll stay out of your way." Shifting my way, he ducked his head and held eye contact. "I owe you after what you said to Owen, and I wanna help. I'm living in limbo right now. I've got nothing and no one. So if you want me to be your husband for a few months while we figure out this annulment process, then I'm game."

For a moment, all I could do was stare at him and consider his words. Over the last thirty-six hours, Cole and I had become friends. We'd come together and connected. Not in a romantic way—granted, things had been very flirty when we were drunk—but maybe we could be platonic roommates? We were both lonely and got along surprisingly well for a jock and a nerd.

"It could work," I said slowly. "If we have ground rules and a plan and maybe a contract."

"How about..." He stuffed his hand into the pocket of his University of Maine sweats, and when he pulled it out, he held it out, palm up. "We roll for it?"

I blinked down at the item. "You didn't."

His grin was positively devilish, the sight bringing with it a flash of our night together. It was no wonder I married this guy. That grin was dangerous.

In his hand between us sat a bright red die. On the side with two markings was a *B*, for the Bellagio, etched in elegant script.

"I swiped it. Couldn't get the other one. But I knew I had to hold on to the lucky charm that had gotten me a wife."

My heart stumbled, even as I let out a laugh. This was beyond ridiculous. How the hell was this my life?

"What do you say? Odd, we fess up. Even, we stay married?"

I could not make a major life decision on the roll of a die. Nope, that was insane. Look what a mess damn dice had gotten me into last night.

No. It was a terrible idea. But the brick of anxiety resting on my chest had me wondering whether this was actually a workable solution.

My life was hectic, so I probably wouldn't even notice being married to the guy, and if it would save my parents embarrassment and stress, that alone would be worth it.

I took in his hopeful face and the shaggy hair falling over his forehead. Dammit. All my caregiver instincts were screaming at me to help this man.

"Okay," I said softly, though my stomach rolled with anxiety. "Even, we do it."

He held out his hand and grinned. After last night, he didn't have to tell me what he wanted. I leaned in, closing my eyes and praying that I wasn't messing things up even worse, and blew on the die.

When I straightened again, he shook it and dropped it onto the comforter. On the soft surface, it didn't roll much, but when it stopped, it landed on four.

"Even."

He waggled his eyebrows. "Okay, wifey. I guess we're calling your parents."

I guessed we were. The clock was ticking, and despite the way I'd been racking my brain, I hadn't come up with a better solution. My parents would be shocked, sure, but if I told them I was in love with Cole, they would support us completely.

The more I considered it, the more it made sense. Short term, easy, no strings, and we'd come out of it better than where we were today. Right?

I held my hand out. "Okay."

Rather than shake on it, Cole threw an arm around my shoulders and squeezed me tight, engulfing me in his warmth and masculine scent. "You should know this about your husband—I'm a hugger. Now make the call."

***

"M-married?" my mother sputtered.

Eyes closed, I took a deep breath. Having Cole's strong

arm wrapped around me was helping more than I'd care to admit.

"Yes," I said, barely holding back the tears. "I've been dating someone. Last night, we got swept up in the moment and had a Vegas wedding. I'm sorry I didn't tell you. It was unexpected, but I'm happy."

"I thought you were in Vegas for Lila's engagement party."

Lila and Owen had invited my parents as well—Lila had been a fixture in our house for decades; they loved her like a second daughter—but my dad couldn't travel, and Mom was too busy managing his recovery like a military general.

"Yes. It wasn't planned..." I inhaled a steadying breath. "We were planning to come home and tell you and Dad properly," I said. "But Gail Thomas took a photo of us and was sending it to people in town. I wanted you to hear it from me rather than through the rumor mill."

My mother scoffed. She had no tolerance for petty gossip. "She hasn't changed since high school."

"I want to tell Dad too, but I don't want to upset him."

"Oh, sweetheart, he will be surprised, but not upset. Your dad only wants you to be safe and happy."

My heart clenched, and my eyes filled with tears. Was I seriously lying to my parents to save face? Had I become the kind of person who shied away from consequences?

"Who is the lucky man?" Mom asked. "Or woman?"

I surveyed Cole, who sat beside me, his eyes totally focused on my face. We'd gone from acquaintances with nothing in common to friends to married in a matter of hours. How was this my life?

He gave me a nod.

"Cole Hebert," I replied, my tongue thick in my mouth.

There was no gasp. No objections. "Okay, then," she said after a pause, her tone curt. She was in therapist mode now. "I'll go get your father."

My dad took it well. He was confused but sweet and requested we come for dinner so that they could meet Cole as my husband—because, of course, he knew Cole and had his entire life. My chest ached at the slowness of his words. He was tired. I should have stayed home. I should never have come to Vegas.

It was selfish. My parents needed me. My patients needed me. This was the last place I should be.

"I love you, kiddo," Dad said. "And I can't wait to see the two of you."

My mother was relatively silent, no doubt choosing to keep her thoughts to herself until she found the right moment. At least this gave me time to prepare for her interrogation.

The moment the call disconnected, I squeezed my eyes shut to keep from bursting into tears.

Silently, Cole rubbed my back while I composed myself.

After a moment, he scooted a little closer. "We fly home tomorrow. I'll try to get our seats moved so we can sit together. We can figure out how we're going to do this, work out the details, on the plane."

"We need a plan," I said softly, overwhelmed by the desire to head home now.

"Yes. For now, the plan is to shower, get dressed, and meet everyone for dinner in"—he looked at his fancy smart-watch—"ninety minutes. We break the news, then we smile and hold hands and eat dinner. Then we get the hell out."

"Okay." Now that the hardest part was over, I had very little concerns about telling everyone else.

Thanks to Aunt Gail, the whole town knew, and they were probably judging us. I wanted to crawl into the fancy bed and hide, but it was time to face the music.

"You're right. We need to own the narrative," I said, my sadness morphing into anger. If I saw Gail tonight, I'd punch her. Then I'd probably punch Owen. I loved Lila and wanted her to be happy, but if he ever looked at Cole like that again, I couldn't guarantee I wouldn't avenge my husband.

"You're making a really scary face right now."

"I was thinking about how mad I am at Gail. And at Owen. If he ever even thinks about giving you shit, I'll knock his teeth out."

He laughed. "I hit the wife jackpot: cute and feisty."

My heart sank, but I forced a smile.

Cute.

If I had a nickel for every time a guy had called me cute. I was always cute. With my round cheeks and green eyes. Never sexy, never gorgeous, never desirable. Just... cute.

I'd been told more times than I could count that I'd be *so* pretty if I lost weight. That line was one of my favorites. Like I was hiding something worthwhile beneath the layers of blubber. I'd worked hard to push past that, to celebrate my body and treat myself with respect. But sometimes, one word could send me into a tailspin.

Cute.

His comment should not have bothered me. Yes, he had

been flirty and handsy last night, and we had kissed a fair amount, but that was where the connection stopped. He was a generic hot guy. That was it. His feelings about my looks should not matter.

So why was I now heading back to my room, determined to look extra hot at dinner?

Chapter 7
Cole

Willa's face looked a little green when she met me in the lobby for dinner.

I hovered close and kissed the top of her head, inhaling the scent of her shampoo. "You look gorgeous, wifey," I said softly.

Two little spots of pink appeared on her cheeks, making her look a little less pallid.

I got the sense that she had not been told nearly enough how beautiful she was. And while I'd keep my mouth shut and uphold my end of our bargain, I couldn't help but admire her. Thick honey-blond hair and an upturned nose. And her lips? Fuck, she had the most kissable lips. Full and pink, with a cupid's bow.

We'd kissed last night. The memories were fragmented, but the sensation of my hand splayed across her ass as I threw dice and the warmth of her body pressed to mine when she threw her arms around my neck in celebration were vivid.

Despite my hangover and the general anxiety about the situation plaguing me, being with her right now felt right.

Even so, I didn't want to walk into that room and announce yet another fuck-up to my family. I especially didn't want to drag Willa down with me. As annoyed as my family would be by my drunken Vegas wedding, they'd be horrified that I'd corrupted the saintly Dr. Willa Savard in the process.

The Savards were good people. The best people. Willa's dad had been the town doctor for decades, and her mother was a psychologist who worked in several area schools. They showed up at every event and every fundraiser, and they were always the first to offer help to their neighbors. The town loved them for it.

I stood a little straighter. So I'd made a drunken mistake, but I was pretty impressed with myself. There was no way I could land a woman as incredible as Willa on a normal day. So we headed down to dinner, ready to face the music.

Unsurprisingly, Owen had gone all out for his fiancée. The same private chef who'd curated an incredible gluten-free meal our first night here was holding a tasting dinner in the private wine cellar at the Bellagio, and as we approached the massive mahogany doors, we were greeted by tuxedoed waiters.

I'd almost nailed my head on the doorframe before I remembered to duck—underground cellars were not tall-guy friendly—but once I straightened, I was blown away by what I saw inside.

The space was filled with priceless sculptures, Renaissance-style carvings, and tens of thousands of bottles of wine, neatly organized and laid out to create a small, intimate space in what was otherwise a medium-size underground cavern.

My family was all here, chatting and milling around. The champagne was already flowing, and a harpist was playing in the corner.

The sight warmed my chest. My family was together and happy. Debbie was beaming, taking photo after photo and chatting with Lila's mom, no doubt making wedding plans. Chloe was sitting on Gus's lap, and he had his hand splayed protectively on her belly. Finn and Adele were standing, telling some hilarious story and finishing one another's sentences.

And then there was Lila. She was tucked into Owen's side, looking radiant in a short yellow dress. Her smile was so big and so genuine, I had the urge to hug her and tell her how happy I was for her.

There was a time when I thought I'd be the man she married. We'd stuck it out for so long together, and she'd given up so much for me. But we brought out the worst in one another. I'd wanted to love her. She was inherently loveable, and for some ridiculous reason, she had believed in me.

So I tried, for many years. But eventually, I stopped putting in the effort.

And I hated myself for that. For not being a better man. The man she deserved.

Lila, like hockey, was another thing I'd lost because I hadn't worked hard enough to earn it.

We'd gotten a few steps into the room when a hush fell over the crowd.

Beside me, Willa went stiff and let out a small squeak.

I squeezed her clammy hand, silently reassuring her. We could do this. We would do this.

Debbie charged toward us, her eyebrows at her hairline.

I braced myself, waiting for a lecture or a tirade. This woman loved me more than anyone ever had, but she had high expectations, and I was sure I hadn't lived up to them. I assumed Gail had filled her in already, but as I scanned the room, taking in all the people watching us, it was hard to be sure.

"Is everything okay?" Debbie asked, giving us a warm smile. "Come get something to eat. The chef has been spoiling us." She turned and gestured to the large table.

Feet rooted to the floor, I turned and assessed Willa. She was staring at her shoes. When she looked up, her eyes were swimming with desperation.

With a deep inhale, I scanned the group again, landing on Lila, the last woman I'd let down. And in this moment, I swore I wouldn't do it again. Nope, I was gonna make this work. Come hell or high water, I would not disappoint Willa.

The silence stretched, only interrupted by the quiet harp music and the sound of Owen's dress shoes tapping on the floor as he strode over. He wore the expression he always had when speaking to me. One that screamed annoyance.

"You okay?" he asked, looking straight at Willa and ignoring my presence.

I reached out and snagged Willa's hand again.

When she gave it a firm squeeze, I cleared my throat. "Actually," I said, looking around at all the eyes staring right at us. "We got married last night."

Immediately, a buzz of voices erupted around the room,

and people closed in on us. I tugged Willa closer as Debbie pulled us both into her arms and squeezed.

"Gail mentioned something," Debbie said, releasing us, beaming. "But I didn't believe it. I had no idea you two were dating."

I summoned every ounce of strength I had to play this right, despite the downright terror flooding my system.

Miraculously, I got through it, repeating the story we'd come up with, keeping the focus on Willa and how I was so in love with her. Every few minutes, I'd pull her close and kiss the top of her head for good measure.

She never left my side. In fact, she was incredible, chiming in with anecdotes about going for hikes together during the summer and our first kiss at Moxie Falls.

I'd always assumed she was the bookish, wallflower type, but I was quickly learning that there were many facets of my wife that I was not yet acquainted with. She was charming and bubbly—the champagne certainly helped—and effusive with her affection, clinging to my arm like a woman in love.

After dessert, I walked her to her suite, where she packed her bag, then brought her back to my room. We'd decided the best way to sell the newlywed story was to cut out early. It'd be natural for us to want to be alone, right? And it would limit the questions and hopefully the suspicion.

Inside my room, I pulled a bottle of water from the mini fridge and chugged it, then dropped to the oversized chair and put my head in my hands. The fake smiling and laughing and thinking on my feet had worn me out.

Willa quietly slipped into the bathroom to change into pajamas and take off her makeup.

After several minutes, she came out with a pillow tucked under one arm. "I'll sleep on the couch."

"No way," I said, sitting straight. "You take the bed."

She shook her head. "It's your room. And that couch is way too small for you." She gave me a once-over that made my heart rate speed up. Damn, I liked the feel of her eyes on me. "Get some sleep," she said, shuffling to the couch, clearly done arguing. "We've got to fly home tomorrow and get our story straight."

"I'm sorry." I wasn't sure why I said it, but the events of the day were hitting me. There was an anvil on my chest, making it hard to breathe, and as this beautiful, kind woman curled up on the couch of my hotel room, I felt like the world's biggest piece of shit.

"Good night," she said firmly, eyes closed.

Clearly being dismissed and all out of fight, I shuffled to the bedroom.

For a long time, I lay in bed, staring at the ceiling, trying to make sense of it all.

What had I gotten myself into? Marriage? With Willa?

I got up for another bottle of water, making sure not to wake my wife.

From the doorway, I watched her sleep, taking in her thick lashes, the blond hair spread out on the pillow, and the curve of her hip under the thin blanket.

I should be panicking. I should be spiraling.

But as I took in every detail of her, all I could think was:

This is my wife.

Chapter 8

Cole

The trip home had been uneventful. We'd landed in Portland this afternoon, then jumped on a shuttle to Bangor. From there, I drove Debbie home.

Though we hadn't had much time to talk through the details since we were surrounded by my family, Willa and I had agreed that I should move into her cottage right away. I had no idea how this was going to work, but I was determined to try. She was the best kind of person, and a single day with me had royally fucked up her life. I owed it to her to do all I could to make this right.

Debbie, exhausted by the busy weekend, was quiet on the drive, but she eyed me suspiciously several times during the trip. To her credit, she didn't ask questions, even as she helped me fold my laundry and pack my limited possessions into a few plastic totes she kept around for craft supplies.

It was already getting dark, but I wouldn't leave until this place was nicer than it was when I'd arrived. It was a challenge, because Debbie took great pride in her house. But I owed her that much. So I took out the trash, vacuumed, and changed the sheets on my bed.

Debbie appeared as I was adjusting the throw pillows in the room I'd been occupying. "You don't have to do all the chores."

"I put fresh batteries in the smoke detectors last week," I explained, keeping my attention on my task. "And I set an alert on my phone to replace them in six months."

"Stop," she said softly, stepping up beside me. She stood silently and waited for me to look at her. Then, pushing her dark blond hair behind her ears, she tilted her head and gave me a soft smile. "It's okay, Cole. Go. Move in with your wife. You don't have to worry about me."

Emotion tore through me, ripping at my composure. I owed this woman so much. A lifetime of repaying her kindnesses wouldn't be enough, and I didn't have the vocabulary to tell her what her love for me meant.

"Thank you," I said as my nose stung and my eyes went hot. That was the best I could do. "For giving me a home, a place to land."

She threw her arms around my torso. "Oh, sweetie. You are my sixth son, and you always will be. And like my other boys, you always have a place here." She patted my arm, sniffling, as she pulled back. "You've been on a bumpy road, but you have such a good heart. I know you'll be okay. Please come have dinner with me every once in a while. And don't forget about knitting club."

Despite the ache in my chest, I couldn't help but smile down at her. "I won't. I promise." I hugged her close again. My whole life, Debbie had been there for me, and she had always treated me as one of her own.

People like her, the kind who had a person's back when the chips were down, were the kind worth holding on to.

I squeezed her hard. "I love you," I said, my eyes stinging with tears.

I'd moved in with Debbie when I hit rock bottom. With nowhere to go. I was recovering from hip surgery, and I'd recently lost my career and my long-term girlfriend, along with all sense of direction. My father had been tossed into prison, my mother had moved away—and hadn't wanted anything to do with me anyway—and I'd alienated every person who'd ever cared about me.

Except Debbie. She didn't scare easily. Even when I was at my lowest, she'd rolled her eyes, given me a list of chores to do, and baked a batch of peanut butter cookies for me.

She never let me feel sorry for myself, and she kept me busy, even if it was only watching *Jeopardy* or going to knitting club.

"I love you too, kid. Now go move in with your wife. I wouldn't give my favorite roommate up for anyone. But I have a good feeling about this. She will keep you on your toes. Not that you need to be any taller."

"Thank you," I said again, because she'd done more for me than anyone ever had. More than I deserved. "I'm not sure I can ever repay you."

"You don't owe me anything. Being a mom is my job. It's my calling in this life. I've been given six wonderful boys to love, and now I've got a couple of grandkids too. I'll gladly do this every day for the rest of my life. Someday you will understand."

THE DRIVE THAT HEADED DOWN TOWARD THE LAKE WAS wooded, and in the evening, the road was dark. But when the woods opened up a half mile in and the light of the setting sun lit up the property before me, it was hard to breathe. Willa had mentioned she was renting a cottage on the water, but this was a spectacular estate. The grounds were meticulously manicured and included what looked like an apple orchard. Old-fashioned style lights lit the long drive that led to a large cottage surrounded by shrubbery. It looked like something out of a fairy tale.

I parked next to a blue hatchback I assumed was Willa's. How strange, that we were married and I didn't even know what kind of car she drove.

Before I'd even turned off the engine, she was out on the porch to greet me, wringing her hands. Clearly, she was as anxious about this arrangement as I was.

"Nice house," I said as I hauled myself out of my truck.

"I'm renting it from Magnolia. She owns the whole estate."

"Course she does." Magnolia Stephens-Thomas was a trust fund baby whose great-grandfather had built a railroad. She lived in New York but had inherited her family's estate up here. She was another person I'd known for most of my life but shared no commonalities with. She was an event planner for the rich and famous, but she was a good friend to Lila and Willa.

"She offered me the big house, but what do I need a seven-bedroom mansion for?" She giggled. "It has a catering kitchen, for God's sake."

The mansion? Apparently, the estate was so large there

was a mansion around here I couldn't see from where we stood.

"She doesn't use it?"

"Only once in a while. Though she's been here more lately. It's been in her family for a long time. You passed the caretaker's house on the ride here—that's Mr. and Mrs. Lewis. You'll see them around. Mr. Lewis has been doing the landscaping here since the '70s."

"It's beautiful," I said as I opened the back hatch.

"Make sure to tell him that. But speak loudly in his right ear. He's still fighting me on a hearing aid."

Grinning, I shook my head. "Noted."

She came down the stairs and rounded the Tahoe. When she was standing beside me, she put her hands on her hips. "Is this all your stuff?"

I nodded, waiting for her to make a comment.

Instead, she sidled up closer and reached for a bin. The move made her scent swirl around me. Vanilla, maybe? It was nice. Even in the cold November air, her proximity made everything feel warm.

She hefted the tote and headed for the porch. Quickly, I did the same, following her swaying hips up the porch stairs and inside. The door opened into an open-plan living room that was anchored by a large fireplace on one side. It was gorgeous. A sort of upscale rustic.

Without stopping, she made her way to the back of the house and nudged a door off the kitchen open with her hip.

"Here's your room."

The bedroom was small, outfitted with a queen-size bed covered with a green quilt and flanked by oak nightstands.

"Perfect."

"Sorry about the queen." She grimaced. "It's all that will fit in here."

There was no stopping my laugh. "I've been sleeping in a twin for more than a year. This is a luxury for me."

She whipped around, her mouth hanging open. "A twin? You? How does that even work?"

I shrugged. "I've learned to make myself fit in a lot of scenarios. This world isn't really made for people my height."

"I guess not." She hummed. "Is that why you've got that monster truck out there?"

Setting the tote on the bed, I shook my head and grinned. "It's hardly a monster truck. It's a Tahoe."

"It's huge." Her eyes went wide.

"I need a car my size." I stuffed my hands into my pockets. "I can't even fit in most sedans, and there's enough room for my hockey equipment."

Her nose wrinkled in the most adorable way. "I knew I smelled something gross."

Chuckling, I rocked back on my heels. "I'll keep it outside."

"Thanks." She spun and headed for the door. "I'll help you get the rest of your stuff."

"It's late."

"Yeah, but it's not every day my husband moves in."

The way she shrugged was so cute I wanted to tug her into my body and hug her. All the drama of this weekend had surely taken a lot out of her, but she was still so kind.

"Once we finish, I was hoping we could chat for a few minutes, establish some ground rules."

I gave her an easy nod. I'd agree to anything right now. I

was here, and we were doing this. Although the circumstances were pretty wild, this felt like a fresh start.

After the boxes were piled up in my new bedroom, I headed out to the living room and sat in an oversized armchair.

I fidgeted on the cushion, working up the nerve to check in on how she was really feeling. "You still okay with me moving in?"

She nodded. "Course. I've got the space, and I'm never home." She pushed a strand of blond hair behind her ear. "I don't mind having a roommate."

"I won't get in your way," I promised. "I can help too."

She'd already said yes, and I'd moved my stuff in, but I couldn't help but feel like I should reassure her that I wouldn't cause any more trouble. That I was worth the risk.

"I'll cook. Debbie has been teaching me," I offered. "My peanut butter cookies are next level. And I can do laundry. She's domesticated me."

A zing of pride worked its way through me. Debbie was loving and kind, but from day one, she'd made it clear there was to be no freeloading. Nope, she had me mowing the lawn, cleaning gutters, and washing my own socks within twenty-four hours of moving in, even while I was recovering from surgery.

And I liked feeling useful. While I doubted Willa would want to be waited on hand and foot—though I didn't know her well, she'd always been a very self-sufficient person—the least I could do was help out.

She rubbed her hands together, a small smile playing at her lips. "That's sweet but unnecessary for this kind of arrangement."

"Maybe so. Guess I wouldn't know. I've never been in a fake marriage before."

She huffed out a laugh. "Technically, I think this is a marriage of convenience."

"Is that right?" I asked, grinning. "And there's a difference?"

"Yes." Her tone was so matter-of-fact. "If we're looking at tropes, we're married for real, not only faking it. And it's for convenience."

"Fair enough."

"So I think a clear set of guidelines and expectations is appropriate, given the circumstances."

I nodded once, resting my elbows on the armrests and lacing my fingers. "Of course. Whatever you want."

"For example. How long are we going to stay married? I'm trying to find a lawyer that doesn't know anyone in Lovewell to help with the annulment process."

That was a good question. With the madness that came after our marriage, we'd yet to even think through the timing.

"What do you think? Six months? A year?"

"I really don't know." She worried her lip. "I figure we shoot for six months? Check in every few weeks to make sure we're both okay with how it's going? Six months would get us into spring. By then, hopefully my dad will have made a lot of improvements. So that could work."

"Hopefully I'll have a job lined up and be moving, anyway."

She twisted the ends of her hair, her nervous tell, I'd discovered. "And I'll be more established and organized at work and be taking better care of myself."

I smiled at her. It was impressive, how committed she was to this town and her patients.

"Let me know what the lawyer needs. I hope you know I won't take anything from you."

"Are you talking about money?" She laughed and then laughed some more, her head thrown back. "I don't have any money," she said, wiping a tear from her left eye. "I'm up to my eyeballs in student debt. I would have made more bartending than I did as a medical resident. If you married me for money, you are in trouble."

"I didn't marry you for money," I said, sitting up straighter.

She waved me off. "Oh, I know. We were wasted."

"Yes we were. But I also married you because I was intrigued by you and got swept up in the moment."

"So..."

I leaned forward, my forearms on my knees. "So, I'm happy to stay married to you. I like hanging out with you. And I think we can help one another. You're a good influence."

"Me?" she scoffed. "The girl who got drunk married in Vegas?"

I huffed. Her tendency to talk down about herself like this irked me.

"You are complex, Dr. Willa Savard," I said, maintaining eye contact so she knew I meant it. "But you are driven, focused, and ambitious. You've achieved a lot in your thirty years. I'd be lucky to be your temporary husband."

One corner of her mouth quirked, but that was the only reaction she gave me. I had a feeling she was not in the habit of being flattered, and I wanted to change that.

"Okay, okay. I get it," she finally said, dismissing my compliments. "But you need to promise me one thing."

"Anything."

"Radical honesty." She tilted her head and assessed me quietly while the words sank in. "This will only work if we're totally honest with one another all the time. I mean it. I'm going to call you out on your bullshit."

Amusement mixed with a little apprehension flitted through me. Still, I nodded. "I welcome it."

"Did you mean all that stuff you told me in Vegas? That you want to grow and find your purpose?" She cocked a brow expectantly, but she didn't wait for a response before she went on. "If I find you unshowered and playing video games on my couch, I'm going to let you have it."

Fiery. I liked this side of her. "Excellent. I'm all for it."

"And, if I'm not sleeping, if I'm eating crap and neglecting my life outside doctoring—"

I held up a hand in promise. "Then I will sound the alarm."

"Good." She nodded succinctly.

"Maybe, together, we can become functional adults."

"Here's to trying. Hopefully we can make it work."

I didn't know whether it was the late hour or how cute she looked in her sweats, but a surge of affection for Willa swamped me. Along with the desire to give her anything she wanted, honestly.

"We'll make it work," I said. "I don't want to fail again. At least not right now. RiverFest was a win, and for the first time in a long time, people are treating me decently. I am slowly earning back the respect of my brothers. And having a quickie marriage followed by a subsequent divorce and having messed up Owen and Lila's engagement weekend for nothing? That's old Cole. I want to be new Cole."

I wasn't in the habit of being so vulnerable. But she wanted honesty, and I wanted to be the best damn husband I could be, even if it was only for six months.

"Thank you," she said softly. "I won't let you down either. There's nothing I hate more than disappointing people. And while we may not live happily ever after, sitting side by side in rocking chairs while yelling at squirrels in fifty years, we can still take this time together and come out better."

She was right. This may have started as a drunken fuck-up, but maybe we could learn and grow from this experience. And looking at her, I knew the last thing I wanted to do was let her down.

Chapter 9
Willa

I took in my tiny cottage, at a loss. I still hadn't wrapped my head around what we'd done.

There was a man here.

He lived here.

And we were married.

I rubbed my eyes, confused. It was five a.m., which in my resident days was practically mid-afternoon.

In another life, I'd be sleeping in, loving life as a fellow, with regular hours and normal daily expectations. I'd sip my coffee and read new journal articles, flagging things to discuss with my mentors over designer salads at lunch.

Instead, I was half awake, tripping over the largest shoes I'd ever seen. I owned snowshoes smaller than these.

This man was an actual giant. Always ducking through doorways and accidentally bumping his head. He was lucky he lived with a doctor. I had a penlight in the kitchen, and I was pretty sure I'd have to use it to check him for a concussion more than once.

My plan was to exercise before I left for work. I'd found

my groove lately, working to prioritize self-care. Without a little morning workout, I wouldn't have the energy to get through a busy day of patients, and I found it was helping me sleep better too. But the thought of jumping on my bike and singing along to Beyoncé in front of him brought a wave of dread with it. Hence the extra-early wake up. I figured I'd exercise, grab a cup of coffee, and shower before he woke up.

Except when I flipped on the kitchen light, I came face to face with my new roommate-slash-husband.

Shirtless.

I froze in place, my mouth instantly watering.

His athletic shorts hung low on his hips, and from behind, a whole slew of muscles was on display, his latissimus dorsi, trapezius, rhomboids, and one of my personal favorites, the levator scapulae. Thank God for anatomy. I could happily trace the lines of fascia under his skin.

He turned around before I started naming blood vessels, but the damage was done.

Because Cole was built. It may not have been surprising, but it was still jarring this early in the morning.

His attention dipped, and a wave of heated embarrassment crept through me. Crap. I'd come out here in nothing but a sports bra and shorts. Despite how I wanted the floor to swallow me up, I had no doubt my nipples had joined the party.

Because *chest hair*.

I'd never had an opinion. It was there. An evolutionary adaptation.

But the dark hair sprinkled across his sculpted chest? It looked delicious. Manly.

And I was hit with an urge to nuzzle him.

Nuzzle? Jesus, I needed coffee and a lobotomy.

"Morning, wifey," he said with an easy smile. "Coffee?"

With a deep breath in, I willed my mind and my body to settle and asked, "You made some?" in a relatively normal voice. It was a miracle.

He nodded. "Couldn't sleep."

"The bed not comfortable?"

He shrugged and held a steaming coffee cup out to me. "Most beds aren't big enough for me, but I'll deal."

I cupped the mug with both hands and inhaled, relishing the rich scent.

With his own mug in hand, he took a sip. "Black, yes?"

Bringing mine to my lips, I nodded. As the flavor hit just right, I asked, "How did you know?"

"I pay attention." He held my gaze in a way that once again had my body temperature rising, but not in embarrassment this time. And suddenly I needed out of this kitchen. As quickly as humanly possible.

How on earth could I have thought this would work? I was barely holding things together as it was. Now I had to dodge through the beefcake obstacle course every morning?

"Go back to bed," I said.

"Nah." A half smile tipped his lips. "I'll keep you company."

I huffed. Seriously? "I'm going to exercise and get ready for work. Mondays are usually ridiculously busy. I'll have patients booked all day, not to mention the walk-ins."

"You take walk-ins?"

"Technically, no. But I also can't let sick people go without care. And everyone knows it."

My dad never said no, even if it meant staying late or

making house calls. So it was impossible for me to swoop in and demand that we close promptly at six.

He sipped his coffee, his brow furrowed in thought. "But you need a break, and you're only one woman. How about this? I'll come down, be your bouncer, make sure everyone makes an appointment."

A laugh bubbled out of me. "Doctors don't need bouncers."

"Ones as pretty as you do." And there were those brown eyes again, staring right at me. "Plus, it'll put my skill set to good use."

"Which one is that?"

He set his coffee mug on the counter and cocked a brow. "The one where I'm intimidating."

Cole Hebert was many things—massive, unexpectedly thoughtful, and weirdly funny—but intimidating wasn't one of them. Maybe it was the shaggy hair or the big brown doe eyes, but when I looked at him, I felt safe and a bit silly. There was a little mischief there for sure, but not intimidation.

"Anyway," I said, taking a step back, ready to extract myself from this early morning interaction. I was supposed to be keeping a healthy distance, focusing on work, and taking care of myself.

"I'll work out with you," he said, clapping his hands. "What's the plan?"

Chatting about my dysfunctional relationship with exercise and my silly little workout routine with an ex-pro athlete and all-around Adonis—whose eight abs were on full display in my kitchen, by the way—was ridiculous.

"It's nothing," I hedged.

"No it's not." He straightened. "You're a doctor. I don't need to tell you how important it is to prioritize your health. I can drive. I'll get my keys."

"I don't go to the gym," I blurted out. "I've never felt comfortable there. Even when I was in better shape, I didn't belong."

He took a step forward, his brow furrowing. "Don't say that. Fitness is for everyone."

"Not for people like me."

He crossed his arms over his chest, making all sorts of things pop and causing my brain to fizzle. "What does that even mean?"

"I don't expect you to understand." I stepped around him and shuffled to the sink. "Bigger people don't have the same type of access to exercise as thin people do. It's part of thin privilege."

I filled up a water bottle, avoiding eye contact. The last thing I wanted to get into with my fake husband at five a.m. was my body issues and societal fatphobia.

I'd given up on the gym long ago. The only way for someone like me to work out in a place like that was to actively and loudly telegraph my self-hatred with baggy clothes and pretend I was there to torture myself into thinness. Shockingly, that wasn't usually an effective strategy to get moving or feel good about myself. So I'd found a workaround.

"I started doing yoga in Baltimore," I explained. "I found an inclusive studio, and I fell in love with it. At the hospital, I walked miles and miles each day. During a fourteen-hour shift, I'd get twenty thousand steps in." I took a swig of water. "But here, I stand in one spot, examining patient after patient. And then I sit for hours while I work on charting and coding. So I've made a point of exercising every day. I know the toll this job can take."

He considered me for a moment, his scrutiny sending a niggle of discomfort through me. Would he laugh? Make a comment about the chubby girl on her silly bike? My head was spinning with all the cruel ways he could respond. Cole was a jock, a bully. By marrying him, I supposed I had given him infinite possibilities to hurt me on a daily basis.

"I can help," he said softly, his dark eyes earnest. "I'd like to help."

My heart stuttered. Seriously?

"I mean it," he continued, roughing a hand through his messy hair. "I enjoy fitness. And I got really into functional movement during rehab after surgery. I do a lot of yoga and Pilates. I could train you."

"No," I demurred. I couldn't imagine anything more painful than being examined by this man while I huffed and puffed and sweated through my clothing.

"I mean it. It would be fun." His lips tipped up. "We could hike, do some strength and agility stuff." Mug in hand once more, he paced across the room, his tone full of excitement. "Yoga, of course, and whatever else you enjoy."

He stopped in front of me, studying me as he sipped his coffee.

"Your job, it takes stamina." He raised one eyebrow.

"Yes," I admitted. "Between the ridiculous hours, the ridiculous number of patients, and the wildly fluctuating days. I've spent my life preparing intellectually for this job, but not physically. And having spent so much time with my dad lately, I realize I need to prioritize my own health."

Dad took care of all the people of Lovewell, but he had no time to do the same for himself. If this was what I would be doing for the next few decades, I needed to get my ass moving.

A wide smile spread across his handsome face. God, now the dimples were popping. Fuck, at this rate I'd be doing push-ups with him at four every morning. I was a sucker for his boyish enthusiasm.

He scratched at his stubble. "You're kind of awesome. You know that?"

Huh? My chest tightened at the unexpected comment.

"You're smart and thoughtful. God, I can't believe I drunkenly married an ambitious doctor in Vegas. How are you so grounded and normal?"

"Me?" I pointed to myself. Normal? I supposed he was right. I was the definition of average. He, on the other hand, was nearly seven feet tall and a hockey star—clearly not the normal one in this marriage.

He rubbed his hands together, grinning. "Okay, wifey. You go cycle, and then I'll lead you through my morning mobility circuit. We'll get you loosened up and get your blood pumping before you spend the day doling out flu shots."

I couldn't say no. Not when he was so fit and healthy and I'd revealed my secret gym shame. I guess we were doing this. And something about letting Cole help me get my blood pumping was strangely enticing.

Chapter 10
Cole

As I settled at the table in the conference room, I took in the space, marveling at how nice it looked these days. Chloe and her team had really turned things around at Hebert Timber. The majority of my dad's absurd art and furniture was gone, making the office feel like a place where people could actually work.

It was strange for me to be summoned to HQ, but a family meeting had been requested. While my brothers probably wouldn't notice or care if I didn't show up, I felt obligated to be here.

I sat back, adjusting in my chair, looking for a comfortable position for my aching body. I was sore and still exhausted from my wild Vegas weekend, a long flight home, and a sleepless night. I hadn't expected to see Willa up so early this morning, but it was nice to have the company. I'd led her through my mobility circuit, then I'd made a peanut butter mocha protein shake for her using my secret recipe. She'd seemed to like it, which filled me with more pride than I should probably admit.

Teaching her and then feeding her gave me a sense of purpose I hadn't felt since planning RiverFest.

Like me, she had tight hips, so we laughed our way through crow pose together. On the drive over here, my mind was flooded with workout ideas. It had been so long since I'd had a fitness partner, and she seemed eager to learn. The view of her in those shorts didn't hurt either. But I had worked hard to keep my eyes off her body.

She was serious, kind, and generous. I couldn't insult her by ogling her like a piece of meat. She was a hell of a lot more than that. But I was a man, and she was gorgeous, so it wouldn't be easy.

"Thanks for coming." Chloe slid into a chair at the head of the table, patting her baby bump and smiling.

I was still wrapping my mind around that bump. Around a lot of things when it came to Gus, really. The revelation that he had been married decades ago and had never told any of us was a big one. Even bigger was that the two of them were together again and they were having a baby.

He seemed happy. Though it wasn't always easy to tell, since he pretty much scowled all the time, there was a softness in his eyes when he looked at Chloe.

Finn and Adele arrived next, with baby Thor in his bucket seat, and then Jude strode in.

Karl, Chloe's assistant, set up a laptop and projection screen, then distributed small notebooks and pens. Already, this was far more official than the meetings we'd had in Adele's sunroom, where half of us had to sit on the floor.

A woman I vaguely recognized from the gym came in next. A friend of Adele's, if I wasn't mistaken. She wore jeans and a black blazer and had an air of authority about her. Military posture, slicked-back ponytail, and a blindingly large rock on her finger.

"This is Parker Gagnon," Gus said.

Karl adjusted the projector, and suddenly, Owen and Lila were on the screen with the view from his office in Boston's Seaport district behind them.

"Glad you could join us," Gus continued. "Parker is a private investigator and former state police officer."

She gave him a head nod.

"We've hired her to help us pursue answers," he explained.

She raised a hand and waved to Owen and Lila. "Thanks, everyone. I asked Gus and Chloe if I could meet with the whole family so I don't have to repeat any of this information."

Ah. It was coming back to me now. I'd heard about her at knitting group. She'd married Pascal Gagnon, and they had a baby. Something like that. Jodie talked incessantly about every baby in town. The only kids I spent time with belonged to Finn, so when it came to others, I often tuned out.

"Two years ago, I was hired by the Gagnons for the same reason, and the work we did resulted in your father's arrest."

What she didn't mention was how that investigation also resulted in her being kidnapped and held at gunpoint by my father. That was a particular family shame we would probably never recover from. I had still been playing at that point and was pretty far removed from it all, but just the thought of my father doing such despicable things made me nauseous.

Sometimes I found myself wondering how he could be

capable of the things he'd been accused of. But then memories I'd worked to repress would creep back in, and it wasn't as hard to believe.

His cruelty toward my mother and me.

Or the long car rides home from hockey games, when he'd spend hours yelling at me, belittling me, and reviewing every play I'd made. He'd accuse me of not trying hard enough and remind me that I was destined to be a loser.

The phrases would play in my mind as clearly as they did when he repeated them.

You'll be pumping gas someday.

Idiots like you can only shoot a puck for a living.

I didn't marry your mother for her brains, and I'm paying the price with you.

And once in a while, it got physical. Mostly, he'd shove me into walls or force me to shoot five hundred pucks in the driveway before I was allowed to go to bed. When those memories surfaced, I swore it was as if I was standing outside with the cold winter air burning my cheeks as I took slap shot after slap shot, trying not to look at the buckets of pucks I still had to get through.

If the abuse had been solely directed at me, I'd have been okay with it. But he'd been terrible to my mother as well—blaming her for everything, yelling at her for making the smallest mistakes.

And if she made a bigger mistake, like the time she dented her new Mercedes? He escalated to physical abuse. That time, he had grabbed her by the hair—her long black hair was her pride and joy—and cut off a big chunk. I remember watching her sit there as he came at her with the scissors, shaking and knowing that I should intervene, that I should fight for her, but being unable to move.

As the memories assaulted me, heat crept through me, and a tingling sensation started in my fingers. Trying to suck in air, I scanned the room. My brothers were all paying careful attention to what Parker was saying, but I couldn't even hear her voice over the rushing sound in my ears.

"Excuse me," I croaked as my lungs tightened further, making it almost impossible to breathe. I stood abruptly and strode to the door. I needed to get out of this room. It was too hot, and there wasn't enough air. With each step I took, my legs came closer to buckling. Finally, I made it into the hallway, but I didn't stop there. Still gasping for breath, I headed straight for the stairs.

"You okay?" Karl, who'd been walking toward the conference room with a tablet in hand, asked.

Without responding, I slammed into the stairwell door. When the cooler air hit me, I collapsed on the metal stairs and gripped the handrail as I put my head between my knees and forced oxygen into my lungs.

Fuck. My hands shook as I extended my fingers to get my blood flowing again. My jaw ached, and my head felt foggy.

"Here."

The voice came from far away, but the bottle of water in my periphery was very close.

"Drink."

Karl sat next to me, adjusting the cuffs of his perfectly pressed plaid dress shirt.

"You're not okay."

I waved him off and took a small sip. I wasn't even sure I could swallow. My tongue felt too big for my mouth. The cool water soothed me, instantly slipping down my throat. Fuck. I closed my eyes and took another sip.

"Now breathe," he said.

We sat side by side in silence for several minutes. Fortunately, he didn't ask any questions. If he had, I wouldn't have been able to explain my weird behavior. I wasn't even sure what was going on.

After a few minutes, I pulled a deep breath in and held it. Then, as I let it out, I stood.

"I better go back," I said without looking at him. "Thanks."

He stood too and held the door open for me. "Cole?"

"Yeah?" I glanced at his face but looked away at the pity etched in every line.

"It's okay not to be okay. Please remember that."

I wasn't sure what he meant, but I gave him a head nod, then shuffled back to the conference room. I wished more than anything I could slip in and take my seat unnoticed, but someone my size didn't have the luxury of sneaking anywhere.

When I returned, they were discussing the fire that had been set in the machine shop. The police had arrested a guy and charged him with arson, but by the way Parker was talking, there was more to this story.

"My contact at the FBI tells me he gave a full confession," she said. "The guy swears he acted alone and was so strung out he doesn't have any specific memories."

"I don't buy it," Chloe said. "It's all connected. The guys who approached me and this guy. I saw the photos. That tattoo."

"Lots of timber people have tattoos," Finn said.

Chloe shook her head. "Nah, this was different, and I've seen it before. It was some kind of tree or shrub."

"I'll pull the photos," Parker said. "We can take a look, and I'll ask around."

"Are the FBI cooperating?" Owen asked on screen.

Parker laughed. "Agent Portnoy is an old friend of mine. You've had the pleasure of dealing with him, I'm sure. For that, I'm terribly sorry. But he is good at his job. Sadly, federal interest and funds vary. It can be hard to sustain a multi-year investigation of this nature."

"But you'll give him a swift kick in the ass, right?" Adele asked.

"Yes. I think it's safe to say my involvement will motivate him." Parker rubbed her hands together. "Owen and Lila have already handed over financial records, and Chloe has given me full access to employee records and contracts. So now my plan is to dig in, start with the paper."

Clearing her throat, she tapped a few keys on her laptop, and a slide appeared on the screen. It was filled with details regarding arrests that had been made. The second slide listed the dates and times of the recent break-ins and thefts, and a third was filled with photos of the various buildings around the campus.

"Following the money is a good way to start. I promised my husband I wouldn't get myself into any dangerous situations." She rolled her eyes like there was a fat chance of that happening.

I'd just met the woman, but already, I couldn't imagine anyone telling her what to do.

"I'll be your fresh set of eyes. Every detail is relevant. Tell me everything and anything. I'm going to create a shared drive on a private server where we can store documents and communications."

"We'll get you whatever you ask for," Gus said. "We need answers, we need accountability, and we need to stop whatever is happening." He put his arm around Chloe, who was seated next to him.

Fuck. I closed my eyes, wishing this would all go away. My oldest brother, the guy who had dedicated his entire life to this company, had finally gotten the thing he had always wanted: a family. But now, during what should be the happiest time in his life, he was being dragged down by this shit.

"I'll be working through evidence and asking questions, and I'll need everyone's assistance."

"We'll do everything we can." Finn straightened. "I'll fly you out wherever you need to go."

"And I can help with the maps and geographical stuff," Jude said, resting his forearms on the table. No one knew these woods like he did.

Gus turned to me, his expression stoic as always. "Cole, you don't have to be involved."

Those few words were like a knife to the heart. "I want to help," I said sharply. He may not have meant that I had nothing to offer, but the comment rankled me just the same. My entire family was rallying together to keep the people they loved safe, but dumb Cole had nothing meaningful to contribute. Story of my damn life.

"What can you do?" Owen asked in a way that probably sounded fine to the rest of the group but was clearly meant as a jab.

And he wasn't wrong. I had nothing to contribute. I

knew very little about the business, mainly by design. My whole life, I'd stayed as far away from my father as I could, and unlike Gus and Jude, I'd never had any interest in Hebert Timber.

From a young age, I'd dedicated my life to hockey and assumed I'd be a famous pro hockey player by now. Living far away and visiting once in a while to show my family how successful I'd become.

But I was here now. And I had more than enough time on my hands. But other than that time and a desire to help, I was worthless. I couldn't read financial records like Owen or advise on the business like Gus and Jude. I didn't have resources like Finn, who could transport Parker and the rest of them anywhere they needed to go.

"Hold on," Parker said. Crossing her arms. She was tall and intimidating. Of course she was. She was Adele's best friend.

She regarded me for a moment, her lips pursed. "Everyone can help. And his help will absolutely be valuable. You planned RiverFest, right?"

I nodded, still tense from being discounted by my brothers.

"Good. Let's chat. I'm thinking we could use your connections with city hall and the mayor's office. Everyone is still raving about all the work you put into it."

My cheeks heated as every person in the room scrutinized me. I knew Mayor Lambert and his staff, but so did everyone else in this town. I wasn't special. Though the earnestness of her comment made me sit a little straighter. I had indeed organized the festival. It had been court-ordered community service, but I'd done a damn good job, and I'd actually enjoyed it.

Awash with gratitude, I gave her a nod. I wanted to hate Owen for his shitty comment, but I couldn't. He had good reason to dislike and distrust me. And while I had little to offer, I'd work my ass off in any way I could to show him I could be valuable to this family.

Parker went through the rest of her plan, requesting records and scheduling a time to fly out to camp with Finn.

After two hours, the group as a whole was restless.

"The entire town will know sooner or later that I'm working for you," Parker said from where she sat at the head of the table. "I'm not concerned. I'm confident we can flush out the people involved. But we need to keep our circle tight and make sure to keep this information from being leaked to anyone outside this group," she explained as she closed her laptop.

"What about your wife?" Owen asked, his tone harsh.

I picked my head up from where I'd been focused on the notes I'd taken. Was he speaking to me? Every head was turned my way, so I guessed he was. It was still strange to think that I had a wife. It had only been seventy-two hours, after all.

Owen's voice was tinny through the speaker as he said, "Why isn't she here?"

That questioned had my hackles raising. "My wife is a busy physician," I said, flexing my hands into fists and trying to keep my voice from shaking. "She has to single-handedly keep this county healthy, so she's got better things to do."

"I think what Owen was trying to say," Lila interrupted, her tone gentle, "was that we need to determine whether to involve her. If we don't, then you need to make sure not to share too much about what's going on."

"Willa is completely trustworthy," I said, glaring at everyone. Then I focused on Lila again. "I figured you, of all people, would know that. I will keep her updated. She's a member of this family now too."

Though I'd spoken the words, the truth hadn't registered until then. And it hit like a brick to the head. She was a member of this family. Our fractured, messy family. The family currently trying to shut down what seemed to be a crime spree. The family that had faced nothing but danger and catastrophe for the past two years. Shit. What had I dragged her into?

Chapter 11
Willa

"Congratulations," Mellie said, enveloping me in a hug, along with a cloud of Chanel No. 5 and her massive mane of black hair. "It's so romantic."

Mellie was effusive and sweet and a lover of all things romance. She was on her third husband, after all. And when I was in high school, she had snuck Nora Roberts books to me, introducing me to happily ever afters.

She'd worked for my dad for almost twenty years, managing the office, doing billing, ordering supplies, and generally keeping the place bright and cheerful.

Dawn harrumphed where she sat, typing on her computer.

She was Mellie's first cousin and total opposite. She was a no-nonsense nurse with a pixie cut, several tattoos, and two rescue pit bulls at home. The woman was pragmatic and focused, so despite her surly demeanor, the patients loved her. Sadly, I'd made little progress in my efforts to win her over with my professionalism and charm. I could not afford to lose an excellent nurse, so I made sure to ask about her dogs, Thelma and Louise, often.

Amazing nurses were impossible to find, and while she was only in her fifties, she was constantly threatening to retire. It typically came up when Mellie was talking her ear off about the *Star Trek* cruise she and husband number three were taking in the spring.

"Why'd you go and do a dumb thing like get married?"

"She's madly in love," Mellie singsonged from her ergonomic office chair. I swore there were literally hearts in her eyes. "And he's so handsome. And tall. Damn."

A little uneasy, I forced a smile. I didn't have the first clue how to even have this conversation. It was so weird to think I was married.

Me, a woman who'd never been in a serious relationship before.

Married.

To Cole Hebert, of all people.

Not that it was going badly. His arrival and our first morning together hadn't been crushingly awkward, as I thought it might be. Instead, he had been sweet and earnest and committed to sticking with the plan to remain married. Nothing I knew about Cole Hebert before this weekend screamed responsible husband material, but his honest confession about not wanting to fail had tugged at my heartstrings. He had a lot to lose as well.

Dr. Walters came in through the front door, and a hush fell over the office. He was wearing his usual wool dress coat over a freshly pressed white shirt and one of a dozen novelty ties he rotated through. He was in his early seventies, and he was tall and athletic. He had rowed crew at Williams, and he never let anyone forget it.

For years, he had been my dad's right-hand man. We had lured him out of retirement and convinced him to mentor me while Dad recovered. He only came in three days a week, but I needed the help desperately. Without him, Mellie, and Dawn, I would not survive even a single day here.

I'd clearly taken for granted how hard my dad had worked. How the hell had he managed to build this practice and take care of the whole goddamn town, while coaching my softball team, taking my mom out for weekly dates, and reviewing my homework with me every night? It was mind-boggling.

The billing alone was exhausting. At this point, I repeated the ICD-9 codes in my sleep.

Medical school had taught me a lot about the body and how it worked.

Residency had taught me how to triage injuries, diagnose illness, and treat patients.

But nothing could have prepared me for the packed waiting room that greeted me every day and the range of people who needed my help.

The endless paperwork, the outdated systems, the needless hoops for preapprovals.

The hospital in Baltimore had teams of people to handle all the behind-the-scenes work. Here, it was me and a small handful of people.

"Blondie," Dr. Walters barked while stirring a packet of Splenda into his morning tea. "Has your generation ever heard an arrythmia, or do you just snaptok about them?"

He loved nothing more than razzing me about my youth

and the failings of my generation. And he was sure to remind me at least once a day that he had been in the delivery room the day I was born.

And in turn, I enjoyed reminding him that he was older than dirt.

"Where were you when Lincoln was assassinated?" was my sugary sweet response.

Brow furrowed, he waved a hand dismissively. "I know you're busy with your new husband—the wife says congrats, by the way—but you can't lose focus."

Mrs. Walters was a delight. In fact, she had sent me a lovely plant for my office as a "thanks for taking him off my hands" gift when we'd convinced him to come out of retirement for a few months.

"Your charting is a mess. You rely on technology too much. Can you even manually take blood pressure?"

Of course I could. But still, I yanked the small pad from my coat pocket and scratched out notes as he spoke. As much as he loved to annoy me, he did take my development as a physician seriously.

"Also, you're on peds today. Waiting room is full of runny noses."

With a grunt, I gave him a mock salute. On any given day between October and May, there was a handful of kids home sick from school, and it was our job to work them in between appointments. Dr. Walters always pawned them off on me, saying he couldn't afford to catch what they were spreading at his age.

"Dr. Savard. You've got a patient in exam room two," Dawn barked, walking briskly down the hall.

At her command, I grabbed a surgical mask and got ready to start my day.

Kayleigh Whitlock was seven and had double ear infections. Her twin brother, Kayden, was sitting on the floor playing on his iPad while I swabbed her for strep.

"So you're a real doctor now?" Mrs. Whitlock asked, her voice high and anxious. "Dr. Walters isn't available."

I forced a smile and focused on examining Kayleigh, slipping the swab into the plastic container that would keep the sample from getting contaminated. "Yes, ma'am. Board certified and all." I wasn't going to launch into a full recitation of my résumé for this woman. At this point, most people in town had fully reviewed my qualifications.

She gave me a tight smile while I examined Kayleigh's glands.

"Dr. Willa." The little girl's voice was scratchy. Poor kid was miserable. "Why don't you have a ring?"

"Hmm?" I asked, mentally noting that her glands weren't swollen.

"A wedding ring." The little girl pointed to her own finger. "My mom said you got married."

"I did." I turned to wash my hands at the small exam room sink.

"And she said your husband is a snack."

"*Kayleigh*," her mother snapped.

My face heated with embarrassment, but at the same time, it took effort not to burst into laughter. This was one of the many reasons I loved treating kids. They said whatever the hell they wanted.

Lips pressed together, I inhaled through my nose and composed myself. When I was certain I could keep a neutral expression, I looked over at Mrs. Whitlock with a raised eyebrow.

"I'm sure he's a fine young man," she said, head down and very concerned with the contents of her purse.

"To answer your question," I said, smiling at Kayleigh as I pulled my prescription pad from my pocket. "I don't have one yet. But we'll get one soon."

Once I'd torn the script from the pad, I explained to her mom that I'd call with the results of her strep test once they were in.

Once I'd ushered them out, I turned and headed to the second patient room. It wasn't even ten, and the day was already off to a roaring start.

I skipped lunch because I was so far behind, and I hadn't even updated charts yet. So while Dr. Walters talked me through which labs should be ordered when the patient presents with hypertension, I shoved a protein bar into my mouth.

"Dr. Savard," Mellie said, poking her head into the office I now shared with Dr. Walters. "Mr. Moran is here for his physical in exam three."

Standing, I threw the wrapper away and picked up my laptop.

When I stepped into the exam room, I was greeted with a wide, warm smile. "My favorite doctor."

"My favorite patient," I said, returning the expression.

Bob Moran had retired from the timber business a few years ago and now drove a school bus in town. He was only sixty-one, but his health was poor.

"Have you started the vitamins we talked about? And added a little exercise?" My dad's notes showed that he'd been trying to talk him into exercise for a long time. Heart disease ran in his family, and his blood work was not great.

"Exercise is boring. Let's talk about the fact that you got hitched."

I rolled my eyes. "Small habits can have a big impact on your health."

He huffed. "You sound like my wife."

With my hand on my hip, I gave him a pointed look. "Your wife is right, but I expect that's most of the time."

"Oh, is that how it is? Now that you're married to the town hockey star, you know everything?"

"About heart health? Yes, pretty much. Multivitamins and fish oil and exercise. I mean it."

"Fine, Doc. But only because you're my favorite."

"I mean it." I eyed him for a long minute so he'd understand I was serious. "And if that cholesterol isn't getting lower in three months, we're adding medication."

As he was leaving, Mr. Moran turned and gave me a wink. "You're doing a great job, kid."

I thanked him, but his compliment did little to counteract the way every other patient questioned my capabilities.

After a case of the flu, a case of eczema, another ear infection, and a few well visits, I collapsed in my office chair and massaged my temples. My massive water bottle sat full on the top of my desk, calling to me. So I picked it up and chugged.

When I'd set it down again, I opened my email, praying I'd find notifications that indicated I had applicants for the job I'd recently posted.

Instead, there was nothing.

My shoulders sank. I was getting desperate. We needed more staff. Sure, my father had always run a lean operation, but he'd worked himself into a stroke. And with the recent closure of clinics in Heartsborough and Millinocket, we were more in demand than ever. Medicine was changing, and in order to offer the best care to our patients, we needed to change with it.

In residency, I'd been introduced to the community care model that had been adopted in a lot of big cities with vulnerable populations. The more I learned, the more I believed that type of approach would be beneficial to rural communities as well. People up here had few options, which made it even more important for me to bring comprehensive care to my patients.

But right now, my grand plans were on hold. There was no time to work out the best way to tackle the problem while I was struggling to keep up with my day-to-day tasks.

Dr. Walters, the cranky pain in my ass, was the key to my sanity. So for now, my number one priority was keeping him happy.

"You were totally right about RSV prevention dosing . Thank you for helping," I said as he put on his coat and headed toward the door.

He snorted. "I may be old, but I know what I'm talking about."

Keeping my expression neutral, I dipped my chin. "Of course."

"And I read. Never stopped. This isn't a job, Blondie. It's a calling. A life's mission. You don't punch out at the end of the day. This stays with you on your way home, while you eat dinner, on the weekends. You carry these people and their lives with you forever."

His words washed through me, a reminder of why I was doing this.

I'd known all this going in. But I couldn't help but hope I could be everything my community needed without burning out and destroying my health and happiness.

"See you Wednesday," he said as he stepped out into the hall, leaving me in my cramped office.

As I input my notes and codes, his words played on repeat in my mind. I'd graduated from med school six years ago, and yet I was still waiting for the confidence to kick in. For the ability to thrive and own this job the way my dad had. To possess the ease with which he approached each day and the tidal wave that came through the door.

So many of my med school friends had dreams of going into specialties with minimal patient involvement. They longed to be the expert who swept in at the last minute to solve the big problem. Or the doctor who triages a patient and then passes them along.

I envied them. They could take off the coat and switch it off. Put boundaries in place to protect themselves.

But me?

I didn't have that luxury. And I was shit at setting boundaries.

The evidence of that was currently living in my spare bedroom. My husband. My platonic roommate. The man who, in the span of a few days, had gone from an acquaintance I barely tolerated to a major part of my life.

While the news was burning through town like wildfire, I didn't waste much time worrying about it. I'd grown up here. I knew how it worked. New gossip would pop up in a matter of weeks, and we'd be old news. Teenagers would spray paint a penis on the side of the water tower, or Bernice would introduce a new flavor of pie at the diner, and my Vegas nuptials would be all but forgotten.

And then we could quietly separate as friends and move on.

Or he could move on. There were very few romantic prospects for me up here, and if the past few months were any indication, it would be many years before I had time to start the whole dating process.

But I'd worry about that another day.

I was almost thirty-one. There was plenty of time to worry about me later.

Right now, my job was my primary focus. And my biggest concern?

My accidental husband.

Chapter 12
Cole

Alittle past seven, Willa finally pulled in, her tires crunching on the gravel. She hadn't been kidding about the long hours she worked.

At the window, I watched her climb out of her hatchback. If my former teammates could see me now, wearing an apron while prepping dinner for my wife, I'd never hear the end of it.

But I was strangely... content? Or something approaching that. After the meeting this morning, I'd been desperate to turn my brain off. Working with my hands, I'd learned since returning to Lovewell, was a great way to do it. So creating a delicious dinner became my goal.

I was not trying to impress Willa. Nope, not at all. And while I baked, I hadn't daydreamed about her short shorts and flushed face while we did yoga together this morning.

She walked in looking weary, pausing inside the doorway. Her honey-blond hair was piled up on top of her head in a knot, and her shoulders were slumped.

"You made dinner?"

I pressed my lips together to contain my pride. A few months ago, I couldn't boil water. And while I was still learning, I'd come a long way.

"Do you like lasagna?"

"Like?" she said, hanging her purse on one of the hooks by the door. "I love it."

Delight lit up inside me. "Good. I made the sauce from scratch. No weird additives that way."

Slowly, with wide eyes, she walked into the kitchen. "How?" she asked, scanning each surface. "Everything is still clean."

"I cleaned up while it was baking."

Her eyes bulged in response, and I couldn't help but puff my chest up a little. Impressing Willa, I was discovering, was akin to scoring a hat trick.

She opened the refrigerator and stuck her head in. "And you got groceries?"

"Least I can do. I went to the health food store in Orono, then stopped at that huge CVS. I used the rest of your fancy shampoo this morning and wanted to replace it. Sorry about that. I picked up two bottles for you."

She closed the refrigerator door slowly. Then she turned and slumped against it, blinking.

"You okay?"

She shook her head. "Yeah. After the long day I had, I think your thoughtfulness broke my brain."

With pride rushing through me, and feeling a bit giddy, I flexed my bicep and winked at her. "One of the many benefits of being married to me. Now sit down and eat."

"One minute." She straightened and pulled her phone

out of her pocket. "Can you do that again? Flex while gesturing to the homemade lasagna?"

I cringed. I probably shouldn't have even done it the first time. "That's a strange request. Why?"

"Do it."

Sighing, I hung my head. "Fine." Despite my reticence, I obeyed, being sure to grin.

She snapped the photo, then, without a word, furiously typed on her phone.

"Uh..." I cleared my throat, worrying that I shouldn't have been so flashy. "Can I ask what you're doing with that?"

"Posting this to TikTok," she said nonchalantly, still typing. "You're gonna go viral. Is husband porn a hashtag?"

My heart dropped right to the floor. TikTok?

She looked up with a twinkle in her eye. "I'm kidding. I sent it to Lila and Magnolia. I wanted to show them what I came home to."

Holding her gaze, I gave her a genuine smile. "You don't have to do that," I said, turning back to the lasagna. "You don't have to go over the top to pretend to your friends."

She strode over to me and stood so close the heat of her body soaked into me. "That has nothing to do with it," she said, her tone sharp. "I'm still upset with Lila. She apologized, and I apologized, but she was dismissive and acted like there was no way in hell I'd marry you."

I didn't say it out loud, but we both knew Lila's assumption was spot-on.

"And as your wife," Willa went on, "I take offense."

There was no denying the small fizzle of pride that swept through me when she declared herself my wife. There were no feelings between us, save for a budding friendship, but even so, it felt really good.

"You really don't have to hold a grudge," I said while I plated our dinner, feeling guilty about the rift despite how her words affected me. "I don't want to come between you and your best friend."

She inhaled deeply. "You're not. We were due for a little dustup. Our lives have changed a lot lately, and friendships go through growing pains once in a while."

I picked up our plates and nodded at the small table, gesturing for her to sit.

"For the last few years, I was in Baltimore," she said, settling in a chair. "I was too busy to return texts, and she was stuck here, trying to put her life together. Now the roles are reversed. She's living in Boston, and I'm the one who's returned home. It's normal that we need some time to adjust. The love I have for her is forever, even if she annoys me sometimes."

I had few friends. It was one of the side effects of playing hyper-competitive sports my entire childhood. When I was home, I was focused on practice, and I traveled often. Tournaments in Canada, clinics in Minnesota, and showcases in Chicago. My teammates changed year after year, making it almost impossible to create solid friendships. The guys I played with were equally competitive and always trying to get an edge over one another.

Willa had no idea how lucky she was to have these long-term friendships. Her love of Lila made me even more determined not to screw this up for her.

I had picked up my fork when she took her first bite.

As she slid her own fork out of her mouth, she closed her eyes. "Mmm," she groaned.

That simple word, the ecstasy on her face, was all it took to get me half hard.

"You made this?" Her tone was full of genuine awe. "Damn, it's incredible."

"It's not a big deal."

"Um. Yes it is," she argued with a fierceness my simple meal didn't warrant. "Today kicked my ass. I had half a stale protein bar for lunch. This is the best way to end the day."

There was no stopping the smile that spread across my face. "Actually," I said. "I know another excellent way to unwind after a tough day."

She froze, and her eyes turned to saucers.

And I had gone and made things weird.

"N-no," I stuttered, waving my fork. "Not that."

She let out a sigh of relief, her shoulders lowering.

Okay, then. Sexual innuendo was not welcome in this marriage. *Noted.*

"I meant *Jeopardy.*"

She perked up at that. "You're a fan?"

"Yup." I nodded once. "Debbie got me into it. I watch every night."

"I love *Jeopardy.*"

"Then get your plate and let's do this."

"Before and After? My favorite category." She squealed.

Watching *Jeopardy* had become a soothing evening ritual

for me. I enjoyed it, and I was happy when I could answer a question or two. But watching it with Willa? Hilarious.

She knew a shocking number of answers about random topics. Fine art? The civil war? I'd always known she was smart, but this was next level.

And the enthusiasm with which she shouted out answers and cheered for the contestants made my insides warm.

"I love the teen tournament," I said. "I actually know more than an answer or two."

"Same. And celebrity *Jeopardy* makes me feel like a genius."

"I think you might actually be a genius," I admitted. "You should be on the show."

"I say that to myself every time I answer a two-hundred-dollar question about medicine, but it's doubtful."

"I get that. When there's a sports category, I get all excited, thinking I'll kill every question. But then they're about the 1972 world series, and I've got no clue."

She turned to me on the couch, bouncing with enthusiasm. "New rule. If we're both home, we watch *Jeopardy*."

My heart clenched. "Deal."

"And we support all contestants, even the ones who finish in the red."

"Yes. Especially the people who get overzealous in the daily doubles and then blow their leads."

"Still can't believe you're a *Jeopardy* fan."

I swallowed thickly, ignoring the pinch of pain that came with that comment. "I'm more than a dumb jock."

"I know that," she said, her tone nothing but serious, instantly bringing my mood back up. "*Jeopardy* has this special place in my heart. During my internship, I used to record it and then watch at two a.m. when I got off shift at the hospital. I'd make ramen and then let Alex Trebek lull me to sleep."

"I miss him."

"We all do."

After the show ended, we took our plates to the kitchen, where Willa insisted on finishing the dishes. "This was amazing. But you don't have to make dinner for me all the time."

"Eh." I shrugged. "I like it. Makes me feel useful. It was a weird day. There's a lot going on at the Timber company, and I want to help, but there's not a lot I can do."

She put the last dish in the dishwasher, then turned toward me, drying her hands. "Wanna talk about it?"

Based on the concern in her eyes, it wasn't a throwaway line. I had the feeling if I needed to unload, Willa would listen. But I didn't want to relive all the drama of the last few years.

"Not really. Basically, yet another situation where my brothers have everything covered, and I'm the chump who doesn't get it."

She squeezed my forearm. "I'm sorry. And for the record, I think you have a lot to offer. If you just keep showing up, sooner or later, they'll realize it too."

I busied myself putting the leftovers in the fridge, ignoring how good those words made me feel. She was right. Showing up mattered. And although they may not want me there, I wouldn't stop. I'd come and offer my support, no matter how insignificant it may be.

"I have practice tomorrow night," I said after the kitchen

was reset. "I made extra, so feel free to heat up the leftovers after work."

"My hero." She beamed up at me. "Also, my parents invited me over for dinner on Wednesday, so don't worry about feeding me then."

"I'm coming with you. You don't have to face them alone."

"It's not like that," she sighed. "I'm not going up against a firing squad."

Head tilted, I eyed her. "We're a team now, so I'll be there. Tell me what kind of flowers your mom likes."

"Tulips," she replied without missing a beat. "And thank you."

I closed the distance between us and covered her hand with mine. "I know this is not a traditional marriage," I said, my eyes locked with hers, hoping she could sense my sincerity, "but I'm still gonna be a good husband. I probably won't get it right most of the time, but I'll try."

She watched me intently, and in the moment of silence that followed, something passed between us. Trust, maybe? There was only one way for this marriage to be successful on our terms, and that was by going all in.

"Besides," I said, pulling away and putting some distance between us—I needed to go to my room and stay there, because I was not comfortable with the warmth that had engulfed me when we were so close—I cleared my throat and pushed away the sensation. "I feel like this marriage is gonna work out. We're gonna crush it."

"Seriously?" She chuckled. "We're one day in."

"Yeah, but you're cool, and I'm cool. Plus, we have *Jeopardy* in common. Some marriages start with even less."

Chapter 13
Cole

What does one wear when "meeting"—because I'd known them my whole life—the parents of the woman they drunkenly married in Vegas? The woman they'd embarked on a marriage of convenience journey with?

If anyone could crush a marriage of convenience, it would be Willa. From what I could tell, she had an incredible ability to compartmentalize.

We'd gotten along well these past few days. Granted, we'd only seen each other while we worked out in the mornings and watched *Jeopardy* at night before I went to my room to knit and listen to audiobooks and she read her medical journals.

So far, it was easy. Honestly, it would probably be a very enjoyable six months. I was more energized and motivated than I had been in years.

Willa could be trusted to stay the course too. She wasn't the type to break rules or cross the line.

I was the weak link here. The guy who'd never met a line he didn't want to cross or a rule he didn't want to break.

But I was working on it, improving myself and figuring out my shit. This marriage was a wake-up call, and I was answering it.

So I dug out a suit, one of many from my hockey days that had gone unused for the past two years.

Putting it on was strange. It was a bit baggy, which was yet another reminder to step it up in the gym. With that reminder came a flood of negative thoughts about how I'd gone from robust pro athlete to pathetic schlub in record time.

I squeezed my eyes shut and willed the negative thoughts to recede. Not tonight. I could spiral later, after I'd met Willa's parents.

In the living room, I sat on the couch, waiting for Willa, with the bouquet I'd picked up on the coffee table in front of me. The moment she had come home from work, she'd run into her room to change.

The pressure was on. She'd made no secret of how much she loved and admired her parents, and I wanted to impress them. It was unlikely, of course, but that didn't change my desire to show them that I'd be a good husband to their daughter.

I was fighting the panic when her bedroom door creaked open. And when she stepped out, all the air escaped my lungs.

She was wearing a soft green sweater over a short black skirt with tights. The look was classy and beautiful while displaying every one of her curves. Her blond hair was down around her shoulders, and her lush lips were glossy.

"Are you wearing a suit?"

I forced air into my lungs so I could respond. "Yes." I stood, brushing off my thighs. "We're going to meet your parents, so I want to make a good impression."

Her lips quirked up teasingly. "You know my parents."

"Yeah, your dad tortured me with flu shots when I was a kid, but this is different."

She sashayed to the coat closet by the door and shrugged on her coat, then tied the belt thingy. Even under the thick wool, the curve of her waist and the swell of her breasts were prominent.

God, I shouldn't be salivating over my wife like I was. We had a partnership, an arrangement.

She had been far kinder to me than I deserved, so I would do the same.

I'd be the best goddamn fake husband on this planet. But first, I had to stop staring at her.

THE SAVARDS MET US AT THE DOORWAY OF THEIR BOXY grand colonial with a brick front and a tree-lined driveway.

"Dr. Savard," I said, shaking the man's hand.

He was smaller and more frail than I remembered. He had been a fixture in my life since birth. A strapping man with thick silver hair and a wide smile. He was much thinner now, and his shoulders were stooped as he leaned on a cane.

"And Dr. Lahey-Savard," I said, bending to give Willa's mother a kiss on the cheek. She was short and plump, with big green eyes and a neat blond bob. When I straightened, I handed her the bouquet.

"Please call me Susan," she said, her cheeks turning pink. "And come inside. It's freezing out here."

Willa had her arm around her father as we entered the house. "How are you feeling?" she asked as Susan led us into the living room.

"Been better," he said with a wave of his right hand. "This one still isn't back up to snuff, but we'll get there."

Willa gave him a warm smile. "Have you been doing the physical therapy exercises?"

"Yes," he huffed. "Your mother makes me every day. And trust me, I'm not enjoying it."

She patted his hand, her eyes dancing with mirth. "Good."

The interior of the Savards' home was spotless but homey. In the middle of the room stood an upright piano covered with framed photos of the three of them. As I got closer, I studied each image. There were several graduation photos of Willa, and in each one, she wore a different type of gown. Damn, how many degrees did she have?

The three of them on skis, playing tennis, and snorkeling.

They looked every bit the happy, loving family.

My chest ached with a jealousy I knew wasn't fair. But my own family had been a shit show my entire life. My mother had taken off to Florida years ago, and aside from an occasional phone call, I had no contact with her. She hadn't shown interest in my life when I was a kid, and it only diminished more after I'd grown up.

Even when I'd played in Tampa for two years, she hadn't come to a single game. I couldn't blame her, really. She deserved a fresh start after all the shit my dad put her through.

My father, of course, was a resident of the federal penitentiary. And as a free man, he'd done nothing but belittle me.

Debbie was the closest thing I had to a loving family.

And she wasn't blood.

Though in her mind, I was her sixth son, and she would not hear otherwise.

"Can I get you something to drink?" Susan asked. "Dinner's almost ready."

"Water would be great," I said with a nod.

Willa helped her dad to the couch. It was difficult, witnessing how slow and shaky his movements were. This was the man who had won the fishing derby every summer when I was a kid.

"We were surprised," Willa's mother said softly when she returned with a tray of drinks.

"I want to apologize," I said, my hands and underarms already sweating. My instincts were telling me to loosen my tie, but I'd committed to the suit, so I'd make it work. "I should have come to you both, declared my intentions and asked for your permission." I reached over and took Willa's hand. "But we got swept up in the moment."

They shook their heads in unison, and Susan smiled. "No, I don't want you to think we're not happy. And please, ask permission?" She arched a brow. "My daughter would have killed you."

Roger laughed. "Just like I taught her."

"Thanks." Willa squeezed my hand. "It felt right."

"I understand, sweetheart," her father said. "I took one

look at your mother thirty-six years ago and knew." He turned to me. "You're lucky, son. Her mother made me wait two years before she agreed to marry me."

The gentleness in his tone imbued me with a sense of relief, and the tension released from my shoulders. While Willa showed them the few photos on her phone of our Elvis-officiated nuptials, I focused on breathing deeply.

These people had every reason to dislike me.

To look down on me.

But they didn't.

They loved their daughter so much that they didn't even consider their own feelings on the matter. If she was happy, then they were too. They did not have their own agenda, and they weren't trying to manipulate her in order to bend her to their will.

I couldn't wrap my mind around it. That kind of unconditional love.

Behind their smiles, they may have had legitimate concerns. But they didn't let them show. For Willa's sake. They put her first.

I thought about my own father, who would spend hours in the car on the way home from hockey games, screaming at me and calling me a loser while picking apart every mistake I had made.

Even on my good days on the ice, he was angry at me. For years, I'd throw up in the locker room while getting cleaned up and ready to head home. Being in his presence brought about crippling anxiety. I was nothing more than a tool used to make him look good. To bring him glory and back slaps from the other hockey dads. Though it was never enough. On top of that, my existence alone was the reason he'd left Debbie and my brothers.

That was a weight I'd carried since the moment I discovered that truth, and I'd always assumed that I'd carry the hurt with me forever. That it was part of who I was. But as I sat at the Savards' table and chatted as we passed the mashed potatoes, I felt some of that load lighten. Just an hour with this happy, functional family made the pain a little easier to carry.

"How's the office? You'll tell me if things are too overwhelming, right? You've taken on a big workload."

"Dad," Willa sighed. "We're not talking about work."

"Is Marty helping?" he asked, ignoring her annoyed response. "He's an excellent doctor, but he'll give you hell to entertain himself."

"I've noticed, and yes, he is very helpful. Every day he's there, he's sure to give me a lengthy list of everything I either did wrong or not up to his standards."

Both the Savards laughed.

"Sounds like Marty."

"Things are great," Willa said, straightening in her chair. "Really. I'm learning and growing. The job is hard, but I'm up for the challenge."

"Of course you are. You're a Savard. It's in our blood."

"Roger," Willa's mom chided.

"I'm not putting pressure on her, Sue," he said, holding up his left hand. "I'm only saying. Our girl was born for this."

He turned toward me, his face the most animated it had been since we arrived. "Willa was diagnosing her dolls at four years old. Did her first appendectomy on a Cabbage Patch Kid at six."

"Dad."

He waved her off, sitting straighter than he had all night and beaming with pride. "Won the state science fair in eighth grade. She cultured and grew a flu virus and tested several household disinfectants to determine which actually killed the germs. We knew then she was destined for med school."

"She went to the national math Olympics in tenth grade," Susan chimed in, clearly catching the parental pride her husband had been infected with.

Willa's face had turned an adorable shade of pink.

Their admiration was clearly very contagious, because I had fallen victim to it as well. She was exceptional. And it was deeply comforting to know that they saw it too.

"So," Susan began as we cleared the last of the plates. "Your father and I want to ask you something."

Willa went stiff as she turned and faced her mom.

I froze, my feet glued to the floor beneath me and my heart in my throat. Did they know?

Had we faked this whole thing for nothing?

My heart took off, and my mind spiraled. God, this family was so close-knit. I couldn't live with the guilt of causing her parents to be angry or disappointed with her.

But Susan didn't look angry.

"Have a seat and don't look so nervous," she chided with a grin.

With a thick swallow, I did as I was told, my legs nearly buckling.

"Your father and I respect your choice of an Elvis wedding, and it's clear tonight that the two of you are in love."

She paused, her silence pure torture.

Panic had begun to course through me when she finally spoke again. "We don't want to pressure you, but—"

"We want to throw you a wedding," Roger cut in. "Something local."

"But only if you want it," Susan added, splaying her hands on the table. "We don't want to overstep."

I turned to Willa and surveyed her. We should have anticipated this and come up with a plan. Lovewell lived for weddings, and given the love they had for their only child, of course her parents would want to celebrate her in a big way.

But what did Willa want? A big wedding wasn't logical. This wasn't real. Someday, she'd find a man she wanted to marry the right way, with church bells and a tent in the town square and blueberry pie instead of wedding cake. Given how beloved she and her family were, Lovewell would be talking about the wedding for years.

She deserved that. To find a great love, have a big wedding, and support of the town.

So why did the idea of it make me feel so terrible?

"Thank you," Willa said, finally breaking the silence. "We're not sure what we want."

"Yes," I agreed when I realized I was expected to participate in this conversation rather than imagining Willa's future with some awesome, faceless man. He was probably a doctor. Probably liked to golf too. Roger and Susan would love him. "Thank you. That is so generous of you to offer."

"We're happy with how we're settling in right now," Willa explained. "But we'll discuss it and maybe think about something in the summer."

"Good," Roger exclaimed. "I gotta get rid of this damn cane before I walk my beautiful daughter down the aisle."

Smiling, Susan clutched her hands over her chest. "You kids let us know. We're thrilled for you both. And I'll have plenty of time for wedding planning while we're in Portland for your father's rehab."

"Mom." Willa grimaced. "Dad is going to need you."

"I know, but I can only yell at him about vitamins, physical therapy, and acupuncture for so many hours a day. And you know I love a project."

The brightness in her eyes had me tempted to suggest she plan a big church wedding and a feast for two hundred guests. Her genuine kindness was scrambling my brains.

Willa's parents were incredible. Sitting here now, it was hard not to picture what holidays and everyday visits would look like. I'd come over and snow blow their driveway, and they'd drop off a casserole when we were busy with work. The more I thought about it, the more I thought I might want that future.

But my wife's body language suggested she felt differently. She was wringing her hands under the table, and her head was tilted to the right, which was one of her tells. She was uncomfortable.

She inhaled deeply and said, "We should get going."

"Sure thing," her dad said. "I want to borrow Cole for a minute. Come to my study, son." Slowly, he rose, using his cane for stability.

Oh boy, I could see where this was going. He was about to give me the speech.

I followed him to a small room with floor-to-ceiling bookshelves, diplomas lining the walls, and two large leather armchairs.

Once we were inside, he silently gestured for me to close the door, then said, "Have a seat."

Silently, I obeyed, steeling myself for this conversation.

"I never wanted to leave her alone," he said as he sat in the second armchair.

I blinked in response to the unexpected confession. Leave her? Alone?

"Walters is a good doctor, but I always believed I'd be there to show her the ropes."

Oh. My chest ached at the pain in his tone. He was talking about Willa running this practice.

He wiped a tear from his eye. He'd barely spoken, and already, he was overcome with emotion. The love he had for his daughter was overwhelming. "Since she was a little girl, it's been my dream to work side by side with my Willa. And this damn stroke has robbed me of that chance."

"If it helps, sir, the whole town is raving about her. She's an excellent doctor."

He smiled, his watery eyes brightening. "She is, isn't she? It's not an easy job. You need to know that now that you're her spouse. It's hard to turn it off, to stop worrying and working and pushing. The job has changed a lot since I was young. It feels like there are even more challenges now than when I started."

Unsure of how to respond, I laced my fingers in front of me and nodded. She'd told me about the challenges already, and I was determined to help her through them.

"What about you, son? What are your plans?"

My stomach sank. Dammit. I should have been prepared

for this. Especially in a family this ambitious and accomplished.

"Working on it," I admitted with a sigh. "Right now I'm coaching youth hockey, and I recently organized RiverFest."

He gave me an impressed frown. "I heard it was a success."

Chin lowered, I shrugged. "I think so, and it gave me a valuable opportunity to develop skills and push myself. All I've ever known is hockey. Now I'm still figuring out my next step."

He sat, head tilted, examining me in a way that had trepidation rolling through my body.

"I know that's probably not what you wanted to hear," I admitted. "But I promise, I will support and take care of your daughter. I have money saved."

He held up a hand. "My daughter can take care of herself. My wife and I made sure of that. But I'm impressed by your honesty. It's okay to take some time and work on yourself. We all move through life at different speeds."

The tightness in my chest only increased with his kind words. "Thank you."

"Willa doesn't need a husband to provide for her financially. She needs a man who will support her, champion her, and listen to her." He swiped at his eyes again. "Help her through the harder parts of her job and life in general. Make her laugh, force her to take vacation time, give her reasons to smile every day."

I swallowed past the lump that had formed in my throat as he listed off each item. "I can do that."

"Love her, son. With everything you've got. Show up for her and make sure she knows it. I don't know how long I'll be around, but I need to make sure she's got the support she deserves."

"I promise," I said, eyes downcast. Fuck, a wave of guilt crashed over me when I uttered those words. Promising like that was a lie. Because she and I had an arrangement. We'd made a plan. And I wasn't even sure I was capable of loving someone in the way he described.

Despite how much Willa deserved it.

After our talk, we said our goodbyes, then Willa and I headed home. The whole way there, a knot of dread tightened in my stomach. The stakes were even higher than I'd imagined.

As we drove back to the cabin, I looked over at her in the passenger seat and vowed I wouldn't let her down.

Chapter 14
Willa

Cole was quiet on the way home from my parents'. I thought it had gone well, but maybe he'd been scared off. They were very supportive and loving, but they could go over the top at times. At various points in my life, I'd been embarrassed by them, but as an adult, I knew how fortunate I was.

He parked in front of the cabin, and when he put the truck in park, he shifted in his seat to face me.

"I get it now." His tone was quiet, subdued.

I tilted my head, studying his expression. It looked like a mix of genuine happiness and pain. How was that possible? "What?"

"How you became you."

"That's oddly cryptic."

He shook his head. "You are one of the best people I've ever known. You're capable beyond my comprehension. And after spending tonight with your parents, I get it. You're special. You all are."

My face heated, but I couldn't take my eyes off him. Where was this coming from?

"Stop that," I whispered. "We're normal people. Yes, they love me a lot, and I adore them, but you're special too."

With a simple shake of his head, he opened his door.

I did the same, my mind a jumbled mess. What had that been all about? One of the best people he'd ever known? We still barely even knew one another.

We headed straight to our rooms, and as I got ready for bed, I tried to make sense of that moment in the car. He was hurting, that much was clear, and hanging out with my parents had affected him deeply. I took their love and support for granted. Though I knew I shouldn't, it was hard not to. It had always been there and always would be. But I could only imagine what it looked like to him.

I changed, washed off my makeup, and paced around my room, replaying Cole's words. It was only ten, and I wasn't sure I could go to sleep. The conversation felt unfinished, and if this were a real marriage, I'd want to talk to him and make him feel supported.

I ran my hands through my hair, pulling it up into a bun as I considered my options. Eventually, my protective instincts won, and I set out for his room.

But he wasn't in his room. When I found him, he was sitting on the couch.

Knitting.

Curiosity bloomed inside me as I watched him work. After a moment, I let it propel me across the room. I only stopped when I stood in front of where he worked. He was on the couch, totally focused on the needles in his hands.

"Whatcha doing?" I asked casually.

"It's called a rib stitch," he replied, not taking his eyes off the yarn.

Watching him was hypnotic. Broad shoulders, rippling muscles, Stubble-covered jaw.

He was knitting away, his massive hands moving confidently as he pulled and looped, his wrist flicking at the end of each row of precise stitches. The muscles of his corded forearms clenched, his friendship bracelets jangling as he worked carefully.

Cole Hebert was a big, burly guy, built for swinging an axe or throwing kegs or hockey.

Yet here he was, delicately knitting, his entire body involved in the most magical way.

I took another step closer. "I didn't know you knitted."

He looked up at me, a bit sheepish, but he never stopped working as he spoke. "Debbie taught me. It's good for my anxiety, and I was feeling anxious tonight."

I sat beside him and pulled one leg up so I was facing him. "Wanna talk about it? My parents can be a lot."

He kept knitting.

"I hope all that wedding talk didn't make you uncomfortable," I prattled on. "Mom would never say it, but I'm their only child, and they love this stuff."

"It didn't."

"I mean it. When Dad is better, I'll let them down gently. I promise."

"It's fine. He is excited to start his therapy."

There was no stopping the way my eyes teared up. "I almost lost him."

All Cole's movements stopped, and he looked at me, not the least bit freaked out or upset about my tears. "You didn't lose him," he said softly. "And I know he will do everything he can to be here for you as long as he can."

For a moment, we watched one another. I couldn't speak, the lump in my throat too big to form words. The gravity of my reality was starting to hit me. I'd been going through the motions, trying to survive for so long, that I hadn't stopped to process it all.

"Debbie dragged me to knitting club when I moved in with her." He changed the subject, as if knowing I needed a moment to compose myself. "I was so annoyed the first couple of times, but she wouldn't let me beg off. Eventually, I learned the stitches, and I find it really helpful."

"It's cool. But you have such big hands; I would think it would make it difficult."

"Nah, it's all about the rhythm and pace. It's basically meditation with your hands."

"How did I not know this about you?"

He shrugged. "I wasn't sure if you'd think it was strange."

"What's strange is my husband not telling me he belongs to a knitting club."

He smirked. "Don't hate on knitting club. We meet in the library rec room every Wednesday night and take turns bringing snacks and tea. These ladies run the town. They are the power brokers."

"So you've spent every Wednesday night for the last year hanging out with the elderly ladies of Lovewell?"

A chuckle rumbled from deep inside him, though his focus was fixed on his knitting again. "They would take great offense to be called elderly. And trust me: they get shit done. I mentioned having trouble recruiting sponsors for RiverFest at one meeting, and the next thing I knew, they were all pulling strings."

"So they've formed a secret cabal that runs the town?" I was giggling so hard my eyes were tearing again.

His lips tipped up on one side. "Joke all you want, but I mean it."

"I'm sorry you missed out on it tonight."

"Happy to do it. Your parents are great."

"What about your mom?" I straightened, watching his expression. "Should we call her?"

I knew very little about the woman, other than that she was really young when she got pregnant with him and she moved to Florida a few years ago. But given the reaction everyone was having to our marriage, it made sense we should probably tell her.

His face was a blank mask. "I'll call her eventually."

"Will she be upset?"

"Doubtful. She's not super involved in my life." The way he said it, so matter-of-fact, made my heart clench.

I inhaled deeply, then slowly let it out. "Radical honesty?"

He paused his knitting and gave me his full attention. "Sure."

"Her fucking loss. You deserve better."

He exhaled heavily. "Wow, that was some powerful honesty."

"I'm serious. If it's any consolation, you can share my parents. They will happily smother you with love."

He said nothing, but his expression was doubtful.

It hurt to see it, how alone he seemed to feel, and every single cell in my body was screaming at me to help him.

"How about I get my Kindle—I'm behind on this book Magnolia has been yelling at me to read; something about a school where people learn to ride dragons—and I'll read while you knit?"

He nodded silently, so I jumped up, put the kettle on, and dashed into my room to get my Kindle.

We settled on the couch, sipping tea and quietly doing our own thing for a while. The couch was large, but so was Cole. He took up so much space that we were always sort of touching.

And I loved it. The comfort of his proximity helped push aside all the bullshit of the day.

Eventually, I leaned into him, my body sagging against his.

As I read, I soaked up his warmth and let his strength anchor me.

He knit, a peacefulness settling over my little cabin. Our little cabin—what was mine was now his, after all.

As my eyes drooped, I knew I'd be paying for staying up too late if I didn't get to sleep.

"I need to go to bed." I stood and stretched wide.

As I turned, ready to head down the hall, he caught my hand, garnering my attention.

Even sitting, he was almost at my eye level. Slowly, he turned my wrist. Then he angled closer and gently pressed his lips to my pulse point.

I couldn't breathe; I couldn't speak. That simple gesture had my entire body screaming with pent-up desire.

He looked up at me, his lips inches from my skin, his dark eyes molten.

The look sent a shiver down my spine.

People tended to underestimate Cole, write him off as unserious or a clown.

But he possessed this intensity, this focus. And the closer we got, the more I saw of it.

My skin was on fire where his rough fingers touched me, and my insides were heating up too. I swore a primal need flashed in his eyes, causing my breath to hitch as I struggled to understand the sensations pummeling me from such minimal contact.

As quickly as desire hit, panic replaced it. Why was he holding my hand and looking at me like that? This was wrong. But was it? A wrist kiss was hardly a display of desire. Though with the way he watched me, it certainly felt like it was. The feel of his lips on my skin was not something I'd ever forget. Never mind the fire in his eyes.

My heart pounded against my breastbone, tapping out a rhythm that told me to leave. I needed space. Yes. Space. Far way. Maybe the next county. Maybe Canada? The border wasn't that far. And my passport was here somewhere.

With a grunt, he dropped my hand, and at the loss of the contact, I took a step back. God, I was too close to him. It was dangerous, this hot, twitchy sensation coursing through me, and if I didn't get out of here, I worried I'd say the wrong thing. Room. I needed to get to my room.

I took another step back, snatching the empty mugs and my Kindle off the table.

"You didn't tell me what you're making," I said, gesturing to the pile of emerald-green yarn in his lap, doing my best to keep my voice from quivering. I was feeling things. Confusing things. I needed to extract myself immediately.

He looked away from me, a blush creeping across the skin above his scruff.

"It's a beautiful shade of green," I said, uncomfortable with the silence.

When he still didn't respond, I turned, put the mugs in the dishwasher, and headed toward my room. He needed space. That was cool. I needed an ice-cold shower and a Valium, but that was another story.

"Willa." His voice was low, rough.

Breath hitching again, I turned in the doorway.

"It's the exact shade of your eyes. I noticed you don't have a scarf, and since it's winter and all..."

He left the thought hanging between us.

When he looked back down at his project, I turned and darted into my room. I didn't want him to see the smile that was almost splitting my face in two.

Chapter 15
Willa

"Y"ou've been avoiding me."

Magnolia stood in my office, wearing a lime-green jumpsuit topped with a black blazer. Her makeup was impeccable, and her trendy asymmetrical haircut was artfully mussed.

"Do you have an appointment?" I asked sweetly, hitting her with a smile.

"I brought lunch, and Mellie confirmed you have no patients until 1:45."

She was right. I finally had a break. And God, was I starving. Also, Mags had been texting me nonstop since we returned from Vegas last week, so it was time to face the music.

My best friend was brilliant, and she had the time and resources to dig for the truth. We'd become friends as kids. Though she wasn't a Lovewell resident like Lila and me, she spent her summers here. She'd regale us with stories of her Upper East Side prep school and bring us old issues of

Seventeen magazine. As we traipsed through town, sunbathing at the lake and splitting milkshakes at the diner, a deep bond was formed.

She was the best kind of people. But she also could read me like a book.

She stepped into the office and closed the door behind her, then she pounced. "Start talking." She pulled out a container and set it on the desk.

"Is this pad Thai?" I asked, my stomach growling at the divine scent filling the small room.

She nodded as she pulled out a second container.

"How?" I asked. "There's no Thai food within fifty miles of this place."

She shrugged. "I got a guy."

"But this is still warm."

"Exactly." She took chopsticks and napkins out of the brown paper bag. "Don't let it get cold."

Obediently, I popped the lid off my container. As a whoosh of warm, heavenly-smelling air hit me, and I moaned. How the hell had she found pad Thai?

"It's interesting," she said. "You live on my property, yet I still can't ever catch you."

"The property is forty acres."

She raised one eyebrow and angled forward. "We don't lie to each other, Willa."

Every muscle in my body went rigid at her tone.

"So." She leaned forward, elbows on my desk, her fingers steepled. "What's going on? I'm worried about you, and I need to know that you're okay."

"I'm okay," I said firmly, looking her in the eye so she could see that was the truth.

"You marrying Cole is strange. You know? Especially because of how much you disliked him when he and Lila dated. That makes me think there's more to the story. Is this a blackmail thing? Coercion? Did you lose a bet?"

I huffed. "Jesus, Magnolia. No."

"Is the mafia involved?" She arched a brow.

"Of course not."

"Okay." She sat back a little and dug into her meal. "Because I know people. You know if you need help, all you have to do is ask. I'd do anything for you."

I didn't doubt that. Her loyalty ran deep, and her job as a party planner for New York's elite had garnered her a lot of useful connections.

"What happened?"

"We got drunk and married," I said, holding my hands up in surrender. "There is no blackmail, kidnapping, or illegal activity at all."

"And you've been secretly dating?" Her face was dubious.

Lips pressed together, I surveyed my friend. The woman who'd hired a private jet to get me from Baltimore to Portland when my dad had his stroke. If she hadn't done that, I would have spent hours waiting for a flight. She literally sent a plane to get me when I thought I'd lose my father.

I couldn't lie to her. I was so tired of lying.

"No," I said softly, deflating. "We were not dating."

"Of course not," she scoffed.

My heart pinched at her tone. Yeah, I wasn't his type, but jeez.

"Cole is a selfish man child," she went on. "If you were dating him, I'd slap you around. I know pickings up here are slim, but really? You could date a pine tree with more integrity and better conversational skills."

Anger flashed through me like a lightning strike. I clenched my fists. "Hey. That's my husband you're talking about."

She frowned, her eyes swimming with pity. "If you need an annulment, I'll call my lawyers. They do shit like this all the time."

I pulled my shoulders back. "Had many annulments, have you?"

She shook her head and let out a laugh. "We both know I attract the crazy."

Sure. Magnolia attracted a lot of things.

Six feet tall with bleached blond hair, she looked like a supermodel, lived like a seventy-year-old socialite, and dressed like a club kid from the '80s. She had a long list of exes, both men and women, and left a lot of broken hearts in her wake.

"It happened," I admitted. "I went to Vegas feeling sorry for myself and needing a break from my responsibilities. I've been feeling trapped and left behind and shitty."

She hummed. "Nothing wrong with cutting loose."

"And trust me, I know what I did was stupid. But I've spent years waiting for my life to begin in New York. Now, that life no longer exists. It's not that I don't want to be here, but I'm still mourning the loss of that version of myself."

"It wasn't stupid. You did all the right things, but shitty things happened and plans changed. You're allowed to grieve the loss of them. The three of us spent years getting ready for our New York era. I get it. We're all sad."

"Not Lila."

"Maybe, maybe not. Just because she's happy in Boston with Owen doesn't mean she doesn't miss what we could have had." She picked up another bite of pad Thai and assessed me. "We're growing up. You and I are thirty, and she's twenty-nine. We've all got adult responsibilities. Shit changes. But you're allowed to be sad about it. You can be pissed. I don't care. Please don't fucking lie to me and go off and get married."

"Sorry. It's..." I blew out a breath, working out how to explain my marriage to Cole. "He's not what I expected."

She rolled her eyes. Her opinion of him, like mine, was mainly based on what we'd learned from Lila over the years. They'd had a long, angsty relationship through most of their twenties, and it had ended badly.

"He's sad and struggling to find his place in the world. And he's kind."

"Sure he is."

"I mean it," I said, rankled by her dismissive tone. "And he's helpful."

She barked a laugh. "Yeah, because you gave him a free place to live."

"He doesn't need it. He's got money," I explained. "I think he needs a friend. He's working on himself."

She slapped the table, startling me. "No fucking way, Willa. God, this is so, so... you!"

I slumped. "You're being a bit dramatic."

"No I'm not. You love a fixer upper. This is your MO. You're a doctor, God complex and all. You think you can fix everyone you meet. Shit, you are in deep." She stood and paced my tiny, cramped office, chopsticks in hand. "I should have intervened sooner. That's on me. We can work on this."

"Magnolia, stop," I said firmly, setting my own chopsticks on my napkin. "We got married, and we've decided to stay married for a bit. Our relationship is strictly platonic, but pretending helps both of us out for various reasons."

She shook her head. "It's platonic for now, but lines will blur. He's a wounded puppy. You'll be fucking him in no time."

Heat flashed through me. "Stop it."

"You've thought about it," she accused.

"No. We've kissed. In Vegas. Nothing since. We don't even flirt."

That was not entirely true. We flirted often—mildly, of course—but Cole was playful and funny. It was like his default setting. So maybe he sometimes put his arm around me while we watched *Jeopardy*. It was all very benign.

And then there was the wrist kiss. I had pushed thoughts of it to the back of my mind because I could drive myself crazy analyzing every facet. Neither of us had mentioned it, and I was happy to pretend it never happened. Unpacking the intensity, the attraction, and the pure lust of that moment would only lead to disaster. Best to ignore it all and keep pushing forward.

"We have firm boundaries, and he's quite respectful."

"Are we talking about the same guy? Cole Hebert? Arrested six months ago for vandalism at his own family's company? Ignored our friend for years, despite how she followed him around, taking care of him and acting as his personal cheerleader?"

"People change, Mags. You said it yourself. We're grown up now."

She'd had a front-row seat to all my romantic humiliation and heartbreak over the years. There hadn't been much, but she'd held my hand through a very complicated situationship with another resident last year. I appreciated her love for me, but I needed to handle this myself.

She shook her head. "I love you. I don't want you getting hurt. If you fess up to your parents, they will forgive you."

"No. I can't do that. They're over the moon. They're thankful that I've got someone looking out for me. You know how overprotective they are. They're so worried I'm in over my head with the practice. I was shocked how relieved they were, knowing that I have a husband looking out for me."

"Gross. I always thought Roger and Susan were more evolved than that."

"Not like that." I chuckled. "They're relieved to know that I have someone to lean on. My dad worked himself almost to death, but he always had my mom to help."

Her expression softened. "Your mom is pretty awesome."

"After Christmas, they're going to rehab in Portland for a few months. Then, in the spring, when Dad is better, Cole and I will separate and start the annulment process. He's trying to figure out his career, and let's face it, there aren't many opportunities here."

"I'll give him a job." She dropped back into her seat and crossed one leg over the other. "In New York. He can assist in planning events. He did a good job with RiverFest."

"He crushed it," I said as pride filled my chest.

She frowned at me. "He's smart and has good problem-solving skills. I'll give him that." She hummed. "I'll give him a job if he promises to get out of town and leave my best friend alone."

My heart sank. Of course.

"I mean it. This is not going to end well. I know in your mind, it's all tidy and neat. But Willa, I've done so much stupid shit. *Please.* Learn from my mistakes."

I raised one eyebrow.

"You're a good girl. You play by the rules. A guy like Cole? He's gonna blow up every single one of them and leave you hurting."

"Wow." My stomach knotted, and suddenly, I'd lost my appetite. "I didn't realize you had so little faith in me. Maybe I can handle myself."

Head cocked, she blinked at me. "You don't exactly have a ton of life experience."

"Sorry I was so busy becoming a doctor I didn't have enough time to date dozens of people."

"I'm not judging," she argued. "You know how fucking proud I am. Recall how embarrassed you were when I hired a skywriter at your med school graduation?"

One corner of my lips twitched without my permission as I nodded.

"Please be careful. And whatever you do, don't sleep with him."

I bit back a guffaw. That was not even a remote possibility. "I promise. It's not like that. There is no attraction."

Her eye roll could rival that of any teenage girl. "Do I need to go talk to him? Make sure he knows if he fucks with you, he will disappear?"

"Please don't tell anyone," I begged, my heart clenching

at the possibility. "I'm protecting his reputation as much as my own."

"I won't. But I don't like this, and I don't trust him. As long as you don't sleep together, maybe there is a chance this doesn't blow up in your face."

"I love it when you're optimistic."

"Only for you, bestie."

Chapter 16
Cole

I laced up my skates, shaking my head at the wild conversations that filled our little locker room. Moms and dads helped with equipment and fixed braids while the girls chattered in pitches so high they had me wincing on occasion.

Never had I envisioned myself coaching children. Mainly because it was something grown-ups did. Men and women who were mature, who had their shit together.

Who possessed patience, wisdom, and the ability to teach life lessons while also reminding the kids three hundred times to keep their sticks on the ice.

Not me. I was not coach material.

But yet, the youth hockey league had wanted me.

And I was still whittling away at my community service hours.

My court-mandated community service had taken many turns. First, I was assigned to volunteer at town hall, but even after the intensity of that experience, only part of my time qualified for my community service hours. It was ridiculous, really, since I'd worked nonstop for weeks planning the festival.

Arthur, the manager at the local rink, had texted me in September, mentioning that they were down a coach for the upcoming youth hockey season. I owed the guy for all he'd done for me throughout my years practicing here, so I told him I'd be happy to help.

I assumed they were looking for a coach for high school boys, or maybe pee wees.

But no, I was coaching the mites. Seven- and eight-year-old girls.

"Coach Hebert," Kali Farrell whined. "Please don't make us skate."

"Sorry, kid." I stood and headed to the door that led to the team bench. "We didn't have practice last week because of Thanksgiving, so we gotta hit it hard tonight. We're playing Lakeville this weekend."

"They are so good," one of the other girls complained.

"Yup," I said, turning and gesturing for them to follow me. "We're working hard today, ladies."

The grumbling was only slightly less high-pitched than the chatter. The girls were hilarious.

Soon we were gliding around the ice, working on edges, turns, and stops, and after twenty minutes of hard skating, I brought out the bucket of pucks.

The whole group broke into cheers, more than one girl losing her balance and falling on her ass.

"Finally," Goldie Gagnon said, putting a hand on her hip. It was hilarious in full hockey equipment, but the sass shone through. She had a lot of talent and led our team in penalty minutes.

"Two lines on the goal line," I shouted. "Give and go, then shoot."

They quickly got to work, the sight filling my chest with pride. The first few weeks had been rocky. There were vast skill differences, but I'd put my head down, done some studying, and stepped up to the challenge of making them a cohesive team. And to their credit, they worked hard and had fun.

"Why don't you ever bring your wife to practice?" Kali asked.

"She's busy."

"We know her," Goldie said, stopping sharply behind me and deliberately spraying me with snow. "She gave me shots."

"She's nice," another girl said.

"Then why'd she marry him?" another one sassed.

"Okay, okay," I said, hiding my grin. These kids never gave me an inch. "We'll finish with sprints, then we're going home."

The rink echoed with groans, making me grin.

"I'VE GOT GOOD NEWS AND BAD NEWS."

I toed off my boots and hung my coat on the rack by the door. Willa had beaten me home, which was rare, so the moment I'd seen her car, I was on high alert, worried that someone had called her out on our lie.

"Hit me."

"The bad news is, we're finally out of Thanksgiving leftovers."

Susan had cooked a feast for twenty, even though it had been the four of us eating turkey and watching football together. We'd brought home a mountain of leftovers and had been living off them for almost a week. If I never saw another mashed potato, it would be too soon.

"But the good news is that I made a healthy dinner, because pie is not a food group, and we could both use a serving or two of vegetables."

"Thank fuck, and yes, I agree. I'm all for vegetables. What did you make?" I tried to hide the hesitation in my voice. Willa was always going on about how she couldn't cook. And I'd fallen into a groove the last few weeks, prepping dinner for us most nights.

Her smile widened and she straightened, causing her oversized U Maine T-shirt to slide down one shoulder, exposing a purple bra strap. Why I was so fixated on that strap was beyond me, but it was damn near impossible to look away.

"Salad," she said with triumph. "But fear not, husband. This is not some basic-ass salad."

I took a step farther into the kitchen, inhaling the delicious scents. Okay, that was a good sign.

"This," she said, theatrically gesturing to two plates overflowing with colorful foods, "is fancy salad. Beets, toasted quinoa, roasted chicken breast, and dried cranberries."

I leaned in and surveyed the dish, impressed. "You said you couldn't cook."

She raised one eyebrow. "I found instructions on YouTube. I'm learning. I can't let my husband show me up every night."

I couldn't help but smile. Goddamn, she was adorable.

When she was in doctor mode, she was all business, focused and intense. But at home, she was a goofball, shouting answers at *Jeopardy*, dancing while folding laundry, and curled up reading her fantasy dragon books.

"So you're competitive, wifey."

"You have no idea. Now grab your plate so we can watch *Jeopardy*."

We'd fallen into a routine, exercising, making dinner, and hanging out. We were rocking this roommate thing. The gossip around town had died down, and though I still felt guilty about lying, I'd found it surprisingly easy to settle into life with Willa. We enjoyed each other's company and had discovered a few commonalities. Despite my initial impression of her, she was one of the least nonjudgmental people I knew, and probably the most supportive. With Willa, I didn't have to be anyone but myself. She was always appreciative of any small act, like picking up her favorite shampoo or taking out the trash barrels on Monday nights. Though it might have seemed silly to most, the recognition felt good. It made me feel useful.

During the commercial break after an extremely challenging Potpourri category, we ran to the kitchen to load the dishwasher and clean up.

"How are the girls?"

"Brutal," I admitted while I rinsed my plate. "They are fierce as hell."

She held out her hand. "Is being back on the ice difficult?"

I shook my head and passed the dish to her to load. "No. It feels normal to be out there. The last year of my life was what felt abnormal. When I lost hockey," I swallowed thickly, suddenly feeling choked up, "it was like losing a limb. I knew it was gone, but the phantom pain remained, nonetheless. I dreamed about hockey. My body still went through the motions, and my hands would itch to hold a stick."

"Wow," she breathed. "That's really powerful."

Of all the talents I could have possessed, in Maine, hockey was one of the best. Up here, people loved the sport. And they loved hockey players.

Once I'd made a name for myself, things came easily. My high school teachers congratulated me on goals I'd scored, and I'd never paid for blueberry pie at the diner.

But then it all came crashing down.

The *Jeopardy* theme song started up, calling us back to the couch.

"This element has the highest atomic number that occurs naturally."

"WHAT IS URANIUM," WILLA SAID CASUALLY, TURNING her attention back to me. "I'm happy that you enjoy it."

"I know it sounds ridiculous," I said. "I love hockey so much. But I struggled to stay focused, to stay the course. I let my love for it and my ambivalence for everything else fuck me up and turn me into a person I didn't recognize, only to then ruin any chance at a meaningful future."

She elbowed me hard. "Stop that."

We sat silently while the final *Jeopardy* question was read.

Often called the "voice box," this organ in the human throat plays a crucial role in speech production.

"What is the larynx," Willa called out before the contestants even began to write. "Now, back to the absurdity you were spewing. Radical honesty?" she asked, though she didn't wait for me to respond before she gave it to me. "You did not ruin your future. I think you might be catastrophizing."

I ran my hands through my hair and huffed a breath. Willa didn't hesitate to call me out on my shit—radical honesty pact or not, I suspected. Often, it was refreshing, knowing she was speaking the truth. But between her and the girls on my hockey team, I did not get a break.

Lowering my focus to the table in front of me, I searched for a way to explain this to her. Why it all hurt so badly. "For most of the guys, hockey is a job. They're focused and determined, and they push themselves every day."

She nodded.

"But hockey was more for me. It was a friend, my sole source of self-esteem, the only constant during a chaotic childhood."

"And that's a bad thing?"

"Like everything else I've ever loved, I pushed it away. I punished myself for loving it too much, and I fucked it all up."

"That's a lot to unpack," she said. "First, let me state for the record that getting injured is not fucking things up. That's a medical event and was probably outside of your control. Second, as your friend, I'm going to remind you that you have a lot to offer. Also, you have to know that if you want hockey in your life, you can choose to keep it."

She was right, of course. She always was. It wasn't the injury. I rubbed my hip absentmindedly. That was the result of not taking care of my body. Not investing in the kind of training, physical therapy, and nutrition required for the physicality of my job.

"I wasn't strong enough. Mentally," I admitted. The thing I wasn't prepared for when I was drafted to the minors? The boredom. Bus rides, plane rides, endless practices, and weightlifting sessions.

And then the downtime. Sitting, waiting, playing video games in a strange, shitty hotel. The game was my life, and every part of my day was structured around it.

"In high school and the three years I spent in college, I lived and breathed hockey. But that was my choice. I still had to go to class, do homework and laundry, all the normal stuff. But back then, hockey was the bright spot in my day. The motivation I needed when I had to be out of bed at five a.m. to deadlift."

"In Florida, though, I was bored out of my skull. Things were different in the minors. Every day, you're up and you're down. You're traded and moved from place to place. It's not worth getting attached to anyone or anything, because it's all temporary. Mentally, it wore on me. Day after day, month after month."

A long winter of travel, practice, weights, stretching, protein shake, game tape, repeat.

I got numb.

"Because my mind is the problem. Yeah, I officially retired because of a torn labrum, and yes, it was painful as fuck, and I'm still recovering more than six months post-op. But my mind left the game long before my body was forced out."

I craved stimulation and novelty. I fell into bad habits,

like partying far too much, which was something I'd never done. My father had been strict, and I, his perfect hockey star son, never wanted to disappoint him.

I was twenty-four when I started drinking. And I really liked it.

It helped the days and nights pass, and it lifted my mood, made things funnier, more interesting, easier to deal with.

It quieted my brain.

Dulled the restless buzz and calmed my itchy fingers.

And sometimes, it even silenced the voice in my head telling me that I wasn't enough, that this life would never be enough.

So I kept drinking. I stayed out late, neglecting my training, my nutrition, and my relationships.

So it shouldn't have come as a surprise that my life went straight to shit.

I didn't tell her that part. I was embarrassed, and I was still working through it. I hadn't had a drink since our wedding night in Vegas, and come to think of it, neither had she.

And, more importantly, I hadn't wanted to. I hadn't even thought about it. I'd been busy coaching, learning to cook, and working out. I was sleeping better, and overall, my days had seemed to level out.

"You don't have to give it up," she said again. "You call the shots. This is your life."

"You may have a point," I conceded. Since my injury, I'd assumed that I'd lost hockey forever. But Willa had a point. Coaching was different, but still a lot of fun. Maybe it wasn't the NHL, but lacing up my skates still sent a thrill through me.

"Of course I do," she said, lifting her chin. "You could coach or scout or run clinics. Or you could sit on the couch and cheer on your favorite team. You get to decide what your future holds."

It was easy for her to say. She'd been the valedictorian, the superstar. She had a lifetime of hard work and achievement to fall back on.

"I have no professional skills," I admitted, my voice thick. It was the first time I'd said it out loud, but the connection Willa and I were building was a solid one, full of trust. I was closer to her than I had ever been to another person, even my brothers. "I have no degree. I'm thirty years old and completely washed up, with no prospects."

We had long since abandoned *Jeopardy*, paying no attention to the responses to the final question. It was long over by this point, and another game show, one I didn't recognize, was playing.

"You are so stubborn," Willa said, her tone stern, no-nonsense. "You are literally the town hero right now. You brought back RiverFest. You know, the event that boosted the economy in a way nothing has in decades? People have hope again. There's talk of a buyer for the inn, and the old flower shop is being turned into a trendy pizzeria."

"It wasn't a big deal."

She scowled. "Now you're pissing me off, Hebert. You have massive potential. You've got an entrepreneurial mind and a knack for problem-solving. And you're a great leader."

"It's the height. People always follow the tall guy."

"Okay, get up." She stood and yanked on my arm.

When I was on my feet, she tugged again, dragging me toward the front door, and grabbed her snow boots.

Brow furrowed, I shoved my hands into my pockets. "What are you doing?"

"Get bundled up," she ordered.

"Why?"

"Because you showed me yours, and now I'm showing you mine."

Chapter 17
Cole

"Where are we going?"

There were several lights on the path to the lake, but the night was so dark, they did little good, and it was freezing.

But she stomped, determined, to the water, without looking back. I followed behind, zipping my coat as I tried to catch up.

I was raw. I'd opened myself up and shared all the ugly inside me, all the insecurities and shame. And she'd listened. She'd called me out when I was veering too far into self-pity and fact-checked some of the assumptions I'd made about myself.

It had exhausted me, yet somehow, impossibly, invigorated me at the same time.

Maybe it was the frigid air stinging my lungs that had woken me up. Either way, I'd unburdened myself and shared things I'd never said out loud before.

I wanted to tell her my secrets. I wanted to be close to her. I wanted her to trust me and depend on me.

She occupied all my thoughts. Her smell and her smile. The way she closed her eyes when she took her first sip of coffee every morning. The fun she brought along with her when we did yoga or went hiking.

I was developing feelings for my wife. Feelings I'd assured her I would control.

It had only been six weeks, but marrying Willa had been the best decision of my life. No matter how impulsive, how rash or stupid, at the end of the day, my life was infinitely better because I was her husband.

Being with her gave me purpose. Talking to her ignited excitement and passion within me I had long forgotten.

She treated me as her equal, even though I was far from it, and she was interested in what I had to say. She wanted to know me, my history, my thoughts.

The way she navigated the world, with so much compassion, but with a spine of absolute steel, was a sight to behold.

I could not fuck this up by falling in love with her.

So I followed her down through the snow toward the lake, unsure of where we were going, but grateful to be along for the ride, then down the path to the main road that led to the big house. Halfway there, we split off and headed toward the dock and boathouse. Behind the big house was a stretch of sandy beach, but here, by the dock, there were large rocks forming a barrier to the water.

Lampposts lined the pathway toward the boathouse, these a little brighter than the ones we'd followed here.

When we got to the edge of the embankment, where the rocky shore tapered off toward the gleaming water, she turned to face me.

"Since you shared your knitting with me. I wanted to show you what I do when I'm stressed."

She crouched and picked up a stone the size of a tennis ball. Then she hurled it into the water. An instant later, it hit the surface with a satisfying splash.

She reached for another, this one slightly smaller, and tossed it. We stood silently, watching the ripples along the surface of the once still water.

"You see these rocks?" She held one up to me.

Stepping closer, I studied it in the lamplight. It was brown and beige, with a bit of pink. Yeah, it was a rock, but an interesting one.

"See the coarse grain? And the small crystals? This"— she hurled it into the lake. She really had an excellent arm— "is granite. New Hampshire might be known as the granite state, but Maine is chock-full of it."

I picked up my own rock and surveyed it. This one was black with beige crystals woven throughout.

"These rocks were once part of something bigger. A majestic mountain. But time and nature have taken their toll. They broke off or eroded or were moved by man." She held up a smaller stone, this one almost black with white veins. "That salt and pepper look? It's mica." She pulled her hat down over her ears, her blond hair spilling out over the shoulders of her puffy coat.

The air was biting, our breath fogging between us. But the moon shone brightly over the water.

"An ancient volcano created this. Hundreds of millions of years ago. And it's only halfway through its life cycle."

She crouched again, this time scooping up sand with her gloved hand. "Eventually, it will be ground down like this, where it will stay. Until the next volcano erupts and it changes again."

For a moment, she was silent, looking out at the glimmering water and the white-capped mountains barely visible in the distance.

"This helps me remember that we are not significant. Our footprint on this earth is so minimal. There are massive natural forces shaping and changing our world and our lives every day."

I found a few stones of my own and threw them into the water in rapid succession. It felt good, the movement, listening to the subsequent *plunk*. But not as good as standing out here with Willa.

She turned to me, her eyes shining. "So when life feels overwhelming, when it's too much, I pick up a hunk of granite and throw it into the lake. Because regardless of the problem I'm facing, the world will keep spinning. The rocks will keep eroding as they become grains of sand."

"Thank you," I rasped, emotion stinging at my eyes. I wasn't sure what else to say. This conversation was about a lot more than rocks. She was showing me parts of herself she didn't normally share.

"Growing and changing is painful. You will look different, think different, be different."

"Like the granite?" I held up another chunk, this one in shades of brown.

"Exactly. It's taken many forms during its life. And the world has changed right along with it. Maybe we're only part way through our journey. Maybe where we end up is miles away from where we started."

I found myself closing the gap between us and pulling her close.

I was acting on pure instinct, but I had to touch her. To ground myself. To assure myself that this moment was real. Thinking that her explanation hit home for me too. That maybe I was actually ready for it.

She dropped the rock in her hand and looped her arms around my neck.

Nothing had ever felt so right. Holding her, touching her, was what I was made to do. Because she saw me, all my darkness and all my faults, and didn't flinch. She didn't push me away. Instead, she'd brought me out into the cold to throw rocks so I'd know I wasn't alone.

"Cole," she said softly, looking up at me.

Want and need and some deeper kind of pull were at play, arcing between us.

"I need to kiss you," I said.

Before I could do it, though, she was pulling me down to meet her lips.

Chapter 18
Willa

D anger. *Danger.*
Code Red.
Kissing.
Kissing Cole.
Kissing my *husband.*

Why did it feel so good? The moment was dreamy. A thrill.

Damn, he was tall. I was on my tiptoes, and he had his massive hands on my hips, and yes.

So.

Much.

Yes.

But also no.

With a hand to his chest, I pushed back, almost gasping for breath. The kiss had shocked me. It was full of so much more passion and desire than the drunken kisses we'd shared in Vegas. And my body had responded on instinct, essentially mounting him on the lakeshore.

Pressing my fingers to my swollen lips, I tipped my head

back and assessed him. Like this, in the moonlight, he was so handsome, his wild hair escaping the hat that I now knew he'd knitted himself.

A slow grin spread across his face as he angled in and pulled me flush against his chest.

For a heartbeat, I melted against him. But then reality set in.

"Cole." I gasped, my body going tense. "We can't."

Slowly, his grin faded, and his eyes turned a dull brown. "Sorry." He slid his hands from my hips, and when he took a large step back, the cold air hit me like a punch. *What was I doing?*

Suddenly, all logic and reason left my body, and I felt like I was going to burst out of my skin. This was bad, so bad. I had to get as far away from this situation as possible.

So without a word, I turned and hurried up the path toward the house, over the rocky ledge and toward the woods, desperately trying to ignore the hurricane of feelings building inside me.

But his lips...

I shook my head. This was not the time to lose focus.

House.

Get back to the house. It was cold and late and—

The world spun around me, and my knee screamed. In my haste, I'd managed to trip over a loose rock on the path and had face-planted in the frozen dirt. Tears stung my eyes, and I wanted to curl up and forget the past hour had happened.

But before I could give up and become part of the forest floor, strong arms were picking me up.

"Willa, are you okay?"

Aw, crap. Now it wasn't only my knee that was hurting, but my entire soul as embarrassment joined the party.

"Please put me down," I said through gritted teeth as he scooped me into his arms, bridal style.

He grunted. "No way. You're hurt and upset, and it's dark out."

"I weigh two hundred pounds. You can't carry me."

He stopped and glared at me, his eyes shining in the moonlight. "I'm a goddamn grown man, Willa. I'm more than capable of carrying my gorgeous wife."

And he did, holding me effortlessly in his arms as he navigated back to the cottage. Under normal circumstances, this would be the kind of romantic moment songs were written about. But sadly, this entire situation was far from romantic.

Once we'd reached the house, I had surrendered to the truth of the moment. He'd carried me. My leggings were torn. And I'd never recover my dignity. I'd done so well these past weeks, but I supposed it was only a matter of time before I humiliated myself in front of my husband. Dramatically running away after he kissed me and sustaining an injury was textbook.

Inside the house, I hobbled to the couch. Yup, my leggings were torn, and my knee was bleeding. Wonderful.

"Do you have a first-aid kit?"

"Bathroom closet, top shelf."

He returned a moment later with my doctor-grade first-aid kit. It was loaded with far more supplies than your average kit, but while this injury looked gnarly, it was nothing a little hydrogen peroxide and a few steri-strips couldn't fix.

He knelt in front of me, untying my boots and easing them off my feet.

"You don't have to do that."

Expression dark, he peered up at me. "Yes I do."

"Give me that." I reached for the box of alcohol wipes he'd opened, but he pulled his arm back. "I can do it. I'm a doctor." I winced at the way those words sounded coming out of my mouth. As if I were superior. But I wasn't that type of person.

"And you're in pain and shaken up."

"I think I can swab at a cut with an antiseptic wipe."

"Doctor Savard," he said, his tone sharper than I'd ever heard. He was usually so soft-spoken.

I froze, my breath catching. He was upset too. I had been so busy wallowing in my own embarrassment that I hadn't stopped to think about what he must be feeling.

I was the worst wife ever. So I shut up and let him clean the scrapes.

He was focused and careful, meticulously cleaning the injury, then applying ointment and bandages. His care was sweet, but it only served to make the boundaries between us fuzzier when what we needed was a clear, concise line. Nothing in my life had gone according to plan, so I needed this marriage to stay its course. We'd gone into this with good reasons. Now I had to resist making stupid mistakes that would compromise all we'd worked for.

"I'm sorry I overreacted," I said as he packed up the first aid kit.

"Don't be. I shouldn't have done that. It was out of line." He kept his gaze averted. His shoulders slumped, and waves of discomfort radiated from him.

Clear boundaries would be good for us both.

I sat back on the couch and inhaled, then let it out slowly, preparing myself for what I had to do. My knee throbbed, reminding me of why this was so necessary.

"We've been married for what?" I asked. "Six or seven weeks?"

He froze, pinning me with his dark stare. "Six weeks and four days."

Okay, then. He wasn't going to make this easy on me.

"I think it's been going well. We set out to do something, and we're doing it."

"Agreed." He nodded once. "I like being married to you."

My cheeks heated at his straightforward answer and the determination in his eyes. I crossed my arms over my chest for fortification. "Okay, so. Um. When we first talked. About everything. Our plan—" I was rambling. *Focus, Willa.* "Well, I never thought to bring up physical stuff."

He raised one eyebrow.

"Intimacy," I clarified, that single word leaving my mouth a bit too loudly. Okay, I was officially making a mess of this.

It had truly never occurred to me to discuss any of this in Vegas. It was laughable, really.

When we laid out the ground rules, I wouldn't have dreamed of even mentioning sex. It was preposterous to even think about.

Him and me?

Please.

I was a realist.

"Okay," I said, forcing myself to get this over with. "I

never said anything about physical stuff because I figured you weren't attracted to me, so it wasn't an issue."

He made a sound under his breath that could have been a growl. "Incorrect," he said slowly, and I couldn't but help stare at his mouth as it formed each syllable. "I'm very attracted to you."

"Cole," I hissed as my heart jumped in my chest. "You can't just say stuff like that."

His brow furrowed in confusion. "Why not? Didn't we promise to be radically honest?"

He had me there. But this was not the time to interrogate levels of honesty. Not when my brain was reeling with the realization that he was attracted to me.

Me. I had to work to contain the inner awkward teenage girl who was positively screaming at this news. I'd learned the hard way not to throw myself at any guy who was interested. After a lifetime of never feeling like the first choice, this type of thing had the potential to send me into a full-blown romantic fantasy. And right now, I could not afford to lose focus.

"I realize I acted impulsively out there." He nodded toward the door. "But I want to be clear. I meant to kiss you. I've thought about kissing you a lot. I regret being so drunk in Vegas because it means I don't remember what it's like to hold you, to kiss you, and to put my hands on you."

My face was flaming now, along with the rest of my body. This was not how I had envisioned this conversation going.

Was I hallucinating? Did I hit my head on a rock when I fell? Maybe I'm unconscious and dreaming. Because the thought of me telling hockey God Cole Hebert he couldn't have sex with me was preposterous. Girls like me did not reject guys like him.

I'd had sex with a fair number of guys.

I understood what they saw when they looked at me.

A lot of fun for a night.

But not a girlfriend. Not someone a man would claim publicly.

Trust me, guys were always all over me after a night of drinking, pawing at my chest and ass. They all wanted to fuck the curvy girl, but none of them ever wanted to keep me. I had a lot of growing and healing to do in the sex and relationships department, and I wasn't about to start now with Cole.

I held up a hand. "If this is going to work, we've got to be just friends."

He hung his head. "I know," he said, his voice once again quiet. "I don't like it, but I understand. We get along so well, and we're actually making this work. We can't complicate matters."

"Exactly." Relief flooded my bloodstream. He got it.

"Yes, we're married, but we're friends. And while I understand it's probably hard for you to not be able to..." I swallowed past the lump in my throat. "To date," I whispered. "We shouldn't become fuck buddies because it's easy."

I wouldn't be an easy lay. I wouldn't be the girl who begged for scraps and settled for affection brought on only by convenience, especially from him. Cole was a good person and a good friend, that I knew for a fact. But I'd seen the way he treated Lila. The man was a shitty boyfriend. So inviting anything more into this arrangement would only lead to disappointment.

"I'm not looking for a fuck buddy, Willa," he said, his tone defensive, his expression pained. "And more importantly. You are not easy. In fact, you are the most complicated and challenging woman I've ever met."

How he managed to make complicated and challenging sound like compliments, I will never know, but the lump in my throat continued to grow.

I needed to be alone. I stood, wincing slightly and making Cole reel back.

"You wanted radical honesty," he said, standing as well.

"I did. I do." As much as it could hurt or confuse, it was the only way for us to survive this marriage.

He took a step closer, towering over me, his hands on his hips. Yes, he could be intimidating, but I had ceased to notice. He was Cole.

He took another step and ducked his head. "Here's some honesty for you. I'm really attracted to my wife. Kissing you was fucking epic, and I'd do it again in a heartbeat."

His words knocked the air from my lungs. Part of me was ready to jump into his arms and kiss him again. But I wasn't that girl. That girl married him in Vegas, and she couldn't be trusted.

I lifted my chin and forced myself to make eye contact. "Do you want to stop?"

"Fuck no. I made a commitment, and I'll honor it."

"Good."

"But I don't want to hear all this bullshit about me not being attracted to you. If you don't want anything more, I respect that. But do not put that on me."

With a nod, I took a step back, but just as I put distance between us, he closed it again. And the closer he got, the more potent the strong warmth of his body was. And the easier it would be to allow myself to give in to the feelings.

So without waiting another second, I turned and rushed toward my room. Space, I needed space. Nothing good would come of this conversation.

"Willa," he said as I crossed the threshold.

I turned, pulling the door mostly closed, peeking out at him from the crack.

"I'm not sure I've ever been as attracted to a person as I am to you."

Without responding, I shut the door hard and slumped against it.

My heart was pounding, and I gasped for breath.

I was fucking this all up.

I was not supposed to be experiencing real lust for my fake husband.

Chapter 19
Cole

Jude was a healthy eater, but like the rest of us, he couldn't resist Debbie's peanut butter cookies. They were perfect, the right blend of sweet, salty, and chewy.

Cookies seemed like the easiest way to go about inviting myself over.

I'd thought a lot about this recently. My relationships. The people in my life.

It was time to start investing in my relationships. I was talking to Dr. Gleeson twice a week by phone now, and she was pushing me to make a bigger effort to connect with my brothers.

"How did you get those?" he asked, taking the container out of my hand and shoving one into his mouth.

I waited until he closed his eyes and groaned before dropping the bomb.

"I made them."

He paused, mouth hanging open, crumbs spilling out, and stared at me.

"Bullshit," he mumbled.

I crossed my arms. "Debbie taught me." I'd also practiced a lot, but he didn't need all the details.

He looked dubious. "So you made these."

"For you." With a smile, I shrugged off my coat. Once I'd hung it up, I held a hand out to Ripley, Jude's dog. She snorted and walked away, clearly not impressed.

Jude crossed his arms over a T-shirt that read: *I'm not procrastinating. It's a side quest.* And glared at me.

"It's a gesture," I said. "I wanted to hang out with you."

He pulled another cookie from the container and took a bite, head tilted in thought as he chewed. "These are fucking great."

I smiled.

"But," he said, heading for his coffee maker, "you don't have to bring me food. Wanna cup?"

I nodded, already feeling grateful that I'd worked up the courage to come. Of all my brothers, Jude was the most approachable. He was quiet and mostly kept to himself, but he had a big heart. He was shorter than me, with thick glasses and a carefully trimmed beard. He spent his free time either hiking in the woods or playing guitar. A couple of years back, he'd bought himself this house. A cape a mile outside of town.

It was small, but super neat, with vinyl and comic book collections meticulously organized and labeled on custom built-in bookshelves.

When he slid a mug over to me, I picked it up right away and took a sip. I carried it with me to Jude's refrigerator, where I studied the photos. Mixed in with his band's practice schedule and a flier for RiverFest were several photos of him and Noah, including one where they were white water rafting. A dull ache throbbed in my chest. I'd never done that before, and it looked like they were having a blast together.

"How's Noah?"

Exhaling, he took off his glasses. While he cleaned them on the hem of his T-shirt, he said nothing, but once he'd slid them back into place, he cleared his throat. "There was a big fire. Back in July."

My heart leapt into my throat. How had I not heard about this? That was almost six months ago. "Is he okay?"

"Physically? Yes. Minor burns and smoke inhalation. He spent a couple of months doing PT for his lungs, but he's good."

"And mentally?"

Head lowered, he gave it a shake. "Not great. He lost a few friends. He won't talk about it and has been avoiding me. I'm slowly dragging it out of him. But you know Noah. He's constantly jumping from one thing to the next."

Noah was more of a concept than a person to me. All I remembered was a boy a few years older than me who was in constant motion, always running, jumping, and disappearing into the woods. He was the risk taker, the kid who'd come home for dinner with a broken collarbone and a cool story.

Jude had always been with him, the cautious, quiet yin to his yang.

But the minute Noah graduated from high school, he was out of here. And in the fifteen years since, he'd visited here and there, but his jobs kept him busy. He worked search and rescue during the winter, and in the summer, he traveled all over the western US and Canada, fighting fires.

He lived a high-adrenaline life with no commitments

and no responsibilities. He loved what he did. The guy had always seemed invincible to me, more superhero than average person.

"Can we help?"

Jude shook his head. "You know what he's like. He'll probably go skydiving or base jumping and get over it. I worry. Not hearing from him for a while shook me up."

My chest tightened at the hint of emotion he couldn't hide. "Don't minimize your worry. He's your brother."

"He's our brother."

Though his tone was sharp, that simple correction ignited a spark in me. I'd never be in the inner circle. I'd always be the half brother. But for Jude to recognize my connection meant a lot.

"He was supposed to meet us in Vegas, wasn't he?"

Jude shrugged. "Yes. I still don't have an answer for why he didn't show up. First it was a work thing and then a delayed flight. But I'm not sure I buy it."

"Have you told Debbie about the fire?"

"Shit no. She'd fly out there and smother him, and then he'd never respond to another one of my texts. You know he needs his space."

Jude helped himself to another cookie and held out the container. I took one, unable to resist the temptation, even though I'd had a couple before I left the house. This batch really was amazing. The first few had been overbaked, but I'd perfected the texture. I couldn't wait to watch Willa as she tried one.

"We can make small talk, or we can get to it," Jude finally said, scratching Ripley's ears. "I'm cool with whatever. I'm a good listener, which basically makes me the family priest. Lay it on me."

I laughed. That was Jude, always straightforward. In another life, maybe we would have been closer. He was only a few years older than me, but he and Noah had always had that intense twin bond, and there hadn't been any room for me.

Even now, he was the only one of us who kept in touch with Noah.

I knew I should keep my mouth shut, keep it light, take advantage of the time I got with my brother. But so many thoughts and feelings were bubbling to the surface, making it impossible to keep them all contained.

I was falling head over heels for my wife. And it was bad. Real bad. I had one job: to be a good fake husband. That's what Willa needed, and she more than deserved it. In the meantime, I was supposed to be sorting out my head, my career, and my goals. Right now, though, there was only one thing I wanted.

Jude sipped his coffee patiently, eyeing me over the rim, as if confident my confession would come eventually.

"I think I'm falling in love with my wife," I finally forced out.

He quirked a brow. "Is this a problem?"

"Yes. Because it's supposed to be platonic."

Jude didn't react, the stoic motherfucker, more than an almost imperceptible widening of his eyes. "Explain."

I gave him the brief rundown—her need to go wild in Vegas, my desire to spend time with her, the wedding and the fallout with Owen, contacting her parents, all of it.

Without a word in response, he walked into the next

room and ran his finger along the spines of his records. Halfway down, he pulled one out and got it set up on the turntable. Not a single move was rushed.

Eventually, melancholic music filled the room, a little folksy and a bit country.

"What is this?" I asked.

"Gordon Lightfoot," he said as he eased onto the couch and set his mug down. With his forearms on his knees, he hunched forward. "Sit down. I need to think."

I sat in the armchair, sipping my coffee while he closed his eyes and tapped his foot to the music.

"You won't tell anyone, will you?" Panic gripped my heart. Why was I just now thinking of that? Dammit. Jude was a trustworthy person, but he was loyal to his brothers.

"Nope. I'm a vault."

Relief rushed over me like a wave. "Thank you."

"But I do have questions." He straightened. "Is this some kind of payback scheme because Owen is with Lila?"

"No," I protested with a huff. "It was a stupid drunken night. Then I got to know her. We live together, and I want to be with her all the time. I want to make her smile and laugh, and I want to cook for her."

His lips tipped up a fraction. "That's why you learned to bake cookies?"

"Kind of. You should see me. I can make all kinds of meals now. I make a killer lasagna."

"Okay, you can cook for me anytime. But first, have you made a move? Is she into you?"

That was the million-dollar question. Was she into me? Willa was supportive and affectionate and kind. But were her feelings for me of the romantic variety? I thought so.

After her reaction the other night, though, I had my doubts.

I felt it, a deep connection, a longing when she looked at me. Saw it in the way she closed her eyes when she snuggled against me on the couch. I caught her checking me out frequently during our morning workouts, and she always made it home in time for dinner and *Jeopardy* with me, even when she had mountains of charting to do at the office.

"I think so," I said. "She kissed me back, and we've always flirted. In Vegas, that night, the connection between us was..." I sorted through the hazy memories, remembering how it felt roaming around the town with her on my arm. Her smiles and laughter. The way she made everything sparkly and perfect. "Electric."

"Kissed you back? So you did make a move?"

I nodded once. "My timing was terrible. She shut it down, and then we had a conversation about boundaries."

He covered his face with his hands. "Shit."

My gut twisted. I'd thought of nothing else for the past two days. Hence my obsessive baking and why I'd shown up here to unburden myself to my brother. She'd never said she wasn't interested or attracted to me. She kept saying we couldn't. That we should stick to the plan.

"Okay, I'm going to lay out a disclaimer. Obviously, I support enthusiastic consent."

"I agree."

"With that said, it sounds to me like she's unsure." He pursed his lips. "The two of you already took a big risk with this marriage, and Willa is not a risk taker."

My heart clenched with affection for her. "It's how it all started. She wanted to be wild. She was feeling like she'd missed out during her twenties since she'd spent them all working nonstop to become a doctor. So I offered to help her cut loose."

"And now you're cooking and cleaning and playing house?"

I couldn't help but chuckle. "Pretty much. But it still feels wild. For me, at least. Depending on her, working with her, spending my days eager to see her. It feels so damn good. I know it's dangerous—"

"It's more than dangerous, dude. You're not only risking a broken heart. You're also risking your relationship with Owen."

I sighed. I'd considered this. But the truth was that I had no real relationship with Owen. He'd always disliked me. At this point, I didn't have much hope that would ever change.

And my feelings? Sure, it would be awful if they weren't reciprocated. But damn if I wasn't falling a little more in love with her every day. And the farther I fell, the more painful it was keeping it to myself.

"I don't care," I told him. "My main concern is that she's the one taking the bigger risk. Her parents mean everything to her. Her job too. You should see her. She is incredible. To lose the respect of the community or disappoint her parents?" I shook my head. The idea of it made me ill. "And not to mention Lila is her best friend."

Jude steepled his fingers and tapped them against his lips. "You really love her."

"I think I do." Chest aching, I buried my head in my hands. I was so fucked. "I should never have kissed her. It was selfish. There is too much at stake to give in to what I want like that."

"Slow down, brother. She did marry you, so you have an in. I think this is a situation where you have to sit back and follow her lead. No pressure, no expectations. Be the husband she needs and bide your time."

I nodded. That made sense. She had a lot on her plate. She didn't need me slobbering all over her while she was up to her eyeballs in responsibilities.

He got up and paced. After a moment, he stopped in the middle of the room.

"You gotta convince her you're worth the risk. Show her the kind of man you are, what you're capable of." He put his hands on his hips. "Keep up with the therapy. It's clearly doing you good. If you're growing and putting the party guy persona behind you, then she will see and appreciate that."

His tone made me cringe.

"I'm not that guy anymore," I said, keeping my voice low and my eyes downcast. "Haven't had a drink since that night in Vegas, and I have no plans to."

"Good for you."

"I want to be better." I looked up at him again. "Be worthy of her. And I want to show her that."

He grinned at me, the expression especially effusive for my reserved brother. "You're a Hebert. I'm pretty sure you can prove it to her."

"You sound like Finn." My middle brother, the prior service Navy pilot, was all confidence.

"You could learn a thing or two from him. He got his girl, and trust me, she put him through the fucking wringer." He smiled. "She's awesome."

He wasn't wrong on that count. Adele Gagnon was a

force of nature, and it was clear in every interaction I'd witnessed that she made the hyper-cocky Finn work for it.

Jude walked out of the room, shouting "get your ass up. I need to move" over his shoulder.

I obeyed, cringing. What was with people forcing me outside in the cold while mid-conversation?

"Now," he barked, heading toward the door with Ripley on his heels.

He put on his Carhartt jacket and boots, and I did the same.

"Where are we going?"

He pulled a wool hat over his head and stepped outside. "To chop wood."

"Why?"

"Because chores gotta get done, and it helps me think," he said, pulling the door shut behind me. "Plus, it wouldn't kill you to chop some wood, brother. You're descended from a proud lumberjack lineage."

He headed down his driveway toward a large shed. He was shorter than me, yet to the rest of the world, he was considered tall. And he hiked through the snow with speed. I followed him, shaking my head. I hadn't swung an axe in years.

Jude unlocked his shed and pulled the string hanging from the ceiling, illuminating the single bulb. Like the rest of his house, this little building was meticulously organized, with a lawnmower and snowblower lined up neatly. Peg boards on the walls held tools sorted into type, scrap wood was stacked on racks, and several chopping tools hung in a row from the largest axe to the smallest hatchet.

He opened a drawer and handed me a pair of leather

work gloves. "This one," he said, taking a large tool off the wall. "This is a small splitting maul. Should be good for you."

Maul in hand, I followed him back outside and around the structure to where a lean-to had been built into the side.

He rolled out a few cut logs. Then he picked up his own maul. "I assume you know what to do with that?"

I nodded, lining up and swinging.

The blade hit the wood, but rather than slicing it in two, it got stuck halfway.

With a laugh, Jude took the maul from my hand and wedged it out with his boot.

"Use your knees," he said, bending his own knees in demonstration. "And drive with your whole body."

I nodded and tried again. This time, the log split, but not evenly. One side was way larger than the other.

"Better. Do it again."

My next swing was better. I threw the cut pieces into the pile and grabbed another log.

While I worked slowly, Jude effortlessly and efficiently chopped half a forest a few feet away. I paused for a moment, watching each movement, trying to understand his technique.

We chopped and chopped, and with each swing, my form improved. My back ached, and I was sweating through my clothes, but it felt good.

"You're not bad," he said, leaning against a tree. "We could train you. Get you competition ready."

I scoffed. "Doubtful."

"I mean it. Gus is incredible with a chainsaw, and Finn can throw an axe with incredible aim. I can climb and have decent speed. But you? You're fast and strong and have those crazy long arms. We could use you on the team."

My heart skipped a beat. Team?

"You guys still compete?"

"Only once in a while. Did that thing last summer against the Gagnons. Bastards beat us, but that was to be expected, with Remy on the pro circuit now. But yeah, once in a while, we get together for town events and charity stuff."

The wheels in my head started turning.

"Would you be interested in doing something at River-Fest next year? A competition or a showcase or something?"

"Sure. You gonna run the thing again?"

That was the big question. The mayor had already asked me to, but I hadn't given him an answer. I wasn't sure where I'd be then. I really wanted to get back to school in the fall, but the idea of walking away, knowing the town could really use the revenue didn't sit well with me.

"I'm helping right now, but they're looking for someone to take over."

"Shame," he said with a shake of his head. "You did a good job."

"Thanks."

Jude picked up his maul and headed back to the shed. Apparently that conversation was over. I neatly stacked the freshly cut wood under the roof of the lean-to so it would stay dry, then I followed.

"Keep that," he said, gesturing to the maul in my hand. "And unlock your trunk."

Frowning, I narrowed my eyes at him. "I don't need it."

Ignoring me, he jogged to the uncut log pile. He scooped a couple up, then strode to my truck.

I pulled my key fob out and hit the button to raise the liftgate.

"You need it now," he said as he dropped them into the cargo area. "Go home, chop some firewood. You've got good form."

"Like to train?"

He rolled his eyes. "No. To impress your girl. Ladies love a lumberjack."

I barked out a laugh. I was many things, but a lumberjack was not one of them.

"I mean it. Women get feral about woodchopping. You wanna know if she's into you? Casually chop wood and then start a fire for her."

"That is pure caveman shit."

Head lowered, he shook it, grinning. "Sometimes you gotta go full lumberjack to get the girl. You own any flannel?"

"Yeah."

He gave me a nod. "You know what to do."

With a sigh, I closed the liftgate, eyeing the logs and the splitting maul as I did. I guess I was going full lumberjack.

"You're not gonna tell me she's too good for me?"

He frowned, a crease forming between his brows. "Cole, you need to believe that you're good enough for her. And I can see you're working on it."

When I headed over here with cookies, I couldn't have imagined this would be where we'd end up. But I wasn't complaining. Sharing this felt good. Jude had always been a good listener, but even so, his consideration had surprised me.

"Show her the kind of man you are," he urged. "Hell, show yourself the kind of man you are. She may want more, and she might not. But you're gonna come out of this a better person either way."

My stomach twisted itself into a knot. "You seem so sure."

"I've watched three of our brothers fall in love. And every single one of them had a hefty dose of personal shit to work through before getting there. You're in it, Cole. You're doing the work. Now it's time to trust yourself."

"Thank you." I swallowed back the emotion burning at the back of my throat. "I really owe you."

He waved me off and turned back to his house. "Go home and impress your girl."

Chapter 20
Cole

Had this been a mistake? Was I going to look like a total tool?

Parker Gagnon had texted and asked if I could stop by, so I headed over to Hebert Timber and met her in the conference room she'd turned into an investigation headquarters of sorts.

Gus and Chloe had stopped by to say hello. The moment they appeared, I was swamped with guilt. They'd been working nonstop with Parker and the FBI for the past few months. There was no way this ordeal wasn't weighing on them heavily. Even if my oldest brother didn't show an ounce of the stress that had to be plaguing him. Honestly, I'd never seen Gus so happy before. He'd admitted a few months back that he'd always wanted to be a father and worried that it would never happen.

Then his ex-wife had come back to town, and the baby was due in a few months.

"I'm going to run through preliminary findings with you, show you a few photos, and ask some questions."

I nodded. "Not sure how much help I can be."

She waved me off, the move making the largest diamond I'd ever seen sparkle. It could have taken someone's eye out. "You'd be surprised what you might know. This is a family company, and our town is small. So many things are connected."

She had me talk through my understanding of the business, her expression one of interest, never making me feel like an idiot for how little I knew. Then she guided me through an org chart of everyone who had worked under my father before his arrest.

"You were close with your father?"

I snorted, my chest tightening painfully. "Not very."

"But of all the brothers, it seemed like he took the most interest in you. I found records for flights and hotel stays he expensed so he could watch you play hockey."

Forearms on the table, I dipped my chin. "Yeah, Dad was a big fan of hockey." And a raging narcissist who would lash out if I didn't play well, if I didn't make him look good. Every time I looked up and saw him in the stands, whether it was on the peewee league or when I went pro, it made me sick to my stomach.

Parker had set up whiteboards on the walls, where she'd listed names and dates. The room was filled with dozens of file boxes too. I couldn't imagine I had any information she didn't already know. Clearly, I was wasting this poor woman's time.

"Did he spend a lot of time with Chief Souza?" she asked, her head bent over a notepad as she jotted down notes.

"Yeah. When I was a kid, they'd go hunting together a lot, and he came over for dinner once a week or so."

"And in the couple of years before your dad's arrest?"

"I wasn't around much then, but I assume they were still friendly."

Humming, she tapped her pen against her chin.

"Can you look through some of these photos for me? I'm curious about the items the feds seized in their forfeiture case. Cars, real estate, jewelry, a few pieces of art."

I flipped through the photos in the binder and stopped on one in particular. "And the watches."

She sat back in her chair and assessed me. "Tell me about the watches."

"My dad was a big watch collector." I pressed a finger to the first of dozens of photos of his collection. The federal government had definitely gotten a good chunk of change for some of these. "Obsessed really. He called them 'timepieces.' That was a bunch of pretentious bullshit, if you ask me."

Parker laughed, the sound warm and genuine.

"He made a big deal about the Holy Trinity, the three best Swiss watchmakers in the world."

The collection began when I was a kid. He bought himself a Rolex for his fortieth birthday and one for my mom after that. From there, he got more and more ambitious.

She nodded at the pictures in front of me. "What are those?"

I was not a watch guy, but I'd spent my entire childhood listening to my dad's lectures, so I could recognize most brands at a glance and could spot the difference between a ten-thousand-dollar watch and a one-hundred-thousand-dollar watch easily.

I pointed to one grouping of photos. "These are less exclusive brands. Rolex, Nardin, Breguet. But this one." I tapped my finger on another image. "This is a Patek Philippe. Super famous. And this one," I said, pointing to a diamond-shaped face casing with complicated mechanics. "That's a Vacheron Constantin. Super old-school." I continued to peruse the pictures, allowing memories to come to mind as I did. Watches were one thing that made Dad happy, and since I craved his positive attention, I always pretended to care. Somewhere along the way, I supposed I absorbed the information. When he gifted me a watch the day I got drafted, I was overwhelmed with the briefest sense of belonging. That was washed away quickly, though, when he launched into berating me about training harder.

"Hold on," I said, flipping through the book. "There's one missing."

"Something valuable?" Parker asked, one brow arched.

I nodded. "It's an Audemars Piguet. He bought me a matching one as a gift. He gave it to me when I got drafted. It's engraved with my name and the date. So is his."

"Maybe he was wearing it when he was arrested?"

I shrugged. That was possible. "It was made of stainless steel rather than precious metals. He said I could wear it to games for good luck." Not that I ever did. It was hard enough not to get my ass kicked on a minor league hockey team without flashing around a fifty-thousand-dollar watch.

But I'd kept it, moved it with me from city to city. Always tucked safely in its fancy leather box. The moment he'd given it to me, I'd felt a sense of pride I'd never experienced. And I was ashamed to admit it, but the gift had made me feel loved. Now, that notion was ridiculous. But I was a nineteen-year-old kid who'd spent my life feeling left behind by my half brothers and striving to earn my dad's love.

Pathetic.

On the bright side, at least I'd have plenty to talk about in therapy this week.

"I'll look into it," she said. "Do you think someone could have stolen it?"

"Not sure." I kept flipping, looking at the cars, his beloved boat, and all the other shit he'd accumulated over the course of his life. How was all this worth the crimes he'd committed?

Nice cars were cool and all, but to obtain them by hurting people, by *killing* people? And destroying his family in the process? The notion turned my stomach.

The longer I looked at photos, the more despondent I felt. No wonder I was such a fuck-up. I never had a fucking chance with this kind of role model.

"You okay?"

Choking back the self-loathing, I nodded. "Sorry, it's that, sometimes, I can't believe this is my life."

"It's okay," she assured me as she scratched out more notes. "The watch info is helpful. I'm gonna call some local pawn shops, see if it ended up in one of them. Could be a good lead. Your brothers didn't know much about the watches."

Huh. A facet of the investigation I had more knowledge of? That felt surprisingly good.

"Anything else I can help with?"

Without stopping her note-taking, she waved her left hand, gesturing to the room. "Feel free to look around, see if anything jumps out at you. I'd love for you to email me the dates and locations of games he flew to over the past few years."

I nodded. I could do that, painful as it might be.

With my hands in my pockets, I made a slow circle around the room, looking through the photos she had spread out on one of the tables before moving to the whiteboards. Most of the information she'd collected was related to the lumber business—names of mills, delivery schedules, buyers the company had worked with, photos of machinery and land.

"What's this?" I asked, pointing to a whiteboard.

She straightened and squinted. "Deimos Industries?"

I nodded.

"No fucking clue. It's a corporation based in Delaware. Supposedly, they're in the merchandising business. Owen and Lila found suspicious financial records connected to them, but we can't trace anything or figure out how they fit. I've spoken to my contact at the Department of Commerce, but they're swamped and haven't gotten back to me."

"I've seen this before. It's familiar."

Parker stood and shuffled to my side, her attention focused on the name. "Where? When?"

I scratched my head. "Not sure. When I was planning RiverFest, I had to look up a bunch of stuff in the archives. Maybe there? Maybe not, but that name is familiar. I'm pretty certain it's connected to this town."

Eyes closed, I took a deep breath and willed my brain to connect the dots. I'd seen it. Somewhere random. While doing something routine. But I lost the thread, came up empty. Fuck.

"Okay. That's still helpful," Parker said, pacing with her hands on her hips. "This is the first lead we've had on this."

Lips pursed, I studied the whiteboard again, looking at the list of dates and dollar amounts, but nothing jumped out at me.

"Could it be a creditor?" I asked.

She shook her head. "There's money going in and coming out."

"So…" I trailed off, unsure of why this was so significant.

"Probably money laundering. Your father may have been using the timber business to launder money for another criminal organization."

Money laundering? That term landed like a punch to the gut.

"And the fire?" I croaked. "The threats?"

"All possibly connected."

Damn. There were people still out there. We knew that. And we knew there were threats. But all this information really made it come into focus.

"I'll find out," I said quickly. "I'll get to the bottom of Deimos."

If there was a chance my family was in danger, then I'd do what I could to protect them. For so long, I'd assumed the fire in the shop had been set by a disgruntled employee. But Gus and Owen had been right. There was a hell of a lot more to this.

My head spun at the implication. I'd been so naïve. So consumed by my own bullshit that I'd failed to register that actual threats to my family existed. Threats that affected Merry, Thor, and Gus and Chloe's baby. Debbie too. And even my mom.

When would this shit end? When would we be free of my father's poisoned legacy? I'd spent all my therapy sessions hashing out my childhood shit, consumed with my own problems, while there was a criminal organization lurking in the shadows.

"Are you okay?" Parker asked.

I swallowed back the bile rising in my throat. "No. I'm not." I grabbed my jacket. "I've got to get to practice, but I will find Deimos. I swear."

She patted my shoulder and smiled up at me. "Investigations take time, Cole. I'm working through this. And you've been a huge help."

That was debatable. But I could do more. I would do more.

I left, my shoulders weighed down by the shame of being a self-centered prick, and hopped into my truck. It was time for hockey practice.

Chapter 21
Willa

I pulled my coat around my body tighter. I'd come straight from work, so I was wearing my lovely professional wool peacoat. It was clearly no match for January in Maine or a Tuesday night at the Lovewell Arena.

But the longer I watched Cole coach these little girls, the warmer I felt.

He was adorable, with his backward hat and the whistle hanging around his neck.

The girls looked so tiny standing next to him, even in all their giant pads.

I'd always been a hockey fan—I was raised in northern Maine, after all—so it wasn't difficult to follow along.

He ran drills, wrangling the girls with more ease than I could have imagined between water breaks. Most of the time, when his back was turned, the girls shot pucks.

Then he guided them through kill penalty drills. He drew out diagrams, then moved each girl into position like they were chess pieces.

This side of Cole was unfamiliar. This man was having

fun. He was smiling as he scribbled on his little board and chatting with the kids as he walked through the plays.

It was adorable. Like ovary-squeezing, heart-meltingly adorable. He wasn't stern or authoritarian. He was supportive and encouraging. Especially to the poor girl playing goalie, who could barely stand with all those pads on.

When practice had wrapped, the girls skated off the ice, wiping off their skate blades and putting their guards on as they went.

The instant their guards were on, two girls headed straight for me. When they took their helmets off, I recognized their sweaty faces—Goldie Gagnon and Kali Farrell.

Goldie, a firecracker with freckles and mischievous blue eyes, walked right up to me and tipped her head back. "So you're Coach's wife?"

"No," Kali corrected. "She's the doctor. You gave me a flu shot a while ago. And a lollipop."

I nodded, unable to hold back a smile as they sized me up. When had eight-year-old girls become terrifying? With my white coat and stethoscope, I had some authority, but here? I was clearly positioned low in the hierarchy.

"Be nice to him," Goldie said coolly, her blue eyes going icy.

"Yeah," Kali said. "He's really cool. And awesome at hockey."

"Yup. And he talks about you a lot." Goldie twirled the ends of her blond ponytail and tipped her head from one side to the other exaggeratedly as she said, "Blah, blah, doctor. Blah, blah, smart."

My chest warmed as her words registered. He was talking to his players about me? I was strangely flattered.

"We only push him around because it's funny and he's kind of afraid of us. Really, we love him. So be a good wife," Kali warned.

"Girls." Henri Gagnon appeared and grasped them both by their shoulders and spun them so they faced the locker room. "We've got to get home. You both have homework."

They groaned, but without another word, they took off.

"Sorry." He gave me an awkward smile. "Goldie is..." He scratched at his beard. "Sassy."

"I can tell." I chuckled. Goldie and her brother had been through a lot in their short lives, but the Gagnons had been incredible with them. "You're doing a great job."

I wasn't a parent, but one thing I'd learned in family medicine was how often they needed to be told they were doing okay.

And it worked, because Henri's stern face brightened instantly. "She loves hockey," he explained. "Tucker's in high school. He won a debate tournament last week."

His love for his children was palpable. I wanted to hug this man. People like Henri Gagnon made life as a small-town doctor more than meaningful. He was also a model patient. His blood work had improved dramatically since I mentioned to his wife, Alice, that he should watch his cholesterol.

"Congrats on the wedding too," he said, flagging another parent to get their attention.

After he stepped away to round up his daughter, I waited for Cole, saying hello to the other parents as they trickled out. I knew most of them. Matt Brown our mailman,

Meg Garcia, who ran the preschool, and of course Becca, my hair stylist and single mom to Kali.

I was in the lobby, wondering why my husband hadn't made his way out yet, when I caught sight of him through the frosted swinging doors.

The man was perched in the seat of the Zamboni, gliding across the ice.

Curious, I walked back into the rink and watched him.

He wore a smile as he drove the big-ass machine, with his hat backward and his head high. He'd traded his skates for work boots and was expertly carving ovals on the ice.

Turning the massive steering wheel with ease, one-handed, effortlessly gliding around.

My body temperature rose, despite the frigid air in the arena. Damn. This was hot.

Strangely hot.

He was full of surprises. At no point in my life had I even considered adding "can drive a Zamboni" to the list of attributes my future husband must have. But at this moment, it hadn't only made the list, but it landed pretty close to the top.

I watched as he exited the ice, presumably to dump the accumulated snow, and then returned.

He swung himself down, and with a grin, he strode toward me.

"You came to watch practice?" His brows were lifted high, as if he were surprised by my presence.

"I wrapped up early, and I wanted to see you in action. Your penalty kill is looking sharp."

"I wish." He chuckled. "But thanks. It means a lot that you're here."

His dark eyes lingered on mine for a moment, his attention causing my thoughts to jumble. Before I could come up with a response, he turned and walked away, closing the boards and latching the gate.

"Arthur asked me to close up tonight. I have a few more things to do."

"I actually brought my skates," I said sheepishly. For days now, I'd had the urge to skate with him.

He whipped around, his eyes bright in the fluorescent lighting. "You own skates?"

I scoffed. "I'm a Mainer. Of course I do."

"Okay," he said, smacking the boards. "Then I'll lace up."

We hit the ice together and slowly made laps. It had been a while since I'd skated, but I was decent on my feet. My wool dress pants were not the best attire for this activity, but I was having too much fun to care. I'd forgotten what it was like to feel the wind in my hair and the crack of a crisp edge beneath my feet.

Cole skated backward, facing me while we chatted. He was so natural, so at ease, it was like he'd been born with blades for feet.

"You're a good skater," he said.

My cheeks heated at the praise. Like any overachiever, I craved compliments. "When I was a kid, I played shinny on the frozen lake with my dad and the other kids almost every weekend," I explained. "After a few hundred falls, I got the hang of it."

He shook his head. "That sounds awesome. I was never allowed to skate on the lake like that."

"Why not?" I frowned. I supposed, now that I thought of

it, I'd never really seen him there, even in high school, when the boys would show off to impress the girls.

"Natural ice messes up your blades, and since my dad insisted I wear fancy custom skates, he wouldn't let me. Also, he didn't want me to get hurt. Would say he spent too much money on my hockey career to risk a stupid injury."

My heart ached for young Cole. I didn't say so, but his dad was an asshole. Some of my happiest memories were of those winter afternoons on the lake. Usually, someone's mom would show up with hot chocolate, and sometimes one of the dads would bring a boom box and we'd skate around to music. Eventually, a group of kids would gang up and start a snowball fight.

"I'm sorry you had to sit it out."

He shrugged.

"The lake doesn't freeze anymore," I said. "But the pond does. I'll take you skating there."

A smile spread across his face. "I'd love that."

With a quick spin, he took off, like his body was itching for that burst of speed.

Those long legs ate up the ice with every stride, his tight butt flexing in a way that made my mouth water.

Holy hell, was this a turn-on.

The way he coached, ever patient with the girls, and the way they teased and pushed him was adorable.

And the man on skates? Damn. It only amplified how gorgeous he was.

Whether it was knitting or reading or cooking or drawing out plays for his team, he could lock in and give 100 percent. And his dedication was hot as hell.

That intensity radiated from him now. We were in a

giant, frozen enclosure, and somehow, this moment felt more intimate than watching *Jeopardy* on the couch while snuggled against him.

He circled back around and linked his arm through mine. "Thank you for coming. Today was weird, and I've been feeling shitty, but seeing you helps."

"What happened?" I blurted, frowning up at him. "Are you okay?"

"Yeah." He dipped his chin. "But can we just skate and talk about nothing for a bit?"

My chest tightened at the vulnerability in his tone. "Sure. But I kinda want to score some goals." I pointed to the big red nets that had been pushed to the side while he made ice.

"Ooh, done." He darted toward the bench.

He pulled out a couple of sticks and a bucket of pucks.

"See which one is the right size for you, and I'll get the net."

We shot around for a bit. My shots were pitiful, but I got the hang of it after a little instruction and started scoring eventually. It was fun, skating and joking and shooting pucks. Cole still hadn't mentioned what was bothering him, but he was smiling and laughing as he whizzed around, doing his fancy moves.

He spun, flipped the puck up, and batted it out of the air like a baseball.

"Ten bucks you can't score like that," I wagered, figuring he probably could but wanting to cheer him up.

"Ten bucks? I don't need your money," he said. "I'll pick my prize."

I shifted uncomfortably on my skates in response to his

flirty tone. I'd done a really good job of ignoring how much this felt like a date for the past hour, but now I was starting to sweat.

He raced around the rink, getting a full head of steam, and barreled powerfully down the ice, cutting in with his outside edge, spinning, then flipping the puck up effortlessly. Between one heartbeat and another, it hit the back of the net with a gentle *swish*.

He raced over to me, stopping abruptly and spraying me with snow.

"I'm here to collect."

The cold air hung between us as my heart raced. If he asked me to kiss him, I was pretty sure I'd do it. There was nothing more irresistible than seeing him in his natural environment. This was Cole at his most relaxed. It was a privilege, I knew, to see him like this.

"Truth or dare?"

The air stuttered out of my lungs. *That* was what he wanted in payment? I leaned back, and I would have fallen flat on my ass if he hadn't grabbed my arm to steady me. His breath fogged the cold air between us, catching my attention and urging me to make a move. But given the height difference and my position on skates I hadn't worn in years, I figured doing so would probably end in catastrophic injury.

"Truth," I said softly.

He regarded me, licking his lips.

My breath hitched. I shouldn't want this. But I did.

He lowered his head slightly, and my heart stuttered to a stop.

Chapter 22
Willa

But instead of pressing his lips to mine, he smiled.

"I need a good truth question," he said, releasing me. Once he was certain I was steady, he skated around me, slapping a stray puck as he went.

A shaky breath escaped me. Had I imagined that?

There had been *A Moment*.

Time had slowed. His pupils had dilated.

What the hell?

I should be relieved, but instead, I felt cheated.

As I watched him skate, a chill rushed through me. When he was close, I'd forgotten all about how cold it was in here. To warm myself, I glided around, getting my legs moving and breathing deep, trying to recover from whatever the hell had just passed between us.

Before I was fully in control of my hormones, he skated up behind me and draped an arm over my shoulders. "I want you to tell me a story," he said.

I frowned at him. "About what?"

"About your first kiss." He raised one eyebrow.

Huh. So now he was thinking about kissing. Where was that train of thought a few moments ago?

I kept skating, not particularly interested in walking down that part of memory lane.

"Come on," he teased. "Who was it?"

I turned toward him and swallowed thickly. "Jonathan Billings."

He stopped skating, his eyes widening. "Seriously?"

Annoyance flashed through me. "You asked."

"Okay," he said, taking off again. "I need to hear this story."

I skated faster, wishing I could escape him but knowing it was an impossibility. I was suddenly filled with a lot of pent-up aggression. Maybe I'd go back to practicing the slap shot he'd been teaching me earlier.

Thinking about Jonathan made my stomach knot and my heart ache. I had been a junior in high school, and he was the first boy who'd ever shown interest in me. "Jonathan and I flirted constantly for several months. He was on the math team too, and we were partners for debate. It was a big year. We qualified for the state championship and were assigned to argue why the metric system was superior and should be implemented in the United States."

"I played hockey in Europe for a few years. I totally agree."

My stomach churned at the memories that flooded me. He would put his arm around me a lot. Make excuses to touch me. All the clues *Seventeen* magazine told me were surefire indicators that he wanted me to be his girlfriend.

"I was used to being ignored by boys. And if not ignored, then not desired like girls like Lila were," I explained. "Sure, they'd stare at my chest and make jokes about my boobs, but no one was asking me out. During the spring of our junior year, I spun out this wild romantic fantasy in my head. Jonathan and I would win the state debate championship, and then he'd ask me to junior prom. From there, we'd naturally make our relationship official. Go to college together and get engaged the day I graduated from med school."

He was skating backward now, only an arm's length away, listening intently. I liked that about Cole. When I spoke, he listened. As much as I did not enjoy telling this story, I appreciated that he was making an effort to get to know me. That he cared about what I had to say. "That's a very specific fantasy," he joked.

Frowning, I shrugged. "One of the disadvantages of having your life carefully planned out for you is that there isn't much room for wild fantasy."

"So what happened?"

"We were practicing at my house one night. Making note cards and researching different forms of government. It was chilly, but he suggested we take a walk to clear our heads before studying for our chem test. So we bundled up and walked through town. The streetlights had come on, and the sun was setting. God, it was perfect. And right in front of Baxter Park, he stopped, took my hand, and kissed me. In that moment, all my teen dreams came true."

Cole stopped skating and crossed his arms, which looked absurd with his hockey gloves on. "Really?" He arched a brow. "Really. Jonathan Billings was a great kisser?"

I waved off the question. "I had no frame of reference, and it felt very romantic at the time."

After the kiss, we walked home, hand in hand, my heart

absolutely soaring. Greatest day of my life. While we studied, my mom made microwave popcorn. As sad as it was, I felt chosen. Special. Like because this boy liked me, I was suddenly worthy.

Pathetic was more like it.

I had been raised by the best people. My mom was curvy, like me. She'd always taken great care of herself and had set a wonderful example of confidence and acceptance. She never once put me on a diet or implied there was anything wrong with me.

In fact, my parents always celebrated me and supported me. They were proud of every single part of me.

If only the world had agreed. Finding clothes was next to impossible, and I had to order old lady bras off the internet by the time I was sixteen. By junior high, I knew that I wasn't the kind of person guys considered desirable. Because of that, it became the thing I wanted more than anything. To be desired. To be wanted and cherished.

God, I was such a sad sack.

Cole was silent, watching me, patiently waiting for the rest of the story. "So then you became boyfriend and girlfriend and you eventually dumped him because he wasn't even close to good enough for you?"

I threw my head back and barked out a laugh. "Not even close. The whole thing was a disaster."

Picking up speed, I pretended to be really focused on skating, head down and locked on the ice ahead of me.

But he wasn't letting me off the hook. "Tell me what happened." A moment ago, his voice had been laced with amusement. Now it was filled with pure concern.

"It's stupid."

He grasped my arm and steered me toward the home team's bench. When we approached, he opened the door and gestured for me to go in.

As I sat, he dropped to the bench beside me, his shoulder pressed to mine.

"Did he hurt you?" he asked, his dark eyes full of fury.

"The next day, I woke up extra early, did my hair and makeup, and walked into school, ready for our debut as a couple, anxious for the entire population of the Penobscot Regional High School to know."

Closing my eyes, I exhaled. In my mind, I could see my outfit and even smell the dab of my mother's perfume I'd applied for the occasion.

"And he ignored me."

Cole went rigid, gripping the edge of the bench on either side of his thighs. "Are you kidding me?"

"Nope. He walked away. I was so confused. I figured we'd be eating lunch together and he'd walk me to class and all of that. You know, boyfriend behavior."

He nodded, his head lowered.

"So I caught up to him in the parking lot after school. We sat in his Honda Civic, and you know what he said? The asshole actually said, 'Do you expect me to be your boyfriend now?'"

"He didn't."

"And me, the total dumbass, said yes."

My face was hot and probably the color of a tomato. It had been fifteen years, and I was still humiliated.

"Then he laughed at me. Actually laughed. Before going on to explain that he could not date me. That he thought we could hook up privately, but he wouldn't be my boyfriend."

Cole hissed. "That asshole."

"He said he couldn't date a chubby girl."

"I will fucking end him."

I put my gloved hand on his thigh. "Stop. It was a long time ago. And trust me, I should have slapped him and taken off. Instead, I sat there and listened to him explain why I wasn't good enough to be his girlfriend." Tears stung at the backs of my eyes. God, this was embarrassing. But it had hurt so much. As he droned on, I had stared out at the parked cars, wondering how I'd gotten it so wrong. How I'd misread all the signals.

With his hand covering mine, Cole rasped, "I am so sorry."

"He was not the last. Over the years, I've discovered that men I'm interested in are very happy to hook up with me, but no one wants to date me."

Head lifted, Cole glowered. "Not true."

"It's fine. I've made my peace with it. I haven't even told you the best part yet."

His eyes widened. "There's more?"

Heart sinking, I nodded. "Oh yes. He then told me he had a crush on Molly Johnson. And asked if I could set him up with her."

"Are you fucking kidding me?" Cole growled. "The guy hooked up with you, then told you that you were delusional for thinking he would date you, *then* asked you to set him up with one of your friends?"

I nodded.

"And Molly Johnson?"

"She's a nice person." I shrugged. "I think she's a dental hygienist in Connecticut."

"Yes. Perfectly nice. But not even in your league."

Seriously? He threw those words out without a moment of hesitation. Like he really believed them. That was strangely comforting.

"Eh. Not to Jonathan. She was small and skinny and didn't have opinions." I shrugged. "You know, the kind of girl guys love."

I stood, keeping my focus averted. It was getting late, and we should probably clean up all pucks before we left.

He stood next to me, his eyes darker than normal and filled with heat.

"No. Not all guys want that."

With one brow raised, I got back on the ice. The Cole I knew was not the man who had dated Lila. That was true. But he was still the guy who'd spent eight years with the local beauty queen.

He was the kind of guy who'd only been seen with beautiful, sparkling arm candy. That was fine. He was a gorgeous man. It made sense. But I really didn't want to hear it right now. Especially after we'd come so close to kissing earlier.

Because this little trip down memory lane had reminded me of exactly why it was imperative to keep my guard up.

It was the story of my life. Ever since I'd filled out an F-cup at fourteen, boys had wanted to hook up with me. Not one of them had ever wanted to date me, to claim me, though. The world gaslit women, telling us it was in our heads. That there was a person out there for everyone. But that was pure bullshit.

My body had been weaponized against me from my earliest memories. Every time I thought otherwise, I ended up sorely disappointed. And right now, I liked Cole too much to risk being let down by him.

Seeming to get the message, he quietly cleaned up the pucks and pushed the nets back into their place.

With the bucket of pucks in hand, he met me at the gate.

"I'm sorry," he said, his voice back to its soft default and his brow furrowed. "I didn't mean to upset you."

I studied him for a quiet moment. He was a good person and a good friend. I couldn't hold him responsible for every injustice I'd experienced with other men.

"It's okay. I'm sorry for dumping all the teen romantic drama on you."

"I'm glad you did," he said, practically boring a hole in my head with the intensity with which he was looking at me. "I want to learn all your secrets, Willa. I never liked Jonathan Billings. You know that? And now I've got an excuse to kick his ass. So thank you."

"Do not." I held up a hand. "It wouldn't be a fair fight."

"He lives near here, right?" Ignoring my command, he clomped over to his giant hockey bag. "Insurance?"

"I'm not telling you."

"It's fine. Can't wait to bump into him in town."

"Cole Hebert, you do not need to avenge teenage Willa's broken heart." That logic came straight from thirty-one-year-old Willa, but inside, teen Willa was positively giddy that a boy was determined to fight for her. Sadly, with the caveman act he was putting on, teen Willa was currently winning.

He tore his gloves off and tossed them into his bag. Then he strode toward me in his skates, only stopping when he was inches away.

With more gentleness than seemed possible from such a big man, he tilted my chin up with his fingers.

"I want to," he rasped. "I hate that he made you feel unattractive and unworthy."

I sucked in a breath at the earnestness in his tone.

"No one treats my wife like that."

Chapter 23
Cole

We'd come so close the other night. At the rink, of all places. We'd goofed around and she'd shared some of her secrets.

And when she looked up at me and closed her eyes, I wanted to kiss her so badly. But I stopped myself.

Before I did it again, I had to be sure.

I was in deep.

I couldn't shake the memory of her lips on mine, the way it felt to hold her. I could barely keep my head on straight most days, and every moment with her was torture.

The way she smiled. How she'd correctly answer Jeopardy questions. The short shorts she wore when we worked out. Her body twisting and bending into yoga positions. The warmth of her at my side while she read and absently twirled her hair between her fingers.

We'd had a very adult, very mature discussion. She was right on every point, of course. A physical relationship would be a terrible idea.

And yet...

My ability to resist her was waning

"Lover boy is lost in space again," Bernice quipped. Our group was small tonight, mostly the die-hards as the weather had been terrible. These ladies had been friends for decades and had lovingly adopted me into their group, but still enjoyed hazing the new guy.

"Look at those stitches," Erica said. "He's knitting the wrong direction."

"And not maintaining proper tension," her sister Steph added.

"Oh, there's tension, all right." Erica snorted. She'd been the first female foreman at the lumber mill and was tough as nails. And she loved to give me shit.

I looked up, finding every eye in the place on me.

We were gathered in the community room at the Lovewell Library, me, along with the usual suspects with tote bags of yarn at their feet and gossip on their tongues. Nothing got by this crowd. I usually sat and listened and moved furniture when asked.

But now they were all focused on me.

Debbie smiled. "Lay off him, girls. He's in love."

That woman was a saint, but some of the others could smell blood in the water.

Bernice harrumphed. "You're ruining that hat."

I tucked my chin and assessed my work. Oh yes, I was absolutely ruining it. Grumbling, I started to pull out the stitches I'd fucked up. I was making matching crimson hats for all the girls on my team, and I was more than halfway through. My fingers usually did the work while my mind wandered elsewhere. But not tonight. Because Willa was taking up every single neuron in my brain.

"You better not be screwing it up already," Bernice drawled, taking a hit from the flask Erica was passing around. "You're still in the honeymoon phase."

Stopping my work, I glared at her. Although I was a fairly mellow guy, my glare usually shut people up. But not the knitting ladies of Lovewell.

"Flowers," Steph said. "Steve always used to bring me flowers."

"A date night. Somewhere nice. Go to Bangor," Jodie added. She'd been my elementary school gym teacher and now single-handedly ran the town's recreation department.

While they went on chattering and making assumptions about my marriage like I wasn't even there, I focused on salvaging this hat. I listened this time, though. Because they weren't wrong. There was tension. A lot of tension.

Although it wasn't the kind they assumed it was, and it definitely wasn't the kind I'd bring up to them.

It was the kind I worked out quietly in the shower after Willa left for work every day.

Because I couldn't afford to take any more risks, especially when it came to the person who was quickly becoming my best friend.

But I couldn't shake the affection that grew deeper every day. The awe overwhelmed me when I was in her proximity. And the attraction to her. Fuck. Most days, it was impossible.

Then there were the thoughts of more. Was it possible for us? Maybe it wasn't logical, but it felt right.

"I'll consider it," I said, pasting on a fake smile. "And I'm doing just fine with my wife." I gave Bernice a glare. "Loretta, have any new photos of your grandkids?"

That got them off my back instantly. Loretta Gagnon had recently welcomed several grandkids, including my nephew Thor, and had approximately one million photos of them on her phone. All the ladies immediately reached for their glasses and soon they were cooing at photos and discussing who was cooking and hosting for the holidays. Eventually, the conversation turned to some show on Netflix about murder they were all obsessed with.

I let my thoughts wander back to Willa.

This wasn't a one-sided attraction. I saw how she looked at me. And there was no hiding the shock on her face when I'd told her that I wanted her. That expression, both surprise and interest, with a hint of heat? God, I had replayed it so many times in my mind, often in the shower.

But Willa wasn't the type of woman to throw everything away on a whim. So I'd have to show her, prove to her that I was a stand-up guy. That I wasn't looking for a shallow fling. That I could make her happy if she'd let me.

And while I wasn't entirely sure how to accomplish that, I was certain it would take time. The last thing I could afford to do was rush. If I did, she'd shut me down hard, just like she had that night at the lake.

No, I'd have to chip away at her defenses. Maybe then she'd be ready to take the next step.

We were cleaning up, resetting the chairs and packing up the snacks, when Loraine Gagnon approached me. She was a lovely woman, but I'd felt strange around her since the moment we found out my father was responsible for her husband's death.

It was one of those wounds that would never heal. The shame would haunt us for all time.

"You're doing great.." She patted my arm, smiling up at me. "Don't listen to the old biddies. They've forgotten what it was like in the early days. It took years of training before Frank stopped leaving his socks on the floor."

I gave her a nod, uncomfortable speaking to her one-on-one. Even being in the same room had taken time to get used to.

She gave me a warm smile. "And remember, play to your strengths."

Frowning, I studied her. I wasn't sure I understood.

"If you're a great dancer, put a record on and twirl her around the house. If you're the poetic type, write her a love letter. That kind of thing. Trust me, keeping the magic alive is work, but it's so worth it."

"Thank you."

"Never stop reminding her of why she fell in love with you."

"I'm sorry," I said. I sounded stupid. Positively asinine. But I had no other words.

She waved her hand. "Nothing to apologize for. You're a good boy. I know because I raised four hooligan children who still keep me on my toes. Now go home to your wife."

I finished cleaning up and headed to my truck, replaying the conversation the whole time. Loraine gave my family more grace and compassion than we deserved.

But her words stuck in my mind.

Play to my strengths.

In the strength department, I was lacking. Especially when it came to impressing Willa.

I opened my trunk, and as I stashed my tote bag full of supplies, I caught sight of the splitting maul Jude had given me a week ago.

Huh.

I'd written off his suggestion of chopping wood as silly.

But my mind was spinning. She certainly didn't mind when I picked her up and carried her around. And she'd complimented my beard several times.

I'd been using the products Jude had given me and worked on trimming it properly.

Maybe playing to my strengths meant going full lumberjack.

I guess there was only one way to find out.

AFTER A LOT OF DELIBERATION AND A COUPLE OF SHITTY nights of sleep, I'd decided it was time to pull out all the stops.

The knitting gals were right. I had to step it up in the romance department. They didn't know the particulars, but the general sentiment was correct. Keeping a woman like Willa took effort.

And while I was trying hard to keep a lid on my feelings, every time I caught her checking me out, it gave me a thrill.

The more I thought about it, the more I wondered if maybe Jude had been right all along. Considering he lived like a monk, I hadn't put much stock in his advice, but all this pent-up energy and tension gathering inside me needed an outlet.

So I went to the garage and grabbed the splitting maul

from the back where I'd stashed it after knitting club. Then I dragged a few logs over to the side of the house. I chose the spot because it was level, but also because Willa could clearly see it from where she spent Saturday afternoons sitting at the kitchen island drinking tea and reading medical journal articles.

The air was frigid, but my cheeks warmed in the bright winter sun. I felt mildly ridiculous, going to all this effort, but the cottage did have a small fireplace, and we had used it a bit lately. So splitting firewood wasn't implausible.

As I set up, I surreptitiously glanced inside. Sure enough, she was reading and sipping tea, looking adorable with a yellow highlighter stuck into her ponytail and wearing a faded UMaine T-shirt that kept slipping off one shoulder. I yanked my phone from my pocket and took a quick photo of her. It was a total stalker move, but she looked so beautiful in this natural light.

After a few trips, I had a dozen or so thick logs ready to split. Jude had taken pity on me and given me wide pine, which would be easy to split.

I used the planks in the garage to create a stable base, then lined up the first log. For a few minutes, I stretched my shoulders out, walking around the grassy area that led to the rocky path to the lake and noting how perfect the spot would be for a patio, maybe an outdoor fire pit.

I could see hosting cookouts here in the summer, enjoying the shade of the tall oaks between dips in the lake to cool off.

Shaking off the thought, I focused on the task at hand. Before I could daydream about that kind of stuff, I had to impress my wife.

So, maul in hand, I staggered my stance as Jude had taught me, and swung, focusing on creating an arc with my shoulders and using my core to bring the axe down.

It hit the side of the log, slicing off only a tiny chunk.

Shit.

I rolled my shoulders and focused on keeping my breaths steady rather than getting frustrated. I needed to do better.

I replayed Jude's instructions in my head and hefted the maul, getting comfortable with the weight of it.

The next time I swung, I focused more on the log and less on looking manly, and the blade came down, slicing it in two perfectly equal halves.

Yes.

I resisted the urge to pump my fist. Now that it was in half, I needed to get it into quarters.

Focus, Cole. Do not look at Willa.

As much as I wanted her eyes on me, I had to be cool.

I took a deep breath and swung again. The blade fell perfectly, slicing the wood.

As I was grinning down at it, a crashing noise from inside startled me.

Whipping around, I squinted, trying to make out what was happening on the other side of the glass. All I found was the back of Willa's head.

Huh.

Maybe she had seen me.

Regardless, I'd hauled all these logs back here, so I might as well chop them. So I set up another.

Thwack. Okay, that felt better. Maybe I'd eventually get the hang of this.

Movement out of the corner of my eye caught my attention. Without turning, I registered the sight. It was Willa. Standing by the window, watching.

Okay, okay. Don't screw this up, Cole.

Swing.

Center hit.

Excellent.

I could feel her eyes on me. And while I had thought I'd feel self-conscious, the attention made me feel like fucking Superman.

Again.

Swing.

Yes.

I was invincible.

Jude wasn't lying; this is an incredible workout. I was already sweating, and my heart was racing. My lats ached, and my abs contracted with each swing.

Just as I'd quartered another log, the sound of a cough drew my attention. I looked up and found Willa standing by the back corner of the house, eyes wide.

She'd pulled a coat over her sweats but still wore her fluffy house slippers, which were probably soaked through already.

Jumping back when she caught me looking at her, she pulled her coat closed around her chest. "What are you doing?"

"Chopping wood." I lined up another log, biting my cheeks to keep from smiling.

"Why?"

"We need firewood." I grunted. This setup was beyond ridiculous, but what could I say? I was willing to make an absolute fool of myself to impress this woman.

I lifted my head and found her gawking. Fuck, if that didn't make me feel ten feet tall. Pulling myself up to my full height, I rested the maul on my shoulder like Paul Motherfucking Bunyan and smiled. "Whatcha doin' out here? It's freezing."

She froze, like a deer in headlights. "I-I needed to check these rose bushes," she said, gesturing to the row of frozen, leafless bushes that lined the side of the cottage.

"Huh. In January?"

Her face flamed. God, I love how easily she flushed. "They're in dormancy, but they still require care." She attempted to sound authoritative, like she did when using medical jargon, but the trembling hands gave her away.

I nodded, rolling my lips to keep from laughing. She had no garden equipment and was wearing slippers, but sure sweetie, the roses needed your attention.

"It's freezing," she snapped, putting a hand on her hip. "Put a coat on."

This time I didn't bother tempering the grin that slowly spread across my face. "Can't. Too sweaty. This is hard work." I patted the handle of the maul. "I may have to take off my shirt."

I propped the maul against the log pile and gathered the hem of my long-sleeved tee, ready to pull it up and give her a show.

Before I could do more than that, she gasped and took a step forward. As she did, she rolled her ankle and tripped straight into the snow.

Abandoning my plan, I darted over to her.

"Fuck," she hissed.

I knelt in front of her. "You okay?"

"Yes," she said, avoiding my gaze. "I'm fine."

Gently, I brushed the snow off her legs, maybe a bit more than necessary.

"You should get inside." I eased her to her feet and held on to her arms until she was steady. "Want me to come in and help you warm up?" I raised one eyebrow and pointed to the pile of freshly chopped wood.

She shook her head, focusing on the ground between us. "I have a lot of reading to do," she mumbled, walking back to the house.

The minute she turned her back, I couldn't repress the ear-splitting grin.

I picked up my maul, determined to finish the rest, certain she'd be watching from inside.

Line up.

Swing.

Chop.

Every few minutes, I caught a glimpse of her in my periphery. Hell yeah, she was watching. So I went for it. I peeled my shirt off and got back to work.

I hadn't made it through the entire pile before my shoulder was screaming. I was fairly certain I'd need reconstructive surgery, but it was so worth it. The way her eyes widened and breathing picked up? Yup, my wife was hot for me.

It felt like the best kind of victory. Until I realized I might have to keep this up and embrace the full lumberjack lifestyle. Shit. Maybe Gus could give me lessons before the baby came?

When Jude found out his trick had worked, he'd be such

a know-it-all about it, but I had every intention of baking him dozens of peanut butter cookies in thanks.

That look on her face alone was worth the ache in my shoulder and the taunting I was bound to be subjected to.

Operation Lumberjack had been a success. Now I just had to stay the course and not fuck it up.

Chapter 24
Willa

Sharing Christmas morning with my husband of convenience may have been the most surreal experience of my life.

Our tree, a little wonky and crooked, was decorated with a mix of things Cole had bought at the gas station and the ornaments we'd made during our hot chocolate and Christmas movie marathon last week.

It looked ridiculous, but also full of cheer. Staring at it made me happy. Purchasing my own Christmas tree was one rung on the adulthood ladder I had not climbed until now. Not when I'd always lived in tiny apartments and was usually working on Christmas.

I'd mentioned it offhandedly to Cole a week or so ago, and that night, I'd come home from work to a small, scrawny tree standing in front of the windows in the living room. He'd already set it up in a proper stand and had even bought the vitamins to keep the needles from dropping.

It was the kind of thing he did. His actions were typically silent and sweet, and he was cognizant of never crossing the line. Since our chat after the kiss that will never again be mentioned, he'd been a perfect gentleman, even keeping his yoga mat far away from me during our morning routine.

We were crushing this fake marriage. We'd gone to my parents' for Christmas Eve, where my mother had made a feast and my dad and I had played chess while Cole helped with the dishes and sang along to Christmas carols with my mom. He'd even knitted matching scarves for them, which they'd worn around the house with pride.

It was so silly, but the way he so easily fit into our little family dynamic meant a lot to me. He asked questions, complimented my mom's cooking, and was genuinely thankful for the small gifts my parents had placed under the tree for him. He seemed to genuinely enjoy them.

I'd always imagined waking up on Christmas morning and rolling over to snuggle my husband. Never had I pictured us in separate beds or the bout of anxiety that hit me while I brushed my teeth.

Despite the routines we'd fallen into, suddenly, I was devolving into a tween girl, questioning whether I should have showered before coming downstairs. Or maybe curled my hair. God, why was I such a train wreck.

And then I saw him.

That motherfucker.

He was wearing plaid pajama bottoms slung low on his hips and a motherfucking Santa hat. And *no* damn shirt.

"Merry Christmas," he said, a smile spreading across this face. Even though his scruff was quickly becoming a full beard, I could still make out the dimples beneath it, and the sight made my heart race.

That bastard. There went every rational thought in my head.

"We said no gifts," I protested several minutes later as I pulled a gorgeous green hat onto my head. It was soft and warm and matched the scarf he had made me perfectly. The frequent handmade gifts were making me feel things. And I couldn't afford that at the moment..

"Do you even know who you married?" he teased, his dark eyes dancing. "I've never met a rule I didn't want to break."

Rolling my eyes playfully, I sipped my coffee. "Since you broke the rules first, I guess I'll give you your present."

Straightening, he clapped. "I knew I wasn't the only one."

I was already regretting mentioning it. What if he was insulted by what I'd chosen?

"You may hate it," I hedged, grabbing the folder out of my work bag. Swallowing past the lump in my throat, I shuffled across the room and held out a manilla envelope. "And I'm not trying to pressure you."

He took the envelope and carefully pulled out the glossy brochures.

Brows furrowed, he peered up at me. "Public policy and administration?"

I nodded. "I made some calls to friends who work in the UMaine system. It's an excellent program, and given the incredible work you've done in town, I thought it would be a great fit."

His eyes widened as he flipped through the pages. I'd taken the liberty of requesting information about several degree programs. He'd mentioned wanting to finish his education more than once, but he'd never been able to articulate a specific direction.

Was I overstepping? Probably. Especially in light of the emotional distance I was trying to maintain. But he was so smart and capable, and I needed him to see that.

"Thank you," he murmured. "I've been thinking about it for so long. I feel stuck. Who goes back to school at thirty? I left college for the NHL draft, and to go back a failure…?" He ducked his head.

"You're not going back a failure. And lots of people have to take time off and come back. I think it's brave."

"I don't want to waste my time or my money," he muttered to his lap. "I don't want to only check a box. I want to really learn things, develop a career path. Find meaning in my life and make a difference."

My heart clenched at the uncertainty in his tone. God. Why couldn't he see how incredible he was? "Then you are the perfect candidate. When you're ready, you will crush it."

He squeezed his eyes shut and grimaced, almost as if he was in pain. "Thank you," he said finally. "This means a lot."

I smiled, though a tinge of unease trickled through me. Had I come off like some kind of educational snob? God, I hoped not. I didn't care about degrees. I wanted to help him find the motivation to take the next step.

He was physically imposing, which many conflated with confidence, but living with Cole every day had shown me that was not the case. He worried and obsessed, and he second-guessed and constantly talked negatively about himself.

If I could do one thing right as a wife, I hoped it would be helping him find his confidence.

"Okay. Get up," he said suddenly. "I have one more thing for you."

"No," I protested, clasping my hands in my lap. "You already made me something."

"It's nothing," he said as he hauled himself off the couch. "It isn't even a real gift. Just put your coat on. I promise."

I blinked at him. What? I was still wearing pajamas. But he was already putting his puffy jacket on over his bare chest. "It'll only take a minute."

Though I grumbled, I obeyed, slipping my feet into my boots and shrugging on my coat.

At least the sun was shining. The trees were covered in a layer of snow, glistening in the bright light of day. The air was crisp, which helped to calm my racing nerves.

Nerves that hadn't settled in weeks. Day in and day out, I was living with this man, slowly getting to know him. And yet, despite our promises of radical honesty, so much had gone unsaid and unsettled.

He led the way down the path toward the lake. In the daylight, it was easy to navigate, and the bare trees allowed the glistening blue water to peek through the landscape.

"Why are we headed down here?" I asked, shivering as a gust of wind hit me.

He turned and raised one eyebrow, which, in his Santa hat, was especially ridiculous, but didn't answer my question.

When we hit the clearing, an object on the rocky ledge came into view.

It was a large bucket. Or a small trash can. With a lid.

"Take a look," Cole said as we approached it.

As I stepped up to it, a pretty sign in the ground next to it caught my eye. It read: *Willa's Rage Rocks.*

I let out a laugh, and a zap of delight coursed through me.

"Open it."

Grinning at him, I took the lid off and peered inside. The entire thing was filled with rocks the perfect size to toss into the lake.

"I collected them for you. This way, you don't have to hunt around in the dark for good ones. You can rage out more conveniently and efficiently."

My stomach flipped at the gesture. Seriously? This had to have taken him hours. And it was just so goddamn sweet. I did spend a lot of time hunting for rocks, and yes, I'd tripped on occasion. Not that he knew that. My heart stuttered in my chest. These were only rocks, but it felt like so much more.

"Come on. You know you wanna."

With my lip caught between my teeth, I removed one the size of a softball and handed it to him. Then I chose another for myself.

"Let 'er rip," I said, hurling it as far as I could and watching with satisfaction as it *plunk*ed into the lake, making a respectable splash.

He threw his rock, managing twice the distance I had. Then we stood side by side in silence, taking in the beauty of the lake. I wanted to talk, to fill the quiet morning, but I had nothing to say. Instead, we existed like that for a few moments. The two of us, wearing pj's and coats, looking out at the wild mountains and forests.

"Honesty?" he asked softly, breaking the silence.

It was a question, not a statement.

"I'm nervous about today."

"Me too," I admitted, turning to head back up to the cottage.

We were headed over to Finn and Adele's house this evening. The entire Hebert family would be there, including Owen and Lila, whom we hadn't seen since Vegas. Lila and I had texted frequently about random things since then, but we'd never talked through the incident and our feelings pertaining to it.

"And I'm worried..." He walked down the path with his head lowered and his hands stuffed into his pockets. With each step, anxiety radiated off him.

If I could, I'd ensure today went off without a hitch for him. He hadn't spent Christmas with his family in years, and he was eager to please them all. He'd gone overboard buying gifts for his niece and nephew, of course, no doubt thinking of the poor little boy he'd once been who'd had no one. That thought alone brought tears to my eyes.

He cleared his throat, the sound bringing me back to the moment. "I'm worried that things between us have been awkward." He looked away, thankfully, since my cheeks had instantly gone hot. "I don't want anyone to question us or cause problems for you."

I closed the distance between us and squeezed his arm. "I'm sorry. For making things weird and for the things I said." I exhaled, my breath forming a white cloud in front of me. "And for not setting the ground rules early."

He straightened. "It's not that—"

I held up a hand. "But I care about you, and I promise to

be the best damn wife at your family's Christmas dinner today. You want mistletoe kisses? Hell yeah."

He smirked.

"You want me to brag about you and demand to see baby photos and bore everyone to death making them feel how soft and amazing my hat is? I'm all over it."

That earned me a snort.

"I mean it," I said. "You've done so much for me. And your brothers are important to you. We're in this together. I'll work on my weirdness, okay? I'm still getting used to being married to a hockey god."

"Ex-hockey god," he corrected, holding out an elbow.

I accepted, and we walked slowly toward the house, arm in arm, stepping over tree roots and boulders along the path.

"Willa." He stopped and turned to me. "Radical honesty?"

I nodded and smiled, giving him permission while bracing myself for what he might say.

"I think you're my best friend."

My heart stuttered at the simple admission, and there was no way I could form words in response.

"I'm not sure I've ever had one. In therapy, I've been working on opening myself up to pursue friendships, to be vulnerable and try to connect with people."

Therapy? He'd never mentioned that before. Color me impressed.

"I get that it probably sounds weird. But I'm working on verbalizing my feelings. So I want you to know how grateful I am for you. The marriage might not be real, but our friendship is, and it means more to me than you can imagine."

The lump in my throat was so big I wasn't sure I could

get oxygen to my brain. We were friends, good friends. We shared interests and supported one another. We were even working together on common goals. I'd written him off because he was Lila's ex, because he was a jock, and because of my own baggage. But he was right. We were connected on a deeper level than I could have ever imagined.

It was so obvious. There was no way I could even second-guess what he'd told me.

"It's a big responsibility," I joked. "Being a wifey and a bestie."

Tilting over, he pressed a kiss to my head. He'd never done that before, and while it wasn't the least bit sexual, it was still incredibly intimate. "I have a feeling you're up for the challenge."

"Oh, I am," I said, adding a little pep to my step. "And for the record, you're my best friend too."

His boyish smile almost split his face in half, causing me to take a step back. He even stood a little straighter. "That," he said, threading his arm through mine again and leading me back to the house, "is the single best Christmas gift I've ever received."

Chapter 25
Cole

The clinic was closed on Sundays, which meant that Willa usually slept in, worked out, and then either read or binged episodes of *Bridgerton*. We'd enjoyed a long weekend due to New Year's falling on Friday, and we'd spent a lot of time attempting recipes from YouTube, doing yoga together, and what had recently become my favorite activity with Willa: knitting—me, of course—and reading a fantasy novel—her—side by side. Most days, she'd put her head on my shoulder, and we'd sit in silence.

But this morning, we'd trekked out to the diner. I'd had a craving for eggs Benedict, and no one made it better than Bernice and Louis. We'd been hanging out at the cottage for the last few days, so the change of scenery would do us some good. Though Magnolia had invited us to some swanky party in New York City, that was not my scene anymore, and Willa's eyes had dulled when she mentioned it. What my wife needed more than anything was a little downtime.

The last thing I wanted was to find myself in a noisy crowd where alcohol flowed. I'd built a safe little bubble here. I was helping out at the mayor's office, planning next year's festival, coaching my girls, and talking to the University of Maine about transferring my credits and applying them to a BA program.

For the first time in years, I felt good. I was sleeping and exercising and doing things I cared about. The best part of it all was spending time with the person I cared about most.

Eventually, my feelings for her would be a problem, but I was choosing to ignore it at the moment, and I was progressively getting better at avoiding my attraction to my wife. Truly, I had developed some kind of superpower. However, it didn't change the fact that I wanted to spend as much time with her as I could.

The diner was packed full of church ladies casting judgmental looks, parents cutting blueberry pancakes into tiny bites for hungry kids, and groups of older men loudly debating the day's hot topic.

I'd avoided the diner for so long. It was the unofficial hub of our town, and I'd been swamped with so much shame and had no interest in the scrutiny I'd receive if I made an appearance. But with Willa? I was proud to walk in, even if I had to duck under the old doorframe to avoid hitting my head.

"Do you have a game this afternoon?"

"Yes. Can't wait." Excitement coursed through me. My girls were kicking ass on the ice. Most of the teams we played were from towns far larger than Lovewell with consistent access to ice time. But my team was scrappy, and moving

Emily to goalie and playing a left wing lock had really turned things around for us.

"Can I come?" It was a simple request, but it made my chest squeeze, nonetheless. She wanted to come watch my team play?

"To my game?" I cringed. Shit. That sounded pathetic. "To see the girls?" I corrected.

"Of course." Nodding, she brought her coffee to her lips. "I'm free all day. You've done every conceivable chore around the house, you've run every errand and even stocked the freezer with meals. Plus..." She wiggled her brows. "Shouldn't the coach's wife make an appearance?"

Yes. The answer was yes. She was always welcome, especially if she went around introducing herself as my wife. The thought of it filled me with pride.

"Sure," I said, trying to play it cool, even as my heart thumped heavily in my chest. "The kids would be excited to have another fan."

She smiled broadly, and though it should have lifted me up further, I was hit with a pang of regret. She'd never seen me play hockey. My family had all seen me play, and people I met along the way were usually impressed by my size and talent. But this was different. I wanted her to see me play because I wanted her to see me, the real me, not the guy decked out in his team's colors.

And there was no realer version of me than when I was on the ice, at least before I went pro and lost my drive. Back when my pulse quickened every time I laced up my skates. I wanted her to know that version of me, not whatever I was now.

"Cole," she said, putting her coffee cup down. Her hands were cupped around it, and she was chewing her bottom lip. It was one of her tells. She was nervous.

My heart sank. "Are you okay?"

"Yes, I'm great. I just wanted to ask—"

A loud crash sounded, interrupting her, and as we both spun. Scanning the space, we found a group of people gathered by the front door.

A loud scream startled me, sending me to my feet. My height gave me an advantage as I surveyed the scene. Immediately, I saw Mrs. Moran kneeling on the floor beside her husband, wailing.

Willa grabbed my arm, and together, we started to push through the crowd. "Back up," she shouted, her tone authoritative.

I followed her, stretching my arms and gently pushing people back.

"It's Bob," a woman near me said, her voice shaky. "He was getting up to leave and collapsed."

Willa dropped to her knees beside him and shook him gently. When he didn't respond, she grasped his wrist and checked for a pulse.

"Help me lay him out," she commanded, her voice calm but firm. "And push everyone back."

Though she hadn't looked up from Mr. Moran, it was clear she was talking to me, so I helped her maneuver him onto his back.

"Let me stabilize his neck," she said, yanking off her sweater. Once she had it tucked under his head, she brought her ear to his mouth and nose to listen for breath.

"Bernice," she shouted. "Call 911. Tell them we have a possible cardiac arrest."

Bernice pulled a phone out of her apron and tapped furiously as she hustled away from the group.

Willa locked her sights on Mrs. Moran. "Your husband is unconscious. Do I have your consent to perform CPR?"

"Yes," the older woman cried, a shaky hand pressed to her cheek.

With a nod, Willa shifted into action. Using her sweater to tilt his head back, she tipped his chin up. She listened for breath again, then moved back to his side.

Hands on his chest, one over the other, she locked her elbows and pushed hard. A hush fell over the crowd as she hummed to herself, her face a mask of concentration. The muscles in her arms tensed with every compression.

"Ambulance will be here in six minutes," Bernice shouted.

Willa nodded, her focus never straying from her patient.

Pinching his nose, she bent down and put her mouth over his. As she breathed air into his lungs, his chest rose. After she'd given a second rescue breath, she went right back to compressions.

She repeated this process several times, her pace steady and her focus unrelenting, compressions followed by two quick breaths, over and over for what seemed like hours.

She never tired or looked away from Mr. Moran. Even as people cried and prayed and shouted updates about the ambulance's arrival. Bernice and I pushed the crowd back, and when the EMTs arrived, she opened the door and flagged them down.

As they jogged into the diner, Willa looked up from her compressions. "Prep the AED."

With a nod, one EMT lifted a small green box-shaped device. The other wordlessly took over compressions and rescue breaths while Willa cut open Mr. Moran's shirt and placed sticky patches on his skin.

"Hands off," she said

Quickly, both EMTs leaned back.

She studied the screen, and a moment later, she said, "Ventricular fibrillation." Then, with her finger hovering over a button on the green box, she called out "clear" and pressed down, sending what looked like a powerful charge.

A hush fell over the diner as she studied the screen again.

"We've got activity," she said. "Resuming compressions. Get the stretcher and the O2."

One EMT rushed away, mumbling into his radio.

When he returned, they loaded Mr. Moran onto the stretcher. Willa never stopped compressions, and she continuously checked the screen.

"Call it in," she said to the EMT who slid an oxygen mask over their patient's face. "Myocardial infarction with V-fib."

She walked next to the stretcher as they rolled it out the door, then helped them load Mr. Moran into the back of the ambulance and climbed in herself, immediately hooking him up to various machinery.

Mrs. Moran grabbed my arm with a shaky hand, her face streaked with tears. "Is he gonna be okay?"

I had no idea how to respond, so rather than speaking, I patted her hand, hoping to offer her a little comfort.

"Thank God the doctor was here."

The EMTs motioned for her to climb in, so I helped her into the ambulance, and then watched helplessly as the doors closed and the bus pulled away, tires screeching.

I was no doctor, but I was pretty sure I'd just watched Willa save that man's life.

Chapter 26

Willa

"Are you okay?" The words startled me as I stepped into the cabin.

Before I could get the door shut behind me, Cole was up and off the couch, grasping my shoulders and pulling me into a hug.

He wrapped those long arms round me in the most intense and comforting embrace.

I closed my eyes and inhaled deeply, soaking in his strength. Every cell in my body ached with exhaustion from the adrenaline that had coursed through me for hours.

When he kissed the top of my head, I almost melted into his body. I needed this. Comfort, warmth.

"You are fucking magnificent," he said, his lips in my hair.

This interaction was crossing several of our carefully drawn lines, but I didn't care.

"I am so proud of you," he gushed. "You don't have to do anything. I've got dinner ready, and then you're taking a bath. Then I'm going to wrap you up in that fancy robe and put you to bed."

All of that sounded perfect. I didn't have the energy to make decisions or even think. I needed to be near him.

I toed off my boots as he gently took the coat off my shoulders.

"Want to talk about it?" he asked, his brow furrowed in concern.

"He's gonna be okay," I said, letting out the breath it felt like I'd been holding since that moment in the diner many hours ago.

He led me to the couch, where I collapsed and pulled my knees into my chest. I'd traveled with the ambulance to the hospital in Bangor. They'd needed to operate, so I'd waited, helping Mrs. Moran understand what the doctors were saying and ensuring my patient was awake and stable before I left.

I'd hitched a ride home with Camden, one of the local EMTs. He lived in Heartsborough, but he'd been kind enough to drop me off.

Cole fed me roasted chicken and glazed carrots—one of those recipes he'd found on YouTube and then effortlessly made his own. And then he drew me a bath, complete with candles, classical piano music, and fancy floral bubble bath. Where he'd procured bubble bath, I didn't know, but it was delightful.

After I was sufficiently waterlogged, I combed out my hair, put on my pajamas, and headed out to the living room. There, I found Cole knitting and two mugs of tea on the coffee table.

"Sleepytime?" I asked with a smile.

He nodded, still knitting furiously. The yarn was a deep red color.

"Whatcha working on?"

"A little something for my team." He smirked. "And you're not getting away with ignoring what I said earlier. You were a fucking superhero today."

His expression turned serious, causing a charge to run through me. Cole saw me, and he wasn't afraid to be honest with me. It was terrifying and a bit thrilling at the same time.

"It's nothing. It's what I was trained to do." I picked up the mug and blew on the hot liquid to avoid his intense stare.

"Stop that. Don't discount how talented you are."

"It's CPR."

He put his knitting down, his brow furrowed deeply. Oh boy, now he was serious. "A lot of people know CPR, but few can manage a crisis the way you did today. You took command, gave orders, provided lifesaving medical care, and then stayed with your patient until he was stable. You are a fucking superhero," he bit out. "And if you ever, for a single minute, think otherwise, then I'm here to remind you."

My heart flipped, but still... "It's my job."

"Sure. Being a doctor may be how you earn a living, but what you did today was so much more than a *job*. It's your calling, Willa. You help, you care, and you jump in when needed. Without hesitation." He roughed a hand over his beard and shook his head. "How were you able to keep your chest compressions so even and steady for so long? How did you control your own heart rate and adrenaline?"

I shrugged. I wasn't sure how to even begin to form a response.

"That's it. I'm getting a tattoo. You, wearing a cape and a

stethoscope. Right here." He pulled up his shirt and thumped his chiseled chest.

Giggling, I averted my eyes. I was exhausted and coming down from one hell of an adrenaline high. My muscles ached and so did my head. I couldn't control what I would do if faced head-on with the combination of those abs, that chest, and that face. He was a deadly temptation. While I could usually resist, in my weakened state, it wasn't worth the risk.

"I was terrified," I admitted, lowering my chin. Try as I might, I needed to unload. Rather than call my mom, who'd always been my sounding board, or Lila or Magnolia, I wanted to share myself with Cole. "I was panicking and struggling to stay focused."

I pulled my damp hair back into a ponytail and focused on breathing steadily.

"I should be used to this. Battle hardened by now. I spent two years in an emergency room. I've seen awful things and treated hundreds of trauma patients. I've lost some. I've seen children with gunshot wounds. Over time, you learn to detach, to be objective, to problem-solve and execute with precision. But today, detaching was difficult."

His eyes softened. "You're not a robot, and when the patients are people you know and love? Cut yourself some slack. Mr. Moran drove us to school from kindergarten until we graduated from high school. He dressed up as Santa at church. He and his wife give out full-size candy bars at Halloween. You're allowed to be scared."

But that was just the thing. I couldn't be scared. I couldn't be human. Not in those types of situations. As the town doctor, my job was to keep everyone healthy all the time, to care for generation after generation of Lovewell citizens. "What if I hadn't been there?" I whispered. "He would have been dead before the ambulance arrived."

"You can't be everywhere for everyone, but you were today. Because of you, Mr. Moran gets to kiss his wife and see his kids again. And maybe that's enough."

I nodded, my eyes welling with tears.

"Let's get you to bed, wifey. You're beat."

I was. And I was in desperate need of a reset. But I couldn't bear the thought of going in there alone. Of not being with him.

"Can you stay with me?" I asked, sniffling.

"Of course. Let me brush my teeth."

My stomach twisted, and my chest went tight as he shuffled away from me. What had I done? I'd invited Cole into my bed?

It wasn't sexual—I was wearing faded old pj's, and my face was red and splotchy from crying, for God's sake—but it was intimate. Regardless, I didn't think I could sleep without him. But was I setting myself up for total devastation by doing this? Because my defenses were crumbling, and my heart had already begun to embrace the man I'd married.

He came into my room dressed in nothing but boxer briefs and a faded T-shirt, his face scrubbed and his hair sticking up funny, like he'd been tugging on it all night.

"Which side do you sleep on?" he asked, his eyes downcast and his cheeks pink, looking boyish. God, that wasn't helping my nerves one bit.

"Right."

Nodding, he rounded the bed and shuffled up to the left side.

It was a queen-size bed, which had always felt spacious to me, but when a six-seven hockey playing lumberjack crawled in beside me, it felt a lot smaller.

He shifted, rolling toward me. "Is this okay?"

Instantly, his warmth radiated through his T-shirt, calming me. With a nod, I reached over and flipped off the lamp on my nightstand.

"Can I tell you something?" he whispered.

Humming, I rolled onto my side so we were eye to eye, our faces only inches apart, though we weren't touching.

"I was thinking about what a treat it is to watch a person when they're at their absolute best. Doing the thing they're exceptional at. Like hearing Mozart play the piano, or Serena Williams play tennis."

My breath caught at the sincerity in his tone while confusion swirled inside me. This was not what I expected at all.

"I know today was a lot for you, and I respect that. But watching you in action made it clear to me that this is exactly what you were born to do."

Huffing, I buried my face in my pillow. "I am not the Serena Williams of doctors."

"Of course not. But Serena is probably the Willa Savard of tennis. Ever think about that?"

I rolled onto my back with a giggle.

"You were even singing a song," he said.

"Oh yeah. 'Dancing Queen,' by ABBA. It's my CPR song."

"CPR song?"

"It's important to keep a consistent pace when performing chest compressions. Usually 110-120 beats per minute. Most people sing 'Staying Alive' by the Bee Gees, for obvious reasons. But my mom is a huge ABBA fan, so I sing 'Dancing Queen' in my head."

"You are literally proving my point right now." He chuckled. "You're one of the greats. Now you need your rest. Get in here and snuggle." He rolled onto his back, pulling me against him with one arm.

I hit his chest and was instantly engulfed in his clean, manly smell. Soap and wood and spice. Total comfort. Not to mention the softness of his shirt beneath my cheek and my palm as I rested a hand on his sternum.

I hadn't been prepared for what it would be like to snuggle such a big, strong man. Lord, was it incredible. He tucked me in closer and kissed the top of my head again. Delight rushed through me. I shouldn't, but I secretly loved when he did that. It was as if the gesture was more for him than for me. Like he couldn't hold back. And that made my heart rate speed up even faster than the sensation of his muscular chest under my hand did.

"Close your eyes," he said, his low tone soothing me in a way that was like magic. "You'll be back at full strength in the morning. let yourself recharge."

The weight of the day pressed on me, and the warmth of his body, the kindness of his words, embraced me. Without my permission, my eyes welled. All the feelings were rushing to the surface, and I had no hope of containing them.

"Can I tell you a secret?" I sniffled.

"Sure."

"I don't think hockey is your thing." Every day, whether he knew it or not, Cole revealed more of his complexity. The more I saw, the more I realized that he had not yet scraped the surface of his abilities.

"No, it was."

"You were good at hockey, but in you, Cole, I see greatness." I tapped his chest, my eyelids heavy. "You just haven't realized it yet. And when you do, look out world."

Chapter 27

Cole

I did not want to be here. I would have much preferred to be at home, sitting on the comfy couch with my wife while she inched closer to me as we watched *Jeopardy*. Then, after we'd brushed our teeth, we'd head to bed, where I'd hold her all night.

We'd never discussed it, but we'd slept that way every night for the last week. I'd been sleeping better than I ever had. Making it through my days more easily too, since no matter what the day threw at me, at the end of it, I got to wrap my arms around Willa.

Even if nothing more ever happened between us, I would be content. She really was my best friend. The person I depended on. The person I couldn't wait to share my funny stories with. And the person I missed the most after a long day.

Our time as husband and wife was limited, so I'd take every second I could get, even if it was while I was asleep.

But I wasn't at home with my wife tonight. Nope, I was at the Moose.

I'd avoided this place, like just about every public place in town, for months. But Jude's band was playing. He'd been such a support to me when I needed him, so it seemed like the least I could do. He was not only keeping my secret but rooting for me to get the girl. So I'd come out to show my support, even if it meant losing a cozy night with Willa.

The Moose was a semi-decent restaurant pretending to be a dive bar. One side was filled with pool tables and dart boards, and the other, vinyl booths filled with families eating burgers the size of their heads.

In the middle was a large stage where the band was warming up.

Willa was chatting with Magnolia, who was in town for a few days. She'd been coming around what seemed like every few weeks. Perhaps it was because of the tiny brunette she currently had her arm around?

I surveyed the room, the crowd, while I sipped my water. Finn was playing pool on the far side with some of the Gagnons, but it didn't look like Gus and Chloe had arrived yet.

A hand landed roughly on my back, giving it a slap and causing me to spin around.

"Good to see you out and about." Chief Souza took a swig of his beer, watching me with a condescending gleam in his eye that said he was not, in fact, happy to see me out.

He'd been good friends with my father for years. But since my dad had been arrested for committing a whole host of crimes right under his old friend's nose, that nose was seriously out of joint.

The chief had been around for as long as I could remember, a stocky guy with a gray mustache and a lot of unearned confidence. He did not hide his how much he disliked me, and I swore he'd taken true joy in arresting me earlier this year.

I could imagine how it chapped his ass that the feds were still crawling around town, infringing on his turf. He was old-school like that. Territorial. And Elliot Ness, he was not. Nothing happened here, and when it did, he was caught unaware, so it wasn't a big shock that he had been asleep at the wheel when it came to my dad.

Most days, he was more concerned with busting high school kids sneaking beers down by the lake or writing speeding tickets off Route 16.

"Congratulations on your, eh, marriage," he said, his lip curled. "Still not sure how you landed the town doctor."

Dick.

He attempted a smile, but it came out like a snarl.

"Neither do I," I admitted, keeping my expression even. "But she said yes, so now I have to keep her."

He laughed into his beer. "You always did have a horse-shoe up your ass." With that parting shot, he sauntered away, headed to talk to someone he surely found more important than me. Asshole.

But before I could spiral, before I could let his words get to me, Willa appeared, smiling up at me. Instantly, the anger dissipated. I put my arm around her shoulder and gave her a squeeze.

"When you're ready to leave, say the code word, and I'll carry you out of here."

She scrunched up her face. "The code word uttered when it's time to leave the crowded bar."

I replied on cue. "What is Final Jeopardy, Alex."

She stood up on her tiptoes as I leaned down. And then she whispered in my ear, "That is correct for four hundred, husband."

We shuffled toward the stage and found a place on the side of the room. At my height, I was always worried about blocking someone's view.

Willa stood in front of me, that delicious ass pressed right up against my crotch, swaying to the music. The bar was crowded, which gave me an excellent opportunity to touch her and smell her hair. Yes, I was in deep. I didn't even care. I'd take every scrap she tossed my way and enjoy the hell out of it.

I'd spent most of my life chasing the next big thing, constantly filled with disappointment because nothing ever lived up to my expectations and because I was always running toward an unknown future where things would surely be right.

This marriage had been a wake-up call. There was no future here. I had no real shot. So all I got were nights like these, pretending in public and enjoying the time I got to spend with her. My therapist had been pushing me to be mindful, to be grateful, and to live in the moment.

And when I was with Willa, those things came easily.

The band was excellent. Jasper was a great musician, but Jude had the most talent. Despite his role as a supporting player, he led every song on the guitar like a pro.

Willa motioned for me to bend down.

"I'm gonna grab another water. You want one?"

"I'll come with you."

With my hand on the small of her back, I guided her through the sea of people back toward the bar and seating area. Away from the crush of the crowd, it was instantly easier to breathe. It was quieter over here too.

I ordered two bottles of water and mentally calculated how much longer I needed to stay in order to check *be a supportive brother* off my to-do list.

Next to me, Willa stiffened. "Oh. Hey, Jonathan," she said, her voice pinched.

I turned around quickly and found Jonathan Billings hovering close to my wife. My eye twitched, and I balled my hands into fists as words Willa had spoken about this man echoed in my head.

The guy was maybe five-ten, balding, and wearing a starched dress shirt to a bar on a Friday night. I wanted to grab him by the collar and throw his preppy ass out into the snow.

"Hi, Cole," he said, his tone friendly.

My response was a glare. We'd grown up in the same small town, but I had probably said five words to the guy in my whole life.

I tipped my chin. "Do you know my wife?" I asked, putting heavy emphasis on the word. "Dr. Willa Savard?"

"Of course." His smile spread.

I wanted to punch it off his face. This man had been her first kiss. And that alone made me want to beat him.

Instead, I pulled Willa close, spreading my hand over the swell of her ass and bending down to kiss her cheek.

Jonathan looked between us awkwardly.

Willa said nothing, just stared at him, her cheeks pink and her green eyes wide.

So I took that as my cue to step up.

"Yup. Not sure if you heard. Convinced her to marry me

in Vegas. I've been obsessed with her forever, but for years, I was sure she'd never give me a chance." I gave her ass another healthy squeeze, the move causing her eyes to widen. "So I had to lock it down quick, you know. Before she realized she could do better."

"C-congrats," he sputtered, scratching at the back of his neck.

I bent down and captured her mouth in a kiss that was far too intense for the bar, and when I pulled back, I grinned, hoping I looked a little feral. "Thanks, man. Fuck, I'm a lucky guy." I turned and stared at Willa, feasting on her with my eyes in a way so blatant that anyone in a one-mile radius could see exactly what I wanted to do to her.

"Anyway, good to see you. I think I gotta get my wife home." I licked my lips and threw some cash on the bar. As I turned and said "we're newlyweds," I punctuated the declaration with a lascivious wink, making sure there was no doubt he understood that I was going home to fuck my goddess wife senseless.

Joke was on me, since that was not gonna happen, but I sure as fuck wanted boring-ass Jonathan and the entire town to know she was mine.

Breathing hard, I pulled her toward the door and snagged her coat from the antler hooks by the door.

She yanked her arm away as soon as we were outside.

"Cole," she hissed, her face pink with embarrassment. "You didn't have to do that."

I pulled her green hat over her head for her and gave her cheek a pat. "Oh, wifey, I sure did."

"You verbally peed on my leg," she huffed. "Marking your territory for Jonathan and the whole town."

Arm crooked, I offered it to her as we walked through the icy parking lot toward my car. "Yup. And I need to do it more often. I think bragging about my hot wife may be my favorite hobby. It's up there even higher than knitting or watching *Jeopardy*."

I gave her ass a firm smack for fun. Shit, I was already getting hard.

"Jesus, Cole. We're in public."

I pulled her close, leaning over so that my lips ghosted over her earlobe. "That ass is legally mine, wifey. The least you can do is let me give it a little smack once in a while."

Her breath hitched. Oh yeah, I wasn't the only one feeling the heat.

"Did you like it?" I asked. "When I manhandled you, claimed you, and made sure Jonathan and his pleated khakis knew you were mine?" My heart was pounding and my cock was hard as stone.

Pulling up short, she peered up at me, her eyes wide and her teeth sunken into her bottom lip.

"I fucking loved it," she said softly. And with that, she shuffled to the SUV, climbed in, and slammed the passenger door shut.

Chapter 28
Willa

The ride home was silent. Except for the sound of my heart beating out of my chest. I was having some kind of physical reaction that I couldn't understand or explain.

The whole way home, I snuck glances at Cole as he quietly drove—the corded muscles of his forearms gripping the steering wheel; the way his eyes narrowed when he was focusing on the road.

Something had changed tonight. When he spoke to Jonathan, my neurons shifted. His words, his tone of voice, even the way he touched me, had changed my genetic makeup, and I'd never be the same.

He'd claimed me.

Publicly.

He'd practically shouted about his attraction from the rooftops. Logically, I knew it was for show. That he was being a good friend and a good fake husband. But logic was not winning this fight. Because my hormones had kicked into overdrive.

And lust had entered the equation.

I was lusting after my husband.

He was gorgeous, and sure, I'd always felt some level of attraction to him.

But this was something else entirely. My body ached for him. My mind was solely focused on him. I wanted to touch every inch of him, experience the kind of connection I had only ever read about in books.

If I were brave, I'd kiss him. I'd climb on top of him and give in to the ache that had been building inside me since he sat next to me on that bench in Vegas.

But that wasn't how real life worked.

He was a good man, and he'd been working hard to figure his life out. In many ways, he was helping me too.

I was getting way more out of the marriage than he was.

What if I came on to him, only to find that he wasn't attracted to me? That I was wildly misreading the signals?

I needed Lila. She'd help me break this down and walk through every possibility.

But I couldn't tell her. I couldn't tell anyone.

I was alone with my lust. And it was going to kill me.

We parked and headed into the house, still ensconced in this bubble of silence. At the very least, I should find my voice and thank him for what he'd done, for the way he'd stuck up for me. To most, it may not have been a big deal, but seeing Jonathan's reaction to Cole's declaration had healed a tiny piece of my teenage broken heart.

But before I could find the words, Cole hung his coat, kicked off his shoes, and headed straight for his room.

My stomach plummeted. Why was he leaving? It wasn't even late. Was he upset? Oh God, I'd been so consumed by my lust that I'd failed to realize that he was upset.

I hesitated in the kitchen, just outside his room. He clearly wanted to be alone. But I wanted to smooth things over. I hated the idea that he might be feeling bad about our encounter with Jonathan and what I'd said to him after.

Letting my hormones take over, I stepped up to his door. We had promised each other total honesty. And I didn't want to go to bed with a weird misunderstanding hanging between us.

As I stood there, working up the nerve to knock, he let out a low groan. Oh shit, he really was upset.

I knocked lightly, desperate to clear the air. To talk about this like adults. We'd done a great job of being open and honest so far. This would be fine.

He didn't answer.

Thinking he hadn't heard me, I knocked again, and when he still didn't answer, I twisted the doorknob. It was unlocked.

With my fingertips, I pushed, and when Cole came into sight, I called his name softly.

His back was to the door, and he was shirtless, wearing only a pair of gym shorts. At the sound of his name, he whipped around, his eyes widening and his mouth dropping open.

I blinked, taking him in. The cut muscles of his chest and abdomen, the V that led straight to his waistband, and—holy shit—the massive erection tenting his shorts.

"What are you doing here?" he choked out.

"Sorry." I squeezed my eyes shut, both embarrassed and intrigued. I was a doctor and had seen some things. But what the hell was happening in his pants? I'd never seen such an impressive show of desire. "I wanted to check on you. You seemed upset."

"I'm not," he said softly. "Just frustrated."

"I shouldn't have come in," I said, lowering my head and stepping back.

"No," he said firmly. "Come in. I want you to see this."

Swallowing thickly, I obeyed, stepping over the threshold. I'd been in his room dozens of times, but tonight, an awareness I'd never experienced hit me as I padded across the hardwood floor.

"This," he gritted out, fisting himself over the fabric of his shorts. "This is how hard my wife makes me."

I gasped at the sight. All the muscles in his abs clenched, his eyes hooded, and his large hand wrapped around whatever that bulge was.

My inner muscles tightened, and at the same time, my legs turned to jelly.

"Take a good look. This is every day of my life. Every single night, I lie in bed next to you, dreaming about what it would feel like to touch you, to taste you. To sink my cock into you and fuck you through that fancy headboard."

My nipples puckered, turning to sharp points I was certain would cut right through my sweater. My heart was racing, and a fire ignited below my skin.

"Every morning," he gritted out, "I wrap my hand around it and hate myself. Because you'll never be mine. I will not mess things up for you. I will not hurt you in any way."

"Cole," I said, overwhelmed by a mixture of need and confusion.

He was so sad, so desperate. I itched to go to him, touch him, give myself to him fully. To experience what it would be like to be his wife in every way.

He was fully stroking himself now, the act making my mouth water. His body was massive and strong, and yet his words were soft and vulnerable.

"We promised each other honesty," he said, forcing the words out. "So here it is. Every day I fall a little more in love with you. I love your laugh and your smile and how incredibly funny you are. And fuck, do I love your body. The things I want to do to you." He bowed his head. "I'll honor our agreement. You've done so much for me, and I don't think you even realize it. So I won't do it. I won't touch you and risk ruining everything you've worked for."

My body was an inferno now, begging me to jump on my husband. To throw all our rules and boundaries and the friendship we'd built straight out the window. How could I control myself when *this* man was standing here, looking like *that*, and saying *those* words?

The attraction I'd been feeling earlier was nothing compared to the simmering volcano of lust inside me now.

We stared at one another, silent. There was nothing left to say. He'd declared himself.

This was the fuck-it moment. The one I'd read about in so many books.

He'd made it clear: He wouldn't touch me. He wouldn't be the one to make the first move.

So now it was my turn.

Chapter 29
Cole

Eyes flashing, she walked slowly across the room, like a lion stalking a gazelle, never breaking eye contact.

I'd done it now. Fully crossed that line. She should slap me. I deserved it.

But as I drank in her gorgeous face, I had no regrets. There was no way I could have lived with this secret much longer. What I told her was the absolute truth. I was falling in love with my wife.

When she stopped in front of me, she gently cupped my cheek. Then, head tilted, she whispered, "I want you too."

My heart took off at a breakneck pace.

Standing this close, the warmth of her body seeped into me. Fuck, I wanted to grab her and pull her into me, eliminate any distance between us forever. But I was frozen, uncertain. This was a significant moment. Maybe the most significant of my life.

In the end, I didn't have to drag her to me. She cupped both cheeks now and pulled me down until our lips met.

God, the feel of her mouth on mine only got better each time.

My hands were on her body, touching her the way I'd always wanted to but was too afraid to try.

With one hand splayed on her ass, I squeezed, pulling a gasp from her. I drank it in, loving the sensation. I wanted to hear that sound over and over again, turn it into the soundtrack of the rest of my life.

"Cole."

Groaning at the sound of my voice on her lips, I kissed my way up the column of her neck, savoring the taste of her skin.

"I want to tell you something."

Slipping my hands under the hem of her sweater, I murmured nonsensically into her skin, too lost in her body to form a coherent response.

"I don't have a ton of experience."

Heart lurching, I dropped my hands.

"Are you...?"

"A virgin?" She huffed a laugh. "No, not even close. But my hookup history is limited, and I worry—"

Angling close again, I put a finger to her lips. "There is nothing you have to worry about."

Cupping her cheeks, I pecked her lips and pulled back, forcing her to make eye contact.

"We can go slow," I promised. "And there's nothing I won't teach you. Nothing I won't give you."

She smiled, reaching down to grip my throbbing erection. "But that's the thing." She bit her lip, and it was almost my undoing. "I don't want to go slow. I want you. All of you."

It took every ounce of willpower I possessed to remain

calm and focused. I wanted her so badly, but more than anything, I wanted to make this experience perfect for her.

"Okay, but I'm gonna take my time." I hauled her up and threw her over my shoulder. I might be wrong, but I had a feeling she'd be more comfortable in her own room.

"Duck," I said as I walked through the doorway and toward her room. The last thing I needed was to injure her.

And as I flipped her onto the bed, she giggled, her cheeks flushed and her eyes bright.

"Not so fast." I pulled off her shirt and tossed it aside. Then sucked in a sharp breath as I was greeted with the sight of her perfect breasts in a black bra.

"Better take off the pants too. Get comfortable," I teased.

With a roll of her eyes, she pushed her leggings down. "You too."

I stripped in a millisecond, leaving myself naked and crazed for my wife. "You are so fucking gorgeous."

A flush crept up her cheeks and down to her chest. Fuck. The sight only amped up my need. I couldn't hold back any longer.

Hovering over her, balancing with one arm, I kissed her while easing her bra straps over her shoulders.

"Tell me what you like," I whispered, grabbing a handful of one incredible tit.

Her breath hitched, and she tensed beneath me. "I'm not sure."

Fuck, I wasn't having any of that, so I kissed her again. "Even better. Then I get to play."

Lowering, I took one nipple into my mouth and sucked, relishing the way she wiggled beneath me.

I kept her pinned down, being sure not to put too much

of my weight on her, and gave the other breast some attention. And then I was kissing down her body, caressing and teasing as I worked my way to her panties.

They were black and fairly plain, and they were standing between me and the thing I wanted most in this world.

So I ripped them off with a swift tug.

She writhed and moaned in a way that made me painfully hard. Fuck, I wanted to rip all her panties up.

"Spread wide for me, wifey," I said, pushing her thick thighs open. "I want to enjoy your incredible pussy."

And it was incredible. She was wet and tight, and the taste of her was addicting. I couldn't get enough. I was a starving man. I'd been lusting after her for so long, and every single moan fueled my desire to make her mine.

"How's that?" I asked as I peered up at her, a devilish grin on my face.

Her head was thrown back as she gripped my hair. "Ah." She shuddered. "Oh my *God*. It feels amazing."

She was close, and making her come became my sole obsession. I slipped a finger into her heat and curled it, and in response, her back arched off the bed.

"That's it, wifey. Come for me."

I dove back in, flicking, sucking, and licking while working my finger and focusing on every sound, taking my cues from her.

And then the dam broke. She cried out, her thighs clamping around my ears, and she came undone.

Once she came down, she sat up, her eyes glazed and her lips plump and well-kissed. Her hair was everywhere, and she had never looked more beautiful.

"Let me," she said, reaching for my aching cock.

I shook my head and kissed her again. "We don't have to do anything else."

"But I want to. You. This." She threw her head back. "It's incredible."

I cupped her face. "Honesty?"

She nodded. "Always."

"Eating your pussy was a dream come true. Making you come and scream my name like that? If I keeled over right now, I'd die a happy man."

She bit her lip and grinned.

"But," I said, "all I want is to be inside you."

Gently, she caressed my cock, peering down between us.

"It's just..." She sucked in a deep breath. "It's so big. I can't even get my hand around it. Will it fit?" In that husky voice, the words alone were enough to have me worrying I was going to blow my load.

"Do you want to try?" I asked, brushing her hair off her face. "I'll never hurt you."

She nodded. "I want to. But I'm a little scared."

With a hand to her chest, I eased her back onto the bed, then slipped one finger inside her, then another.

"You're soaked and ready. I'll be gentle. I promise. You're gonna love it." It would take all my control to go slow and not fuck her senseless on the first go, but she was worth it. "Let me get a condom." I sat up, instantly missing the contact. Dammit. Why hadn't I thought to bring one with me?

She pushed up on her elbows, and as her tits bounced, all semblance of logic left me. "I've got an IUD," she murmured. "I'm healthy."

I was on top of her, covering her body with mine and kissing those breasts before she could utter another word.

"Got tested," I said, unable to keep my mouth off them. Fucking delicious. "All clear."

"Then I want it. I want you inside me."

I brought my face to hers so only inches separated us and watched her eyes flash. "You want my cock? Say it for me."

"I need my husband's cock." She wiggled beneath me. "I hope it fits."

I pushed her legs open wide and notched myself in place.

God, this was going to be a tight fit, but if I took it slowly, I'd make every second of it good for her.

I gently pushed in, keeping my focus fixed on her face. And when her eyes widened, I took a nipple in my mouth and laved at it, helping her relax, and pushed in, inch by inch.

"Cole," she cried, her nails digging into my back. "Fuck. You're so huge."

I stopped and sucked in a breath. "Does it hurt?"

"A little," she panted. "But it's so good."

Heat licked up my spine. "You're doing such a good job. My wifey takes my cock so well."

"I'm so full, and I love it."

My balls twitched in response to her words. "It's gonna be over too fast if you keep talking like that," I said, gently thrusting. I was on a hair trigger, and her screams, her bouncing tits, and her tight grip on my cock were not helping matters.

She relaxed beneath me, allowing me to easily slide in another couple of inches. Fuck, this was bliss. I could die a happy man right now. Because fucking my wife was the single best thing I'd ever done.

But there was no way I'd last long, so I spread her legs wider and set a pace I could maintain while using my hands and mouth to make sure no inch of her was neglected.

"How can I get you off again?"

She shook her head. "I don't know. I've never..."

My hips stuttered, throwing me off rhythm. "You've never?"

"No. Not like this. Not from, you know, penetration. other stuff."

I closed my eyes and said a silent prayer that this woman would keep me long enough to make up for all the shitty sex she'd had in the past.

"That's okay. Can I try something?"

She nodded, her eyes never leaving mine.

I held out my thumb, and she eagerly sucked it into her mouth. Fuck, it was so hot I got momentarily distracted from my mission.

I slipped my hand between us and lightly circled her clit with my thumb.

Instantly, she clenched around me.

"You like that?"

"Yes." Her nails were digging into my back again, a good sign that this was working.

I hitched up one of her thighs for better access, then I got to work, timing my thrusts and using my thumb to tease her clit as she writhed and moaned. Excellent.

"Such a good girl," I murmured. "Look at this view. Play with your tits, wifey."

She obliged, clenching around me as she did. Hell yeah, victory was in sight.

"That's it," I praised her. "Come on, greedy girl, come for your husband. Come on my cock. Let me be the first."

That was all it took. In the next moment, the most beautiful thing happened.

"Cole," she screamed, writhing and clenching. "Oh my God, Cole."

There was no time for celebration, because the way she pulsed around had me coming immediately.

And as my own orgasm hit, I knew without a doubt this woman was it for me.

Chapter 30

Cole

I had a spring in my step, and even the bitter winter cold couldn't keep me down. Willa had gone into the office, so after a morning spent cuddling and making her come a few more times, I got out of bed, showered, and got to work.

Jude, being Jude, wouldn't accept my offering of peanut butter cookies alone. Not only did he shove a cookie into his mouth the moment I arrived, but he also insisted on going snowshoeing. I would have preferred to stare out the window and count the minutes until Willa came home, but with Jude, outdoorsy shit would always be on the agenda.

It was only ten, yet he was already on his third cookie. "I take it from the goofy grin, the cookies, and the circles under your eyes that tell me you didn't get any sleep last night that things are going well at home?"

I bent down to give Ripley a scratch behind the ear. She was Jude's constant companion and best friend. I swore he spent more time talking to his dog than he did humans. Not that Ripley minded. He'd found her in the woods a couple of years ago, a little puppy that he'd cuddled in the cab of his crane for the rest of the day, then nursed back to health.

That tiny, sick puppy had grown into an imposing mini horse. She was black, with a little shock of white on her belly. We thought maybe Bernese mountain dog with some Great Dane, but Jude claimed she was his dire wolf, whatever that was.

All I could do was smile at my brother.

He shook his head. "You love her?"

I nodded. "Pretty sure I do."

He nodded into his coffee cup.

"Lemme guess. You chopped wood."

"Twice. And I'm man enough to admit you were right."

He held up the container I'd filled with three dozen cookies—though it was probably closer to two dozen by now; he had made quite a dent. "So these cookies are an official acknowledgment of my superior seduction skills?"

I gave him a mock bow, further feeding his ego.

Before I could blow more smoke up his ass, Ripley barked and skittered to the door, where she growled loudly. That was unlike her. Despite her hulking presence, she was usually pretty calm.

Jude strode to her and ran a hand down her back, trying to comfort her, but when a knock sounded on the door, she barked again, this time incessantly. It was pretty quiet up here on the mountain. People didn't wander by Jude's house and knock to say hello, so he and I were both instantly on guard.

Without a word, I grasped Ripley's collar, and Jude went to the door.

As he pulled it open, we came face to face with two men

wearing suits and sunglasses. Both were of medium height and an average build. Wholly average looking.

"Jude Hebert." The man who spoke had close-cropped hair and was clean shaven. His posture indicated a steel rod had been shoved up his ass. Definitely feds.

He held his badge up, confirming my suspicions. "Special Agent Bryce Portnoy, Federal Bureau of Investigation."

My entire body tensed. I hated law enforcement. Instantly, I broke out in a cold sweat.

Jude, on the other hand, was perfectly Zen. "I know. We've met several times. Can I help you? You looking for a hiking trail or something?"

"We came by to speak to you."

Rather than letting the men in, Jude gestured for me to step out on the porch, then did the same and shut the door behind us so that Ripley didn't run out. By the way she was acting, I couldn't be sure she wouldn't attack these guys.

"This is my brother Cole," Jude said.

"We know," Portnoy replied.

The other shook his head. Maybe he wasn't allowed to speak?

"Should you call a lawyer?" I asked my brother as anxiety coursed through me.

Portnoy glared at me. "We've recently picked up a missing persons case. You're not a suspect."

I unclenched slightly, but the fear and apprehension remained. Who was missing? Jude mainly hung out with members of our family, and we were all accounted for as far as I knew.

"Have you had any recent contact with Mila Barrett?"

Jude tilted his head and frowned. "I'm sorry, I don't know that person."

Portnoy cocked a brow and hummed. "We've got several eyewitnesses that say you two were acquainted, and the security camera outside the local bar shows the two of you leaving the bar together on May 11th of last year."

Portnoy held up his phone, displaying a photo of a young woman with chin-length hair and a bright smile.

In an instant, Jude went from loose limbed and laid-back to coiled tightly like a snake. His muscles bunched in a way that surprised me. I knew he was an active, outdoorsy guy, but the way he held himself made me wonder what he was capable of.

"I know her," Jude said in a soft voice. "What happened? Is she okay?"

"She's been reported missing. Have you heard from her? Has she contacted you recently? When was the last time you saw her?"

"That night. The one from the video. She came home with me and then left. I didn't get her number, and she told me her name was Amy."

Portnoy studied him for a long moment, as if determining whether he was telling the truth. Then, with a sigh, he reached into his jacket and pulled out a business card. "If she contacts you, call me immediately." With that, he and his associate turned to go back to their black SUV.

Jude stepped forward. "She said she was from Portland. Why are you asking around up here? It's been almost a year since I met her."

Portnoy paused. "Mila Barrett is the older sister of Hugo Barrett."

That name sounded vaguely familiar, but I wasn't sure why.

"Oh fuck," Jude hissed.

I looked from one man to another. All three were staring at one another. I was missing key information here, but Jude's face looked stricken and he was gripping the business card so tightly I thought it might turn into dust.

Portnoy looked at me, his lip curled up in annoyance, clearly sensing my ignorance of this matter. "Hugo Barrett is an employee of the Maine Department of Fish and Wildlife. He was attacked on the campus of Hebert Timber back in April."

I remembered the details now. It was around the time I'd been arrested for vandalism. Lila had found the guy almost beaten to death, and Owen and Gus had spent months working with law enforcement to figure out what had happened.

"He remains in a medically induced coma in Portland, under round-the-clock police protection."

"So Amy—"

"Mila," Portnoy corrected. "We have reason to believe she was spending time in Lovewell and Heartsborough before her disappearance."

Jude took off his hat and ran a hand through his hair. "God."

"Call me if you hear anything at all."

And then they were gone, climbing into their SUV and rolling down the wooded drive.

I put my hand on Jude's shoulder, startling him out of a stupor. "Come inside, it's freezing."

I led him into the living room and gently pushed him

onto the denim blue couch. Ripley was immediately by his side, nuzzling him for comfort.

"Are you okay?"

He stared ahead vacantly, his jaw slack. "She said her name was Amy."

"And you met her at the Moose that night?"

He shook his head. "No. I met her at the dojo last year."

"Dojo?"

He patted Ripley's head, still shellshocked. "Yeah, I'm a brown belt. Been studying martial arts for years."

That was news to me. Though it was so like Jude to take up an intense hobby and get really good at it but tell no one. "Do the guys know? Debbie?"

He shook his head. "Just Noah."

Of course. "You told him with your psychic twin connection?"

He turned and glowered at me. "No dumbass. On the phone. Well, over text, I hate talking on the phone."

"And you met this girl there?"

"Yeah. Sensei does free self-defense classes one Saturday a month. I help out sometimes. She came in, introduced herself as Amy, and we chatted. She was pretty and nice and that was it."

"And then?"

"A month later, she's at the Moose. I was playing that night, but after, we talked, and things progressed."

"You had a one-night stand with her."

He glared at me, pushing his glasses up his nose. "I'm a single thirty-two-year-old guy. I'm allowed to bring girls home. You're getting judgy now that you've wifed up."

"Sorry." I shrugged. I guess I was, but I didn't care. I was delighted to be wifed up, thank you very much.

"She was incredible. I would have loved to hang out with her again, but she slipped out while I was sleeping and didn't even give me her number." He put his head in his hands. "And now she's missing."

I patted his back. "The feds are on it, and it may not be related to what happened to her brother. It could be a misunderstanding."

He looked up at me, his dark blue eyes blazing. "It's all related. And it all comes back to our fucking father."

Dammit. We'd never be free of this. We'd forever live beneath the cloud of our father's crimes. The fucker had been behind bars for more than a year and yet, horrible stuff kept happening.

While I sat with Jude, I closed my eyes and replayed every moment of the meeting I'd had with Parker Gagnon. She believed I could somehow help. Was she right? Or was I only wasting her time? Deimos Industries. Business connections, deposits and withdrawals. My thoughts bounced from one to another, then back again.

When I left Jude's, I headed straight into town. I'd promised to do my part, but I'd been too distracted to really put any effort into it.

This would never end unless we put a stop to it ourselves. How many years had the fucking feds been lurking? And Chief Souza was useless. Year after year, this town had been in danger. We'd been living with criminals in our midst. My dad had taken the fall, but he was clearly only one cog in a bigger wheel.

My family needed me. My brothers and their wives and

my niece and nephew. And Willa. The thought of her being pulled into any of this made me sick to my stomach. This had to end. And Parker was our best shot.

My contributions may not be major, but I had to do something. I needed to get to the bottom of this shit.

Chapter 31

Cole

"So good to see you, son." The mayor's smile was blindingly white, almost as white as his hair.

I shook his hand and gave him an easy smile.

"So I take it you've considered my offer?" He arched a brow. "To join my staff?"

Honestly, I hadn't considered it. But I couldn't tell him that, not right now at least.

"Thinking about it, sir," I said firmly. "I'm working on going back to school and need to line some things up first. But I'm happy to stay on in a volunteer capacity."

He nodded, clearly a bit put out that I hadn't instantly jumped at the chance to work for him.

"I'm actually here on official business today," I said. "Arlene from the library has really blossomed in her role as finance director of the festival. She and I are strategizing about partnerships and sponsors to reach out to."

That lit his face right up. There was nothing politicians loved more than free money. "Of course, of course. That's very prudent. You're doing a great job, kid." He was already losing interest now that I was talking about actual work. Mayor Lambert was a good enough guy, and he really enjoyed being mayor. But he didn't seem to like all the nitty-gritty details, like paperwork, budgeting, and local ordinances, of the job. His administrative assistant, Marcus, did the lion's share of the work and got no credit.

"Talk to Marcus. He'll set you right up."

With a nod, I headed to the open area where the admin desks were set up. Marcus was in his forties and had twin toddler boys at home. Naturally, he wore an air of pure exhaustion. He'd set me up with a login to the town records system last year and was content to let me do my own thing.

As I neared him, he gave me a nod and went back to his spreadsheets. So I grabbed an extra chair and opened my laptop.

City hall was halfway through the long process of digitizing. A lot of records were still in paper form, and since I didn't want to rouse too much suspicion by poking around, it seemed best to set up shop and pretend to be working on festival financials.

I started with sponsors, vendors, and contacts from last year, thankful that Arlene and I had kept decent records. Though those searches yielded nothing. From there, it looked like I'd have to poke around in the file rooms.

Once I'd surreptitiously slipped into the large space, I worked to retrace my steps. Last spring, I'd pulled documents for previous town events and festivals, so I started there. But after hours of searching, I'd found no mention of Deimos, and I was getting more frustrated by the minute.

Was my brain playing tricks on me? I was beginning to think so. Where had I seen that name and why had it stuck out to me?

Needing a minute to clear my head, I put the box I'd finished looking through away and walked over to the new coffee shop to clear my head. The Caffeinated Moose belonged in a much trendier town than Lovewell, but that didn't stop me from falling in love with the specialty coffee, sandwiches, and baked goods. Lila had gotten me hooked last year when I was recovering from surgery. She'd bring honey oat-milk lattes to me on occasion, like some kind of fancy coffee fairy. We'd been broken up for months by that point, but she still showed up, always worried about me.

I cringed when I thought of how I'd spoken to her then, how I'd disregarded her even before that point, and how I'd failed to appreciate her kindness and generosity for years.

As I sipped my latte, a sense of dread filled me. I'd been a shitty boyfriend to Lila. I was selfish and distracted and had never even considered her needs.

Fuck, that was a hard pill to swallow. Dr. Gleeson and I had discussed it, of course, but it wasn't until I sat at a small table, with the stupidly delicious latte in my hand, that I realized how badly I'd fucked up.

Not because I still loved her, but because she was a wonderful person and I'd caused her so much pain.

Would I do the same to Willa? My gut clenched. I loved her. I knew it in my bones. And I wanted to be everything she needed and wanted. But was that even realistic, given my track record?

All this time I'd been sailing along in a bubble, deluding

myself into thinking that I could take our accidental Vegas nuptials and turn them into a real and lasting marriage. But the coffee cup in my hand said otherwise. I'd already fucked over one lovely person, and the thought of hurting Willa was like a sucker punch.

"Cole."

I was pretty deep into my shame spiral when the sound of my name hit me. Blinking back to reality, I scanned the shop. The man was only feet away when I finally saw him.

Dennis Huxley. I disliked him immensely.

His smile was fake, his tan was fake, and those teeth probably were too. They were far too sparkling to be anything but veneers.

"Dude, how do you even fit in that chair?" he asked, his tone pure condescension.

I glowered at him, squeezing my cup until it dented, startling me.

Dennis was a small, cruel man. Years ago, his father had been a state senator, and for as long as I'd known him, Dennis used this as an excuse to be a nightmare.

Thankfully, he'd gone to a private high school when his father went to Augusta. But for some reason that defied logic, he was back. His father was the classic politician. Fake tan, capped teeth, and empty promises. He wasn't a bad guy. He had a really high opinion of himself. He'd taken Debbie out a few times, which had made my brothers furious. But from what I'd seen, he was mostly harmless.

His son, however, was a straight-up sociopath. He was thin, with light hair and beady eyes, and he seemed to think we had something in common. At least I assumed that was why he was always trying to draw me into a conversation.

"Good to see you in town. We should hang out sometime."

I blinked a few times, swallowing back the words *fuck off*.

"I'm super busy," I explained instead, holding up my left hand. "Newlywed."

That didn't deter him. "Oh, right." Without an invitation, he pulled up a chair and sat opposite me. "How is my ex-girlfriend treating you?"

An alarm sounded in my brain as anger roiled in my stomach.

"Sorry," I said, clearing my throat. "You must be mistaken. I'm married to Dr. Willa Savard."

"Oh, I know." His cocky smile made me want to punch his teeth out. "I know her *really* well." By the way he emphasized the word *really*, he was clearly implying that they'd slept together.

That wasn't possible. It didn't make sense. Not at all. Willa and this bozo? No way.

"I was surprised to hear she'd married you," he continued, dunking his tea bag aggressively into his mug. "Seems off brand for her, but then I heard it was a drunk Vegas thing, and let's face it, that's definitely your brand." He raised one eyebrow.

My eye twitched much more violently than when we had run into Jonathan. This wasn't just disgust. It was revulsion.

I stood abruptly, almost knocking my chair over as I did. "I need to go." If I didn't get away from this asshole, I might knock his teeth out. He was messing with me, and implying that he'd fucked my wife was a great way to do it.

Breathe, man. He was baiting me and insulting me and my wife, and I didn't have to take it. I wasn't a violent guy. I was aggressive on the ice, but never off it. And my self-confidence had taken a nosedive today.

I made a beeline for the door, bumping my hip against a table in my haste. *Shit, that hurt.* My brain spun. I needed to get back to city hall. I wasn't leaving until I found those files. But how many pieces of paper could I comb through on my own? There had to be a better way.

As I strode down Main Street, breathing in the brisk air, an idea struck. So I turned my ass around.

THE ADMINISTRATIVE STAFF LOVED COOKIES. THE Caffeinated Moose had several specialties, including molasses, blueberry cardamom, and maple cream. I bought several dozen—without bumping into Dennis again—and took them back to city hall. This impromptu cookie break was the perfect opportunity to chat about the festival and possible sponsors. Everyone had suggestions, and my notepad was filling up fast, but so far, I hadn't gotten a single lead on Deimos.

Dennis Huxley was still in my head, so I took a chance.

Marcus had been busy showing me photos of his kids, so I figured he'd have my back. "Do you know Dennis Huxley?"

He snorted, and the way his face puckered said it all. He sure did.

"I ran into him at the coffee shop. Man, that guy is such a jerk. Do you know why he's back in town? What does he even do for work?"

Marcus shrugged. "Beats me. He came back when his father moved back last year. Has a house up on Maplewood Lane, but last month, when he came in to scream at me about his parking tickets, I pulled the deed. Turns out his daddy bought that giant house for him."

Interesting.

"His dad bought him a house? Wild."

"It was through one of his companies. Charles and Dennis have registered like half a dozen corporations in Maine. He does everything that way. Helps avoid the tax man." He raised one eyebrow, telling me what he really thought of these entitled jackasses.

The wheels in my head creaked, then started turning.

"Interesting. What do the companies do?"

"Own real estate mostly. A few properties up here and down downeast. It's hard to find them. The way they set them up is shifty, for sure. The mayor made me do a deep dive a couple of years ago. Charles donated to his campaign through one of his companies. But for our federal election filings, I had to chase down the details. Took me forever. That guy is slippery."

My stomach flipped. Charles Huxley, beloved politician who acted like he was God's gift to Lovewell, had convoluted business entities? Fuck yes.

"This is gonna sound weird, but I'm working on reaching out to businesses to sponsor the festival. Would you mind sharing the info you found about him? I know he's got deep pockets. Maybe he could help out."

"Sure thing. They all have weird names. Greek, I think." He scratched his head.

Fuck me. Greek names? Like Deimos? Could this actually be possible?

"I'll dig out the file on my laptop later and send it to you."

I gave him a nod. "Thanks, man. Appreciate it."

Chapter 32
Willa

"Do you want extra butter or kettle corn?" Magnolia asked, holding up two boxes of microwave popcorn.

Lila raised her wineglass. "Both. And bring the M&M's too."

We were camped out in Magnolia's living room. Scratch that. *Living room* was too pedestrian a term for this space. A great room would be more fitting. It was a massive cathedral that opened up to the lakefront, with several seating areas, a wet bar, and a projection screen that descended from the ceiling with the push of a remote.

We'd pushed the couches together and created a fort with her Hermès cashmere blankets and pillows for girls' night. We'd been doing this since middle school, camping out here and watching movies while eating snacks and talking all night.

It had been ages since we'd done it, but Lila was on winter break, so Magnolia declared it girl time.

I was reclined, wearing monogrammed silk pajamas—

Magnolia had brought each of us a matching set—with a facemask on while the girls busied themselves in the kitchen.

I'd missed this. The carefree fun of being with my friends. It transported me to a simpler time. Back before adult responsibilities had taken over.

Magnolia had inherited the house from her mother, a disgraced New York society heiress who'd had a torrid affair with Magnolia's father, a starving artist, and had caused her prim and proper family great shame. She was barred from the family compound in Kennebunkport and was instead given this home in the "stick," as Magnolia's mother called it. She hated it here, so she stayed away. But when school was out each summer, she would send Magnolia up with her nanny. Eventually, her mother gave it to her as a twenty-first birthday gift.

It was way more house than any one person needed. A massive clapboard colonial on twelve acres, with several outbuildings, one of which I lived in. There were at least seven bedrooms in this house, and the dining room sat twenty. It was just down the road from my quaint little cottage, but when I stepped inside, I instantly felt as if I were a world away.

But Magnolia loved it. She'd furnished it with pieces that fit her eclectic style, and she continued to support the caretakers, Mr. and Mrs. Lewis, who'd become like grandparents to her. This place was part of her, and despite her New York career and roots, I knew in my bones she'd come back here for good someday.

Tonight Magnolia had cooked for us, and after we'd eaten, we'd played several hyper-competitive rounds of Uno and then changed into our pj's and settled in to marathon the

Hunger Games movies. We'd all been obsessed with the books in high school—another thing we'd bonded over.

"Liam really is the hottest Hemsworth brother," Lila mused.

I rolled my eyes at her. "He's no Thor."

"I mean it." She slapped the cushion beside her leg. "He's underrated."

Magnolia plopped down next to me with a fresh bottle of wine. "Look at the Doc over here." She nudged me. "She couldn't appreciate Liam's hotness if she tried. She has eyes only for her husband."

My face heated as I darted a glance at Lila.

"She's in deep," Lila mused, one side of her lips tipping up. "I've never seen her clam up about a guy. Usually she tells us all about her hookups."

"I'd say she's dickmatized." Magnolia raised her pierced brow, the expression full of subtle judgment. I'd sworn to her I wouldn't let things get physical, and although I hadn't told her anything, she knew. It was her superpower.

They didn't even know the half of it. I was completely infatuated with Cole. And while I'd never held back with details about the few guys I'd dated, this was different.

What had happened between us was precious, special, and I wasn't about to spill all the gory details. He was my husband, after all.

Huh. It felt weird to think of him in that way. We'd been married for over two months, but typically, I thought of him as my friend, my roommate, Cole.

Legally, though, he was my husband. And I was his wife.

I stared down at the ring on my finger, the one we did eventually purchase, and tried to piece together how my feelings had changed in such a short time. The last guy I ever thought I'd trust had turned into the one person I'd opened myself up to entirely.

"She's got that dreamy look in her eyes," Lila said, wrapping a blanket around herself. "She's in love."

God, I felt terrible lying to her while Mags glared at me. Lila was a far better friend than I could ever deserve. Cole was her ex, after all, and despite the shock and tension in Vegas, she'd been supportive, never saying a single bad word about him. My stomach clenched at the thought of her discovering the truth. But now, the lines had become so blurry I wasn't even sure what the truth was anymore.

So I did what any person who didn't want to face the consequences of their actions did. I redirected.

"What's going on with the inn?" I asked Magnolia as I grabbed a handful of popcorn.

She had made some noise about buying it and renovating it, and she certainly had the money to do so, but there was a good chance she'd changed her mind. The woman didn't keep the same hair color for more than a month.

She steepled her fingers like a Bond villain. "Things are moving along."

"Way to be vague," Lila complained. "Come on."

"It's a massive project. The place has been closed for almost a decade, and it's probably a terrible investment."

Lila dipped her head. "But?"

"But I love it." Magnolia sighed. "It's old and romantic, and now that this town is slowly growing and evolving, I think it would be a good time to reopen the inn."

"And so you're gonna buy it?"

She shrugged. "My lawyers are doing their thing. If I get the price I want, then yes."

This was so her. Pivot on a whim, throw money around, and push herself into new challenges when she felt like it. I admired the hell out of her bravery, though I couldn't help the flicker of jealousy that flared once in a while. My future had been so set, so certain. I didn't have the luxury of trying something new because I felt like it.

My mind spiraled back to work and the need for help. Could I sustain my current pace for the next few decades? Probably not. I wasn't sure I wanted to, anyway.

"Everything okay at work?" Lila asked gently, pausing the TV. It was the reaping, and we always shouted "I volunteer as tribute" together. It was tradition.

"Yes and no. I'm doing okay, but I know there's a better way. In Baltimore, community health clinics were open seven days a week, had all kinds of services, and employed different types of providers. I look at my dad and what happened to him, and I can't help but wish for that type of practice. Where I had support and my patients had a broader spectrum of care."

"How can we help?" Magnolia asked.

I shrugged. "Know any nurse practitioners who want to move to rural Maine? What about clinical social workers? Ultrasound techs? Phlebotomists? This area is ridiculously short on medical personnel, and rural hospitals and clinics keep shutting down."

I pulled my hair back and sighed. "It's a struggle to fit in exercise, six hours of sleep, and moderately healthy eating most days, and I'm only doing all of that because of Cole."

It hit me hard then that I'd be a mess without him. He'd

gently helped me get healthier and make more time for rest and fun, and he'd inspired me to come home earlier instead of spending all night in the office, catching up on paperwork.

I was stronger, fitter, and laughed more than I had in years.

"You want more," Lila said softly.

"What do you mean?"

She scooted over and put her arm around me. "We've watched you push yourself with single-minded determination since we were kids. Being a doctor has always been your calling. Maybe even an obsession. I envied you so much for a long time. You knew who you were and what you were going to do with your life."

"I was so jealous of you," Magnolia admitted, popping a piece of popcorn into her mouth. "You are the most driven person I know."

Tears stung my eyes as I looked from one friend to the other. God, they were the best.

"But you're in love," Lila said, giving me a squeeze. "It's okay to want more—more time, more experiences, more people to love. I felt the same thing. That's how I knew I was in love with Owen. I wanted my life to expand. Suddenly, I didn't want to be single-minded anymore. I was ready to make room for more people, experiences, and love."

Now I was fully crying.

And I wasn't the only one.

Magnolia sat on the other side of me and wrapped her long arms around both of us.

"Guys, we're growing," she said with a sniffle. "And there is no reason we can't all achieve our dreams."

We sat on the couch huddled together for a while before

turning off the movie. Magnolia made tea, and we talked through our various challenges. Lila shared her struggles with balancing her course load with her growing responsibilities at the foundation where she worked. Magnolia worried about her event planning business and how the hell she'd figure out how to be a rural innkeeper.

The three of us did what we'd been doing since we were kids. We worked it out together. We brainstormed, made suggestions, conducted random Google searches, and laughed as we dug deep.

My heart ached the whole time. I'd missed this so much. This was what I'd looked forward to during those long hours in residency. This was why I'd wanted to move to New York so badly, to experience life with these two extraordinary women by my side.

But these women were no longer all I needed. Now, I craved the comfort and presence of someone else.

Around two, we crashed, sprawled across the couches under mountains of blankets and sleeping bags.

But I couldn't sleep. I missed Cole. I'd become so accustomed to snuggling with him that sleeping alone felt wrong. It was late, and I should be exhausted, but my brain would not stop spinning.

So I dug out my phone and shot off a text.

WILLA

I can't sleep without you.

COLE

neither can I. I'm just staring at the ceiling and sniffing your pillow because it smells like you.

I swooned a little. The girls were right. I was in deep. And while I knew I should think all this through and prepare myself for the possibility that this wasn't sustainable, my heart didn't care in the least.

There was no way I'd sleep a wink without him, and after the intensity of the night, all the tears and laughter I'd shared with my friends, I needed him to ground me. That's what he did. He helped me make sense of my life and brought me back to myself every time.

WILLA

I'm gonna sneak out and come home

COLE

Miss me that much?

WILLA

Yes

COLE

I don't want you walking over here alone.
Give me ten min. I'll come get you.

My heart expanded. The thought of sneaking out to see him filled me with a wild thrill. Like I was back in high school. Except I'd never snuck out with cute boys back then.

I got off the couch, folded the blankets, and tiptoed toward the kitchen where I'd left my bag, wide awake and buzzing with excitement. I'd seen Cole this morning—he'd done pushups while I rode my stationary bike, and then he'd given me an X-rated kiss goodbye—but it still felt like too long.

I was putting my coat on in the mudroom area when Magnolia appeared, hair mussed and arms crossed. "Are you seriously sneaking out right now?"

I nodded sheepishly.

"Willa." She let out a resigned sigh. "I'm worried about you."

I looked at her. "I'm sorry. I owe you a full explanation, and I promise you'll get it. I just need him right now."

Her shoulders dropped. "Fine. Do you want a ride?"

"He's walking over now," I said.

I swore her lips quirked just a little. "Good man. You're totally in love with him, aren't you?"

There was no way I could answer that question. I'd never been in love and never thought I would be. My life had changed so dramatically in such a short time. It was impossible to verbalize any of this, especially in the middle of the night.

Lips pressed together, I shrugged.

"I'm bummed you're leaving. You're gonna miss the mimosa bar tomorrow morning. But I guess you can go home with your man."

I rushed forward and pulled her into a hug.

"Thank you for protecting me," I said as she squeezed me hard. "But I need to take a risk right now."

With a pat to my cheek, she walked me to the front door, where Cole was waiting, wearing pajama pants, winter boots, and one of his knitted hats.

"Watch yourself, lover boy. If you hurt my girl, there will

be consequences." Magnolia had no coat or shoes on, but she stood in the snow and stared Cole down.

With his focus fixed on her, he swallowed audibly. "Of course."

"I mean it. I know people. No body, no crime. You get me?"

He nodded, his brow furrowed in confusion and maybe terror.

"She's all yours," Magnolia said. Between one blink and another, her expression turned sweet, and she waved as she shut the door behind her.

"Hi," he said. He had clearly been rushing when he shoved his hat on his head. It was lopsided, and his hair was sticking out adorably. "That was... something."

I shrugged. She wasn't wrong. I had no doubt Magnolia could dispose of a body efficiently.

He pressed me up against the side of the house and kissed me deeply. His mouth was warm and tasted like peppermint.

Instantly, my core heated and my breath quickened. "Take me home," I said.

"My pleasure, wifey." He turned around and motioned for me to jump on his back.

"You can't give me a piggyback," I protested.

"It's the middle of the damn night, and we're both in pj's. Just climb on."

Huffing, I jumped up. Once I'd gotten my arms securely wrapped around his neck and he had a good hold of my legs, he took off down the road toward the cottage. It was frigid, but the sky was clear and the stars glowed above the lake.

"Are you sure I'm not hurting you?" I asked, resting my chin on his shoulder.

"Pretty sure I can carry my wife home," he said. "I was a pro athlete."

"But I'm heavy," I pleaded. The last thing I wanted was to hurt him.

He stuttered to a stop and put me down. When I'd found my balance, he turned and grasped me by the shoulders. "When will you get it, woman? This is not a hardship. I love it."

"It's just—"

"Stop right there." He squeezed my arms. "I'm a big guy. God made me six-seven for a reason. For a while I thought it was to play hockey, but now I know better. It's so I can carry my wife home and then ravage her."

Before I could respond, he scooped me over his shoulder, slapped my ass hard, and took off jogging toward the cottage.

Chapter 33
Willa

He had me on the bed, naked and ready to go, within minutes.

The sheer power of his body and the way that naughty grin got my panties off in record time continued to amaze me.

He was already kissing my neck and trailing his fingertips over my breasts.

But as much as I wanted to let myself go, give in to all of it, my chest tightened and nerves skittered through me.

He pulled back, wearing a worried frown. "Are you okay?"

I nodded and inhaled deeply. How the hell could I put into words the insecurities plaguing me? Cole made me feel so desired and cherished, but I couldn't help but worry that I wouldn't be enough for him.

"Um. I just—" I squeezed my eyes shut, resigned to getting it all out. "I haven't had a lot of relationships. And physical stuff without trust can be limiting."

He nodded, his expression looking more confused than worried now.

God, I was rambling and making no sense. "I'm afraid that I'm inexperienced."

He let out a laugh, the deep sound blasting through some of my fears. "Willa, I don't care about that. We've already had sex many times, and it's been incredible."

I blushed and averted my gaze. He wasn't wrong. Things had been hot and heavy between us since that first night.

But my insecurities were clouding my judgment.

"Sorry. It's just, there's so much I've never done before you."

"I do particularly enjoy watching you come on my cock."

God, how could I explain this to him, a good-looking athlete with plenty of experience? How did I tell him that, for most of my adult life, I'd been begging for scraps, so grateful when a man expressed attraction that I put my needs aside and settled for unsatisfying hookups?

"I've never been able to ask for what I want or to try things," I admitted. "Mainly due to lack of confidence. I was so busy worrying that I wasn't sexy that the thought of doing something new terrified me."

He bent down, taking a nipple into his mouth while his fingers teased their way down my stomach to the sweet spot between my thighs. "We've established this. You are unbelievably fucking sexy. I want you all the time. And fuck, I've never been so sexually attracted to a person in my life."

How he managed to say such swoony words while licking my nipples and expertly fingering me was a true wonder. I could barely form coherent thoughts.

"I've never been on top," I blurted, my face flushing. "I've been afraid to try, but with you, I really want to."

He looked up, a wide grin spreading across his stubbled cheeks. "Fuck yeah. I'd love nothing more than to watch you ride me." With a groan, he stroked his erection. "Just the mention, and I'm ready to explode."

He lay back on the bed, putting one arm behind his head and winking at me.

"I'm yours for the taking, wifey."

With a mixture of fear and need racing through me, I straddled him and kissed my way down his chest, loving the feel of my nipples dragging against his chest hair. God, he was so perfect.

I'd never been willing to try this position. The idea of putting my body on display, with everything hanging out, had always made me panic.

But as I kissed Cole, as he slid one hand down my side and gripped my hip, I suddenly couldn't think of a single thing I wanted more. And rather than scared, I felt turned on.

Exhaling, I sat up and leaned to one side to switch off the lamp.

"Excuse me," he said, grabbing my wrist. "No fucking way." With a huff, he switched it back on. Damn his long arms.

"I need to see you when you're riding my cock."

"But—"

"Shh." He held his fingers up to my lips. "Not nego-tiable, wifey." Then he rolled his hips, teasing me in a way that sent sparks arcing through me.

Breath hitching, I grasped him and lowered myself,

relishing the sensation of him at my entrance. Like it had every night, it felt impossible, despite how wet I already was, that he would fit. But I took a deep breath and sank down slowly.

Tingles tore through my extremities. Fuck. I threw my head back. Oh my God, the pressure.

I put one hand on his chest to steady myself so I could breathe through the reaction, because hell, my inner muscles were already clenching.

He raked his gaze down my body, his expression full of so much heat it made me feel like a goddess. "That's it. Take what you need."

And I did, rocking slowly as I took him deeper, feeling full and on the brink after only a moment.

"That's my good girl."

Without stopping my movements, I squeezed my breasts and rolled my nipples between my fingers, knowing how much he loved it when I played with them.

Slowly, I worked myself over him, soaking in the way every bump and ridge of his shaft hit me in all the most sensitive spots. My pace was slow, but I savored the control I had in this moment.

"You're doing great," he rumbled. "Can I touch you?"

I nodded, and an instant later, he was gripping my ass cheeks and spreading them wide, allowing him to go even deeper.

With a moan, I threw my head back. It was such a turn-on, the way he manhandled me and used me with those big hands while I was in control of our pleasure.

"Yes," he growled. "You were made for this. You were

made to take my cock. But you know that, wifey. You know this pussy is mine."

I cried out, clenching around him. Jesus, his words hit me with such physical force.

"Oh yes. Now ride me. Tell me about all your dirty fantasies. Everything you want me to do to you. I'll fuck you and make you come any way you want."

As his words drove me higher, I increased my speed, reveling in the all-consuming sensations taking over. I played with my nipples and let my body figure it out, shifting and adjusting until I found an angle that hit me just right.

"I want you to fuck me somewhere public," I admitted, a heated flush washing over me.

"Oh yes, dirty girl," Cole said, clearly turned on rather than appalled by my request. "What else?"

"Tie me up. Blindfold me."

He groaned. "Anytime. As long as you promise to tie me up and have your way with me the next time."

I smiled down at him, meeting his dark, glassy eyes. My vision blurred, and my pleasure bloomed larger until all I could feel was him inside me, his hands on my body. I was building and building, but not sure to what. I'd never experienced this combination of sensations before.

"What else, wifey? I'm gonna make all your dirty fantasies come true. I'll teach you and make you come so hard you forget your own name."

My breaths were coming in sharp pants now. I could barely speak. How was he able to keep up a steady stream of dirty talk when this felt so good?

"What else? Don't hold back on me."

I closed my eyes. This was a big one, and despite how incredible I felt, I was scared to say it.

"I want you to—" I snapped my mouth shut and froze. "You know."

He cocked his head, and one side of his mouth quirked up. "Come?"

Swallowing, I nodded. "On me."

He sat up and took my mouth, biting down on my bottom lip. "Anywhere you want, but you have to be a good girl and say it."

With my heart pounding in my ears, I took a deep breath. "I want you to, um, come on, um. My tits."

He squeezed his eyes shut and froze. "Shit. I almost came because of your words alone."

His hands were all over me again. "It would be my fucking honor. I'm the luckiest guy in the world. I get this greedy, dirty girl all to myself. But I need you to do something for me. I want you to rub your clit while you ride me, because I'm holding on by a thread here."

I snaked my hand down to where we were joined and gently flicked the bud. Instantly, electricity shot through me. Using the pad of my thumb, I rubbed gentle circles, and pressure built hard and fast, ramping all the way up to a breaking point.

"That's it," he praised. "Now ride me. I wanna watch your tits bounce as you come."

I obeyed, rubbing and riding, and when a toe-curling orgasm rocked through me, I threw my head back. I was levitating, and all that was keeping me grounded were his hands on my hips and his cock pulsing inside me.

Wave after wave, I ground against him until the pressure that had mounted inside me ebbed.

When I finally collapsed on his chest, my throat ached from screaming.

He wrapped his arms around me and kissed the top of my head.

"Jesus, wifey. You are quite the sexy student. I came so hard my vision is spotty."

"You should get that checked out," I teased, lifting up and grinning.

"Good thing my sex kitten wife is a doctor."

Chapter 34
Cole

"You won't believe what happened today," Willa said, breezing into the kitchen in her sensible blouse and hauling her massive tote bag.

It was mid-January in Northern Maine. The sun set before five, and the temperature frequently dipped below zero. But the minute she walked into the cottage, the space lit up as if she were a beam of pure sunlight.

Her hair was pulled back in a messy bun, and her mascara was smeared, but as she pushed up on her tiptoes to kiss me, my body warmed.

"Go change," I said, slicing grilled chicken to put on top of the massive salads I'd assembled. "Dinner is ready and I've got tonight's *Jeopardy* cued up. Tell me during the commercial break."

Side by side, we sat on the couch. Willa had changed into short shorts and a tank top, making it hard to keep my eyes on the TV. Her black bra strap was right there in plain view, tantalizing me.

I wanted to throw her down and lick her clit while she

answered *Jeopardy* questions, but I kept my hands to myself. She'd been honest about her lack of experience in relationships, and I wanted to give her the time and space to get comfortable before we got in too deep.

Because already, this relationship was all-consuming.

I craved her, morning, noon, and night. I couldn't get enough of her taste, her smell, or the sound of her voice.

This was uncharted territory for us both, and I was trying hard not to scare her with the intensity of my obsession.

"I have a good feeling about Alexandra tonight," she said, sauntering back in from the kitchen with two glasses of water as the theme song played.

"Yeah, she whiffed that question about Genghis Khan last night, but I feel like she can keep the streak alive."

We ate dinner, shouting out answers—more wrong than right—and fast forwarding through the commercials.

"What was it you wanted to tell me when you got home?" I asked after the show was over and I was heating water for tea.

She turned around and threw a dish towel over her shoulder—she was doing the dishes, refusing to let me help, as usual, because I cooked. "Max, the pharma rep, brought donuts in today, but he tripped in the waiting room, sending donuts flying all over. Poor Mellie spent an hour cleaning powdered sugar off the walls."

I burst out laughing. Good, I hated that guy. And the guy from the medical supply company who came on Tuesdays. Basically, I hated any man who talked to my wife. "Oh, Jesus. Couldn't have happened to a better guy."

"Yup. Walters kicked him out. I had to hide in the back

because I was laughing so hard. He's so smarmy. Always offering to set up an intimate dinner where we could talk about the new products."

"That's a threat." My eye twitched. "You should get a restraining order."

Huffing, she put her hands on her hips. "The guy is doing his job. He's annoying."

I shook my head. "Nah, he's trying to get into your scrubs."

She rolled her eyes. "How many times do I have to explain this? Pharma reps educate us on their products in the hope that we'll prescribe them to our patients. It's annoying, and I absolutely hate it, but it's part of my job."

I clenched my fists to tamp down my annoyance. Willa was so oblivious to the effect she had on people, especially in her doctor's coat. She was competent, beautiful, and sexy as fuck. I was already hard watching her bend over to load the dishwasher.

"You're being a jealous husband."

I rounded the island and grabbed her by the shoulders.

"Only because my wife keeps forgetting how fucking gorgeous she is. Men look at you and drool. Just because you've conditioned your brain to incorrectly assume otherwise doesn't mean it's not happening."

She lifted her chin, defiant. "Then I guess it's good I have a giant husband to scare them all off."

Grinning, I smacked her ass hard. "Correct. I'll have to stop by and make sure he and all the other bozos know you're spoken for."

She threaded her arms around my neck, pulling me down to kiss me softly.

"I love having a giant husband to scare off lesser men."

Though she was being sarcastic, her words still sent a zing of arousal through me. If she only knew what I'd like to do to any man who even looked at her.

"That's it," I said, picking her up and placing her on the counter. "Now I'm going to eat this sweet pussy until you agree with me. In fact, your white doctor coat is too sexy. Do you think you can practice medicine in a nun's habit?"

I slipped my hand under the hem of her tank and cupped one luscious breast. "I fear it's the only way to hide these incredible tits."

She giggled and squirmed, but I held on tight and kissed her again, rocking my erection straight into her core. Within seconds, her shirt was off, and I was lapping at one nipple, then the other. God, I didn't know what I had done to deserve this woman, but I sure as hell was not taking one minute for granted.

I pulled back, enjoying the glazed look in her eyes. "You know what? This isn't working for me."

I threw her over my shoulder and headed for the bedroom. "I want you to sit on my face, wifey."

"Cole," she gasped, then followed it with a giggle.

I spanked her again for good measure, then I dropped her onto the bed and tugged her shorts down her legs.

"Would you look at that." I licked my lips. "So wet for me already."

"Cole, I am not sitting on your face."

I dropped onto the mattress and pulled her on top of me. "Sure you are. Just hold on to the headboard and let me do my thing."

Eyes swimming with uncertainty, she sank her teeth into her bottom lip. "I'm not sure."

I cupped her beautiful face. "If you don't like it, we stop. But I think you're gonna love it."

She nodded tentatively. "I don't want to hurt you."

I pulled her up until her dripping pussy hovered above my face and inhaled her scent. Fuck, I must have died and gone to heaven.

"Good girl," I said, nipping at her inner thigh. "Now sit."

She lowered herself, but only long enough for me to get a quick lick in.

I grabbed her thighs and pulled her down. "No hovering," I commanded.

"But my big ass—" she pleaded.

"Is fucking delicious," I gritted out. "I'll eat that next. Now be a good girl and ride my face, wifey."

Without another second of hesitation, I dove in, making sure to hold her in place. I was determined to make this the best orgasm of her life. That way she wouldn't hold back next time.

And fuck, was I up for the job. Pleasing my hot doctor wife was my favorite chore.

Chapter 35
Willa

The office, thankfully, closed at one on Saturdays, meaning I could relax a little this evening. At some point, when I'd hired more staff, I would take Saturdays off altogether.

"Apparently norovirus has hit the preschool," Dawn declared, tossing her latex gloves into the trash can. "I love winter."

I couldn't help but chuckle. Late January was peak time for the cold and the flu in Maine, and generally, toddlers were ground zero for all infections.

"In fairness," I quipped, "I saw several ear infections today too."

Dawn grabbed her coat and bag and gave me a salute. "See you Monday, boss."

After she'd disappeared, I sat back in my chair and breathed, eyes closed, thinking about how things had evolved around here. This office was running smoothly, and we were working as a team. Even Walters was noticing the positive changes I'd put in place.

Little did he know I had grander plans.

It would take time, but I could do so much more for the people of Lovewell. I hadn't become a doctor to get rich, and I'd rather make less money and give myself and my patients better quality of life. So I was cooking up plans and had been in touch with some of my mentors from my residency days.

I never could have done this much without Cole's encouragement. He patiently listened to all my complaints about the state of rural healthcare and asked helpful questions. His curiosity about my career was honestly flattering. He wasn't only interested in the medical stuff, but the how and why behind it all. I was used to being taken seriously at work, but never in my personal life. Not until Cole. My romantic entanglements had mostly been hookups or friends-with-benefits arrangements, and those guys hadn't been super interested in my opinions.

They hadn't been super interested in my orgasms either, I was now realizing.

And Cole could not be more different in either aspect. He was very interested.

My face was heated as I climbed out of the car, since I'd spent the drive home thinking about him and what we'd gotten up to last night.

Inside, I threw a load of laundry into the washer, and when I emptied my lunch bag, I noticed that the dishwasher had already been emptied, so I rinsed the containers and put them in. Then I headed to my room to put on my yoga clothes, still smiling about Cole and how far we'd come since that wild night in Vegas.

Despite the way I floated an inch off the ground while

daydreaming, one tiny doubt still niggled in the back of my mind.

What would happen in the future?

We'd been thrust into this arrangement, and though something real had grown from it, we'd only agreed to stay married for six months. Could this last in the long term? Was Cole even interested in trying? I was tied to this town and to my job, but more than once, he'd talked about moving and starting over. We were halfway into this marriage, but that small doubt surfaced every day. It was only a faint whisper, but it was enough to make my heart sink.

For now, I pushed my doubts away and focused on my yoga mat. I'd been craving a deep stretch all day and loved the way it made me feel.

My YouTube yoga class was wrapping up when he came home, bearing flowers and a smile.

I stood, sweaty and disheveled, but my state didn't stop him from pulling me in for a kiss.

"I brought you these." He thrust a large, colorful bouquet at me.

Grinning, I brought them to my nose and inhaled.

"Where did you get these?" I took another whiff. "These are not from the gas station."

"I have connections," he said with a smirk. "And I would never buy my wife gas station flowers."

I pulled him down and kissed him again.

"Thank you. No guy's ever bought flowers for me before."

He stiffened, a glower overtaking him. "You can't be serious."

I shrugged. We'd talked through my lack of serious relationships, but I'd never brought up this detail. Why would I? It hadn't bothered me very much.

He shook his head as though he could not comprehend how I could be treated so egregiously. "Anyway," he said with a heavy breath tout. "I brought you the flowers because I was hoping to take you out tonight."

My heart flipped. "Out?"

"Yes, wifey. On a date."

"We're married. You don't need to take me on dates. Also, we're sleeping together."

He rolled his eyes and let out a dramatic sigh. "Willa, I want to take my girl out and show her off. It's nothing fancy. Jude's band is playing at the Moose again, and I want to go support him. He mentioned he may play one of the songs he's written. So I thought we could go together, make a night of it."

I wrapped my arms around him and put my head on his chest. "I'd be happy to make a night of it."

The big boyish grin he gave me made my heart clench. Being the recipient of this smile was an honor. "You could wear something sexy. Maybe that green dress. You know, the one you wore to our wedding." He wiggled his eyebrows.

"That dress is way too fancy for the Moose. I normally wear jeans."

"Not tonight. I'll dress up too. I'll wear a suit."

"You can't wear a suit to the Moose. You'll be laughed out of Lovewell."

He put his hand over his heart. "I don't care. I wanna look good for my lady."

I scoffed, dismissive, and turned so I could change. Into jeans.

"There may be another reason." He grasped my wrist gently, stopping me.

I spun, perking up. "What?"

He took a big breath, his dark eyes flashing with excitement.

"Okay, here goes. I met with the dean of the public policy school at UMaine last week. And I'm applying to the public administration program."

A zap of pride coursed through me. "That's wonderful. Are you excited?"

"Terrified," he confessed, his shoulders lowering. "The plan is for me to audit a few classes this spring to get myself started. Then I'll do some intensive summer courses. They have a lot of nontraditional students, and the dean thought I could be an asset to the program."

This felt like a big step forward. He'd been stuck for so long.

"That's so fantastic," I said, still proud and elated for him. Though the fears I'd pushed away earlier surfaced too. And...

"Is this what you want?"

I'd given him those brochures for Christmas and talked up the program. I hoped I hadn't pressured him or made him feel inadequate.

"Because you're amazing with or without a degree."

He dipped his chin. "This is what I want. I've been keeping a journal—my therapist's recommendation—of things that inspire me, make me proud, or excite me. And besides you, one of the things I'm passionate about is this town. I like our rural way of life. I love our traditions and our history, and I'd love to develop the kind of skills that would allow me to help make it even better."

His words hit me hard. He was always so thoughtful. His ideas were so much deeper than anyone realized. And he put me in the same category as his life goals?

"Watching you move throughout the world has inspired me. You're confident yet humble. You possess skills that save lives, but you always make time for others. And you've shown me that it's possible for a person to carve a path for themselves that works. You can honor who you are and what you want and still be of service. You are my inspiration. My everything."

Choking back tears, I stepped forward and pulled him down for a kiss. This man. Every single day, he surprised me.

He broke the kiss and gave me a hard slap on the ass. "Now go shower and get dolled up. I'm taking my lady out tonight."

With a whole lot of swagger, he headed toward the bathroom.

"You don't need to work that hard. I'm already sleeping with you," I said as he went into his room.

"That's where you're wrong, wifey. I gotta work extra hard to keep you."

I RARELY CAME TO THE MOOSE. MAINLY BECAUSE I'D see a lot of my patients, and by the end of the night, I'd be looking at people's moles or hearing about their constipation issues.

I didn't want to practice medicine during my precious off

time. Really, all I wanted was to be home, naked, wrapped around my husband.

This new phase of our relationship had been the highlight of my life so far. Touching him whenever I wanted to. Kissing him. Waking up next to him stretched out across my bed.

Even tripping over his massive shoes made me smile.

I was not wearing my wedding dress, but I had put on a slinky black cocktail dress. It hugged my curves and showed only a tasteful bit of cleavage. Paired with thick black tights and booties, it was mostly winter-weather appropriate. Cole had whistled when I'd come out into the living room. Then he'd immediately grabbed my ass, so I was calling it a success.

But my husband had truly stepped it up. He'd donned a pair of gorgeous charcoal dress pants, a crisp white shirt, and a vest. A motherfucking *vest*.

I swore that vest, which matched the soft Italian wool pants, was the hottest thing I'd ever seen. It had made me want to drop to my knees right then and there.

Even now, I kept sneaking glances at him. It was disorienting how good he looked. I was hot and bothered by the time we walked into the bar, and that was an achievement, as it was twelve degrees out.

Only in places like rural Maine would the Moose and other establishments have a special spot for snowmobile parking in the winter. Mainers did not get intimidated by snow. Quite the opposite, in fact. They usually relished the chance to get out and make Mother Nature their bitch.

The moment we stepped into the warmth, Cole wrapped an arm around me. I'd never figured him for the possessive type, and I couldn't remember a single time I saw him hanging all over Lila, but he'd hear no complaints from me. Since we'd started sleeping together, he'd let his inner caveman out, and I liked it.

There was a group in the corner by the dartboards, and by the look of them—the height, the flannel, and the beards—it was his family.

Finn, who had his sandy brown hair pulled into a man bun, was gesturing with his pint glass as he turned to greet us.

And he was wearing a baby.

"Are you wearing a suit to a bar?" Finn guffawed.

"Did you bring your baby to a bar?" Cole countered.

"This is a family dining establishment," Finn corrected. "And Adele is at girls' night with her friends, so Thor and I decided to come out and see Uncle Jude. Plus, I packed protection."

He pointed to the mini noise-canceling headphones that Thor was sporting.

For eight months old, the little guy was massive. Unable to help myself, I stepped up close and squeezed one of his chunky denim-clad thighs. He looked exactly like Finn, except toothless, and he couldn't quite rock the man bun yet. I had a feeling he'd be a lot of trouble when he grew up.

"Ah, Dr. Willa is here," Gus added, leaning forward to kiss me on the cheek. "Which is good, because Chloe keeps dancing in her heels, even though I told her not to."

"She's off the clock," Cole gritted out, pulling me into his side.

I smiled down at the chubby baby. Gah, he was damn

cute. He gave me a toothy grin, happy to look around at all the goings-on around him.

Finn, a big Viking with a baby on his chest, was getting a lot of attention. Every uterus in a five-mile radius was staring at him. But I was far more enamored with my husband.

And the vest.

Shit, would he leave it on later? Would it be weird of me to ask?

"It's fine," I said, patting Cole's arm. "Gus, you can't dictate your wife's footwear choices."

With a huff, he lowered his head and nodded.

"You know Adele has been working hard to sleep train," I said to Finn, giving him my best serious doctor face. "So leave at a reasonable hour."

"Yes, Doc," he said, also hanging his head.

Before I could get caught up in more doctorly lectures, Cole steered me toward the stage, giving them both the finger.

"Your suit is ridiculous," Gus shouted as we walked past.

"It's a vest," Cole shouted back. "And I don't give a shit what you think. I like to get dressed up for my wife." *That* admission made a few heads turn.

My face heated at the attention. My brain wasn't quite making the connection that I was the wife being publicly discussed. In fact, my brain had not been functioning optimally at all tonight. I blamed the vest and lots of hormones. I was a doctor, after all. I had earned the right to blame science.

The band was good. I'd known several of these folks for most of my life, but in an environment like this, when the music brought them to life, it was like seeing them through a new lens.

Jude Hebert was quiet and withdrawn, the kind of guy who nodded when you said hello. Whether that was a product of his childhood, when Noah—his more boisterous twin, usually spoke for him—or what necessitated Noah's input in the first place, I wasn't sure.

So watching Jude play guitar and sing backup while keeping time was like watching him transform into a totally different person.

He moved as he played, swaying, his fingers gracefully sliding over the fretboard of his guitar.

"Your brother is talented."

Cole hummed, the sound rumbling through me. "Debbie begged him to think about music school, but he went to work for the timber company instead."

"It's incredible to watch him on stage."

Cole laughed. "Just wait until they take a break. He'll flip the switch and be back to his normal self. Mostly silent, and when he does speak, it's in sarcasm only. He loves writing and playing music. The guitar changes him."

He wrapped his arms around me from behind as we gently swayed to the music. It felt so good to be enveloped like this, wrapped up in the safety of his arms in public. To feel his hot breath when he leaned down to whisper in my ear. Even though we stood out in our fancy clothes, being here with him was like a dream.

It was only the Moose, a place where people came for waffle fries and draft beers after a long week at work. A place I'd been hundreds of times throughout my life.

But being here with Cole made the experience almost

magical. Listening to a great band while a hot guy pawed at me easily topped the list of my top teenage fantasies.

When the band took a break, we headed to the bar for another round of waters. Cole kept me close, always touching my body.

"Have you ever thought that maybe when you're doing the thing you love the most, the thing you were made for, that you do become different? A better version of yourself?" he asked, those dark eyes focused only on my face while we waited for Jim, the bartender and owner of the Moose, to bring our bottles of water.

My heart pounded out a rhythm at the intensity with which he watched me. I wanted to grab him by the hair and maul him. I'd never been this girl. I kept my expectations low. I never pushed or acted clingy, and I was grateful for any scraps thrown in my direction.

But standing here with him made me want so much more. He made me feel like I deserved it.

"No, I've never thought about that. But I think you're right. Did you ever feel that way when you were playing?"

"Sometimes. But hockey for me wasn't about finding my Zen or leaving it all behind. If anything, I carried a lot onto the ice with me. I let my fear, my anxiety, fuel me. Control me. So the stakes felt higher. Even as a kid, it didn't feel like play. It felt like work."

I stroked his hand, intertwining our fingers. "I'm sorry."

He shook his head. "Don't be. My experience has made me love coaching. The memories encourage me to make it fun. I want these kids to fall in love with hockey and being part of a team."

It was pointless even trying to fight what I felt for him

anymore. How could I not fall in love with him when he was being so introspective and self-aware?

"You're doing a great job," I said. "Those girls love you. And look at it like a do-over. You are the coach you wish you'd had. The coach who lets the kids be kids."

He smiled. "Thank you for saying that. It means a lot."

For a moment, we were locked in place, the crowded, noisy bar falling silent. I studied him—the scruffy jaw, the intense dark eyes, and that damn vest—and realized that I was even more obsessed with the man beneath the gorgeous façade. The sweet, earnest man who woke up every morning wanting to be better.

We could have stood there all night, never breaking eye contact. Except I was itching to head to the car and tear his clothes off.

Eventually, the spell was broken by a feminine voice. "Cole. Great to see you."

I blinked back to the moment, and when I opened my eyes, I found myself staring at a tall, athletic-looking woman who was rocking trendy baggy boyfriend jeans and a crop top like she'd stepped off the pages of *Teen Vogue*.

And she was throwing her arms around my husband.

Hugging him.

And lingering.

My stomach clenched. Why was she touching him? Even after he stepped out of her embrace, she kept her hand on his arm.

I blinked rapidly, unsure of how to proceed.

"Aspen, hi. What are you doing in Lovewell?"

She nodded at the stage. "My friend Lola is on the drums."

I followed her line of sight to the small, angry-looking woman sitting behind the drum kit. Come to think of it, she wasn't the usual drummer. But Jasper's band had a rotating cast of musicians who popped in to play when they were in town.

Turning back, I surveyed this stranger, wondering who the fuck she was and whether I could throw her ass out into a snowbank. She was tall, but I'd been working out a lot and was pretty damn strong.

"You never called me." She grabbed the front of his vest and yanked playfully. "I thought we'd hang out more." Her tone was teasing, but there was a hint of hurt there too.

Rage ignited in my every cell. *She touched the vest.* That bitch touched the vest. Who did she think she was?

That's all it took for me to push closer and put my arm around Cole's waist.

He draped his arm over my shoulders and drew me in, kissing the top of my head.

"Willa, I want you to meet Aspen Clark. Aspen, this is my wife, Dr. Willa Savard."

The woman extended a hand and gave me one of the firmest handshakes of my life.

"Congrats," she said, though her awkward tone belied her well wishes. "I didn't realize you had a wife."

"We're newlyweds." I rested my head on his chest. I felt like an idiot, pawing him like this, but when the alternative was aggravated battery, it was the safest choice.

"Aspen's a hockey player," Cole explained. "We've trained together since we were kids. She was on the national team."

"A few years ago," she said with a wave. "Damn shoulder. But now I coach."

The two of them chatted about hockey—I only understood every other word—while I sized her up.

She was pretty. And definitely sporty. From the stud in her nose to her sleek ponytail, she screamed *I do push-ups for fun.*

As I tuned out of their conversation, my mind wandered. *Had they dated? Had sex?*

The thought made my breath hitch. He'd said he was single when we were in Vegas.

But a guy like Cole? Well, who knew?

Lila had sworn up and down he'd never cheated. That he'd been a distant asshole. But I'd put a lot of trust in him when we entered into this arrangement.

Though I tried to tamp it down, jealousy ripped through me, making me doubt him. I may have never considered myself a jealous person before, but then again, I'd never been married to a ripped hockey god either.

I was a good girl, a planner. I was careful and precise. But I'd married Cole, become friends with him, developed feelings, and started sleeping with him. All in the span of three months.

What if I'd gone too fast? Ignored red flags? What if this was the kind of woman he wanted? The kind he would go for if he weren't stuck with me for now?

I hadn't had a drop of alcohol, but my brain slowed as if I was drunk. I was nauseous and lost.

A whole slew of emotions swirled through me, and I had no idea how to manage them.

Because I'd never let myself experience this kind of connection, this intensity.

Love, my brain screamed.

I was in love with him.

Shit.

Chapter 36
Cole

Willa was quiet on the ride home, and I was stuck in an endless thought loop.

Did I say something wrong?

Did I do something wrong?

Is this vest totally ridiculous?

While it was more likely I'd done something dumb, I was beginning to blame the vest. Sure, the flowers and fancy night out were overkill. But as I discussed with Dr. Gleeson during my session yesterday, I had been struggling to find the words to express my feelings to Willa.

Hell, I couldn't even wrap my head around them all. Emotions I'd never experienced. That I didn't know even existed. As I was learning in therapy, I was terrified of saying the wrong thing and ruining something so incredible.

For the most part, the night had been perfect. There had been moments when it felt like it was only the two of us in the bar. I'd only had water. Hell, I hadn't had a drop of alcohol since our wedding night. I didn't need it. I felt giddy being there with her. Touching her and whispering with her and experiencing a place I'd been to a million times in a new way.

With the moon so bright over the lake, I had the perfect idea. "Wanna go throw some rocks?" I asked, trying to draw her out, as I parked in front of the cabin.

She shook her head. "I'm going to take these clothes off."

I wanted to offer to do it for her, but considering how quiet she'd been and how I hadn't been able to pull her out of her shell, I couldn't help but feel that would not be welcome.

So I followed her into the cottage, wishing I had the words to fix whatever I'd broken, and hung up my coat.

My instinct was to head to my room and avoid the discomfort altogether, hoping that, by morning, it would have blown over. But if I did that, I'd be pulling away, putting distance between us instead of closing the gap.

"Willa," I said softly.

She looked up, her face drawn.

"I'd really like to talk about tonight."

"Sure."

I paced the kitchen, rolling up my shirtsleeves, as she stood with her hands clasped in front of her. It felt almost impossible to open my mouth. But looking at her beautiful face, I knew I had to do it.

"Before... when I was with Lila," I started, fighting like hell to get the words out, regardless of how awkward they felt, "if things didn't feel right, I'd retreat. Ignore the problem. You and I were having such an amazing time tonight, but then you went away. And if I did something—"

"No," she interrupted, lifting her chin. "You didn't do anything."

I stepped up close and pulled her against my body. "Then where'd you go?" I asked, placing a soft kiss on the top of her head.

She hugged me back, the small act instantly easing a little of my fear. "I'm embarrassed," she said into my chest.

I pulled back, placing my hands on her shoulders.

"Why?" I asked, throat thick. "Is it the vest?"

She laughed, the sound watery. "*No. I love the vest.*"

I raised my eyebrows.

"Yes. *Love.* I've had a hard time focusing on anything but it all night. If I had my way, you'd wear a vest every day, even when doing mundane tasks."

I stroked her cheek. "Then I'll make sure to wear it while folding laundry tomorrow. But why are you embarrassed?"

She dipped her chin. "This is so dumb."

"Nothing is dumb. I care about you, and I want to understand how you're feeling. I've done so many things wrong in my life, and I'm still figuring out why in therapy, but I want to do this right. So if you're willing to talk, I want to listen."

Instead of responding, she buried her face in my chest.

I took a deep breath, telling myself I could handle whatever she was feeling. Even if it meant she didn't feel the way I did.

"I got jealous," she said softly, her voice muffled by my vest. "Of that girl at the bar."

The admission was like a physical blow. *Jealous?*

"Of Aspen?" I asked? Frowning, I carefully replayed the interaction. It had been friendly, not flirty.

"Yes. She's beautiful. And the way she was looking at you and touching you made me so mad." Her face was red, and she was clenching the fabric of my shirt and vest at my sides. "She was totally flirting with you. Lusting after my husband."

I smiled. When she called me her husband in that possessive way, all my primal instincts were unleashed. I stood taller and pulled her closer, palming her ass. "Now you know how I feel every day."

"No," she scoffed. "It's more than that. Seeing her speak to you and the way you looked together made me feel insecure and silly." She stepped back, putting distance between us and crossing her arms.

Fuck. This was not good.

"We're married, sure, but we were drunk and making stupid decisions. Now you're stuck with me. I was feeling so good about us, but then I saw her and realized that she's the kind of woman you should be with, and then I started to feel awful."

My stomach lurched. "Stuck with you? You believe that?"

She was pacing now. All I wanted was to kiss her to shut her up and make her never feel this way again, but she was on a roll. "I want to be above petty jealousy. I want to be above being hurt when pretty girls flirt with you. But I was so mad. And then I felt like an overdressed idiot at a bar on a cold Saturday night."

"You look gorgeous," I insisted, stepping toward her. "And let me be very clear. I am not stuck with you. Marrying you was the best decision I've ever made."

She stopped and dropped her arms to her sides. "Cole," she said, her voice so fragile and sad.

Pain lanced my chest. Shit, I had to fix this.

"Look at my phone," I said, pulling the device from my pocket. Once I'd unlocked it, I handed it over. "Go to my photos."

She picked it up, eyeing me skeptically.

"Now click on the album titled *Wifey*."

Head lowered, she tapped the screen a few times, and then her eyes widened. Slowly, she scrolled through the photos. Even more slowly, recognition dawned on her face.

"You took all these photos of me?"

"Yeah." I ran my hand through my hair. "I realize it's creepy. We can unpack that later. But sometimes I look at you, and you're just so damn beautiful. I want to remember the way you looked in that moment forever, so I take a picture."

She kept scrolling, past photos of her reading on her Kindle, throwing rocks, and doing yoga. Photos of the two of us hiking and one of her posing in front of the Zamboni at the rink.

"Then I put the photos into this album, and any time I feel like a complete loser or a waste of space, I look through them and remember that you married me. Even if you never love me like I love you, and even if this ends in a few months, I'll always look back at these photos and know that though it might have only been a blip in time, there was a point in my life where I did something right."

"Cole." She looked up, her eyes misting. "There are so many."

I shrugged. "I may fail at everything else. But I am going to work hard every day to be the best damn husband I can be for as long as you'll have me. I want you fiercely. And I want a future with you. But I have to earn it. And I will if you give me a chance."

She jumped into my arms and kissed me hard. Heart thumping wildly, I pushed her up against the wall and kissed her back with just as much passion.

This. This is what I've always needed.

Chapter 37
Willa

He loves me.

The thoughts bounced around my brain as we kissed, my body wrapped around his, supported by his strength and overtaken by the sheer power of his lips.

It was like a dam had burst in my heart. All the things I'd been holding back came rushing forward, and no amount of kissing could express how I felt about this man.

I'd spent years developing these insecurities and building up my defenses. All my life, I'd absorbed messages from the world, being told that I wasn't ideal. That I wasn't right. That men didn't want me.

Men had treated me like I was worthless, and other women had made nasty comments about my big breasts or how my clothes fit. I'd settled for friends-with-benefits situations with partners who didn't want to be exclusive because they were holding out for someone "more their type." It had been far easier to believe all the lies than I would like to admit. To convince myself that I didn't deserve what others had and to lower my expectations.

But in only two months, this man, my husband, had laid waste to it all, making me feel like the most treasured, desired, and powerful woman on earth.

"Naked," I breathed while he kissed my neck. He had me pushed up against the living room wall, and his erection was pressing against my core. This wasn't enough. I needed to see all of him, feel all of him, let myself experience this. Fully unburdened and ready to embrace whatever came next.

Nodding, he gently lowered me to the floor. The moment both feet were planted, I tugged at his pants, pulling them down to get what I wanted.

I bent at the waist, my mouth watering and my heart racing, and grasped his hips, then took him into my mouth.

"Jesus," he said, bracing his hands on the wall.

I smiled up at him. One of the advantages of being with someone so much taller than me was that there was no kneeling involved. I'd be licking his knees if I did.

I took him to the back of my throat, letting instinct take over and pushing away concerns about my lack of experience. I wasn't putting on a show. I wasn't strategically hiding parts of my body. I was giving myself to my husband. And the sensation was fucking amazing.

"Fuck, Willa." Gently, he gathered my hair and tugged.

In response, a jolt of electricity shot straight to my clit. *Interesting.*

"You're gonna kill me, Doc," he whispered, the rough pads of his fingers caressing my neck. "You need to stop."

With one hand wrapped around his shaft, I shook my

head and swirled my tongue around his tip. With every lick, with every caress, my arousal amplified. And when he slipped a hand down my top and squeezed my breast hard, the ache was almost unbearable. I clenched my thighs together, desperate for relief, though I didn't stop.

"That's it," he said, clutching my shoulders and forcing me to release him. "I can't wait any longer to be inside you."

He pushed my dress up around my hips and then yanked my panties and tights down my legs. When they tore, it only ramped up my need for my husband.

"Bra," he said through gritted teeth as he dropped to his knees.

I obeyed, pushing my sleeves down my arms and unclasping my bra with shaky hands.

"Oh, fuck yes," he said, drinking me in.

I was probably a mess. My hair was no doubt wild from being tugged on. The top of my dress was pushed down, causing my tits to spill out, and the skirt was hiked up, exposing my lower half.

"My beautiful wifey."

Whimpering, I grabbed his shirt collar. "I need you to fuck me."

He gripped my hips and tugged. "Let me warm you up first."

"No. I'm ready," I breathed. "Now."

With a nod, he stood. Effortlessly, he picked me up and set me on the kitchen island.

As he nudged my entrance, I buried my face in his neck, inhaling and trying to relax.

Slowly, he pushed his way in. The pressure and pain were exquisite, the fullness liberating.

When he was seated, he kissed me hard. "Look at you. Dress pushed up, taking your husband's cock. Fuck," he groaned. "I love you so much."

I leaned back on my hands so he could feast on my breasts, flying higher than I ever had before. He wasn't slow, and he wasn't controlled. He was frenzied, and so was I.

"Look," he commanded, his tone dark. "Look where we come together and tell me that isn't the hottest thing you've ever seen."

As I obeyed, my breath caught. Damn. It was hot. The sight of him pushing inside me, the way my body stretched to accommodate him, was unlike anything I'd ever witnessed. In this moment, I felt even more connected to my body and to his. We were in perfect sync, and I was already hurtling toward my release. And the fire in his eyes? God, I'd never get enough.

I kissed him again, closing my eyes and letting instinct take over as I climbed higher.

He slid his hands from my breasts to my hips, anchoring me to the stone countertop as he thrust harder, making me cry out.

"That's my girl. You're close. I can feel it."

Nodding, I bit down on my bottom lip. He was hitting all the right spots, causing sensations I'd never experienced before. Maybe it was the angle or the intensity of his thrusts. Maybe it was the way he was gripping me on the counter. Whatever it was, I could barely string words together. Just a chorus of *yes* and *more* as I spiraled.

"That's it," he whispered, threading his hands up my neck and gently tugging on my hair. "Come for me."

I obeyed, screaming and gasping and shaking. Completely free and wild and in love.

He followed, grunting and pulling me close.

With his forehead pressed to mine, he grasped the countertop, steadying us both, and panted.

He still had his dress shirt and vest on, and my little black dress was probably destroyed, but I was consumed by his breath on my skin and the frantic pulse of my own heart.

We stayed like that for a few minutes, catching our breath and grinning at one another.

"Cole," I whispered.

"Mmm."

"I want it to. A future." My thoughts were jumbled, making it impossible to seize the words to explain the intensity of my feelings. But his declaration, coupled with whatever had just happened between us, had me ready to declare myself, no matter how inarticulate I might be in my post-orgasmic haze.

"Good. Because I want forever." With a kiss to my sweaty forehead, he scooped me into his arms and strode for the bedroom.

"And wifey? Know this: I'm not taking no for an answer."

Chapter 38
Cole

"Be patient," Willa said, turning off Main Street. "We'll be there in ten minutes."

I let out a grumble. "I hate surprises."

"No, you don't," she corrected. "chill." Behind the wheel of my Tahoe, she navigated carefully through town.

"It's Sunday," I pouted. "I wanted to spend the morning with my wife, but you dragged me out of bed."

Her lips tipped up. "It'll be worth it."

She pulled up near Baxter Park and parked off the side of the road near the pond.

"Come on," she said, opening the liftgate and pulling out my hockey bag.

"We're at the pond?" I asked as I scanned the park. It was a clear, chilly day, and the sun was shining.

"Yes. We're playing pond hockey. Come on."

I took the bag out of her hands and followed her, appreciating the view—my wife in black leggings that left little to the imagination, one of old my UMaine hockey hoodies, and the hat I'd knit for her. She looked delectable. Damn if I didn't want to throw her down into a snowbank and bury myself inside her.

I surveyed the trees, the playground, and the park as we continued. I'd never been down here in winter. The park was a hub of activity during the warmer months, but at the moment, we had the place to ourselves.

Around the edge of the frozen pond were several small wooden benches made from cut logs, and on the embankment were two nets.

"So people really play here?" I asked, striding to catch up to Willa.

She peered over at me with one brow arched. "Yes. For generations. And it's time we initiate you. Skating is even more fun outside. When you miss a shot, you have to go dig the puck out of the snow." She threw a bright orange puck at me.

"Is that why the puck is neon?"

"See?" she said brightly, spinning and walking backward while she smiled at me. "You're already learning."

The ice was bumpy, and it sloped in certain spots. It was certainly nothing like the surfaces I'd trained on in some of the country's best hockey facilities.

But Willa was right. It was damn fun.

We raced across the pond, spraying snow at one another when we hit spots that hadn't been cleared. After we'd dug our sticks out, we passed the puck, making it jump and skitter over the ice and into the snow.

For a little while, we played passing and shooting games. But mostly we skated. I'd never experienced such innocent, pure fun. I was used to the pleasure of moving fast, of gliding and feeling the world still as my body accelerated. But when paired with the warm sun on my face, the icy breeze on my skin, and Willa's mitten-clad hand clutching mine? It was thrilling.

And then, just as my heart was full and I didn't think I'd ever had a more perfect day, I got hit with a snowball.

Thrown by my beautiful wife.

From that moment, it was on. We skated and slid and ducked as snow flew in every direction. Her aim was good, but I was faster. I crouched and spun quickly to avoid another hit and snagged her with one arm, tucking her into my body as we fell, sliding together into the mountain of snow.

Her face was pink and her eyes bright. My heart was pounding. I couldn't help myself.

"I fucking love you so much," I said, pinning her to the ice and kissing her.

"So you like pond hockey?" she asked when I came up for air. She wiggled beneath me, making me go instantly hard, despite the frigid temperatures.

"It's the most fun I've ever had," I said honestly as I dipped in for another kiss.

"Cole. I'm losing feeling in my ass." I'd lost myself in her mouth, the experience of kissing her on the ice fulfilling so many of my fantasies. "But I don't want to stop."

Hovering over her, I took her in. She was panting, and her eyes were glazed. Fuck, she wanted this as much as I did. "Let's go to the car."

I hauled myself up and then helped her to her feet. We skated for the benches and pulled our skates off in record time, then jogged toward my truck. I dug my key fob out along the way and had the truck running and the liftgate open by the time we made it to the parking lot. Once I'd tossed all our gear in the back, I pulled her to the driver's door.

I pushed my seat all the way back, grateful I'd bought such a big car, and then pulled her on top of me and shut the door. We kissed frantically, only stopping to pull the sweatshirt up over her head.

Hockey and skating and this woman. It was a deadly combination, and when she ground against me, I was ready to explode in my pants.

"You are incredible," I said, lifting up her T-shit and practically drooling at the sight of those perfect tits in her sports bra. "Fuck, I need you."

She pulled the bra over her head and tossed it into the passenger seat. "Then take me," she said, lifting off my lap and hovering above me. "Because I'm yours."

My cock surged as I unbuttoned my jeans. Tilting my hips, I pushed them down my thighs. I was already straining my boxers, and my balls ached as I buried my face in her tits. I bit one nipple, then the other, loving the sound of her gasps.

"You better be ready. I need to fuck you." I growled as she tugged my hair, sending a tingle down my spine.

She leaned on me and used one hand to shimmy her leggings down. "Then it's a good thing I forgot to wear panties."

I palmed her ass, my eyes rolling back. God, it would be a miracle if I lasted two minutes.

With a groan, I slid one finger inside her, making her cry out. Then I quickly added a second. "You're so needy and wet. Look at you."

She ground down against my hand, making her tits

bounce in my face. Fuck, this really would be fast. I'd have to get her off first, because once I was inside her, I would be done for.

I rubbed her clit with my thumb, slowly fucking her with my fingers.

"Cole," she pled. "Please. I need you."

"You need my cock, don't you, wifey?"

She threw her head back, her chest heaving. "Yes. Yes. I need it."

"So greedy." I hissed. "We've come a long way from being scared it wouldn't fit."

She laughed, but the sound quickly turned to a moan. "What can I say? I'm a size queen now. I need my husband's big, thick cock."

She tightened around my fingers, sending a surge of pure heat through me. With one nipple between my teeth, I tugged. God, she had gone from timid to so deliciously dirty in a matter of weeks. "That's my good girl. It does fit perfectly. This cock was made for you, wifey. Now come on my fingers so I can fuck you hard after."

She nodded, picking up her pace. Within seconds, she was shaking. God damn. This was my favorite thing. Watching my wife come.

As I applied more pressure to her clit, her leg muscles tightened and her pussy spasmed. She was bouncing and yelling and—what was that?

I paused and held my breath. Had the car been moving?

Above her labored breathing, there was a strange huff.

Willa gripped my shoulders. "Why did you—*Ahh*," she screamed.

Heart racing, I hugged her close to my chest. "What the fuck?"

On the passenger side of the car, a massive moose was leering, head bent so we could see one black eye and a big rack of antlers.

"Is that a fucking moose?"

She pulled back and studied the creature. "It's licking the salt off the front of your car."

"You've got to be shitting me. How do we get rid of it?"

It nudged the car, making the whole thing rock.

"Jesus."

"Relax," she said, giving my shoulders a reassuring squeeze. "It will walk away."

"Have you seen my car? It's covered in salt. We could be here all day." I reached around her and leaned on the horn.

She jumped, but the moose was unbothered. Fucking beast.

"They need the nutrients in the winter," Willa explained with a small smile. "That's why they go for the salt."

She climbed off me and leaned over to look out the back window, sending panic through me. I grasped her and pulled her back to me, squeezing my eyes shut.

"There's a scar on his flank. Looks like Clive," she said, as if that made this all better somehow.

Clutching her closer, I asked, "What if I start the car?"

"Don't. If you spook him, then he could cause a lot of damage. Look at the antlers."

I didn't want to examine the damn moose or his antlers. I wanted him gone. Better yet, I wanted him dead.

"It is hunting season?" I asked. "I need to shoot that fucker."

"Why?" She pulled back and slid over to the passenger seat.

"Because he saw your tits. The fucking moose got an eyeful of my wife."

She chuckled. "Cole, he's a moose. Chill."

I shook my head, shaking from the built-up testosterone flowing through me. "We could mount his head above the fireplace."

She pulled her shirt back on. Again, this kept getting worse. "You can't hurt Clive. That's not how things work in this town."

I sat up and grasped the back of her neck, pulling her face to mine. "These tits belong to me. No one gets to see them."

She studied my face, her eyes moving over every inch, before bursting into laughter. Wild, uncontrollable laughter.

And then I started laughing too. The entire thing was beyond ridiculous. I had been cock-blocked by a moose. It was the kind of ridiculous thing that could only happen in this crazy-ass town.

"He's a fucking menace," I said, hiccupping.

"I swear he's evil," she agreed, wiping the tears from her eyes before kissing me again.

"But there's no one I'd rather be stuck in a car with."

Chapter 39

Willa

We'd closed the office early today because a major storm was coming. The snow had started around breakfast, light and fluffy and not unusual for this time of year. But by lunch, the winds were fierce, and visibility was minimal.

Up here, we got snow from October to May. People didn't even blink. It was a fact of life. School kids hiked through waist-deep snow to get to the school bus without a second thought. Snow was dangerous, but wind was deadly. Once or twice a year, we'd be hit with a nor'easter, a storm that combined high winds with record snowfall. Those were the storms Mainers took seriously. We'd all heard horror stories of people being caught out in the snow, losing power without a backup generator, or being stranded without supplies.

Thankfully, Lovewell had an excellent community network, spearheaded by Bernice and several of the other older ladies who made sure the seniors and parents with young kids were checked in on. The whole town was sharpening their plow blades and gassing up their generators in anticipation.

On many occasions, I'd ended up buckled in next to my dad in the old pickup he kept for plowing. After big storms, we'd plow the neighbor's driveways and sometimes the hill that led up to the elementary school.

My heart clenched at the memory. My parents were safe down in Portland, but I missed them fiercely.

They had always prized hard work, dedication, and self-lessness. Growing up, I had watched my father step away from the table on Thanksgiving Day to help someone in need. He'd leave sporting events or even the grocery store—and a cart full of groceries. The entire community relied on him and trusted him to help.

My mom too. As one of only a handful of psychologists in this county, she was inundated with patients and was always visiting hospitals. Thankfully, when I was in elementary school, she opened her private practice. That cut down on her travel, but she was available twenty-four seven to anyone who needed her.

Service was in my blood. More and more, I was realizing that my ideal version of service looked a little different from my parents'. But I had a way to go before making that leap. Dr. Walters's niece was finishing her social work degree, and I'd recently been talking to her about the possibility of an internship at my practice. Having mental health support would be huge. I was still searching for the unicorn physician assistant or nurse practitioner who could take some of the patient load, but Cole's positivity had kept me from giving up hope.

While I took on all the responsibility at work, it was such a relief to have someone to share it with at home.

This afternoon, he greeted me at the door with a kiss.

"We should probably hit the grocery store before it gets bad," I said, standing in the entryway in my coat and boots. We'd need to get through the pre-storm checklist ASAP.

"Already done," he said, heading toward the kitchen.

"What about—"

"Gas for the generator? Done. I also charged our devices —but plug your phone in now; there's a charger set up in here—and the battery bank is full of juice too. I also put fresh batteries in the flashlights."

He gestured to the kitchen counter where several flashlights were lined up.

My heart stuttered. "I don't think I've ever been so attracted to you."

He winked. "You've got plenty of time to show me just how much you like me, wifey. This is gonna be a multi-day storm."

Once I'd plugged my phone in, I stepped into his arms and let his warmth and familiar scent flood my senses. Though I'd spent most of my life too busy to even think about marriage, I was luxuriating in it now.

But there was a little nugget of guilt that I couldn't shake. The sore spot in my brain that I kept poking at. Lila. Our friendship. The lie I'd told her. I didn't want to betray Cole, but I also wanted to come clean and tell her everything. Move on. But it wasn't only my story.

He cupped my face and ducked down. "Something is wrong. Work?"

I shook my head.

"Tell me." He kissed my forehead and pulled back, brow furrowed. "You can tell me anything. Radical honesty, remember?"

I took a deep breath, my heart beating a little faster. "I want to tell Lila the truth. About Vegas and how things started. I hate lying, and she's my best friend. She's been supportive and happy for us, and I want her to know the truth."

He dipped his chin, his eyes never leaving mine. "Then tell her."

"Cole." He was making it sound so easy. "What about Owen?"

He took a step back and ran his hands through his hair. "Sure, we got wrapped up in going wild in Vegas and things went further than we anticipated."

I hated the way that sounded. It was the truth, of course, but we'd come so far since that drunken night.

"But it turned into the most incredible thing in my life. Maybe we shouldn't diminish it by ignoring how it started. I love you. I want you to feel good about what we're building together."

That hit me right in the heart.

"But Owen?"

He shrugged. "I can live with Owen's judgment. We've never been close, and with or without telling him the truth, I can't see that ever changing. I'd rather have him hate me than make you lie to your best friend. You are the most important person in my life."

My heart panged. God. This man. He was giving me permission to tell a story that was only half mine. To expose him to the judgment of his older brother so we could move forward together.

"For so long, I've done all I could to avoid consequences. I've dodged and weaved and evaded." He blew out a breath. "But you've taught me that facing things can be liberating."

I threw my arms around him, burying my face in his chest.

"Go call her," he said against the top of my head. "Say what you need to say. You don't need to protect me."

It took me an hour to work up the courage to make the call. We chatted casually for a few minutes, but I was a nervous, sweating mess, so I pretty quickly cut to the chase.

"I need to tell you something," I forced out. "I'm terrified that you'll hate me, but the thought of lying to you for any longer is scarier."

"Willa," she said, her tone concerned. "Nothing you could say would make me hate you. What's wrong?"

"I love you so much. And I can't bear the thought of not being truthful."

"Okay..."

With a deep breath in, I spewed out a brief summary of the Vegas situation.

"What the fuck?" she screeched, the sound bringing tears to my eyes. God, I hated disappointing her. I was a shit friend.

"We decided to pretend. Just for a little while. Mainly

because of my stuff. I didn't want to upset or disappoint my parents." And now I was fully crying.

"Willa." She sighed. "They love you so much."

My heart ached. "I know. But we almost lost Dad, and the thought of admitting to a tequila-fueled wedding to the town bad boy was just too much."

"So you figured it would be easier to pretend to be in love with him instead?" She snorted.

"I realize it sounds ridiculous. But he was so worried about his brothers' judgment. And honestly, it made sense. At the time, he needed a place to live, and I was lonely and overwhelmed."

"And now?"

"It's amazing," I said, a smile spreading across my face.

"How long did the faking go on? If you were pretending when you snuck out of our sacred sleepover to be with him a couple of weeks ago, you did a damn good job."

"That wasn't pretending. I fell for him. Hard."

"Of course you did. He's perfect for you."

Cheeks heating, I laughed. Had she seriously just said her ex was perfect for me?

"I mean it. Things went badly between us, but it wasn't all his fault. Trust me, I did plenty wrong too," she promised. "It seems like being with you has helped him grow up and face some of his demons. And you need to cut loose, have fun, and let yourself be still sometimes. And he's great at that. You two balance one another out."

Tears pricked at the backs of my eyes. God, I didn't deserve her friendship. "I'm so sorry," I said as the tears crested my lashes and tracked down my cheeks. "I have felt so guilty and shitty and awful. We made a pact long ago never to let guys come between us, and I feel like I've betrayed you. I love you so much."

"Shit, now I'm crying too now." She sniffled. "I'm hurt." Her voice was a whisper. "I won't deny it. And I need to process all of this. But you're still my best friend. I want you to be happy and well cared for."

I swallowed back the emotion swamping me. "Thank you. I'm so sorry."

"But." She paused and sniffled again. Then she cleared her throat. "I can empathize. Owen has been working through a lot of baggage his father piled on him. They've all had to deal with a lot. But Cole's comes with another facet related to his brothers. He's always longed for their approval. So I'm sure it hurt that Owen was so angry when he found out you got married."

"I hope we didn't ruin your engagement weekend."

"Not at all. He was so stressed about making everything perfect for me. But the wild stories and the imperfections are what made it incredible." There was a smile in her voice now. "And if you guys really do live happily ever after, then I'm taking full credit for all of it."

A giggle bubbled out of me. "I'll allow it."

"Did you tell Magnolia yet?"

"She guessed." I cringed. "Only took her a few days."

Lila huffed. "Of course she did. That woman's bullshit detector is next level."

We chatted longer, about her classes and the charity gala she and Owen had attended recently, along with all kinds of gossip about Boston's biggest sports stars, of course. Apparently, her circle now included professional athletes.

She was equal parts happy and tired and fulfilled. It

warmed my heart. Because Lila had been through so much and had worked her ass off to realize her dreams.

By the time we hung up, it was dark and the snow was falling hard. When I stepped into the living room, feeling lighter than I had in weeks, Cole was crouched in front of the fireplace.

He was so handsome and kind. It would behoove me to remember that our origin story was not a shameful secret, but the start of something special.

Chapter 40
Cole

"I've gotta go."

Willa came out of the bedroom, pulling a sweatshirt over her head.

I put my hands on my hips and exhaled. "Look outside. We're in the middle of a nor'easter, remember?"

She ignored me, opening the hall closet and pulling out a large military-style duffel bag.

"Willa," I said, striding over to her. "We've been stuck inside since yesterday. There is a literal blizzard outside this door. What's going on?"

She shook the bag out, not bothering to look at me. "It's Kara. She's bleeding."

Kara? From high school? Bleeding? Before I could ask a follow-up question, she whipped around.

"She's only thirty-four weeks pregnant. And she's terrified."

The weather was awful. Honestly, we were lucky we hadn't lost power. There was no way I was letting her out in this weather. "Have you seen the winds? What the fuck, Willa? That's dangerous. You can't drive. There's two feet of snow on the ground."

She gave me a withering glare. "I'm not gonna drive. I'll take the snowmobile."

My stomach lurched. "Do you even know how to drive it?"

She shrugged. "It's been a few years since I've been on one, but I'll be fine."

I picked up the bag and slung it over my shoulder. "What's a few years?"

"High school." She said it without an ounce of shame.

She was already piling on layers, twisting the scarf I'd knitted around her neck.

"Willa," I pleaded. "This is crazy."

Her eyes flashed with rage. "Listen to me. Kara has been a friend for years. Her husband is out at lumber camp and can't get out. She's alone and scared. I'm her doctor and her friend, and I do not take orders from you."

My lungs seized up. All right, then. I was equally terrified and impressed by my wife.

"Fine," I said, opening the closet and grabbing my own jacket. "I'm coming with you. I have a lot of snow mobile experience. I'll drive."

"Not necessary."

"Yes, it is," I gritted out. "You're my wife, and if you're going to drive miles up a mountain in a fucking blizzard, then I'll be by your side the whole way. It's my job to protect you."

She threw her arms up and dropped them heavily with a

smack against her thighs. "I don't have time to fight with you about the patriarchal insanity of that statement."

"Good. You can kick my ass later. Now move. I need to get my boots."

Of all the nights. I shook my head. The snow had been pelting the side of the house all day, and it was bitterly cold. I wanted to be curled up in front of the wood stove, not role-playing one of those weird survival shows Jude loved to watch.

We headed out to the garage where she threw the cover off the snow machine.

It was a large touring model, thankfully. That meant there was room for both of us.

She set the medical bag on the back, along with a wilderness survival kit, and covered it with a tarp, then secured it with bungee cords. Every one of her movements was controlled and confident. I couldn't help but admire her. She was determined, and nothing was stopping her.

"Okay, it's secure." She pointed to a gas can. "Fill her up."

I poured gas into the tank as she double-checked the bungee cords.

As I worked, adrenaline pushed through me. I did not want to do this, but the thought of her being out in this weather alone ignited some instinct inside me that I could not identify.

I wanted to protect her, keep her safe, and deliver her to her destination.

As a native of rural Maine, I knew my way around a snow machine as well as this town. Even so, this wouldn't be easy.

Before I mounted the damn thing, I grabbed my phone and sent a quick text to my brothers, just in case.

COLE

Willa and I are heading out on the snow machine to see a patient. If you don't hear from me in a few hours, call for help.

FINN

We'll come look for you

GUS

Are you sure? It's dangerous out there

COLE

She's a doctor man. She's not gonna let someone suffer

FINN

I've got snowshoes. We'll rescue you. Give us the address so we know where to look.

JUDE

Good luck

GUS

Remember, wide turns so you don't roll into a snowbank

COLE

Don't tell Debbie, and please come find my body if necessary…

ONCE WE'D DONNED OUR HELMETS, I STARTED THE engine.

She settled behind me and wrapped her arms around my waist. "Stay focused," she said. "I don't know what I'm going to find when I get there, but in this situation, the most helpful thing you can do is stay calm. Do you understand?"

I patted her arm. "I got you, wifey. Let's go see this patient."

The long, wooded drive was rough. The snow was deep and wet, which actually made for decent driving, but the wind was biting, and every cell in my body was screaming at the cold. With Willa at my back, though, steady and focused, pointing out intersections and navigating as I kept us upright, I eventually found my groove.

The roads improved as we made it into town. The plows had come through a few hours ago, meaning we were able to pick up speed.

We passed through town, the blizzard conditions and wild snow drifts making the lights hazy. When we reached Route 16, we headed up past the river toward the mountains. Jude lived up here, on a winding country road where people had acreage and privacy. It was beautiful but hard to reach in the snow.

I slowed as the road forked to ensure I remained in control, and from there, the path narrowed, making it difficult to see.

When Willa squeezed my arm and pointed to the right, I eased forward slowly, wiping my visor with my sleeve. My arms were coated in wet snow, but I ignored the chill and pushed forward.

We drove by several cabins and a few larger homes before finding a small cape in a clearing.

I got as close as I could to the front door, then killed the engine. Willa hopped off the back, unlatched her bag, and jogged through the snow without a word. The drifts were knee high for her, but she wasn't deterred.

Kara Mosely was a small woman who'd graduated a year or two before us. She worked at the post office and her husband, Jack, was a crane operator for Gagnon Lumber. We'd played hockey together in high school. I'd always liked the guy.

The instant she opened the door, it was clear she was in distress. Despite the frigid temps, she was sweating and shaking.

"Blood," she said. "There was a lot of blood."

Willa rushed toward her and guided her to a chair. Once she was settled, my wife dropped to her knees, and as she took her pulse, she asked Kara to describe her symptoms.

Wearing a mask of calm, Willa looked at me. "Glass of water."

I hustled to the kitchen without a word and searched the cabinets until I found a glass. I filled it to the brim and carried it back to the living room with shaking hands.

"I'm only thirty-four weeks," Kara cried.

"I know. And it's going to be okay. Let's talk about the last twenty-four hours. Tell me every single thing you felt. Then I'll examine you."

"My back." Kara moaned, doubling over.

"Okay, I'm going to examine you, and we can talk through it all." Willa shot me a look that I took as a silent request for privacy. So I snagged the bag from the foyer, then took her coat from her and moved back out toward the front door to hang our gear to dry.

As I was untying my boots, Kara moaned. That poor woman. She looked so relieved when Willa walked in the door. I closed my eyes and said a silent prayer that she would be okay.

"Kara," Willa said, using the calm doctor tone she'd mastered, "you're in labor."

"No. Not possible."

"Yes," she soothed. "What happened is called a bloody show. It's the shedding of your cervical cap. That means your body is getting ready to deliver the baby."

Kara whimpered, the sound so forlorn it hurt my heart.

Willa, speaking a little louder, called my name.

When I stepped back into the living room, Kara was sitting up, wincing, with a hand braced on her back.

Willa turned toward me. "Call the hospital. Tell them we've got an OP thirty-four-week delivery coming and see how long it will take them to get there. Then call Jack and tell him we've got everything under control. No need to do anything dangerous."

I nodded, having been given my marching orders.

"And I need latex gloves from my bag."

I fetched them, making sure to open up the bag so she could reach all the other supplies.

"What does that mean?" Kara cried, her face etched with pain. "OP?"

Willa squeezed her hands. "It means the baby is in the posterior position. We call it sunny side up." She traced her hands over Kara's stomach. "You feel this dip above your belly button? The baby is turned around and descending into your cervix, causing your back pain."

"Is the baby going to be okay?" Kara asked as I headed for the foyer again.

"Yes," Willa said, her tone full of reassurance.

Once I'd made both calls, I stepped back into the living room. "Ambulance said it will take an hour. I spoke to the emergency department, labor and delivery, and the ambulance dispatcher. They're going as fast as they can. The roads are bad, but plows are out."

Kara whimpered, and the sound quickly turned into a cry.

"It's okay," Willa explained. "You're only seven centimeters. We've got time. We can let you dilate and try to turn the baby, or if the ambulance gets here in time, we can get you to the hospital for a C-section."

With tears streaming down her face, Kara hiccupped and sobbed.

My heart broke at the sound. Breathing through the emotion, I looked out the window at the swirling snow, taking a moment to compose myself.

"And Jack?" she asked, garnering my attention.

"Waiting patiently for the winds to die down." I gave her a sympathetic frown. "When they do, there's a truck ready to bring him back to town."

The tears fell as she hiccupped and shook.

But then Willa was grabbing her hands and squeezing hard. "Look at me," she said firmly. "It's okay to be terrified. But today is gonna be one of the best days of your life. You're going to meet your baby. Maybe the circumstances are shitty, but you're gonna have a hell of a birth story, mama."

Kara smiled through her tears. "I'm so scared."

Willa pulled her into a hug. "I know, but I'll be here with you until the ambulance comes. We're doing this together." Her tone was so confident that even I felt comforted.

"Now, let's time your contractions and practice your breathing."

Chapter 41
Willa

The ambulance barely made it up the driveway, but by the time they were out front, we had Kara bundled up, and Cole was carrying her outside to the paramedics, who were ready with a fetal monitor and oxygen.

The wind had died down, and visibility had improved greatly. Still, it was bitterly cold and dark. Kara was in better spirits, and the timing of her contractions indicated she'd likely make it to the hospital before that baby made his or her debut.

When we were alone, Cole wrapped his arms around me, knowing exactly what I needed.

"I was so terrified," I admitted into his chest. "It's been years since I delivered a baby."

He tipped my chin up. "You? Terrified? How? You were so calm. You knew exactly what you were doing."

"It's my training. I've had lots of practice. By now, it kicks in and takes over. But, shit." I put my forehead on his chest and exhaled. "That would have been a difficult delivery. She needs to be in a hospital for it."

"You were incredible."

I tried not to bristle. His praise felt misplaced. I hadn't done much. In fact, the only reason I'd made it here alive was because of him. There was no way I could have driven the snowmobile in these conditions. After tonight, I only had more respect for my dad, if that was possible. He'd gone out in many snowstorms to help patients and friends in need.

I patted his chest. "Let's clean up here."

We set to work, throwing the towels into the wash, quickly cleaning the floors, and turning off all the lights. I texted Jack to let him know Kara was en route to the hospital and things were going well.

"Thank you for coming," I said as we locked up. "Having you here helped me stay calm."

He blinked at me, surprise flashing in his eyes. "But I didn't do anything."

"You did," I insisted. "I felt safe with you here. It's because of you that I could be strong for Kara."

His eyes softened and he pulled me down for a lingering kiss. "We make a good team. Now can I drive my wifey home?"

I nodded wearily. It was almost four a.m., and I was beat.

We secured the bags again and slipped our helmets on.

Eventually, we'd have to dig out and I'd go to work, but right now, all I wanted was a warm bed and this man by my side.

I climbed on, and as he fired the snowmobile up, I held tight to my husband.

The snow had let up a bit, and as we drove, I couldn't

help but marvel at the strange beauty of this winter night. Though I was sure Cole was as eager to get home as I was, his driving was careful, every move controlled and deliberate. As always, he put all his effort into caring for me. God, the thought made my heart squeeze.

My body had almost completely frozen when lights up ahead caught my attention. I squinted and—were those people?

I tapped Cole's shoulder and pointed. With a nod, he headed in that direction. As we crept closer, the sign for Mountain Meadows, the trailer park in town, came into view. Just outside it on the embankment was a whole slew of construction equipment.

I steeled myself. Dammit, I hope no one was injured.

Cole slowed to a stop, the lights doing little to illuminate what was happening. A large pickup truck sat on the side of the road, and there was a snowmobile parked near it.

Once Cole cut the engine, I hopped off, removing my helmet as I rushed to the side of the road.

I waved my arms as I approached. "Excuse me. Do you all need help? I'm a doctor."

Cole came up behind me, his long strides unbothered by the thick snow.

"Can we help?"

As we got closer, a person in dark clothing hopped onto the snowmobile. The engine roared, and then it took off at high speed.

My stomach twisted as I watched its taillights fade. That was odd.

"Can I help you?" a man barked as we got closer.

Cole pulled out his flashlight and shone it ahead.

Even out of uniform and with a winter hat pulled down, I recognized that face.

It was Chief Souza.

My throat tightened, and I walked faster. "Chief," I said. "Are you hurt? We can help."

The police chief, dressed in a thick gray ski jacket and hat, gaped, his jaw unhinged and his eyes wild.

"What are you doing out here?" he barked.

The man next to him backed up. In the dark, I couldn't make out his features. He was shorter and leaner. He was dressed in a black snowsuit and had a small bag in his hand.

The chief stepped forward, his chest puffed out. "Go home."

"We wanted to make sure you're all right," Cole asked. He was standing in front of me now, shielding me. But from what? What the hell was going on?

"I should have known it'd be a Hebert out here causing trouble," the chief said.

The other man chuckled.

At the sound, I pushed in front of Cole and shined my light at the other man, who was inching away from us.

"Dennis?"

He squinted and shielded his eyes with a hand, but it was definitely Dennis Huxley. God, that guy had always given me the creeps. "Are you hurt?"

He trudged forward through the snow. "We're fine. Just having a meeting."

"On the side of the road at four a.m. during a blizzard?" Cole asked.

Dennis stared at him, saying nothing, still clutching the bag.

"Now, before things get ugly, go on home," Chief Souza said.

Ugly? What the hell was he talking about?

"Yeah," Dennis added, his tone strangely menacing. "This is my property. I own Mountain Meadows. I could have him arrest you for trespassing."

I shook my head. Was the cold messing with my brain? I'd known the chief since I was in diapers, but it sure felt like he was threatening us.

The chief took off his thick gloves. In the light of our flashlights, a large wristwatch glinted, catching my attention. Then he slid his bare hand into his coat. Fuck. Was he reaching for a gun? Why did this feel so strange?

Cole pulled me behind him, his grip tight. "We were only checking to make sure no one was injured. I need to get my wife home."

"Good idea," Dennis snarled as Cole pulled me back toward our snowmobile.

"Listen, I'm going to drive by slowly. Can you shine the light at the truck and snowmobile? I think we're missing something," he whispered. "See if you can catch the license plate."

Nodding, I slipped my helmet back on. Once we were settled and Cole was navigating past the truck, I shined the flashlight at the truck, looking at the plate and committing it to memory. The vehicle was huge and, despite the snowfall, looked new. The bed was filled with plastic storage totes covered in a dusting of snow.

I repeated the letters and numbers in my head until we got back to our cottage.

"Write it down," Cole said as he helped me off the machine.

While he unstrapped my med bag, I ran into the house, dripping with snow, still wearing my coat and boots, and scribbled the plate number on a Post-it, my mind still buzzing.

Cole came in a minute later, his cheeks red and his eyes wide. "I need to call Parker now."

"What was that?"

He shook his head. "Not sure, but I saw some things."

"Did he have a gun?" I squeaked, the realization of how much danger we could have been in settling in.

He blew out a breath and tugged his hat off his head. "I think so. Did you see the watch on his wrist?"

I nodded. "It was huge. Looked really fancy."

"Exactly," he said, already dialing. "And he knows we saw it."

Chapter 42
Cole

I met Parker at her house before sunrise. She lived with her husband and baby near town on a cul-de-sac filled with enormous newly built homes. The driveway was clearly heated, as there wasn't a flake of snow on it when I pulled in.

"Walk me through again," Parker said, bouncing her baby on her shoulder.

"Charles Huxley owns Deimos," I explained, pulling up the email Marcus had sent overnight, where he'd attached a list of over three dozen corporate holdings.

"The trailer park is owned by Phobos Management."

She nodded.

"Which we know is owned by Charles and Dennis Huxley. And in Greek mythology, Phobos was the brother of Deimos."

"That doesn't prove anything."

"I know. But these receipts for campaign contributions do. Look." I turned the laptop around so she could study it.

"Mayor Lambert is subject to federal campaign contribution laws. His aids spend months preparing these reports. Marcus told me that the Huxleys always contribute to local political and charitable campaigns. Usually as individuals, but occasionally from their corporate entities."

Nodding, she slowly scrolled through the documents.

"And last year, someone screwed up and sent a payment from a bank account held by Deimos Industries. Which sent Marcus and the mayor's staff on a wild adventure to determine ownership so their boss wouldn't get investigated by the FEC."

"And do you know what they found?"

"Deimos is owned by Scylla, Inc. I'm not great at understanding incorporation paperwork, but it appears to be an entity of Phobos Management."

"And they own a ton of stuff."

"Yeah, lots of real estate up here and on the mid-coast. Phobos shows up in FEC databases all the time. They are a politically active family, but someone messed up with Deimos."

She was grinning now. "And the police chief?"

I slid the Post-it with the license plate number on it across the table. "I could swear I caught a glimpse of a fancy Swiss watch on his wrist. And my wife grabbed this plate number from the truck parked by the side of the road. It was a black F-350. Really fancy."

"On it," she said. "I can make a call to run the plate and put out some feelers. If we've connected Deimos to the Huxleys, then they have a lot of explaining to do. Not just for me, but with the FBI."

"Good." All of this—the corporate holdings, the late-night meetup—was raising red flags left and right.

"And you think the chief might be involved? I've had my suspicions since I started working with the Gagnons, but I've never found anything to indicate he's not above board."

"It could be my dislike of the man." I shrugged. "But there was a clear vibe. At one point, he took off his gloves and reached into his coat."

"Fuck," Parker hissed.

"Exactly. This wasn't some innocent roadside run-in. There was a third person too. But they peeled out the moment we arrived. And there were boxes in the bed of the truck. Gray plastic bins. And why would he take off his gloves—it was ten degrees out and snowing—if he wasn't reaching for a gun?"

Parker pinched the bridge of her nose. "This could get ugly."

"What could get ugly?" Pascal Gagnon sauntered in and scooped the baby girl out of Parker's arm. "You promised no danger," he growled.

She smiled up at him innocently. "My sweet husband is still traumatized from when your father kidnapped him."

My heart plummeted. Fuck. When would we be free of my dad and all he'd done? His actions were so far-reaching I struggled to believe a day would come when we wouldn't have this black cloud hanging over our heads.

"I'm so sorry," I said, looking from Parker to Pascal and back. "I know it's not enough."

"Not your fault," Pascal said, his tone neutral, as he bounced the baby.

"Still." I roughed a hand down my face. "We all feel terrible. Hopefully Parker can help us put an end to all of this once and for all. The entire town needs to heal after all my father did."

Pascal gave me a curt nod, and Parker patted my hand.

"You've given me a lot to work with. Go home, dig out, and wait to hear from me. I may need you to go back to the town archives and pull some things."

Nodding, I stood.

"We're close," she said as she pushed her chair back. "This is so much bigger than anyone bargained for, but you've been incredibly helpful."

Terror filled me at her comment. Was my family in danger? Was Willa in danger? The thought left me cold. I wouldn't let anything happen to her.

"Are we in danger?"

Parker paused before responding, not usually a good sign. "I don't know. After all that's happened over the past few years, it's always possible. So just lay low. Hopefully this is the break we need. I'll be in touch after I speak to the FBI."

I nodded and stood to leave.

"Cole," she warned. "I mean it. Lay low, speak to no one, keep your nose clean, and wait for my instructions."

***

My mind was spinning. The roads had finally been cleared, and the people in town were slowly emerging. Willa had texted that she was headed into work to see her afternoon patients, so I headed into town to grab a cup of coffee and think.

Unsurprisingly, the Caffeinated Moose was full. After a morning of shoveling, it was no wonder everyone wanted to gorge on muffins and lattes. I said hello to a few people while I waited for my order, then found an empty table and mulled over all the things I'd learned. My mind kept circling Chief Souza. What the hell had he been doing out there?

And why had he reached inside his coat?

My heart thundered in my chest at the thought of what could have happened. But my thoughts snagged on the glimpse I'd gotten of his wrist.

That watch.

My spidey senses were tingling. I needed to get a better look.

I headed up to the counter and gave Raeanna, the owner, a smile. "I'm headed over to visit my friend, Chief Souza," I explained. "What is his usual order?"

Armed with a skim-milk peppermint mocha, I headed for the public safety building, determined to get answers. I could pop over to town hall across the street and do some digging around in the records, but my curiosity would not be sated. I'd been forced to listen to my father drone on and on about *timepieces* for years, and I couldn't shake the feeling that this one was important.

Martha, the dispatcher, greeted me warmly as I walked in. Her granddaughter played on my team, and she and her husband never missed a game.

"I brought a treat for the chief," I said, my tone friendly. "Can I drop it off?"

She pointed me toward his office, where I knocked gently on the door.

"Come in."

Souza's face soured the moment he saw me. I had to duck my head under the frame to fit, but I walked right in and sat down without being invited to, both cups of coffee in hand.

"Raeanna said you enjoy a good peppermint mocha. Since you didn't get much sleep last night, I figured you could use it."

"Thank you," he said curtly.

I studied the man I'd known since childhood, the guy who used to go on fishing trips with my father, who coached the high school baseball team once upon a time. He was tall and sturdy, his uniform crisply pressed and his face freshly shaven. He didn't look worse for wear, despite his late-night snowstorm activities.

I placed the cup on his desk, far enough away that he would have to reach for it.

And that's exactly what he did. The move caused the cuff of his uniform shirt to slide up just enough for me to spot a thick stainless-steel band etched in a familiar pattern.

He sipped the coffee and eyed me suspiciously.

"That's quite a watch," I said casually. I would know. It matched the one currently residing in my sock drawer.

He froze, his eyes narrowing, and my pulse quickened.

He knew I knew. I had no doubt. "You know a lot about watches, son?"

Channeling all the calm I could muster, I leaned back and sipped my latte. "Enough to know that small-town police chiefs don't usually wear fifty-thousand-dollar watches."

"Watch yourself," he growled. "You don't know what you're talking about."

His red face and clenched fists told me everything I needed to know. I'd hit a nerve. He was hiding something, and that was definitely my father's watch.

"Maybe not." I stood and shrugged nonchalantly. "But I know an Audemars Piguet when I see one. Did your friends at Deimos Industries give it to you?"

He stood abruptly, knocking his peppermint mocha over. "Get the fuck out of my office," he yelled as the dark liquid seeped across the papers on his desk.

Having gotten what I needed, I gave him a mock salute. "Have a great day, Chief."

Chapter 43
Cole

"Mom, you look great. I think city living agrees with you," Willa said, smiling brightly.

We were FaceTiming with Willa's parents, who were still in Portland so that Dr. Savard could work with rehabilitative specialists. Willa missed her parents and texted with them daily, but they had asked to see us tonight, so we'd made the time.

"The condo we've rented looks out over the ocean, and I've been taking long walks every day," her mother said. "Your father says we should get a dog."

Willa laughed. "Dad, you look amazing. And you barely even need your cane anymore. Maybe a dog is exactly what you need."

"They're working me to the bone over at the rehab hospital. It's practically around the clock." He chuckled. "I feel like I'm training for the goddamn Olympics."

Susan elbowed him gently. "Don't listen to him. He's doing great. And sitting on the couch gets old after a while.

It's warmer here than in Lovewell, and we mostly get rain rather than snow because of the ocean."

"Are you turning into a city girl now?"

She huffed a laugh. "Your father and I take walks and we go to little cafés. We've met up with a few friends who were in town, and next weekend, we're taking a little road trip down to Boston. *Six* is playing there, and your dad bought me tickets as a surprise," she gushed, her smile wide.

Roger beamed. "You know your mother loves the theater, and she's been so wonderful, taking care of me, so I'm taking my girl out and doing it right."

The two of them smiled at one another in a way that made my heart clench. They'd both had long, demanding careers, and even after decades of marriage and raising a child on top of it all, these two people still loved one another deeply. Willa was lucky to have had this example of what a loving, functional marriage could look like. My heart ached with the longing to experience that for myself.

They chatted for a few more minutes, Willa's smile growing as she updated her parents on the town and my team's recent victories. They were so supportive and interested in every detail of our lives.

"Willa, sweetheart, I love you to bits, but could I have a moment alone with my son-in-law?" Roger asked.

My stomach lurched when he called me his son-in-law. It felt like a huge responsibility, and he was the kind of man I'd never want to let down.

Willa blew him a kiss and headed off toward the bedroom.

"I wanted to check in with you and see how my Willa is really doing."

"She's doing great, sir," I replied. "Working hard."

"I hate that I had to leave her with the practice like this. I never intended to drop this kind of responsibility on her so early in her career, and I worry about her."

"She's doing an incredible job. There are good days and bad, and I know she's looking to hire more help, but she cares so deeply for every single person in this town. She's making it work."

"Thank you for saying that." He ran his hand through his gray hair. "I shouldn't have given her all this responsibility so early. A few years ago, I was given the opportunity to sell the practice, but I turned it down. I wanted to save it for my Willa. But she's young. You're young."

He shook his head, clearly getting emotional. "The two of you are so in love. You should be out experiencing the world together instead of being saddled with enormous responsibility in a small town that could never fulfill you." He wiped a tear from his eye. "My daughter deserves the world."

"I agree." I couldn't say it out loud yet, but I intended to give it to her. I had a lot of work to do and a lot of things to learn along the way, but she made me want things I had never allowed myself to even consider having before.

"I didn't do all the things I should have done, and I wasn't the man I could have been. And that's because I gave every part of myself to my job. I don't want that for my little girl. I want her to have a full life with a family and a partner. I want her to travel and spend time with friends. Find hobbies and prioritize her health."

"She will," I assured him. "If there's anyone who can do it all, it's Willa. And I'm right here to support her. We exercise together, and I make sure she gets enough rest. We go out and see friends. I swear to you, I will do everything in my power to keep her healthy and happy every day of my life."

He cleared his throat, choked up. "Thank you, son," he rasped. "You have given us such a gift. Please take care of my girl."

"She's our girl now," I said. "And I will take excellent care of her."

Chapter 44

Willa

As I pulled up in front of the cottage, I frowned. Where was Cole's car? He had practice tonight, and he always closed down the rink for Arthur on Thursdays.

But it was after eleven. He should have been home hours ago.

I walked inside, flipped the lights on, and called his phone.

Straight to voicemail.

With a huff, I kicked off my shoes. Then I changed my clothes and paced around the house, as if I'd find an answer hidden in a corner or behind a piece of furniture. This was so unlike him. He always texted if he was going to be late.

Maybe he'd stuck around to skate and shoot some pucks? He did that a lot, and I knew how much he loved having the ice to himself.

Even if that were the case, I couldn't imagine he'd stay out past nine. Practice had ended hours ago. Had he had an accident? The roads were incredibly icy. It was February, for God's sake.

Unease wound through me, upsetting me to the point that I called Jude.

"Have you heard from Cole? I went to dinner at Magnolia's house and just got home."

"Not since this morning. Doesn't he have practice on Thursdays?" he asked, his casual tone irking me.

"Yes." I nibbled on my thumbnail. "But it's so late."

He sighed. "It's not even midnight, Willa."

"Midnight?" I bit back far too loudly. "Midnight in Lovewell, Maine, is like three a.m. in a normal town."

"He could have run into someone and struck up a conversation. Or maybe he went to the Moose?" Jude offered. "Or maybe he was hungry and drove to Heartsborough to get Wendy's. He's not the most responsible, and phone batteries die…"

I pinched the bridge of my nose, annoyance joining the party worry had started. "You know, your version of Cole sounds very different from mine. The man I'm married to comes home on time, texts on the rare occasion that he'll be late, and never lets his phone battery die."

I was pacing now, my stomach clenching painfully. I didn't have time to lecture Jude about the man his brother had become. I had more important shit to do.

Like find my husband.

So I hung up without saying goodbye, threw my boots on, and grabbed my keys. If I had to drive around all night, I'd do it.

My heart was pounding in my ears as I drove into town. *God, please let him be okay.*

Deciding to start at the rink, I headed past town hall and down Route 16. When I pulled off into the dimly lit parking lot, I held my breath. Immediately, his Tahoe came into view, where it was parked sideways, taking up two spots.

I pulled up, cut my engine, and jumped out.

What the hell?

Cole was in the driver's seat, slumped across the center console, unconscious.

Hands trembling, I tore the driver's side door open and reached across his body to feel for a pulse.

Okay, strong pulse. Good sign.

And then the smell hit me.

Alcohol.

Heart racing, I scanned the interior. Quickly, I discovered two empty bottles of whiskey on the floorboard and another, this one unopened, in his cupholder.

What was going on?

"Cole," I said, shaking him. By the way his body was contorted, he hadn't just fallen asleep.

"Cole." I shouted, grabbing his shoulders forcefully and pushing him with all my might.

One of his eyes opened, and I shook him even harder.

I needed to get him out of the car and examine him.

Just as I was trying to figure out how to maneuver his giant shoulders out the door, sirens wailed in the distance.

"Cole," I said, pulling him onto the cold ground and silently thanking him and my own determination for the strength I'd built over the last few months. The jostling and the cold asphalt were enough to rouse him, thank God, and give me access to examine him fully.

As the sirens got louder, I peered over my shoulder. Had

someone called 911? It wasn't a bad idea. Who knew what could have happened to him.

The police and fire trucks were pulling into the parking lot when another odor hit me. A terrible smell that made my nostrils burn, like gasoline and chemicals.

I waved, hoping to get their attention, but they passed by and didn't stop until they'd pulled up to the side of the building. I straightened and took off for the emergency vehicles. It wasn't until I was a few yards away that I noticed a massive hole in the side of the building and the Zamboni on its side in the embankment of snow by the parking lot, with shorting lights and sparking wires and hoses and valves leaking and spraying icy chemicals in every direction. Oh my God. What had happened?

"Ma'am," a voice called out. "Please step back."

The man was decked out in turnout gear, so it took a moment to recognize him as Matt Graves, whose kids were my patients.

"It's Dr. Savard," I said, shoving my freezing, shaking hands into my pockets. "What happened?"

He shook his head. "Dunno. But we need to secure the scene. Please step back."

With a nod, I spun, eager to get back to Cole. As the Tahoe came into sight, my heart stopped.

Chief Souza and his deputies were standing next to the vehicle. I took off, slipping on the ice but catching myself before I fell.

The chief stood over Cole, who was slumped against the driver's side of the Tahoe, his hands on his belt and a look of pure pleasure on his face.

"Oh boy," he said to Office Fielder. "Take photos. Do you see all those bottles?"

He tapped Cole's leg with the toe of his boot and shook his head. "My, my. What kind of shit have you gotten yourself into now, boy?"

"Excuse me," I said, stepping directly in front of Cole—who was awake but clearly not lucid—and forcing Chief Souza to take a step back.

"Dr. Savard, did you see the mess your husband made?"

Behind me, Fielder took photo after photo. With every click of the shutter, my eye twitched. Damn, I wanted to stomp on his phone. I didn't know what they were implying, but this was not what it looked like.

"Hebert here got blackout drunk and drove the Zamboni through the building. And then did God knows what else. From what the fire crew is saying, the condensers are shot, and there are leaks everywhere."

"I didn't do anything," Cole said slowly.

"You did." The pompous prick stood over us, trying to intimidate us. "You have a record of petty crime. You're only coaching hockey because of legally mandated community service, isn't that right? And you just destroyed the place, meaning the rest of the season will be canceled for all those kids. Such a shame."

"I love coaching," Cole said, clutching his head, his eyes squeezed shut in pain. "And I love this rink. It's where I grew up. I would never."

Shit. I had to intervene. He clearly didn't have all his faculties. Who knew what he might say.

I grabbed his shoulder and squeezed hard. He took the hint and closed his mouth.

"My husband did nothing wrong," I said curtly. "He is ill, and I'm taking him home." I had no legal experience, but every instinct I had was telling me to get him the hell out of here.

"No, ma'am. I'm afraid I can't allow that. This is a crime scene."

"No." I crossed my arms and lifted my chin. "That—" I waved in the direction of the rink. "Is a crime scene. This is a parking lot, and we're going home."

The chief took a step toward me, his face softening. "Willa, I've known you your whole life. I have great respect for your parents, so I'm going to be honest with you. You married a drunk and a criminal. I know that's hard to hear, but you're a young woman with a bright future. Don't ruin it by hitching your wagon to a Hebert."

Rage flaring inside me, I took a step toward him, resisting the urge to throw a punch. "Do not talk about my husband like that." I hissed. "You have no evidence, and he's ill."

"If you leave, then I'm gonna have to go wake up a judge and get a warrant. Then I'll come all the way out to your house to arrest him."

I glared at him. "There will be no need. You have no evidence, and he's done nothing wrong. Looks like the environmental police have arrived." I nodded at the vehicles pulling into the lot. "You should probably go deal with them."

I squatted and draped Cole's arm over my shoulder. Then, using all my strength, I got him to his feet. We did it, and I vowed never to complain about our morning workouts again.

Slowly, I walked him to my car, taking care not to slip, my mind spinning.

I pushed him into the front seat and peeled out of the parking lot. A mile down the road, I pulled over.

"What's going on?" he asked as I fired off texts to his brothers. This was bad. Really bad. As I looked at his confused face, I knew in my bones he wasn't drunk.

"Stay here," I said, hopping out. Since the house call I'd made to Kara's, I'd been keeping my medical kit in my trunk. I had everything I needed to perform field surgery if necessary.

"Take your shirt off." I sanitized my hands and wiped everything down with alcohol pads.

"What are you doing?" he asked.

"Here." I thrust a small container of ammonium carbonate near his face.

He gagged, his eyes going wide. "What is that?"

"Smelling salts," I explained. "Shirt, now."

He took off his layers, his movements still slow.

When he'd finished, I wiped him down with alcohol and tied a rubber tourniquet around his bicep.

"What is that?" he asked as I popped the top off the butterfly needle with my teeth.

"I'm drawing blood," I said, steadying his arm. "You'll feel a pinch."

He dropped his head back against the seat and closed his eyes. "Why?"

"Shh," I said, focusing on making sure there was adequate flow into the collection tube.

I popped out the first one and shoved a second in for

good measure. Then I disconnected, slapped a Band-Aid on his arm, and wrote the date and time with a Sharpie on each.

"Drink this." I shoved a plastic bottle of Pedialyte at him. "I may need a urine sample too."

"Why do you need my blood?"

I shot him a look as I maneuvered through town.

"And where are we going?"

"Bangor," I explained. "I have a friend at the lab who owes me a favor. I took your blood to test so we can figure out what happened to you."

"I don't remember. We had practice. I put the girls through some drills." He shut his eyes again and breathed deeply. "Then I had to make ice. I wasn't feeling well, so I made sure to drink extra water. I close up on Thursdays and then..." He trailed off.

His speech was slow, but he was coming out of the fog.

"Drink your Pedialyte," I instructed. "And then try to rest. I'm calling your brothers. God knows what was done to you."

"Done to me?" He frowned, his eyes glassy. "Do you believe me? I swear I didn't drink. I haven't had a drop since our wedding night."

I glanced over at him again, taking in his drawn, sallow skin. I suspected he'd been drugged, but I'd let the lab confirm that. "Of course I believe you. You're my husband."

Chapter 45

Cole

"How did this happen?"

"Explain it again."

"What the fuck?"

My head spun as I sipped water and did my best to follow the conversation. Willa had called all my brothers, and after we went to the lab in Bangor, we headed home, where they were waiting.

"Why were you there?" Gus asked again, his hands on his hips. His beard was mussed, and his flannel shirt was partially untucked.

"He had practice," Willa snapped from where she hovered at my side. "Catch up."

"Sorry, I've been up all night, and I still can't understand how the ice rink got destroyed and why my brother was found unconscious in the parking lot."

They were all trying their best to understand, but I could see the doubt in their eyes. I could taste the questions lingering in the air.

I was asking myself the same damn ones. I knew I hadn't

bought any whiskey, and I certainly hadn't drunk any. Willa was convinced I'd been drugged, but why and by whom?

I tilted my head back and closed my eyes as they continued to argue.

The world around me blurred. Just getting up from this chair felt insurmountable. The irony was that I hadn't even had the urge to drink since our wedding. Ever since that day, I'd wanted to be better, both for myself and for Willa.

And the rink? I had learned to skate in that arena. Arthur used to let me come in, day or night, when I had no place to go and home was unbearable. It was the place where I'd found myself and learned countless lessons. The thought of it being ruined, that my kids wouldn't get to finish the season, was unbearable.

Willa thrust another glass of water into my hand, which I dutifully chugged. I'd never seen her so angry and fierce. Some of the details were foggy, but I recalled her yelling at Souza and then picking me up and putting me in her car before doing a blood draw by the side of the road.

Even now, she was firing back at Gus, pacing around, and demanding they help me.

She believed me. That alone was my saving grace. She held not even an ounce of hesitation. Unlike in my brothers' eyes, there wasn't even a shade of doubt in hers.

By now, the entire town had probably heard. No doubt I'd already been condemned in the court of public opinion. But Willa wasn't buying it. She had done nothing but work to protect me since she found me.

A surge of love for her tore through me as she bossed my brothers around, making phone calls and forcing me to hydrate. I'd spent my life looking for this. My person.

Someone who didn't look at me like I was a disappointment. Someone who believed in me even when I wasn't at my best.

Silently, I thanked those Bellagio dice. Because with one roll, I'd won this fierce woman.

Several glasses of water and four pieces of toast later, I was beginning to feel more like myself. Finn was asleep on the couch, Gus had gone home to Chloe, and Jude was making scrambled eggs in the kitchen.

When the phone rang, Willa answered and immediately paced the room, asking questions in doctor's speak.

When she hung up and looked at me, her features had hardened.

"Flunitrazepam," she said, shaking her head.

"In English, please?" Jude asked.

"Cole was dosed with a benzodiazepine to make him sleepy and confused."

"You got roofied?" Finn asked, almost rolling off the couch.

"I fucking knew it," she said, stomping her foot. "Those fuckers are going to pay."

My thoughts were still jumbled and foggy. Why would someone drug me?

"The good news is, it was a small dose. Well, it was probably a dose that would have done damage to the average person, but luckily, you're a giant. God, the existence of this shit makes me insane."

"What does this mean?" Finn asked.

"Cole was set up," Willa said, snapping her fingers at Jude. "Call Parker. Tell her we need to get in touch with the FBI."

When he hesitated, she glared at him until he abandoned his eggs and grabbed his phone.

"You," she said, pointing at me. "Hydrate more. Your liver is angry right now, and you're going to be feeling sick for a while."

"What about me?" Finn asked.

"Call your ex. We need a good lawyer."

"I like this one." Finn gave me a wink. "Bossy. Reminds me of my Adele."

Snarling at him, she strode across the room, headed for me. When she got close, I pulled her into my lap, kissing her head and whispering thank-yous in her ear.

"You were set up." She shook her head.

It was because of the watch. I knew it. "I think it may have been Chief Souza."

Her mouth dropped open. "Because we saw him the other night during the blizzard?"

"Yes. And because I went to his office yesterday and asked him point-blank about the watch."

Her eyes widened. "Shit."

My brain was fuzzy and aching, but I knew in my bones the chief was involved. Whatever we'd stumbled upon that night during the storm, it was something he did not want known. And the look on his face when I identified the watch only made it more clear he was up to something.

So this was how he planned to get me out of the way.

Willa closed her eyes and took a deep breath. "We will fight this," she said under her breath.

"Parker is on her way," Jude reported.

"Good." Willa snapped up straight. "We're gonna need the FBI too. And probably the whole damn town."

Burying my face in her hair, I inhaled deeply. "Thank you. For believing in me."

She turned toward me, cupping my face. "I'm not the only one. You think you're alone, Cole, but you're not. We will fight this."

"You don't have to."

"I'm your wife," she whispered, and I swore my heart seized up in my chest. "I'll never stop fighting for you."

Chapter 46
Cole

I was sent to shower and nap while Willa bossed people around. I'd progressed from the brain fog stage to the vomiting stage of recovery and had spent most of the day with my head in the toilet. That FBI agent, Portnoy, who'd been at Jude's house had stopped by briefly. He was a complete asshole. Smart, though, and Parker seemed satisfied with the questions he'd asked me. I wasn't sure how helpful I was with the way my thoughts had blurred, but at this point, I had nothing to lose.

The rage boiling up inside me—not just for me, but for all the kids who'd lost their hockey arena last night—didn't help.

The ice rink was more than just an ugly building from the '70s. For decades, it had been a home for so many kids like me who needed an outlet, who needed a place where they could find themselves.

Whether I was headed to jail or not, my primary concern was the Lovewell kids who'd lost that special place. I doubted Arthur had the money to fix it, and I'd be surprised if he had an insurance policy hefty enough to do much good.

My chest tightened painfully with guilt. Yes, I'd been drugged, but the damage had been done, and regardless of who the mastermind behind it was, I was responsible for it. I couldn't imagine the rumors that had been flying around town. I'd worked so hard to earn the respect of my community over the last year, but I was the son of Mitch Hebert, so it had probably been a waste of my time from the start.

Whatever happened, I'd deal with it. Right now, I was too tired to even think. So I lay in my lonely bed and closed my eyes.

I'd just drifted off when a clatter outside had my eyes flying open. I remained prone, too tired to move, and after a moment, let my lids lower again.

"Cole."

I looked to the doorway, where Willa was standing. Even blurry, she looked like a beautiful angel.

"Cole, get up."

"What's wrong?"

"I think you need to see this for yourself."

Groaning, I hauled myself to sitting, and when I stumbled to my feet, I stretched, smacking my hands on the ceiling beam above me.

Willa shuffled in and embraced me. "Come," she said, pulling back and grabbing my hands.

I staggered out behind her, letting her lead me to the front door. She stepped into her boots and motioned for me to do the same. Leaning against the wall, I slid one foot in. She helped adjust it, then we repeated the move with the other boot.

When I straightened, she pulled open the door, revealing a crowd of people. On the wraparound porch, and in the driveway, there were people everywhere outside our little cottage.

"What's going on?"

She looked around, her lips tipping up. "I made some calls."

I stepped outside, instantly finding my team.

"Coach," they squealed. The girls were dressed in their jerseys, wearing the knitted hats I'd made them, holding hockey sticks.

"We're here to defend you," Goldie Gagnon declared.

The other girls nodded, their faces serious. Some of their parents were sipping coffee and chatting on the porch.

There was no stopping the grin that spread across my face.

"You didn't do anything wrong." This from Olivia. "We know you'd never hurt the rink."

"You love hockey more than anyone," Kali added.

She was right. I did love hockey. But for so many reasons I never would have imagined before these last few months. I loved what it could do for all these kids. I loved the community it created. And I loved the dreams it inspired.

Out in the yard, my brothers were building a fire, and Debbie was chasing Thor, who was waddling around in his snowsuit.

At the end of the driveway, a group of older ladies were passing a flask around. Bernice had a large thermos and was joking around with several of the other knitting club ladies—Jodie, Steph, Erica, Gayle and MaryJo.

Erica broke into a large grin and waved when she saw me.

I waved back.

"All these people are here to support me?"

Willa squeezed my arm and nodded. "There were some unfortunate rumors spreading around town, so I took it upon myself to set the record straight. Bernice was outraged and said she'd rally the senior citizens."

Emotion clogged in my throat. "I don't know what to say."

"This is your town. You belong here. You've convinced yourself otherwise, but look at all these people who love and support you."

It was jarring, the sight in front of me. For so long, the story I'd told myself was that I didn't belong. Not here, not anywhere. That I was destined to be the odd man out forever.

My eyes went hot, and my chest went tight.

But this heartwarming display of affection was interrupted by sirens.

I braced myself as the noise got louder.

And when two police cars pulled up, my heart sank.

The crowd of rowdy seniors refused to move from the end of the driveway, forcing law enforcement to park at the end of the driveway.

Chief Souza exited first, putting his hat on and striding up the icy drive, his focus fixed firmly on me.

Unsurprisingly, the various people milling around did not get out of his way, forcing him to navigate around them comically. As he approached the porch where we stood, Willa reached down and squeezed my hand.

"Mr. Cole Hebert," he said at the bottom of the stairs while holding up a piece of paper. "You are under arrest. You—"

"You're not arresting our coach," one of the girls hollered.

The declaration was followed by a chorus of *yeah*s as the girls crowded around him with their hockey sticks. A few of their parents snapped videos with their phones.

"He's innocent," Kali yelled. "We're not letting you take him to jail."

The chief barked a vicious laugh. "You've got children fighting your battles, Hebert? Good God, you're pathetic."

"No, what's pathetic is you targeting and framing my husband," Willa shouted. "We know what you did."

Glowering, he said, "Watch yourself."

His deputies had finally made their way through the crowd and stood next to him, hands on their tactical belts, looking confused and shaken.

Willa stepped between two of the girls on my team, glaring at the chief. "You put a controlled substance in his water bottle to incapacitate him and frame him for a crime he didn't commit."

A gasp went around the crowd.

"You have no idea what you're talking about," he hissed.

"Actually, I do. Because despite how good you've become at lying and manipulating over the years, Chief, you can't control science."

He took a step toward her, which spurred me into action. I stepped closer, growling. No one looked at my wife like that.

"I don't want to have to arrest you too, Dr. Savard," the chief bit out.

Willa smiled. "That won't be necessary. Now please leave my property."

He looked around at the crowd, who was unmoved by his threats. "I'll arrest you all."

"You can't arrest us," Merry said, stepping forward. "We haven't broken any laws, and we're on private property. And my mom, who is standing right there"—she jabbed a finger toward Finn's ex—"is a lawyer."

Alicia crossed her arms, gazing proudly at her teen daughter.

Merry lifted her chin. "So you should probably leave."

"Yeah," the girls shouted in unison.

"Get out of here," Kali hollered.

"And find the bad guys who did it," Goldie added. "Not our coach."

There was no wiping the smile from my face, despite the real possibility that this asshole was going to haul me in.

"You should go home," Souza bit out. "This is no place for little girls."

I almost laughed. If this man only knew what little girls were capable of.

"Our coach taught us that we're stronger as a team. So we're not going anywhere," Goldie declared.

The chief's face was getting redder by the moment, and his deputies were looking around, frowning, without a clue as to how to handle this situation.

In front of me, Willa popped up on her tiptoes and waved. The crowd in the driveway parted, and a black suburban pulled in.

The doors opened, and several men in dark suits exited.

"Agent Portnoy." Willa smiled. "Right on time."

He strode through the crowd, wearing an expression so inscrutable, it would be easy to believe the guy was here to pick up his dry cleaning rather than interrupt a standoff between a rural police chief and a gang of elementary school girls with hockey sticks.

"John Souza," he said, a brow cocked at the angry man who had just threatened a crowd of children. He held up a badge. "Agent Portnoy, Federal Bureau of Investigation. I need to ask you a few questions."

Chief Souza glared at him. "I'm here to make an arrest. It can wait."

He stepped in front of him, blocking me from view. "I'm afraid you are not."

"I have a warrant," he said, holding up the paper.

"Not anymore. I just got off the phone with Judge Quimby. Since you lied on the affidavit, this warrant is invalid."

He took it out of his hand, tore it neatly twice, and then let the paper flutter to the ground.

"And like I said, we'd like you to come with us."

Another handful of federal agents had stepped out of a second SUV and were milling around, totally conspicuous in their identical dark suits, earpieces, and sunglasses.

One big, beefy guy crossed his arms and grunted. That finally got the chief moving.

"Shame on you," Bernice yelled as he headed toward the blacked-out Suburbans.

Others followed.

"How could you turn on our community?"

"Corrupt, corrupt," Debbie chanted.

Quickly, the whole crowd was joining in, chanting "Corrupt, corrupt, corrupt" as he ducked his head and slid into the waiting Suburban.

The scene was surreal. My head still ached, and I struggled to understand what had just transpired, but one feeling won out. Love.

For my community.

For my family.

And for my wife.

Breath hitching, I looked at Willa.

"Did you do this?"

She shrugged. "I had a lot of help."

Epilogue
Cole

3 months later…

It was freezing. Though it was almost May, this weather was typical. We were all bundled up, waiting for the photographer to stop taking photos. I was uncomfortable with this level of publicity, but my brothers had insisted it was good for the town.

My team was here with me, wearing their jerseys and hats and holding signs. It was adorable. We'd fought to keep the hockey season from being canceled. Thankfully, Heartsborough had lent us some ice time to host home games, and we'd made do with the pond for practices.

I'd also started hosting a Sunday morning skills clinic on the pond for everyone from toddlers to high schoolers. It had been challenging, but Willa had convinced me that my love for hockey could get us through it.

But spring was coming soon, and although hockey season was over, I had kids from around the region wanting to continue their training. The damage to the rink had been substantial. But between Owen's construction company and my hockey industry contacts, we'd gotten repairs done in a matter of months.

A few weeks after the FBI took Chief Souza in for questioning, I'd driven down to Portland to meet with a rare watch dealer. He had found a buyer for my Audemars Piguet, and I happily sold it to pay for the repairs to the rink. I'd been holding on to that ridiculous thing for years, clinging to some kind of hope that my father had loved me and been proud of me.

It took me far too long, but eventually I realized that I cared more about possessing integrity and grit than I could ever care about what my father thought. So that money came in very handy, especially when it was time to buy a new Zamboni. A state-of-the-art electric model that drove like a dream. And I drove it a lot, mainly because it made my wife very hot and bothered.

Arthur and I had worked out an agreement where I'd buy and take over the rink. He was ready to retire, and I wanted to use some of my NHL contract money to give back to the community that had lifted me up and had my back when I needed it.

So we remodeled and expanded, adding indoor training areas, a basketball court, new locker rooms, and a homework lounge. The goal was to create a place for kids to spend time playing hockey and also just being kids. My team helped me design it. They were very vocal about their preferences.

And now we were here, ready to cut the ribbon.

The past few months had been a blur. I'd started auditing classes at UMaine, all while coaching and remodeling the rink. I was still in therapy, doing the work and pushing myself to learn and grow from my past mistakes.

"This is so exciting," Willa squealed, clutching my arm. She looked beautiful, wrapped in a thick scarf I'd knitted for her. She'd been by my side through every step of the process.

Her quick thinking that night, stopping on the side of the road to draw my blood, had helped cement the evidence against Chief Souza and connect him to other outstanding investigations. We were still waiting for the official charges, but as of right now, he was on leave from the Lovewell police department and under the FBI's surveillance.

The watch—which was, in fact, the one that belonged to my father—had been seized. I still had no idea how he had come into possession of it, but Parker had assured us that the feds were connecting the dots.

I smiled as the mayor walked toward us with his giant scissors. He'd no doubt prepared a long-winded speech, but I was anxious to cut the ribbon and get everyone inside.

"You nervous?" Willa asked as I waited to thank the town and give my brief remarks. Public speaking scared the hell out of me, but we'd been practicing together.

I nodded.

She popped up on her toes and tugged my arm, silently signaling me to come closer. I leaned down and shivered when her lips grazed my earlobe. "I'm proud of you, and I love you. I also can't wait to go home and tear all your clothes off. I've been thinking about sucking you off all day."

My face heated, and a current of electricity shot down my spine.

"Willa," I whispered. God, she knew just how to take my mind off things.

She winked at me. "Go get 'em."

THE LOBBY WAS FULL OF PEOPLE, ALL OF THEM mingling and eating and laughing. For a long moment, all I could do was drink it all in. Finn had organized a silent auction to raise money for the town hockey programs, and we'd had an overwhelming number of donations.

I still couldn't believe we'd made all this happen so quickly. But I was learning that when Lovewell set its mind to something, it would happen.

Especially my hockey team. Those girls, who I was already set to coach next season, were making the rounds. With Goldie leading the charge, they were shaking down the adults for donations and forcing them to bid on auction items. On the ice, they were powerful; off the ice, they were unstoppable.

My entire family was here, including Owen and Lila, who had driven up from Boston. We had been spending more time together recently, and Owen's construction contacts had been invaluable. Despite the bad blood between us, he had stepped up to help the town, and for that I would always be grateful.

In the far corner, Debbie was busy chatting with Loraine Gagnon about the upcoming wedding. In a few weeks, Finn and Adele would officially be tying the knot. It had taken him a while to wear her down, but the two of them were outrageously happy.

No one knew quite what to expect from their wedding—

planes, throwing axes, and heavy machinery were all possibilities—but we were excited, nonetheless.

I was posing for photos with the ladies from knitting club when a commotion near the door caught my attention. One of the advantages of my height was the ability to see over crowds.

Debbie cried out, and then she was rushing to the door and throwing her arms around a man. Jude stalked to the entrance next, and as he approached and Debbie stepped to the side, a familiar head of sandy brown hair came into view.

Noah.

He was weeks early. He'd arranged time off from work to come out for the wedding, but that was still almost a month away.

Granted, showing up unannounced was Noah's MO. He lived on his own timeline and put little stock in the importance of holidays and special occasions. I'd only seen him a handful of times in the last decade and a half, and only when he'd come to a game when I played on the West Coast. I wasn't sure he'd even set foot in Maine since he'd graduated from high school.

I made my way through the crowd, accepting hugs and congratulations, keeping my focus trained on where my family had congregated.

Noah was tan, and his face was covered in stubble. As always, he wore a daredevil air.

But that wasn't all he was wearing today.

On his chest, in one of those carrier things Finn liked to wear Thor in, was a baby.

A chubby, smiling baby with dark curls and a gummy smile.

"Cole," he said, stepping toward me and offering his hand. "Congratulations."

Blinking, I worked to make sense of what I was seeing.

Debbie, Gus, and Finn seemed to be doing the same. Jude had his arm around Noah's shoulders, seemingly unsurprised by the infant.

The baby was cute. Not a newborn, but not as big as Thor. Based on the pink fleece onesie thing and the polka dot pacifier attached to a bright ribbon, I assumed it was a girl.

Noah looked down at the happy baby on his chest, his expression warming.

"This is Tess, my daughter."

Bonus Chapter

Want more Cole & Willa?

Grab the Bonus Chapter

Warning: it will make you laugh, cry and swoon!

Acknowledgments

Thank you for taking this trip to Lovewell with me! My 17th published book, and one that is so near and dear to my heart. I poured a lot of myself into Willa, and a few of her war stories are my own. And in Cole, I got to share my love of hockey with my readers.

Few know this, but I grew up in a hockey family, played for many years, and even played in college. My life revolved around the sport for so long, I've been waiting for the right book to share some of my hockey passion.

Writing a book is difficult, writing it while camping in the woods of Maine with no childcare and lots of mosquitos is even harder. And like all my books, it would not have been possible without the support of several talented and dedicated people.

There were moments when writing and producing this book felt impossible. But thankfully, I have some wonderful people in my corner who will not let me quit.

This, or any of my other books, would not exist without my team.

Morgan Leigh, I asked for help and you jumped in with both feet, quickly becoming the MVP in my life and the person who keeps me organized and on track. I treasure your friendship and your positive attitude. No one is more willing and more capable of learning new things than you are, and I am pinching myself that I get to call you mine.

Erica Walsh, thank you for being my friend and cheerleader for all these years. From cover design to finding photos and editing blurbs, you are truly in my corner every single day. We have cried and laughed and yelled together over the past three years, and I am a better person and writer because of you.

To the incomparable Jenni Bara, you are so talented, humble, and kind. Your friendship is a true gift. I continue to be amazed by all the things you manage to do while never losing your sunny attitude. Every book I write is better because of your ideas and energy. Thank you for being a true friend and for teaching me to just roll with things.

Beth, thank you for your thorough editing. I am amazed by your patience, professionalism, and kindness. You've worked through this series with me, tolerating my late add-ons and last-minute changes. Your careful work has helped bring these characters to life, and I am truly in your debt.

To my oldest friend, the indomitable Caroline, thank you for using your eagle eyes (and four literature degrees) to proofread this book. But more importantly, thank you for igniting my love of romance by introducing me to Jane Austen (and Colin Firth in a wet shirt) at the tender age of fifteen. My entire romantic worldview has been shaped by our shared love of happy endings and your friendship for these last twenty-seven (!!!) years is a true gift.

Amarilys, you are the kindest, most positive person I know. I cherish your friendship and feel so lucky to have you on my team. Thank you for believing in me.

Amy Jo, you are loving, hilarious, and incredibly talented. Thank you for sharing your creativity with me.

Becca, thank you for your professionalism and excitement about this series. You and the Author Agency have been such wonderful partners throughout this process.

Catherine, getting to know you has been one of the highlights of my year. Thank you for your marketing expertise, your passion for books, and your invaluable TikTok wisdom.

Sue, thank you for the gorgeous cover. You took a simple idea and elevated it with your immense talent. I am so grateful to get to work with you.

To my hype teams, thank you from the bottom of my heart for loving these books and this crazy world I've created. Most days, I pinch myself that I'm surrounded by such an amazing group of positive, kickass people.

Thank you to my mother, who always pushed me to do my best and believed in me even when I did not. I am the kind of person who decides to write books in my nonexistent free time because of you.

To Claire, my IRL friend and confidant. Your love and support mean so much to me. A greater power brought us together, and I am thankful every day for your humor, wit, and heart.

Thank you to my family for being hilarious, loving, and silly. To my children, G & T, you push me, challenge me, and surprise me every day. Being your mom is my life's greatest adventure. Thank you for never going easy on me. To G, my mini-me, you are my #1 fan and I can't wait to share my author journey with you as you grow.

Thank you to Craig, my handsome, supportive, and most

importantly patient, husband. Thank you for the inspiration and endless support. You are my original Alpha Roll.

And finally, I'd like to thank Taylor Alison Swift. For getting me through, not only the production of this book, but through all of my life's challenges for the past decade. You have taught me, and countless others, how to harness my creativity, and, most importantly, how to invest in my potential. Your work has made me a better mom, writer, entrepreneur, and person. Thank you.

Also by Daphne Elliot

LOVEWELL

The Lovewell Lumberjacks Series

Wood You Be Mine?

Wood You Marry Me?

Wood You Rather?

Wood Riddance

The Maine Lumberjacks Series

Caught in the Axe

Pain in the Axe

Axe-identally Married

Axe Backwards

Axe-ing for Trouble

THE MOM COMS

Mother Hater

Also by Daphne Elliot

HAVENPORT

The Quinn Brothers Series
Trusting You
Finding You
Keeping You

The Rossi Family Series
Resisting You
Holding You
Embracing You

About the Author

In High School, Daphne Elliot was voted "most likely to become a romance novelist." After spending the last decade as a corporate lawyer, she has finally embraced her destiny. Her small town steamy novels are filled with flirty banter, sexy hijinks, and lots and lots of heart.

Where to find Daphne:

daphneelliotauthor@gmail.com

Stay in touch with Daphne:
Subscribe to Daphne's Newsletter
Join Daphne's Reader Group
Follow Daphne on TikTok
Like Daphne on Facebook
Follow Daphne on Instagram
Hang with Daphne on GoodReads
Follow Daphne on Amazon

www.ingramcontent.com/pod-product-compliance
Lightning Source LLC
Chambersburg PA
CBHW060423310726
48977CB00001B/22